DEAD TO THE LAST DROP

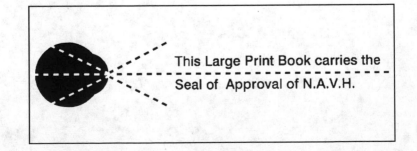

This Large Print Book carries the
Seal of Approval of N.A.V.H.

A COFFEEHOUSE MYSTERY

DEAD TO THE LAST DROP

CLEO COYLE

THORNDIKE PRESS
A part of Gale, Cengage Learning

GALE
CENGAGE Learning

Farmington Hills, Mich • San Francisco • New York • Waterville, Maine
Meriden, Conn • Mason, Ohio • Chicago

GALE
CENGAGE Learning®

LIBRARY OF CONGRESS CATALOGING-IN-PUBLICATION DATA

Names: Coyle, Cleo, author.
Title: Dead to the last drop / by Cleo Coyle.
Description: Large print edition. | Waterville, Maine : Thorndike Press, 2016. | © 2015 | Series: A coffeehouse mystery | Series: Thorndike Press large print mystery
Identifiers: LCCN 2016014468| ISBN 9781410491664 (hardcover) | ISBN 1410491668 (hardcover)
Subjects: LCSH: Cosi, Clare (Fictitious character)—Fiction. | Women detectives—Fiction. | Murder—Investigation—Fiction. | Large type books. | GSAFD: Mystery fiction.
Classification: LCC PS3603.O94 D42 2016 | DDC 813/.6—dc23
LC record available at http://lccn.loc.gov/2016014468

Published in 2016 by arrangement with The Berkley Publishing Group, an imprint of Penguin Publishing Group, a division of Penguin Random House LLC

Printed in Mexico
1 2 3 4 5 6 7 20 19 18 17 16

To Wendy McCurdy, our longtime editor, for her brilliance, her patience, her kindness . . . and her belief in us.

ACKNOWLEDGMENTS

My first thank-you is to my husband and cowriter, Marc Cerasini. *Dead to the Last Drop* marks the fifteenth book in our long-running Coffeehouse series, and I couldn't ask for a better partner in writing — or in life.

Our nation's beautiful capital city of Washington, DC, is second on my thank-you list. My DC experiences — interning as a newspaper reporter, studying at American University, and enjoying the nightlife of Georgetown — stayed with me for years and helped inspire key elements in the story that you're about to read.

For coffee inspiration, Marc and I thank Holly O'Connor of One Good Woman coffee and teas from around the world, onegoodwoman.com, along with her Baltimore-based master roaster, Shannan Stroble, of Source Coffee for taking the time to share details of their life and work.

Special thanks is in order for Thomas Blanton, national security archive director, GWU, for his eye-opening appearance at the Washington National Press Club, which fueled and informed a subplot in this mystery, including the "thirty-year gap" in government e-mail archiving. See the appendix of this book for helpful links to learn more about this archiving gap and the National Security Archive, the U.S. National Archives, and the FOIA (Freedom of Information Act).

Thanks to author Ronald Kessler for information on guarding the children of the President. To learn more about the lives of U.S. Secret Service agents, read his informative book *The First Family Detail.*

Props must be paid to the Smithsonian Institution and especially its beautiful National Museum of American History, americanhistory.si.edu. If you have never been to the Smithsonian Museums, put it on your bucket list. You won't be sorry.

Many years ago, I hosted a radio program on WRCT FM titled "Alice's Jazzy Restaurant," which allowed me to celebrate brilliant jazz artists, who also inspired what you're about to read. My thanks goes out to those artists, especially my old friend George Gee, georgegee.com, and the clubs that keep jazz alive, including: Blues Alley in Georgetown, bluesalley.com; the Blue Note, bluenote.net; and a tiny club called Smalls, where you can join me nightly in watching live jazz because its website streams directly from its Greenwich Village stage, smallsjazzclub.com.

Cheers to everyone at Berkley Prime Crime who had a hand in creating this beautiful finished book, especially our longtime editor, Wendy McCurdy — and our new editor, Kate Seaver! Our grateful appreciation goes out to assistant editor Katherine Pelz for cheerfully keeping us on track, production editor Stacy Edwards for her tireless efforts, and copyeditor Randie Lipkin for her kind diligence. We also thank our talented designers Rita Frangie and Kristin del Rosario, and our Coffeehouse Mysteries cover artist for the original publisher's editions Cathy Gendron, a brilliant painter to the last drop.

Last but far from least Marc and I send a triple caffeinated thank-you to our friends and family, our fantastic readers, our tireless booster Nancy Prior Phillips, and our dedicated agent, John Talbot, for their continued faith in us.

In closing, Marc and I invite you to join our wonderful Coffeehouse community at coffeehousemystery.com, where you will find recipes, coffee picks, and a link to stay in touch by signing up for our newsletter.

May you eat, drink, and read with joy!

— Cleo Coyle

Coffee, the favorite drink of the civilized world.

— Thomas Jefferson

Ethics are more important than laws.

— Wynton Marsalis,
artistic director, Jazz at Lincoln Center

PROLOGUE

He stomped the brake and glared at the BMW swerving into his lane. *I could smash this idiot's bumper, but it won't get me to her any faster . . .*

Suppressing the urge to turn this SUV into a battering ram, he laid on the horn instead. It worked. The Beemer swung out of his path and he hit the gas, running the next two yellow lights.

Thanks to the Cherry Blossom Festival, the DC streets were flooded with a sea of rentals, complete with drivers rattled by Washington's infamous traffic circles.

Built for an era of horses and buggies, the circles were a rite of passage for newcomers, as confusing as many of the rules for navigating this town. His first boss at Justice had tried to warn him about some of those twists and turns before the cancer killed him.

Now she was his prime concern.

Fingers strangling the wheel, he feared the worst, that he might be too late. Seeing congestion ahead, he cut the wheel, swinging onto 31st, a Georgetown residential street that gave him clearance to fly. Then two quick lefts and he was exactly where he needed to be, Wisconsin's 1200 block.

He double-parked, reached into his suit jacket, and popped the thumb snap on his holstered Glock. *Whatever it takes to keep her safe . . .*

The Village Blend, DC, was beyond busy, its line spilling onto the sunny sidewalk — locals, college kids, selfie-taking tourists.

"Hey!" A boy with a backpack poked the air. "Cutting the line's *not* cool. You can't —"

A single, arctic stare was all it took to freeze the kid — because in this city, a dead-eyed look from a big guy in a suit meant one thing . . . federal agent. In this case, *armed and pissed* federal agent.

Inside the shop, he looked for her, his body and soul relieved to find her busy behind the espresso bar. Green eyes brightened at the sight of his approach. Lips parted in surprise and then melted into that special smile, the one reserved only for him.

"Mike, I'm happy to see you, but I'm in the middle of —"

"You're coming with me."

"What?"

"Right now, Clare."

Confusion wiped her smile. She didn't want to go. *But she will,* he thought, *even if I have to cuff her and carry her out.*

"Can you tell me why?"

"No time." He extended his hand. "If you trust me, you'll come . . ."

A moment's hesitation and she took it.

He pulled her outside, practically pushed her into the vehicle, slammed their doors, and peeled out.

"Whose car is this?"

"Not mine and not yours — and that's the point. If you have a mobile, we have to toss it."

"It's back at the coffeehouse, in my handbag!"

"Good. At least they can't trace us. I've already disabled the LoJack."

"Mike, what is going on?"

He swung off the crowded avenue and zigzagged his way toward the Potomac. "Open the glove compartment."

She did, saw a travel guide, sunglasses, and a .45. "Now you're scaring me."

"Why? I taught you to shoot. You don't have to be afraid of it."

"I'm not afraid of *it.* What's scaring me

15

is *you*!"

"I'm sorry, sweetheart, but lives are in jeopardy."

"Whose?"

"*Ours.* And we've only got a narrow window to change that."

Glancing her way, he saw her struggling to process his words. For a rare minute of time, he realized Clare Cosi had been rendered speechless.

The afternoon sun was unforgiving, revealing the crow's-feet at the edges of her eyes, the tiny wrinkles around her down-turned mouth. But the golden light also burnished the red strands in her dark chestnut hair. And though her ponytail was coming undone, she wasn't.

The woman he loved was strong, one of the most resilient spirits he knew, and one of the most stubborn, but it was her loyalty that made her one of the best partners he could have in this situation — that and her innate nosiness.

"Clare, I need you to talk to me about Abby."

"Abby? You mean —"

"I need to know everything."

"But you know most of it already."

"Most of it, not all of it, and I need you to go over it all, even the parts you think I know. No matter how trivial a fact may seem, tell me. Remember, Clare, details matter . . ."

Leaning back, she took a breath. "Then I suppose I should start with *Nox Horrenda.*"

"What?"

"It's how I think of it: *that horrible night.*"

"The night of the first homicide?"

"Yes — although I didn't know it was murder. Not then. And it wasn't the first time I saw the victim, that was a week before. The same night I spotted two armed men in my coffeehouse."

"Back up, sweetheart. *What* armed men?"

And that's where her story began . . .

ONE

"Gardner, get off the phone."

"Why?"

"Just do it!"

Still panting from my upstairs sprint, I counted the seconds, waiting for my young co-manager to end his call.

Like the rest of this former bakery, the top floor of our rented building felt as big as a barn. Tall windows bathed the place in sunshine — when the sun was up, that is. Nights were a different story.

None of the fireplaces were working yet, which made this high-ceilinged beauty impossible to properly heat; and on this moonless February evening, in heels, hose, and a little blue dress, I hugged myself to suppress a shiver.

Our DC location hadn't always been a bakery. Around 1865, it became a confectionary shop with an ice cream parlor so beloved that the Smithsonian's Museum of

American History preserved a portion of its interior in its Hall of Everyday Life.

My everyday life wasn't nearly so fixed.

At first my move here had been a joy. My elderly employer had found me an elegant situation, house-sitting a historic George-town mansion.

Madame Dreyfus Allegro Dubois had made flocks of influential friends in her eighty-plus years running her New York coffee business, so I wasn't surprised that among them was the absent owner of said mansion.

Madame had even bunked with me for a few weeks to help us open our DC doors — and cut some red tape for a temporary liquor license. Then she headed back to New York, and for the next two months, I settled into a routine with my co-manager, a talented African American jazz musician named Gardner Evans who'd worked for years as a part-time barista in our New York shop.

Hailing from the Baltimore area, Gard had harbored a childhood dream to open a jazz club in Washington; and, given the longtime success of the legendary Blues Alley (just down the avenue from our DC digs), our elderly owner was thrilled to give the concept her blessing, as well as her funding.

After all, Georgetown was a picturesque, historically preserved neighborhood with collegiate ties and bohemian leanings, much like the Greenwich Village location of our original Village Blend. It seemed the perfect way to expand our century-old family business, a dream Madame had been fostering in recent years.

As for my dream, it had less to do with business than a man named Michael Ryan Francis Quinn — NYPD detective by trade, training, and instinct — who was now on temporary assignment at the United States Department of Justice.

The protracted duration of Quinn's supposedly "transitory" duty was compelling enough for me to relocate. In plain speaking: *I missed the man.* As a result, I'd agreed to help Gard get this DC branch of our Village Blend coffee business up on its feet — unfortunately, after eight weeks of coaxing, this promising baby was still on its knees.

I handled the day-shift coffee business on the first floor, which was decent, but it wasn't brisk enough to carry the jazz club, which was hemorrhaging money.

Gardner managed the club, and we agreed the music wasn't the problem; it was the food. (One recent devastating print review and a dozen online reviews concurred.)

That's why he'd asked me to stop by this evening and evaluate the menu issues, which I'd been doing, table by table — until I spotted the man with the gun.

Keeping my cool, I moved slowly to the stairs and raced up them.

Now I stood before Gardner in our small office on the third floor. He and I shared the space. The rest of this large top floor served other purposes, including a small apartment that Gard used and a "green-room" for the performers he booked. At the moment, however, I regretted the floor plan didn't include an armory.

"Okay, talk to me —" Gardner said, putting down his phone. "What's up?"

"I think we're about to be robbed."

"What?!" His espresso-hued eyes went wide. "Have you called the police?"

"No!"

"Why not?"

"Because nothing's happened yet."

"Then what makes you think —"

"Remember that holdup in the news last week? The bistro on Connecticut Avenue? Two armed men took wallets, smartphones, and jewelry at gunpoint. The perps waited at separate tables for the right time to strike. Well, I think I've spotted them downstairs."

"In the coffeehouse?"

"No, the club. As I was chatting up customers, I came upon this man, sitting alone, wearing a baseball jacket. He's not eating or drinking alcohol, just sipping a Coke. He's scanning the room, hardly paying attention to the stage."

"Is that all?" Gardner smoothed his goatee. "There could be any number of reasons why —"

"Except a big, bald guy, at the opposite end of the room, is doing the same thing — and making occasional eye contact with the first man. When I moved closer, I saw the gun in the big guy's suit jacket!"

"He's strapped?"

"Yes!"

"Did either of these guys notice you noticing them?"

"I could feel their eyes on me as I crossed the dining room, but I don't know that they know I know."

Now Gardner was on his feet. "Do they look Middle Eastern?"

"Why does that matter?"

"You never heard of prejudiced profiling? We call the cops and we're wrong, they could sue us for discrimination, defamation, harassment!"

"I suppose the guy in the baseball jacket could pass for a Saudi."

Gardner moaned.

"Let's not panic," I said. "We'll have to involve the police, but we can do it carefully. Business has been pretty lousy around here without bad publicity killing it completely —"

"Or a lawsuit!"

"I have an idea."

"I'm all ears."

I explained my plan, and Gardner nodded. "Let's do it. But I still hope you're wrong."

"That makes two of us."

Two

I led the way down the stairs to our second floor Jazz Space. Sweet music flowed from the low stage, where three members of Gardner's own band, Four on the Floor, were wrapping up their first set.

We entered the dining area behind the polished coffee and wine bar. Our young, Italian bartender was helping out on the floor, along with our sole server for the evening.

To keep us from spooking these robbers, I directed Gardner to turn his back on the customers and gaze instead into the ornate mirror mounted behind the long bar. The LED light star field on the twilight blue ceiling and opposite wall were reflected there, along with tonight's sparsely occupied tables.

As Gardner prepared a drink, I pretended to help.

"Where do I look?" he whispered.

"By the exit to the restroom. See the big bald guy in a suit? He's the one I know is armed . . ."

As Gardner observed the man, the band ended their set.

Stan "Sticks" McGuire, the band's wiry new drummer, grabbed his Hoover cane. Stan had a permanent limp, unruly brown hair, and tremendous energy. Despite his leg injury and visual impairment — a blind eye, which he masked with a Captain America eyepatch — he moved smoothly off the stage, unassisted.

Jackson placed his bass into its stand and grabbed the microphone.

"Thanks, folks. Now it's time for us to clear out so you can listen to our Open Mike favorite. Join us on a musical stroll down the piano keys with the extraordinary fingers of Miss Abby Lane."

Gardner nearly dropped his glass.

"Don't panic," I cautioned. "You might alert the robbers."

Gardner didn't reply. He simply melted into barely stifled laughter.

"Have you lost your mind?"

He shook his head. "Clare, I'm sorry. I was burning up the phone lines, looking for next Saturday's replacement act, and I forgot Abby was playing tonight."

"Abby? The girl at the piano?"

A serious-looking young woman in a long, funereal black dress sat down behind the Steinway. Her pale features were obscured by black glasses with thick, retro-1950s horn rims and a curtain of shiny ebony hair. With a silent dip of her head she acknowledged the applause, which was enthusiastic.

Clearly, Abby had a small but loyal following. As she began to play, I knew why. Her music immediately captivated, her style was playful yet soulful. And she was a delight to watch. The notes seemed to illuminate her spirit with a joy so radiant that it burned through the industrial-strength eyewear.

I faced Gardner, who'd finally managed to tamp down his uncontrolled mirth.

"I'm confused," I said in a loud whisper. "Why are you laughing?"

"Because we're not being robbed." Gardner's gaze met mine. "Take another look at the woman behind the piano — a good look."

Still baffled, I faced the stage again.

The young musician appeared blissfully immersed in her music. I noticed the hint of a tattoo peeking out from under her sleeve, but lots of young women had tattoos, so it wasn't much of an identifier.

27

"Is she a celebrity? A famous musician?" I snapped my fingers. "That's it! She's a musician, and the two armed men are really her bodyguards."

"You're half-right. So you don't have to worry. We're not going to be robbed by a pair of Secret Service agents."

"Secret Service?"

"That's right."

"Then the young woman, onstage . . ."

When words failed, Gardner finished for me.

"She's the President's daughter."

THREE

After watching Abby for fifteen minutes, I tugged Gardner's sleeve. I had a potful of questions and didn't want our conversation overheard, so we climbed back up to our third-floor office.

"Why didn't you tell me?"

"I'm sorry, Clare. I *wanted* to, but . . ." Gard leaned back in the desk chair and rubbed his long neck. "Knowing the truth about Abby comes with a lot of responsibility — rules and worries and procedures. You already had your hands full with the dawn-to-dusk coffee business on the first floor; and Abby only comes to the Jazz Space at night. I wanted to spare you."

"Do your bandmates know?"

"They didn't at first, but they do now . . ."

He leaned forward and switched on the house speakers so we could hear more of the live performance of First Daughter Abigail Prudence Parker, who apparently enjoyed appearing at the Village Blend, DC, under the stage name Abby Lane.

"Has she been performing long?"

"She showed up at our very first Open Mike. But she didn't sign up until week two. She's played every week after that."

"She obviously has passionate followers. I tried to engage a middle-aged couple, ask them about our menu, but they insisted they were only here for Abby Lane."

"I didn't notice them," Gard said.

"They were sitting next to the star field wall, near the stage. The man looked East Indian. Beautifully tailored suit, monogrammed tie. The woman was a brunette; hair pinned up; wrapped from head to toe in House of Fen; and her bag was that new five-hundred-dollar Fen Pouch fashionistas are drooling over. A real power couple."

"Sounds good . . ." My co-manager nodded. "Maybe they'll tell some of their well-heeled friends about us."

"And did you notice that olive-skinned hipster with the gray beard and ponytail? He couldn't tear his eyes away. I've never seen him around, either, at least not in the coffeehouse."

"I know that guy. He only comes on the nights Abby performs. Always alone. Last week he sat at the front table." Gardner snorted. "Fan or not, he's in for a surprise if he tries to get any closer to that girl."

"What do you mean?"

My co-manager replied with the story of how he discovered Abby's true identity . . .

"The first time she got up the nerve to play at our Wednesday Open Mike Night, I was impressed with her ability. She stayed for the Open Jam Session and Stan worked with her, helped ease her into improvising with other musicians. Over the next two weeks, I noticed she came by to listen to my group. After her third Open Mike, I decided to invite her for a talk over coffee. But when the Open Jam Session ended, she hustled down the stairs and out the door. I hurried to catch up, down to the street, where I saw her climbing into the backseat of this big SUV. I called out her name and ran toward her . . ."

He shook his head at the memory. "Huge mistake! Two beefy guys came out of no-where, and *wham*! I got T-boned and then pinned to the pavement. Man, I hurt for a week."

"What happened next?"

"Well, there I was on the ground, rasping like Louis Armstrong, and suddenly Abby is standing over us screaming, *'Don't hurt him, don't hurt him!'* "

The overzealous Secret Service agents released Gardner, and the misunderstanding was cleared up.

"Now I don't feel so bad," I said.

"What do you mean?"

"You didn't recognize Abby's bodyguards as federal agents, either."

"Don't worry about it. They're trained to mingle with the public."

"I would have expected navy blazers with joe-obvious earpieces, you know the kind, with curly wires running into hidden radios —"

"They have wireless earpieces now, shoved so deep into their ear canals they have to be removed with magnets. And their jackets do hide communications equipment — smartphones. That's how they talk to each other." He snorted again. "Thanks to Abby, I've learned more than I ever wanted to know about the dos and don'ts of the Secret Service."

"I gather you and Abby had that coffee talk, after all."

"That very night. That's when Abby told me who she was, and swore me to secrecy. And the band, too, once they figured out the score."

"When did they catch on?"

"A week after I did. It was Stan who saw it first."

"Saw?"

"That's right, Clare. For a near-blind guy, he never misses a trick."

"Did Abby tell you why she's keeping her identity a secret?"

Gardner shrugged noncommittally, but I got the impression he knew more than he was letting on. Meanwhile my own mind was racing.

A piece of news like this, released into social media, could go viral — even global — overnight. My eyes glazed envisioning the paparazzi and journalists of this town lining up at our door, not to mention the curious public. We'd be packed for a long time to come.

"Is there any chance Abby would be okay with us telling the truth about her Open Mike appearances?"

"Doubt it."

"Would you at least let me ask her?"

"I don't know, Clare . . ."

"Please?"

Gardner released a hard breath. Then he fell silent, tuning back in to Abby's performance. Finally, he cocked an ear at the speaker. "She's about to finish her set."

"How do you know?"

"She always wraps with 'Cool Reception.' It's an original piece."

I listened until the final notes of the haunting song faded into applause. Though the crowd was small, the reaction was wholehearted.

Gardner rose. "Let's go . . ."

"Back downstairs?"

"Yeah, it's time you met our First Daughter."

FOUR

After introductions were made, we led Abby upstairs for a break in our greenroom. Not that it was completely green. I'd painted lush trees against walls of a pale, powder blue that turned luminous when the sun poured through the skylight. At night, stars twinkled above and the room's floor lamps bathed the space in a warm glow.

Couches and armchairs littered the perimeter of the room, but we all took seats around the circular dining table. Gard called refreshment requests down to the bar and kitchen. His band settled in, and Abby fidgeted in her chair, still pumped from her performance.

I started off by asking the young woman about her musical training.

"I've studied classical piano since I was six, Ms. Cosi. Once upon a time, I dreamed of becoming a concert pianist. But as my mother loves to say, 'Most dreams turn into

35

nightmares, Abigail. Better to keep both eyes open . . .' "

Stan gave a disapproving grunt.

Either he didn't care for her reference to both eyes being open — given that his military service left him with only one — or he disagreed with the statement philosophically.

I absolutely disagreed with it philosophically but, for the moment, I held my tongue. Gardner had more experience with DC than I did, and he advised me early on to keep my opinions to myself. *"If you want to stay in business in this town, Clare, don't stir the pot. Just pour from it . . ."*

In theory, I agreed. Factions came to Washington from every state in the union and every region of the planet. But I wanted our DC Village Blend to remain a blend, true to the basic principle our country was founded upon —

Everyone was welcome.

Unfortunately, *everyone* included disapproving bodyguards, like the young female Secret Service agent posted next to the greenroom's open door.

The athletically built woman had been among the downstairs audience from the start, but in her jeans and Windbreaker she blended in so well that I hadn't noticed her

36

until she introduced herself as Secret Service Agent Sharon Cage and insisted on checking the greenroom before Abby went up.

With a golden ponytail as high and tight as her on-duty posture, Agent Cage's frowning gaze studied everyone at the table, though she focused most of her attention on me. Obviously the woman didn't care for my questioning Abby.

Well, last I checked, the First Amendment was still in force . . .

I asked about her studies, and Abby told me she was a political science major at American University. I couldn't hide my surprise.

"You're not pursuing a degree in music?"

The girl shrugged. "It's no use."

"Why?" Gardner jumped in. "Come on, Abby, admit it. You're great and you know it."

The girl laughed. "So *you* say. No offense, Gard, but I've had some of the best instructors in the world, and the consensus was always the same. I'm good, but nowhere near good enough to be taken seriously."

I couldn't believe my ears. "Everyone who enjoyed your music tonight certainly took you seriously. And anyone can see you love playing."

"That's true, Ms. Cosi. Music touches me the way that nothing else does." She hugged herself, one hand absently touching the musical notes tattooed on her arm. "I have a digital piano in my dorm. I've used it for years. It's got hammer-weighted keys so it's got the feel of an acoustic . . ." She shrugged. "I always play with the headphones on, you know, so I won't bother anyone . . ."

When her voice trailed off, I leaned closer. "You know, Abby, back in New York City, I employ young artists. They work as baristas to make ends meet while they pursue their love of painting, acting, writing, dancing. And do you know what I've learned from them?"

"What?"

"The practice of any art is a worthy pursuit. Whether you're the world's best at it or not is beside the point."

"Excuse me?" Abby's brow knitted. "But isn't that the whole point? Aren't we all supposed to be striving to be The Best?"

Stan grunted. "You mean like the best rental car company?"

"Or best football team?" Jackson laughed. "We're number one! We're number one!"

Stan pulled out his sticks and found a beat. The band hooted and clapped and chanted in time. "Best, best, best of the rest!"

Abby laughed, and they finally settled down — all except Stan, who launched into a Miss America drumroll. "Step right up, son, and accept the prize for *The* Best Half-Blind Jazz Musician to Play the Table in a Washington, DC, Coffeehouse, *hooah*!" The room fell silent, and he grinned at Abby. "At last, my life is complete."

"All right, you got me." Abby returned Stan's smile. "I never thought of it like that."

"Well, you should," Stan said. "There is a massive metaphysical difference between striving to be THE best and striving to be YOUR best."

"Darn right." Jackson held out his fist and Stan bumped it. Then Theo did.

But Gard didn't join his band. Instead, he folded his arms.

"You don't agree?" I asked.

"I do. But let's face it, most of the public doesn't."

"What's that supposed to mean?" Stan challenged.

"It means, as much as I hate to say it, Abby's point is valid. The public's been conditioned to think of every art form as some kind of sport." He exchanged a glance with me. "Or political race."

Abby nodded. "Sometimes it feels as though everyone and everything in this country is rigged to be in some kind of competition."

"Not everyone," Stan insisted. "And not everything. True art is not about competition. It's about expression."

I leaned toward Abby. "That's exactly what the people in my New York coffeehouse community believe. If art feeds something inside you, then you should practice it. That's it. That's the only measuring stick you need."

"Look, I can see you're all trying to help me with this, but . . ." She shook her head. "Coming here was a real leap for me. Gard and Stan and the other Open Mike musicians have all been really supportive, and I've been so happy playing. But this can't be part of my real life."

"Why not?" I pressed. "I'm sure Gardner is dying to give you a paid performance slot."

Gardner nodded. "That's true."

"Come on, you guys know why I can't do that." Abby glanced around the whole table, then at me. "You know who I am, Ms. Cosi."

"I do now."

"So you know I'm not a private person anymore. I live in a bubble and I have a responsibility to my family, my country, and someone else, too. I can't embarrass them. They know best, and they want something better for me."

"What on earth could be better for you than something that makes you so deeply happy?"

My blurted words appeared to cast a serious shadow across Abby's face.

For heaven's sake, I thought, *how could the simple idea of being "deeply happy" bring on such darkness in a bright young woman?*

Then Abby's hand slid down her tattooed arm, and for the first time I noticed something that shook me up — and shed some light.

Raised white scar lines marred the tender skin of Abby's left wrist. The girl was right-handed and those scars were unmistakable. Abby had attempted suicide.

There was one more thing I noticed: the lines were vertical.

When Abby tried to end her life, she meant business.

FIVE

I said nothing, but I couldn't stop the shock from crossing my face.

Thankfully, Gardner spoke quickly to cover my reaction. "I think what Ms. Cosi meant is that you're very talented, Abby, and it bothers us all to see you belittling your gift."

"Really, you're fussing too much. I'm nothing special."

"But you are," Gardner fired back. "The people in your past who decided you weren't good enough were judging you by the wrong music. You told me you've been studying jazz on your own, and it shows. Replacing Bach with bebop is exactly what you needed."

"It does feel good. I mean, I love the improvisation with jazz, you know? It's so freeing."

Gard nodded his approval. "Just keep up your playing with other musicians — instead

of all alone in that dorm room — and you'll
be a shining star. You aren't going to
'embarrass' anyone, if that's what your family is worried about. They *should* be proud."

"If you were my daughter, I'd be proud,"
I assured her. "Consider us your *musical*
family — and if you ever want to perform a
full evening of jazz, we'd all be thrilled to
host you."

"Really?"

"Yes, really!" Gard and I practically
shouted together.

"I can't promise anything, but . . ." Abby
chewed her bottom lip. "I will think about
it."

"No," Stan said.

No? Stunned at Stan's discouraging word,
I opened my mouth to argue until I saw the
young man's hand reach across the table to
affectionately squeeze Abby's fingers.

"Don't *think* about it," he said. "Because
jazz isn't about thinking —"

"— it's about feeling," she joined in,
finishing the saying in unison. "About taking what you know and letting go."

As the pair laughed together, Agent Cage
redirected her frown from me to Stan.

Abby didn't appear to notice. She just
continued laughing. Then she started talking with Stan about a duet they were work-

ing on. I noticed how animated she became and felt myself smiling — until she brushed away an errant strand of dark hair and I caught another glimpse of those pale white scars.

I didn't know much about the First Family. President Parker had been a centrist senator for years, rising in his party, and taking the White House without much drama. During the election cycle, it was Abby's handsome, outspoken older brother, Kip, who'd been the media darling. Abby had remained far in the background — quiet, studious, private. The photos I did recall of her had little in common with her current look, and I couldn't remember any stories, positive or negative, about her personal history.

My thoughts were interrupted by Luther, our older assistant chef, who appeared with a big smile and a generous tray of savory selections from the kitchen: Sticky Chicken Wings glazed with his special sweet and tangy Carolina Mustard Barbecue Sauce; hot, crispy steak fries; fat, crunchy onion rings; Mini Meat Loaves with Smashed Baby Reds and Roasted Garlic Gravy; Sweet-Hot Honey-Chili Chicken; and, for dessert, Coffee Cups of Warm Apple Crisp with an Oatmeal Cookie Crumble Top, each waiting to be finished with a scoop of his No-Churn Cinnamon and Vanilla Bean Ice Cream.

I wasn't surprised that Abby and the band had chosen items from Luther's Wednesday chalkboard specials. Most of our customers were doing the same, and I didn't blame them, given the items on our young executive chef's fussy, pricey standard menu —

Pork Belly & Octopus on Black Rice; Honeycomb Tripe in a Chorizo-Pimento Nage; Oslo Creamed and Pickled Herring; Tuna Burger with Wasabi Mayo; Olive Oil Gelato with Rosemary Shortbread . . .

Not that I had anything against bacon and seafood, cow's stomach, Norwegian delicacies, or a tuna puck with green mayonnaise. And truth be told, the man's olive oil gelato was absolutely delicious.

But receipts didn't lie.

While five years ago Manhattan's food critics may have crowned Chef Tad Hopkins a "culinary prodigy," here and now, in our Georgetown Jazz Space, the man's gourmet fare was a resounding flop.

The only nights that our kitchen made a profit were Tuesdays and Wednesdays, the chef's days off, when *Luther* ran the kitchen — and whipped up his down-home daily specials.

Several times I tried to speak to our executive chef about his menu, but he refused to listen. So tonight, I'd come in to hear customer feedback with my own ears.

In the meantime, I noticed Stan talking into Gard's ear. A few minutes later, my co-manager swallowed the last of his sticky wings, wiped his lips of the tangy-sweet goodness, and cleared his throat.

"So, Abby, what do you think of coming back next Saturday night? To perform, I mean?"

"But there's no Open Mike on Saturdays."

"Our headliner canceled, so this would be a paid gig. Besides, Sticks insisted I ask." Gard nudged the drummer until Stan grinned behind his Captain America eye patch. "I think he's hot to play that duet you two have been working on."

"Oh, that would be awesome!" Abby cried, then turned to Stan. "But are we ready? There are still some rough spots."

Stan shrugged. "So we'll practice every day. We have a week."

I could see the excitement in Abby's eyes. "I'd like to . . ."

"Then do it," Gardner said. "You've got the chops —"

"And the butts," Stan added.

Abby blinked. *"Butts?"*

"Butts in the seats!" He leaned close. "You have fans, girlfriend. If Gardner puts up a sign downstairs that Abby Lane will be playing a full set next Saturday night, these folks — and more — will be back to hear you perform."

"Say yes," Gard urged. "My band can back you, right, guys?"

"Heck, yeah!"

Abby grinned and silently nodded. *Yes!*

"See that, Clare, my booking problem is over . . ." Then Gard gave them a taste of their future introduction. "And now, ladies and gentlemen, the world premiere of *Abby Lane with 'Three' on the Floor!*"

As the boys applauded, I joined in. Only one person in the room lacked any cheer — Agent Sharon Cage.

The wider Abby grinned, the deeper the Secret Service agent frowned.

Six

"And you only learned about Abby that night?" Mike Quinn pressed, eyes on the road. "You weren't aware she'd been coming to your Jazz Space for weeks?"

From the passenger seat, I shook my head. "My primary management responsibility was the coffee shop trade — early in the morning to late afternoon. I was only there that night to help Gard sort out the problems with our dinner menu."

"It's hard to believe nobody recognized her."

"No, it isn't. Not with those big, retro glasses. And her hair was so different. In the few photos I remember from her father's campaign, she had curly blond hair. As Abby Lane, her hair was straight and ebony black . . ."

As I paused to clear my throat, I tumbled into a tailspin of coughing.

Quinn reached a hand into the backseat

48

and produced a clear plastic bottle. "Sip this, Clare. You've been talking nonstop since we left Washington . . ."

The stark glare of the setting sun rays revealed the deep lines etched into his face. Brown stubble, a shade darker than his sandy hair, now dotted his jutting chin. I knew he was getting tired, but his steady blue gaze never left the windshield.

I stared at the bottled water he'd given me. "I'd really prefer a double espresso with my primo Sulawesi."

"If you crave caffeine, we can stop at one of *those* places."

Quinn jerked his head in the direction of a billboard for the most ubiquitous coffee and pastry franchise in the USA.

I frowned. "You said making a stop would be dangerous. In this instance, I agree."

He cracked a smile and then the window, filling the vehicle with the cool whistling wind of fresh country air.

I unscrewed the bottle and took a gulp. The water was lukewarm, but it soothed my talk-tired throat. Quinn must have been reading my mind.

"You want to give your vocal cords a rest for a couple of minutes?"

"What I want is for you to do some talking."

"Me?"

"I've shown you plenty of trust. How about you return the favor?"

On a long exhale, Quinn nodded and finally gave me a briefing on our situation. And *brief* was the word.

In a nutshell, I was a wanted woman.

Now most women my age would consider that a compliment. I would, too, if it didn't involve the possibility of a "Wanted" bulletin being issued to every police precinct in the country. To be painfully specific, Mike learned that I'd become the primary suspect in a case of cold-blooded murder.

And that was the better news.

"What else?" I pressed. "You're holding something back."

"I'm sorry, sweetheart, but the feds want to bring you in for 'questioning,' too."

"On what? The DC murder?"

"No. Conspiracy to kidnap the President's daughter."

"What?!"

We discussed the situation for many more minutes. But the bottom line was an ugly truth — the local charge would reinforce the fed's belief that I was a "bad guy."

"If it were only the homicide charge, I would have brought you a top lawyer," Quinn said, "but the federal involvement makes it too heavy. Once they take you in for something like that, I'd have no chance of contacting you, helping you sort out the real truth, and . . ."

"And? And what?"

He took a breath, blew out air. "I know the kind of tactics they'd use to loosen your tongue."

"Aggressive interrogation?"

"I can't let you go through that. Or let them railroad you on a set of circumstantial evidence."

"They're going to find us, Mike. They're going to track us down. You know that, right?"

"I know. But this little flight of ours will buy us time."

"Enough time to find answers? To hand the authorities the truth instead of me?"

"And me. We're in this together now. I'm helping you evade the police. Whatever they think you did, they can call me an accessory . . ."

I squeezed my eyes shut, wanting to scream. Instead, I filled my lungs with the fresh country air.

I hated that Mike was putting himself in jeopardy like this. But I trusted him. If we were on the run, then we needed to be — and there was no easier way to straighten out this colossal tangle.

When my eyes opened again, I felt calmer, though there wasn't much to see. A lonely stretch of trees and guardrails. A small town came and went. Weeds, guardrails, and more weeds — fitting, since we were in them. Then a sign appeared, and Quinn made a turn.

"What's our destination?"

"Baltimore."

"Baltimore?!"

We'd been on the back roads since we left DC. Certainly, the Baltimore–Washington Parkway would have been a much easier route. I mentioned that to Quinn.

"Easier to be found, too," he said. "Remember, this isn't my vehicle, and that should keep us off the radar. But the feds have facial recognition tools and ungodly tracking resources. If they see us on a highly traveled highway, we could be tracked by helicopter, traced by a Stingray tower, or pursued by a drone."

At a red light, Quinn turned to me. "They'll be looking for us on those main highways. It's the last place we should go."

Quinn continued to stick to the roads less taken.

"So what's in Baltimore?" I finally asked.

I heard a crack as Quinn stretched his neck.

"Rest and a change of vehicles —"

"Speaking of which, whose SUV is this, anyway? I hope to heaven you didn't steal it."

"Borrowed. A co-worker had to take personal leave unexpectedly — flew to another state to be with a sick parent. I agreed to get his vehicle out of the shop for him, so I had his keys. No one else knows."

"We're car thieves, too?"

"I fully intend to get his property back to him."

"Without bullet holes, I hope."

"That's the idea."

"Is that all we're after in Baltimore? Rest and a new vehicle?"

"There's a good lead, too, I think . . ."

He took back the bottle and drained it.

I touched his arm. "The tension is tiring you. Why don't you let me drive?"

"What I want is for you to grab another water from the backseat, and tell me more."

"About Abby?"

"About the second time you saw her. When was it exactly?"

"A week and a day after I met her. Remember *Nox Horrenda*? Well, *this* was that horrible night."

"What night of the week was it?"

"Thursday — and it didn't start off badly. Gard and I had talked all day about Abby's big headliner debut on Saturday. We were ready, except for the fact that our menu was still a major problem, which is why I broke into my own coffeehouse."

"You *what*?"

"Okay, technically I didn't. But I did."

"What happened? Did you forget your keys?"

"On the contrary, I brought every passkey with me."

Quinn shot me a glance. "Okay, Cosi, I'm officially intrigued. Better take it from the top."

After a long swig of water, I did.

SEVEN

Wearing black boots, black jeans, and a black trench coat, I disarmed the security system and slipped through the front door.

The table and chairs on our deserted first floor appeared cobwebbed with shadows, but I avoided turning on any lights; and when a Metro DC police cruiser rolled down Wisconsin, I hid in the gloom until it slipped out of sight.

While I had a perfect right to enter the business I managed, tonight I didn't want witnesses. So I moved with extreme stealth until a noise on the second floor froze my feet.

First came laughter. Then a few bright bars of jazz . . .

Gardner and his bandmates must be having an after-hours jam session.

Explaining to Gard what I was doing here would be uncomfortable, but it was far better than another shouting session with my

55

hotheaded chef, who I prayed was long gone.

Moving to DC seemed an exciting change, and I naively assumed that things would go swimmingly. They *might* have, too, except for one giant shark in the tank — a beady-eyed shark with a blond buzz cut, a juvenile smirk, and a great white jacket.

It was Chef Tad Hopkins who pushed me to this new low in my management career — snooping around my own coffeehouse.

I passed through the swinging kitchen doors, turned on the lights, and blinked against the fluorescent glare.

I was now in forbidden territory.

After our disagreement earlier, Hopkins barred me from his kitchen "for life." There was little I could do about that banishment, or anything else I saw as wrong. As the loudmouth chef pointed out, he was under a two-year, ironclad contract, which included "complete control" of the kitchen and costly penalties if we "violated his terms."

The problem was: I didn't hire the man, and I couldn't fire him. That privilege belonged to our employer, Madame Blanche Dreyfus Allegro DuBois, who was presently far away from the fuss, in her New York penthouse.

It wouldn't be easy changing Madame's opinion of this twenty-nine-year-old "prodigy" who she'd been tickled to "hook." But if I could find evidence that Hopkins had violated his contract, then we could kick him *outta here,* and a better man could run the kitchen — namely, Luther Bell.

Though Luther was the assistant chef, he was much older than Tad — not that chronological age was the issue. The problem with Tad Hopkins wasn't age, it was his lack of maturity.

Luther was a well-grounded gentleman who could stay calm and focused, even in the face of Tad's tirades. Luther also possessed a kindness in his soul that everyone responded to, and that sweetness was reflected in his cooking.

Like the passionate notes of jazz playing every night on our stage, each bite of Luther's food seemed to carry the love of the man who prepared it.

Sure, Chef Hopkins was talented. But ambition and ego had blinded him, and his loss of perspective had become toxic. This wasn't a trait he'd revealed initially, which is how my kindly old employer had been fooled. The chef could be funny and charming when he needed to be; and for far too long, I believed I could penetrate his thick shark skin.

That belief ended with our first argument of the day.

Once I show Tad the evidence of his failed menu, he'll change his tune!

Or so I'd thought. But the hotshot chef didn't see his menu as a failure. He blamed Gardner and me, claiming we weren't attracting the right kind of clientele who would appreciate his cuisine.

"What the Village Blend really needs is intelligent management and a highly paid publicity team," he'd declared and named two of his friends for the job.

Ready to strangle him, I not so gently pointed out that this was a club that showcased jazz, not a temple to one gourmet chef.

My observation didn't exactly help the situation, and the chef promptly barred me from his domain.

But with Abby's big debut coming up, I was determined to feature Luther's down-home chalkboard specials on Saturday — our busiest night.

So despite our nasty encounter that morning, I waited until late afternoon before pushing my way through the swinging doors of Tad Hopkins's kitchen, for one more try at talking some sense into our senseless chef . . .

"Clare! Where have you been keeping yourself? It's been too long!"

The warm greeting didn't come from the chef. It was Luther who'd welcomed me with a broad smile and a voice that rumbled low under the high clatter of stainless steel.

"We both know Chef Hopkins doesn't like me butting in," I reminded him.

"Well, I don't feel that way. And the chef isn't in the kitchen right now, so come on in!"

I hesitated. My business was with the chef, not his assistant. On the other hand, I hadn't eaten in hours, and the sizzling skillet was sending out tempting aromas.

Without thinking, I moved forward like a thirsty nomad toward an oasis, licking my lips with anticipation . . .

EIGHT

With a rainbow of splashes decorating his white jacket, Luther's russet brow glistened from the heat, and his cropped silver hair displayed the same hue as the lid he used to clap over his giant skillet.

"Do I smell wine?" I asked.

"Hard cider."

With a wink he lifted the pan's lid and revealed culinary magic: chopped bacon, Vidalia onions, and bright red peppers, all blended with pounds of fresh green string beans caramelized in a succulent, sweet-tart glaze.

"You want a taste?"

"Does a cat want nip?"

Luther directed me to a corner table, where he proudly presented me with a sample bowl.

The first delicious bite made my mouth salivate beautifully. The sweet-tart flavor came from a combination of hard cider and sweet apple juice, a brilliant pairing with the smokiness of the bacon, richness of the caramelized onions and slight crunchiness of the al dente beans.

Next, Luther set down a plate of Buttermilk Fried Chicken Wings.

"Is that a combo, or what?" he crowed. "I must have made fourteen tons of coleslaw working at those federal cafeterias. Now, don't get me wrong — nobody can say that Luther Christian Bell doesn't enjoy a good slaw. But it might be time for a change, and I think these string beans pair perfectly with my grandmother's buttermilk fried chicken. I did wings to keep the price down, and it gives the folks more pieces on their plates."

I nodded. "Little bites on the plate work much better for a nightclub."

Luther's instincts were spot-on, but then he'd been working in the food preparation business for thirty years; first in the Marine Corps, then in New Orleans, and finally at various United States government cafeterias in the DC area, including a stint at CIA headquarters in Langley, Virginia, and the famous U.S. Senate Dining Room.

His natural home was the kitchen, and I never knew anyone who enjoyed cooking more. According to Luther, that love was born on the knee of his great-great-grandmother, a former slave from South Carolina.

"These are scrumptious," I managed between chews. "The chicken is crispy on the outside and juicy on the inside. And these string beans? That fresh brightness with all those vibrant flavors is the perfect complement to your fried chicken."

Luther's smile outshined the gleam of the spotless kitchen.

"So when are you adding these Hard Cider Green Beans to the menu?"

"Next week. Tonight is a test run for the staff dinner."

"Why not try them out for *tonight's* chalkboard specials?"

"That's not up to me, Clare . . ."

Of course, I knew that. When Chef Hopkins was working, he created the specials. But they never sold as well as Luther's.

"So what *are* Chef Hopkins's daily specials?"

Luther suppressed a chuckle. (I suspected he got a kick out of my endless rounds with Hopkins over the menu, and he likely knew the specials were going to ring the opening bell of our next toe-to-toe match.)

"As I recall, the first special is Pomegranate Pork Chops."

"With or without those annoying crunchy seeds?"

Once again, Luther suppressed a laugh.

"What else?"

"Squab with Black Pepper–Strawberry Compote."

I turned away, pretending to be ill.

Luther snorted.

"Okay, I'm over it. Hit me with another one."

This time Luther held my gaze, expression deadly serious. "He's got Sea Trout Stuffed with Cranberry Chutney in the freezer, ready to go."

"Are you kidding me?"

"Do I look like I'm kidding?"

"I know *fresh* sea trout was delivered yesterday, because I paid the supplier —"
Too much, I silently added. "How and why are they suddenly *frozen*? Is freezing some step in Chef Hopkins's 'prodigy' preparation?"

Luther folded his corded arms. "All I know is the chef loaded the trout into his minivan last night. When he came back this afternoon, he stuffed the freezer with preprepared servings."

"That makes zero sense. How does he want you to cook it?"

"He told me to zap it in the microwave.

The chef said the trout steams in the bag."

"You're telling me all that lovely *fresh* trout is now encased in plastic? To be steamed — in a microwave? And why would he take the fish away, only to bring it back?"

Luther showed me his palms. "It's his kitchen."

"For now," I said. "Would you mind showing me that fish?"

Luther waved me to the walk-in. Shivering in the big freezer, I glanced over the preprepared fish, trying to weigh it with my eyes. It seemed to me this was roughly half the order I paid for.

"What are you doing?" Luther asked.

"Checking something . . ." I unwrapped one of the chef's prepped fish and frowned. *Freezer burned? In less than twenty-four hours? I don't think so . . .*

Despite the walk-in's zero degrees, my blood started boiling.

"Luther, where exactly is our executive chef?"

"He had a personal appointment," Luther replied. "Said he'd be back later."

Now, why is my highly paid executive taking personal time during dinner prep? And why did he take these fish off the premises? Where is the other half of the order? And why do these fresh mid-Atlantic catches look like they were sitting in a North Pole snowbank for the past month?

At that point I made a vow to get some answers, and hung around after my day shift to confront the chef when he finally showed up again.

No surprise, Hopkins blew his stack for a second time. He absolutely refused to allow Luther's specials to go on Saturday's menu, or explain his suspicious activity with all that beautiful sea trout.

And *that* was why I returned to the coffeehouse in the dead of night. If Chef Hopkins wasn't giving up answers, I'd sniff them out for myself!

NINE

At 1:00 AM, I was back in Hopkins's kitchen.

Except for the soft hum of refrigerators, the room was quiet — and spotless, I had to give him credit for that.

I passed the gleaming silver counters, the heavy-duty ranges, and the dumbwaiter that took food up to the second floor. Rounding a corner, I stepped into a short hall, where Chef Hopkins had turned a small storeroom into a private office, which he always kept locked.

But I'd come prepared with my giant ring of manager's passkeys, all twenty-two of them. I inserted the key into the knob lock, but it didn't turn.

Oh, you're kidding me. It appeared the chef had changed the doorknob and lock.

I was already suspicious of Hopkins. Now alarm bells were going off in my head, until I heard an even more startling sound —

Bam!

Bam-Bam-BAM!

Someone was pounding on the back door, and I immediately recalled a story Gardner had told me.

Coming down from his third-floor apartment in the wee hours, he found the kitchen occupied by Chef Hopkins, who was speaking in hushed tones with a thuggish, middle-aged man in a long, black leather coat. This man had pale, craggy features, a receding hairline, and an Eastern European accent.

My co-manager asked the chef what was up and was immediately told to "forget what he saw and mind his own damn business" (*that's the sort of charm Chef Hopkins exudes*).

Of course, Gardner recounted the incident to me.

After years in New York, I'd learned about chefs who did quasi-illegal things in this insanely competitive restaurant trade.

One head of a Michelin-star Manhattan kitchen traded in smuggled caviar from Russia. Another illegally demanded a cut of his waitstaff's tips. And then there was the proprietor of a Chelsea gastropub who obtained certain items at a cut-rate price, after they "fell off" a big restaurant chain's trucks.

67

Now I knew the Village Blend didn't serve caviar, bilk its baristas, or pay off truck drivers to misplace a case of frozen lobster tails.

So who was the strange Eastern European man? What was his business in my coffeehouse? And could that be him at the back door right now, looking to find Chef Hopkins for some nefarious purpose? Like, oh, say, buying up a big order of fresh sea trout at a discount price — and covering the crime by replacing it with half the amount of cheap, prefrozen fish?

Expecting to discover the truth, I decided to answer the back door (couldn't wait, actually). If I could subtly question this mystery man, I was sure I could get him to reveal some kind of net to catch and cook our resident shark.

First I grabbed a big meat cleaver (in case the man got nasty). Then I released the door's dead bolt. The loud click sounded, and the pounding abruptly stopped. But before I could pull the steel door wide, it burst inward.

On a cold blast of night air, a well-dressed gentleman rushed inside with astonishing force, slamming me backward. My rear hit the deck and the cleaver flew out of my hand and across the spotless floor.

With his eyes wide and hands shaking, the

intruder stared down at me.

His face was clean-shaven, his features refined, his skin a milk chocolate hue. He looked East Indian, maybe Pakistani — and definitely *not* the pale, leather-jacketed thug whom Gardner had seen come through this back door.

He also reeked of alcohol!

"I am s-s-o s-sorry," he slurred, "but I've got to find it! I know it's here . . ." (The words came out sounding more like "I gosh to fine ish" — but I got the message.)

I raised myself on both elbows and met his ink-dark gaze. He wore no coat, just an exquisite pin-striped suit, yet his shirt was sloppily opened with a few buttons missing. His thick, dark hair was disheveled, the white dress shirt matching his temples, a sharp contrast to his dark complexion.

As his undone tie slithered to the floor beside me, I realized —

I've seen this man before!

"Who are you?" I asked, trying to sound calm. "What do you want?"

"I've gosh to fine ish," he simply repeated and frantically scanned the kitchen. When he spied the swinging doors leading into the coffeehouse, he bolted.

TEN

"Wait!" I cried, but the man shot past me, colliding with a food caddy on the way. A stainless steel shower of forks, knives, and spoons pelted me as the cart toppled.

Undeterred, he crossed the kitchen in a weaving run and plowed through the swinging doors.

I was on my feet and on his trail, bellowing —

"Help! Gardner! Anyone!"

Bursting out of the kitchen, I spotted the maniac man heading for the staircase.

"Help!" I called again. "There's a crazy drunk in the coffeehouse!"

The second floor is where we kept the alcohol, and I assumed he was heading to the bar.

As I raced up the steps after him, I heard a table crash in the Jazz Space, followed by an ominous silence. I hurried through the archway to find a shocking tableau in the middle of the dining room —

Stan "Sticks" McGuire was holding the intruder at bay with his white Hoover cane. Onstage, First Daughter Abigail Prudence Parker stood fearfully, mouth agape.

What in heaven's name is Abby doing here at this hour?!

My frantic scan of the room gave me another shock, a dreadful one.

"Abby, where is your security detail?"

Eyes wide, she shook her head.

Oh, my giddy aunt. The President's daughter was here *alone* with a half-blind, jazz-drumming army vet — and *without* Secret Service protection, which could only mean one thing. The frowning agent Sharon Cage and her heavily armed security detail had *no idea* their charge had slipped away from her college dorm in the dead of night.

Exactly how Abby had managed this feat, I was determined to find out, but this was not the time to ask.

"Stay back," Stan commanded, controlling the drunk.

"Stan, be careful!" Abby cried.

Hearing Abby's voice, the well-dressed drunk turned his gaze toward her, and the fight went out of him.

"Your father . . . your father," he slurred. The words were difficult to make out. I moved closer. "The truth . . . I have it. It's right . . ."

With that, the drunk dropped to his knees and then toppled forward. His forehead struck the hardwood with a sickening thud.

"Omigoodness, what is going on?" Abigail whimpered. "Who is this guy? And what did he say about my father?"

Stan and I bent over the fallen man.

His breath was ragged, but at least he was breathing. With Stan's help, I turned him onto his back and checked him for injury or a throat blockage. I couldn't find anything, but I could see he was in distress.

"I'm calling 911," I said, grabbing my smartphone.

"I can perform CPR," Stan offered. "I learned it in the army."

"And I learned it in the Girl Scouts," I returned. "If he stops breathing, I'll handle it. Right now I want you and Abby to leave."

"But —"

"You listen to me, Stan McGuire: If the President's daughter is found in this club, after hours, with a crazed intruder in this state, and *without* her Secret Service detail, you will never see her again. I guarantee it."

"Dang, Ms. Cosi, I think you're right."

"Now, get her out of here!"

"Yes, ma'am!" Stan grabbed Abby's hand.

"C'mon!"

"Unlock the front door," I called after them. "So the paramedics can get in. But leave through the back alley! You hear me?"

"Roger that!" Stan returned.

As the pair hurried down the stairs, I heard Abby cry out.

"Thank you, Ms. Cosi!"

With a gurgling moan, the intruder stirred, and I dialed 911.

For three long minutes I sat with the stranger, concerned for his life. As his ragged breathing continued, my mind began to work, and I finally remembered where I'd seen him before — *right here,* a week ago.

He'd been sitting at a table with that stylish, middle-aged woman, swathed in the latest Fen suit, part of what I'd assumed was a "power couple" who'd come here specifically to watch Abby perform.

But how in the world did he know Abby was here at this hour? And what did he mean about the President? *"The truth . . . I have it. It's right . . ."*

Checking his vital signs again, I knew there was nothing more I could do for him, so I did something for Abby. She wanted to know who this man was, and so did I, so I went through his clothes.

The man's pockets held little, a half-empty pack of cigarettes, a few after-dinner chocolate mints (from J., an excellent local chocolatier), and a fine leather wallet, which contained loose bills, credit cards, and a U.S. State Department ID.

I found nothing else on him — no "truth" as far as I could see.

That's when I heard the siren in the distance.

I put everything back where I'd found it and waited for the paramedics.

ELEVEN

The ambulance came and went, spiriting the unconscious man to Med-Star Georgetown. Only two DC Metropolitan policemen remained.

I'd already dealt with Sergeant Reginald Price, a heavyset African American police officer. He took my written statement and then began wandering around the building from the first-floor kitchen to the second-floor club.

I was left in the care of a rookie cop who came after all the others. He was so fresh-faced with his boyish dimples and eager smile that he seemed to have skipped his junior prom to play dress-up in a blue uniform and badge. When he told me his name was Patrolman Tom Landry, I thought my hearing was off.

"Yes, ma'am, that's my name."

"Did your parents name you after the coach?"

75

"What coach?"

"Head coach of the Dallas Cowboys. He led them to Super Bowl victories in 1971 and '77."

He shrugged. "Far as I know, I was named after my granddaddy. He mostly played golf."

"Sorry. My mind makes odd connections when I'm nervous . . ."

I was careful to leave out the fact that I grew up in Western Pennsylvania with a pop who ran a sports booking operation out of the back of my nonna's little Italian grocery. Sure, it was Pop who made a living on the wrong side of the law, not me. But why give him a reason to question my veracity?

The truth was — I hated the idea of giving false statements to the police, especially one as sweet and polite as Patrolman Landry. But that's exactly what I had to do for Abby's sake.

I said that I was alone in the coffeehouse. *False.* But nearly everything else I told Landry and his sergeant was the truth, including the man's drunken rantings about the President and the fact that I went through his pockets, although I fibbed about the reason. (I said I was looking for an asthma inhaler or any type of medication.)

"You know, ma'am, you were lucky you

76

weren't hurt," Patrolman Landry said, "I mean, being alone and all."

Instead of replying, I poured the young officer a cup of coffee — because making coffee is another thing I do when I'm nervous.

After a loud slurp he sighed contentedly. "This sure beats the stuff I get at my regular joint."

"Is that right . . . ?" (I couldn't help myself.) "Where do you usually go for coffee?"

Landry named America's most famous burger-and-fries franchise. Then he blissfully drained his cup.

"Awesome," he declared.

"That's our Wake Up Washington blend. And I'm glad you liked it."

"Liked it? I'm in love." Landry smiled. "I'll be back tomorrow."

"I'll be glad to see you. We could use the business."

He smiled wider. "Then I'll spread the word."

"Thanks."

He nodded. "So . . . you didn't know Mr. Varma?"

"Afraid not. Until I looked in his pockets, I didn't even know his name. What is it again?"

"Varma . . . Jeevan Varma," Landry replied. "Forty-seven years old. Mr. Varma works for the government, according to the IDs in his wallet."

Not just the government, I thought. *He works for the State Department.* But what I said was —

"Oh, really?" Then I gave Landry my best "puzzled citizen" look. "Don't you think it's odd that a man who works for the government would go crazy like that?"

Landry appeared to stifle a laugh. "You haven't been in this town long, have you?"

"A few months."

"Well, ma'am, the District of Columbia is a government town, so people here tend to work for the government — sane and insane alike."

"I see."

"Ma'am . . . don't you have any idea why Mr. Varma pounded on your door and raced up here?"

"He said he knew something was here . . ."

The President's daughter, maybe? But I couldn't say that. Instead, I muttered: "I assumed he was looking for alcohol."

"Because . . . ?"

"He smelled of alcohol. He was slurring his words. And when he burst through the door, he ran up the stairs toward our beer

78

and wine bar —"

"Except he didn't stop at the bar, did he, Ms. Cosi?"

The gravelly voice belonged to Sergeant Price, who seemed to materialize out of the shadows.

"What do you mean, Sergeant?"

"The paramedics found Mr. Varma on the floor in the middle of the club, correct?"

I nodded. "He'd collapsed. That's where I found him. Then I checked his throat for blockage and monitored his breathing until the paramedics came."

"Very commendable . . ."

As Sergeant Price's voice trailed off, he closed his deceptively sleepy-looking eyes and added —

"But I wonder if you realize, Ms. Cosi, that to reach the middle of the club, Mr. Varma had to pass the bar entirely? He never even touched all those bottles lined up behind the counter."

Now the sergeant's eyes were wide open and fixed on me.

"Looks like your intruder was running toward *the stage,* not the bar. But since nobody was here but you, that doesn't make much sense, does it?"

TWELVE

It was hard not to flinch as Sergeant Price's ebony eyes bored into mine, but somehow I managed to keep my cool.

"I'm sorry," I said, "but I couldn't tell you what Mr. Varma was after." (And *that* was absolutely true.)

"By the way, I found this on the kitchen floor." The sergeant dangled a gallon-sized Ziploc bag he'd purloined from our supplies. Inside, a blue and white tie was curled like an exotic snake.

"You didn't write anything about the intruder losing a tie, so I wasn't sure if this belonged to Mr. Jeevan Varma. That is, until I saw the monogram — *JV.*"

"Oh, yes, I'd forgotten about the tie. Sorry about that."

Price tossed the bag onto the polished coffee bar. "Now, Ms. Cosi, tell me *again* why you opened the door for this man, whom you didn't know, in the middle of the night."

"It's all right there, in my statement . . ." I pointed to the pages tucked into his dark blue police jacket.

"Tell me again anyway."

I took a breath. "My executive chef has been known to frequent the kitchen at odd hours, and I understand he entertains acquaintances after closing. I thought the man pounding on the door was there to see Chef Hopkins. I didn't anticipate trouble."

Sergeant Price's eyebrow lifted. "Then why were you holding a meat cleaver?"

I cleared my throat. "Meat cleaver?"

"Your kitchen is spotless, everything in its place. Yet I found *this* on the floor near the door —" The sergeant produced a second Ziploc bag. Inside was the meat cleaver I'd been clutching. "Now, whose fingerprints are we going to find on the handle, do you think?"

Gritting my teeth, I blinked hard. "You'll find mine. I admit it. When I heard the pounding on the door, it alarmed me. I grabbed the meat cleaver in case I needed to defend myself."

"Why open the door at all?"

"I'll level with you, okay? I don't trust my chef. I'm not sure what exactly he's up to at odd hours, and I was hoping to find some answers on the other side of the door . . ."

My explanation seemed to soften Sergeant Price's stony expression.

"I think I'm beginning to get the picture. And if what you say is true, then what you did was foolhardy, Ms. Cosi, considering you were alone in the building."

"You're right," I said because I couldn't admit that I wasn't alone. Not without landing Abby and Stan, and (at this point) myself, in hot water.

Price offered me his hardest stare. "You seem nervous. Do you find my questions disturbing?"

"Yes, I do, because . . . well, I have questions of my own."

"Ask away."

"Not questions for you. For my night manager and my bartender. Until I question them, I won't know if the poor man who barged in here tonight was a regular customer. I won't know if he was here earlier this evening, if he'd been drinking, or how much alcohol he was served." Now it was my turn to stare. "You and I both know this business could be held culpable if one of my employees poured Mr. Varma a few too many."

"Where is your night manager, Ms. Cosi? You say he lives upstairs, but he's not there now."

"I'm sure Gardner and his bandmates are hitting some after-hours spots so they can keep playing. The members of Four on the Floor are passionate about their music, and they don't usually hit the sack until seven in the morning. That's why Gard is the night manager."

Sergeant Price gazed at a poster of our house band, propped on a tripod near the staircase. "I'm going to have to check out Mr. Gardner Evans . . . and his bandmates."

"Do you think they did something wrong?"

Sergeant Price cracked what passed for a smile, then he shook his head.

"I want to hear them play, that's all."

Patrolman Landry had been silent throughout his sergeant's tricky interview. Now he let out an audible sigh.

"I think that will be all, Ms. Cosi," Sergeant Price concluded. Then he tucked the meat cleaver and tie into his bag, and slung it over his shoulder. "I'm heading back to the precinct to file the report. If you need the case number, for insurance purposes or any other reason, let me know."

He laid a card on the counter and wished me a good night.

So it was that easy, I thought. *A seasoned law enforcement officer had accepted my*

obfuscations as truth . . .
   Or had he?

THIRTEEN

Although I lived only a few blocks away, Officer Landry insisted on giving me a ride home.

"It's late, ma'am. I don't want you walking the streets alone."

"That's very kind of you, young man . . ."

Eesh, I sounded like a little old lady. But it was certainly how the officer viewed me, and humoring the police was my objective tonight. So I smiled sweetly at him as I filled a disposable cup of French-pressed coffee and locked up the building.

Climbing into the front seat of his Chevy Impala police cruiser, I heard him radio something about a 10-7.

I sat back, happy this was a short trip. I was totally talked out, and I had far too much to ponder to continue chatting up the young cop. For one thing . . .

I couldn't stop wondering how Mr. Varma had recognized Abby, despite his inebriated state. *A mystery in itself.* Blind drunk, you might recognize a friend or family member, but would you so quickly recognize a seldom-seen First Daughter who took pains to disguise herself?

And what was he trying to tell Abby about her father?

Did "the truth" involve a scandal? A danger? Or some kind of threat? Or was Mr. Varma nothing more than a half-crocked government worker on a sloppy bender?

Officer Landry had advised me to think of this as a company town. Maybe Varma was simply spouting off about his boss, who also happened to be the President. Maybe "the truth" was nothing more than a workplace grievance.

"Here we are, Ms. Cosi, home sweet home . . ." The police cruiser rolled to a stop in front of my N Street address. Landry craned his neck. "A very nice home, too."

"Thanks. Unfortunately, it's not mine. I'm only house-sitting."

"Really? Must be lonely."

"Well, I'm always busy, and —"

"You know, you still seem a little shaken up." He turned off the engine. "I can hear the tension in your voice."

"You can?"

"How about I escort you to the door, see

86

you inside? Tuck you in?"

Tuck me in? "That's nice of you, Officer. But I'm fine." I waved the idea away with my left hand.

"You're not married, are you?"

"Excuse me?"

"I don't see a wedding band on that pretty finger."

Then he leaned closer, and despite the dimness in the car, I suddenly saw the young man's "friendly" smile in a whole new light.

"Um, Officer Landry —"

"Call me Tom."

I blinked. "You're kidding, right?"

"Don't be embarrassed, Clare. All night long, you've been smiling at me, making small talk about my name, fixing me amazing coffee. A blind man could see you're interested." He checked his watch. "Look, I already called in an 'out of service.' We have an hour, give or take. What do you say?"

"I say I'm old enough to be your mother!"

"So?"

"So you should find yourself a nice *young* woman, you know, one closer to your *decade.*"

"Aw, girls my age are a pain in the — you know. Whereas older ladies, like yourself . . ." He waggled his eyebrows. "You're

87

so together, so confident. You go right after what you want. I respect that."

"Believe me, what I *want* right now is to say *good night.*"

"Oh, I get it. You're tired."

"No. I had a nap earlier. I'm wide awake. That's not the reason."

"Another time, then?"

I popped the car door and lunged onto the sidewalk. Landry called after me —

"Hey, Clare, I didn't forget. I'll be sure to tell them!"

I tensed. "Tell who? Tell them *what*?"

"My friends. I'll tell them how awesome your Village Blend coffee is."

"You do that. Now go back to work, Officer!"

I slammed the door and, for the first time in hours, exhaled with relief — but not until the police cruiser disappeared around the corner.

What a horrible night!

FOURTEEN

"Mike, are you *laughing?*"

"I'm sorry, Clare . . ." Behind the wheel, Mike Quinn shook his head. "It's just . . ."

"What?"

"Tom Landry made a pass at you. In any other context that sentence would have to involve a football."

"Please. I'm embarrassed enough."

"Why? Don't 'older ladies like yourself' have a sense of humor?"

After years of detective work in the NYPD, Quinn had developed a poker-face approach to human interaction. Over time, I'd schooled myself in reading his subtle emotional cues. But this? This wasn't subtle. The man's shoulders were shaking.

I punched his arm.

"Ow!" The squawk came from me. Quinn's biceps were made of granite. I rubbed my knuckles.

"Assaulting me will get you nowhere,

sweetheart. I'm armed. But I promise to stop laughing — in a minute."

"You know what, Mike? I think you're cracking up because you're cracking up."

"I'm fine."

"No, you're punch-drunk. You've been driving these back roads for hours."

"I'm not risking Baltimore until night falls."

"Well, we've got to stop. You're tired, hungry, and in need of caffeine — and so am I."

"Look, I told you. Restaurants, gas stations, and convenience stores have security cameras."

"Okay, fine . . ."

I banged open the glove compartment. Quinn's .45 sat beside a pair of sunglasses and on top of a mid-Atlantic travel guide. I grabbed the guide, checked the index, and then the map.

"There's a mom-and-pop donut shop a few miles from here."

"Clare, they'll have a security camera, too. I guarantee it."

"It's way off the beaten trail. Warm donuts and hot coffee. *We're going.*"

Minutes later, Quinn was parking around the corner of the little white clapboard shop. He donned a baseball cap and Windbreaker from his bag, and I handed him the glove-compartment sunglasses.

"Everything go okay?" I asked when he returned to the car.

"They had a security camera, but I kept my head down. And the teenager who rang me up barely noticed me. The line was out the door."

"Really? Must be good stuff . . ."

We dug into the pastry box and were soon moaning with bliss as we sank our teeth into the pillowy piles of fried yeast dough dipped in delectable honey glaze. The four giant cups of coffee were hot and highly caffein-ated. Quinn practically chugged one of them.

"Pretty good for roadside coffee, don't you think?"

I took a test sip. "Colombian. Large batch. City or city plus . . ."

"Plus what?"

"Sorry, occupational hazard."

"Don't apologize. You're a master roaster. I expect you to have an opinion on the brew."

"I do, and . . ." A flash of color in my side mirror froze my tongue — and then my bones.

"Clare? What's wrong?"

I told him.

Pulling up behind us was a local police cruiser. The cop at the wheel was staring right at us and placing a call on his radio.

FIFTEEN

"Mike, start the engine. What are you waiting for? Get us out of here!"

"Relax, Clare. Sit back and *relax.*"

"Don't you see the cop behind us? Look in your mirror!"

"I don't have to. I expected this."

"Excuse me?"

"The guy's a good cop. He saw me in the donut shop with the sunglasses and ball cap, trying to avoid the security camera. I figured he and his partner would run our plates. And we're going to let them. So why don't you educate me?"

"Educate you? On what?!"

"On the coffee. I want your mind — and eyes — off that mirror. So tell me what a city roast is."

I cleared my throat and closed my eyes, willing myself not to gawk into the mirror. It wasn't easy. I couldn't stop picturing those uniformed men walking up to our

SUV, guns drawn.

"Clare, talk to me *now.*"

"Right, okay . . . uh, city roast. You've heard me say roasting different coffees is akin to cooking different foods?"

"Sure."

"Well, a professional roaster chooses what level of cooking best suits a varietal's profile. Vienna, French, Italian, Spanish, those are . . ." I clenched my fists, trying not to picture Quinn and me in the back of that cruiser wearing handcuffs.

"Keep talking, Clare, what about them?"

"Uh, those are the darker end of the spectrum; they come after the second crack. On the lighter end, you've got city, city plus, full city, and full city plus. They come after the first crack and before the second."

"Crack?"

"The beans make a popping sound as they're roasted. That's how we judge the cooking time. We call it *crack.*"

"In my business we call something else crack. But I'd rather get my jolts from caffeine."

"Then you're in luck with this donut shop coffee. A light roast like this preserves more caffeine than a darker roast would." I gulped down half the cup and whispered, "Are they still there?"

"Yes, but now the officer behind the wheel is shaking his head, laughing with his partner. He's starting his engine, and . . ."

Zoom! The cruiser rolled by my window and disappeared around the bend.

I slumped back. "They're gone."

"Yeah, and I'm not surprised."

"Why?"

"Because these plates don't belong to me. They belong to a federal employee who resides in DC, and that radio call would have confirmed it. He probably figured me for a hotshot agent out here on a fact-finding jaunt, and off he went."

"Why didn't he come up to your window and check your driver's license?"

"Because his coffee was hot, his donuts were warm, and he didn't feel like dealing with federal arrogance, or . . ."

"Or what?"

Quinn shrugged. "Or he saw me get into this SUV with an attractive woman, miles away from my home and work, and decided the sunglasses served another purpose."

I was about to ask *what?* when light dawned. "A married man with his mistress wouldn't want to be recognized."

"Sorry, sweetheart."

"Hey, whatever it took for him to leave us alone is fine with me, and — wait a second.

If the DC police or federal authorities *are* out looking for me, or you and me, they're still doing it within the Beltway. That cop wouldn't have driven off if there was a nationwide APB out describing us."

"Exactly right. It's good news. For now." He regarded me. "So what do you actually think of the coffee?"

"It's fine."

Mike raised an eyebrow.

"Okay, it's one-dimensional and a little flat, but it has a pleasant nuttiness and it's freshly brewed — an acceptable choice for serving with donuts this good; after all, they're the star."

"I'll say . . ." Quinn garbled, mouth full. By now he was on his third. "Too bad this place is so far from DC."

"Tell you what, if we actually get out of this mess *alive,* I'll ask Luther for his recipe and make you a dozen. He makes fantastic glazed donuts for the staff."

"Positive thinking. I like that. A *reason* to get out of this mess alive."

"Donuts aren't the only reason . . ."

As I touched Mike's cheek, his gaze melted. My fingers were sticky from the honey glaze, but he didn't care. He turned his face enough to taste the sweetness. Then I reached around his neck to pull his kisses closer, and we held on. We both needed it.

"Baltimore," he finally murmured against my lips.

"I know . . ."

He started the engine and pulled away from the curb.

By now, night was falling fast. Soon the trees looked black to me, the road ahead unbearably dark — until Quinn flipped on the headlights and asked me to go on with my story.

"Which part?" I asked. "You know the State Department factors into this, right?"

"I know. And a member of the White House staff. And that computer flash drive you told me about, the one you've been hiding . . . on your person. But don't get ahead of yourself, Clare, because most of these early details are new to me. Keep the events in order."

"Okay. Where did we leave off?"

"With Tom Landry." Quinn's eyebrow arched. "I believe he fumbled his pass at you. Or did that slip your mind already?"

"No. Older ladies like myself find caffeine boosts our memories . . ."

And with another hit of hot city roast, I refreshed my boyfriend's memory on the *second* pass that came at me that night.

Sixteen

Hugging myself against the February chill, I waited for Officer Landry's cruiser to disappear around the corner. Then I turned to face my temporary home, one of five stately brick structures beautifully situated on a shady section of N Street.

Though I was an art school dropout (by way of an unplanned pregnancy), I was still captivated by distinctive architecture, and this lineup of town houses, known as Cox's Row, was one of the country's finest examples of Federal period design. I couldn't help admiring the solid brick construction, exquisite dormers, and graceful white swags beneath the tall, black-shuttered windows.

The builder, John Cox, was a merchant, importer, and former mayor of Georgetown. He'd even served in the War of 1812, the same war in which Francis Scott Key, his M Street neighbor, wrote our national anthem. Soon after, the building I occupied became part of the Underground Railroad, that network of secret routes and safe houses run by brave abolitionists who'd defied the law to help slaves flee northward to freedom.

That's what I loved about this DC neighborhood. Like Greenwich Village, every block seemed to have a tale to tell. But there was a difference. In New York those tales were about artists and writers; in Georgetown, the stories filled me with national pride.

Unlike most of the buildings in the area, the Cox's Row homes were set back from the street, allowing patches of greenery to cheer up the severity of the lines.

In the wee hours of this morning, however, as I walked up the little dooryard of evergreen boxwood shrubs, I didn't feel cheered. What I felt was trepidation — as if someone were watching me.

I'd left the porch light off, not wanting to call attention to my nocturnal activities. I now regretted that, as I fumbled for my keys in near-total darkness.

The Canadian hemlock shrouded the small raised porch in shadows and I felt a shiver. Was that the whisper of tree branches swaying? Or a stranger's heavy breathing?

When I spun to find out, my spine turned to ice.

A man's silhouette was leaning against the front wall's red bricks. His broad-shouldered form had been hidden by the greenery, barely illuminated by the street-light's distant glow.

"Who's there?!" I cried as my fingers frantically fished around my handbag. "Don't come near me. I have Mace!"

"I know you have Mace, sweetheart. I gave it to you last Valentine's Day."

Out of the gloom stepped Mike Quinn.

"For heaven's sake, Mike, you stopped my heart! What are you doing here?!"

"For starters? This —"

His palms were warm on my cheeks, his lips soft then hungry, like a man who'd been deprived for days. I didn't mind the scratches from his five-o'clock shadow, but when his hands dropped lower and began to roam I caught his wrists.

"Mike, the neighbors . . ."

As I broke our embrace, the sandy stubble of his unshaven cheeks looked even darker in the gloom. But that true-blue gaze was alive and bright as it focused on me.

He'd been gone for a week and his presence tonight was, like our relationship, something of a miracle. After all I'd been through, and all my tortured thoughts, part of me was thrilled to see him — but another part was still agitated by the events of the night, and a little annoyed he hadn't warned me of his change in plans.

"I was expecting you tomorrow. What happened?"

"I missed you." His worn expression cracked a sheepish smile. "So I took a late flight out of LA and came straight here from Reagan."

He jerked his head toward a Pullman behind him, leaning against the front wall. "Unfortunately, I left my keys to Scarlett's mansion back at my apartment — where I was about to go, until I saw you roll up in a Metro DC cruiser. I thought I'd duck out of sight, surprise you."

"Congratulations, you did."

"So why the police escort? Did they release you on your own recognizance?"

"Something like that . . ." Turning quickly, I busied myself with unlocking the front door.

"Clare? What happened?"

"Nothing. A little trouble at the coffeehouse."

"What kind of trouble?"

"A drunk broke in and collapsed, but the paramedics took care of him."

"Why were you there so late?"

The front door opened onto a long hallway, and I busied myself with hanging up our coats. "Are you tired?" I called from the closet. "Because I'm wide awake."

"I slept on the plane — and you're evading a direct question."

"You know, I could use a midnight snack. How about you? Are you hungry?"

Quinn caught my arm. "Cosi, what have you been up to?"

"Look, some things at the coffeehouse are broken. Tonight I was trying to fix them."

"That's pretty vague."

"I know. But I don't want to rehash it right now, okay?"

He studied me. "Okay. And the answer is *I'm starving.*"

"At last, something I *can* fix. Come on . . ."

SEVENTEEN

I led Mike down the hall, through a pair of white columns, and into the elegantly furnished double parlor. The space was magnificent, with high ceilings, two fireplaces, and a display of eclectic souvenirs from the owner's world travels.

In fact, evidence of the former ambassador's extraordinary life was scattered all over her five stories, six bedrooms, seven baths, finished basement, and whimsical checkerboard patio. At the moment, however, I was leading Quinn beyond her double parlor and through a small connecting den. This led to a formal dining room, and finally —

"The kitchen!" I announced, flipping on the lights.

"Is that an echo?" Mike put a hand to his ear.

"I know. It's a cavern . . ."

Mrs. Bittmore-Black's gourmet kitchen

was also a cook's dream, decked out with a built-in Sub-Zero, a professional double gas range, and miles of countertop.

Mike didn't care. "I prefer your cozy kitchen back in New York."

"Me too. But you have to remember, this wasn't a family kitchen. Mrs. B. used it for catering her Washington parties, which, according to Madame, were legendary . . ."

As I went to the fridge, Quinn moved with me.

"So, what are we having?" he asked, snaking his arms around me.

"Well, since I was expecting you tomorrow, I already made a succulent prime rib roast . . ."

Quinn made yummy noises in my ear, a ticklish delight as I pulled out the tray of beautifully cooked beef. Unfortunately —

"Houston, we've got a problem. No bread. Your premature homecoming came before I had a chance to shop."

"No problem," he murmured, "just give me a fork."

Back in New York, I would have used split *tortas* for the sandwiches. The Latino population had made them popular in the city and the chewy little flatbreads made amazing French dips. Here in Georgetown, baguettes were easier to find, and I was going to buy fresh-baked loaves — but Quinn failed to give me a heads-up.

This begged a return to a question still bothering me.

"Mike, why did you *really* come home early?"

"What?"

The sudden tension in him said it all. "Okay. What aren't you telling me?"

"Sweetheart, I missed you," he claimed again. Then he gave me the boyfriend pout. "Aren't you glad I'm here?"

"Of course . . ."

But I had a strong suspicion that I was dying to check out.

"Tell you what, you get comfortable," I said, pulling off his blue blazer and draping it over a chair, "and I'm going to make you my Thirty-Minute Dinner Rolls."

"Oooh," he moaned, loosening his tie. "I do love your fresh bread . . ."

"The smell of it baking?" I asked, moving to get the flour.

"Oh, yeah."

"Or the butter melting on the hot, warm crumb?" I purred, taking out the mixing bowl.

"Oh, hell, now you're just torturing me —" He grabbed my hand. "Let's go upstairs."

"Not yet." I tugged my appendage back. "I'll need this hand to mix the dough."

"Clare, you're not really baking bread at three in the morning."

"Why not? That's when most bakers make it. And like you, I'm wide awake. After what I went through tonight, I'm also wired. Baking the rolls will calm me down."

He hooked my waist. "I can think of something else that will do that."

"I know, and I'm looking forward to it — *after* we eat."

"You're sure you want to wait?"

"Yes, Mike," I said, breaking away to preheat the oven, "because I know exactly what will happen if we rush upstairs like we usually do. You'll still be starving; and after we, uh — spend our energy — you'll come right back down here to raid the fridge. Let's try taking things in a civilized order tonight, shall we?"

"When the lady's right, she's right. Be right back . . ."

It wasn't easy letting Mike depart. As his long legs strode across the room, he pulled off the leather straps of his shoulder holster, and I couldn't help noticing his muscles move beneath his dress shirt.

I quietly sighed.

Baking rolls was a ruse. What I really

wanted was to follow him upstairs and help him off with that shirt. But tonight my curiosity trumped my libido. And, besides, my evil plan was hatching perfectly.

Quinn had left his blazer on the kitchen chair.

It took me one minute to stir together the warm water, oil, and sugar, and sprinkle on the RapidRise yeast. As the mixture proofed, I dried my hands and fished around the coat's side pocket to find — handcuffs? *Whoops.* Not what I was looking for. I tried his other pocket without any luck. But in his breast pocket — *bingo!*

Quinn's mobile phone.

I fired it up and (unlike Chef Hopkins's private office) found it unlocked.

Okay, Mike, in the interest of truth in our relationship, let's see what you're hiding from me . . .

EIGHTEEN

Fifteen minutes later, Quinn returned looking comfortable (and distractingly masculine) in his NYPD sweatpants and tee. But there was now an intensity in his blue eyes that wasn't so comfortable.

He accepted the cup of French-pressed Sumatra I'd made him (bold but smooth with a comfortingly thick body) and sat down at the center island to watch me blend salt, egg, and flour into the yeast mixture; knead the dough smooth; break it into pieces; and shape it into dinner rolls.

Quinn's steady gaze was unnerving, but I ignored it. And as the pale white dough balls waited out their quickie rise in the greased pan, I heated up slices of the prime rib on the stove with some of my special American-style au jus. Then into the oven the rolls went, sending the heavenly aroma of fresh baked bread throughout the house.

Minutes later, they came out golden

brown, and (much like Quinn) crusty on the outside, fluffy and tender in. He split two of them warm, slathered butter like crazy, and inhaled them before we settled into the formal dining room.

"Table for twelve?" he quipped, looking down the long expanse of polished mahogany. "I think the Walton family is missing."

"Walton's Mountain never saw a dining room with four sets of bone china, a wall of priceless paintings, and sideboard that once served Abraham Lincoln."

He raised an eyebrow. "You think my bottle of beer is outclassed?"

"No. It's got a coaster."

"But no opener."

"Oh, sorry. I'll get it."

"Allow me," he said, gently pushing me back in my chair.

"Top drawer, next to the fridge!" I called.

Some grumbling ensued about not being able to find it, but before I could get up again, he reappeared with something that was definitely *not* a bottle opener.

"Mike, what in the heaven's name are you doing with those?"

"You'll see . . ."

In one swift move, he closed his handcuffs around the neck of my frosty bottle, angled the metal edge upward, flipped off the top, and handed it back to me.

I blinked, staring at my open bottle.

"It's an old beat-cop trick," he explained.

"I hate to ask where you learned it."

"Stakeout, of course. Upper Manhattan."

"You were drinking beer on a stakeout?"

"No, old-school Coca-Cola from a Mexican bodega. But after the job was over . . ." He smiled as he flipped open the cap on his own beer and took a long, happy swig. Then he dug into the food and went quiet until every bite was gone and his fingers were licked clean.

That's when Quinn's laser gaze was back on me, and I uncomfortably turned my attention to Mrs. Bittmore-Black's Smithsonian museum of a dining room.

"If these walls could talk . . ." I mused.

"You don't know how many times I've thought that on homicide investigations."

"I can imagine."

Quinn looked over the antiques. "If you could choose one item in this room, just one, what would you like to hear talk? That cuckoo clock?"

"A gift from a German chancellor," I informed him. "And I've heard it talk already. Can you imagine that clock going off during the formal dinners here? Eccentric lady."

"Or a very wise one."

"What do you mean?"

"Consider the pontificating that must have gone on here among officials and bureaucrats. The sound of a cuckoo bird every hour would have been a brilliant reality check on pompous speeches." He lifted his beer bottle. "So how about the Lincoln-era sideboard? You said this house was part of the Underground Railroad, didn't you?"

"It was, but that's not what I would choose."

"What, then?"

I gestured to the ornate tray on top of the sideboard.

"The silver coffee service?"

I nodded. "It was a gift to Mrs. Bittmore-Black from Jacqueline Kennedy."

"Really?"

"I understand they were lifelong friends. Did you know Mrs. Kennedy lived at two addresses on this street? First in a town house with Jack, before they went to the White House, and then . . ."

"And then?"

"After the President was assassinated, Jackie moved back to Georgetown. This street served as a launching pad for her highest heights and in a stunningly short time —"

"Her crash pad for god-awful depths."

I shook my head. "That poor woman. The whole thing must have felt surreal."

"The whole thing was a monumental crime, Clare, that's what it was. A conspiracy to commit cold-blooded murder."

"Conspiracy? You don't think Oswald acted alone?"

"At this point, few detectives I know do. And if it wasn't a conspiracy, then it was a conspiracy of dunces."

"You mean the Secret Service not properly protecting the President?"

"Members were either in on it — or incompetent."

"Either one is hard to believe."

"Why? They're not robots. They're human. They make mistakes. And they can be corrupted like anybody else in government. Power corrupts, sweetheart."

"Even good people?"

"Without checks and balances and transparency — what we in the crime-fighting trade call *witnesses* — power corrupts . . ."

"Absolutely?"

"No. *Insidiously.*"

I studied him. "You're not talking abstractly, are you?"

"I've got . . . shall we say *problems* . . . at work."

"Yes. I know. I've known for a long time. What I don't know are the specifics. I've been waiting for you to open up."

He drained his beer bottle and set it aside. "How about we start with what you know."

I shifted uneasily, but then leaned forward.

"I know your work is classified, some special DOJ task force focused on corporate wrongdoing that utilizes your years of drug enforcement expertise. I know your new lawyer boss — that Katerina creature — is trouble. And it's not simply about snapping her fingers, and calling you at all hours, and forcing you into unpredictable overtime."

Quinn's steady blue gaze remained on me. "Well? I'm waiting."

"For what?"

He gestured to the Kennedy coffee service. "Don't you think Jackie listened in on a few of Jack's phone calls?"

"Excuse me?"

"Clare, don't you want to talk to me about what you learned after raiding my pocket?"

Oh, crap. "Mike, I'm sorry —"

"Don't be." He leaned back and folded his arms. "That's why I left my mobile phone in my jacket — and my mailbox unlocked."

NINETEEN

"Tell you what . . ." Mike tossed me his phone. "Let's review it together."

I turned the phone back on and reread the text messages . . .

Thur. 6:30 PM — Katerina Lacey, Esq.

Great work, Michael. You are the man! Late meet tonight, your room. Work review + bubbly to celebrate. You deserve it. When the cat's away! On Rodeo now. Facial and shopping. Expect me at 9.

Mike's reply came two hours later:

Fri. 8:30 PM — Michael R. F. Quinn

Apologies. On standby @ LAX. Must get back. Urgent, personal. C U in DC.

I handed the phone back to him. "Can't

you complain to someone? File a grievance?"

"For what?"

"Sexual harassment. That's obvious, isn't it?"

Quinn grunted. "Not so obvious. Her text message mentions work. We were on a business trip."

"What about the 'bubbly' and that 'cat's away' remark?"

He shrugged. "Is that any different than my NYPD CO buying me a few beers after a stakeout?"

"Then it's down to 'he said, she said'?"

Quinn nodded.

"What about what I say?"

He actually smiled. "I love you, you know that?"

"Mike, I'm not kidding. There's something I never told you. Katerina and I had a . . . well, a verbal exchange at your place."

He leaned forward. "When was this?"

"My first week in Washington . . ."

When I initially arrived in DC, Madame was bunking with me in the mansion, so I confined my love life with Quinn to his high-rise apartment, across town. That Friday evening, I was already dressed for dinner, waiting for Quinn to shave and change.

"There was a knock at your door," I explained. "You were in the bathroom, so I answered. Standing there was Katerina Lacey . . ."

"Excuse me, do I have the right apartment?" she asked.

Tall and slender with blunt-cut bangs and supernaturally straight, strawberry blond hair, precisely sliced mere millimeters from her narrow shoulders, Katerina spoke with a cultivated accent; and while her words were polite, her tone and manner were drenched with disdain.

"Aren't you Mike's superior?" I asked.

Her pea green eyes narrowed. "And you are?"

"Clare Cosi, nice to finally meet you." I extended my hand.

In high heels and a belted coat, she clutched a briefcase in one hand, a bag of Chinese takeout in the other — and didn't bother freeing either to shake mine.

"Oh, that's right," she said instead. "You're the little waitress."

My hand dropped. "Master roaster, actually, and general manager, and, as of this week" — I gritted out a smile — "DC resident."

"Oh?" She pursed her glossed lips and

looked beyond me. "Well, Michael didn't deem that information significant enough to share. *Where* is he?"

"Changing. We have dinner reservations."

"I see." She looked me up and down, and smirked — as if my simple little black dress and the classic pearls my daughter had gifted me were some kind of joke. "I suppose the work can wait. Over lunch on Monday. That's when Michael and I will, you know" — she raised an eyebrow — "*do* it."

"That piece of work!"

Quinn was on his feet and pacing, a dangerous look in his eyes.

"She knew you were moving to DC. I never stopped talking about it! And she knew about our Friday dinner plans. I remember turning her down for some invitation and informing her why. I can't believe you didn't tell me about that!"

"I didn't want to ruin our evening. And that's obviously what Katerina wanted — the two of us fighting all night about whether you two were having an affair. And, Mike, I knew you weren't. I never saw a man so happy as when I told you I was moving here to be closer to you."

He exhaled hard and took a breath. "Well,

I appreciate your finally telling me that story. But face it, *she said, she said* isn't much stronger than *he said, she said.* And if you examine the words she actually said, it could all be explained away as a misunderstanding."

"Fine, I get it. The woman knows how to cover her bony ass. But if that's how she operates, it makes me sick. So how about quitting? I know you wanted those generous paychecks for your kids' college funds, but you've put plenty away by now. And you know the OD Squad is waiting for you back in New York."

"It's not about the money, Clare. Not anymore."

TWENTY

"If it's not about the money, then why stay?"

"Because I don't like the way things are going, and maybe I can do something about it."

"Well, I don't like her hitting on you."

Quinn grunted. "Her passes I can ignore or evade. What I won't tolerate any longer are her methods."

"I don't understand."

He sat down. "When I was a cop our stings caught bad people doing bad things. We knew they were doing bad things, all we had to do was catch them doing it and show the evidence to a grand jury."

Quinn rubbed his forehead. "Under my first boss at the DOJ it was the same, only we were catching bigger bad guys doing worse things. But when he died and Katerina took over, things got ugly. She expanded the operation exponentially, a wider net to catch bigger fish. Now she's practically pushing entrapment. Her tactics are too aggressive, not to mention legally dubious. She has to be stopped."

"What about the other people on your task force? Don't they want to stop her, too?"

"No. Some are as ambitious as Katerina. Catch a big fish, and you're on the fast track."

"And the others?"

"They're scared of her. Reading between the lines, she has some kind of hold on them."

"So Katerina wants to use your years of experience running drug stings to help her advance her career with high-profile entrapment cases? And she keeps her team in line with promises of advancement or threats? Is that what you're telling me?"

Quinn nodded. "And it gets worse. I'm sure she's breaking the law to obtain confidential information."

"What makes you think that?"

"Entrapping good people, which is what we're doing, isn't as easy as catching bad guys. You have to find their weaknesses and exploit them. You have to use their needs and desires, their fears and phobias against them."

"But to know all that, you'd have to get

really close to them."

"Yes, you would. And yet Katerina seems to know — for every case. She's constantly providing shadowy intelligence from 'unnamed sources' and 'confidential informants' who are never revealed and never come forward to testify."

"So is Katerina making this evidence up?"

"I wish. A frame job would be easier to prove. But her intel is spot-on and ninety-nine percent accurate — and she always comes up with a way for me to exploit it in my stings so it will get her an entrapment prosecution. In law enforcement, it's called *parallel construction.* You might obtain information illegally, but you don't use it in court. You use it to find other evidence, and you prosecute based on that — which is why Katerina is in love with my ability to create effective stings. It shields her from a 'fruit of the poisoned tree' charge."

Quinn got quiet again . . . too quiet.

"What else?" I pressed. "What could be worse than using illegally obtained information to entrap otherwise good people?"

"I did a little digging," he confessed, lowering his voice as if he feared someone was listening. "And when I stepped back from all of our prosecutions, it seemed to me there was a pattern. Many of the people

Katerina targeted have either openly campaigned against the current President or given large amounts of money to his opponents."

"You mean . . ." My whole body went cold. "Your boss is using the Department of Justice for political payback?"

"It's not an easy case to make from the outside because her targets are across the political spectrum. But from the inside, what I see is a woman who owes her position to the current President and is looking to advance herself through a reign of terror on his rivals, followed by a government-funded guillotine. I can't prove it yet, but I think Katerina used those same 'mysterious connections' to dig up dirt on President Parker's opponents before his first election."

"Hold on a second. Isn't opposition research legal?"

Quinn's blue eyes turned glacial. "Not when a government official abuses the power of her office to do it. Then it's a felony."

"Mike, do you realize what you're telling me? If that woman is using your years of experience to help her do political dirty work, then . . ."

I closed my eyes, seeing an image of Mike, walking into a congressional hearing room, cameras rolling, his distinguished NYPD career over, reputation shredded, the college savings for his kids in the pocket of defense attorneys. And that was the *good* scenario. Worst case? The man I loved, this very good man, would be heading to federal prison.

"There's no dodging it, Clare. No walking away. I'm guilty, too. My fingerprints are on some of her most recent prosecutions. I didn't figure out her game until it was too late."

"There *must* be something you can do!"

"I can. And I will. But I need hard evidence, not just theories and accusations."

"Does Katerina know you're onto her?"

"That's why she keeps making passes. She doesn't care that I'm in love with you. She wouldn't care if I were married. She figures if I'm in her bed, then she can keep me in her camp and manipulate me any way she pleases."

My stomach lurched remembering my only encounter with that woman. At least I had a little toughness in my soul, and a lot of trust in Quinn. I felt terrible for the wives or girlfriends she may have played that number on before me.

"There's got to be a way to bring down someone as powerful and connected as

Katerina. There's got to be . . ."

"This town isn't kind to whistle-blowers, sweetheart, but I'm working on it."

He moved his chair closer to mine. "And while I'm working, I want you to know how grateful I am to have a woman like you in my life. Trusting me, loving me, backing me."

"You've got it as long as you want it."

Quinn touched my cheek. "How about forever?"

"Sounds like a plan."

We smiled, despite our troubles. And then we were kissing — sweetly at first and then not so sweetly.

I didn't want to resurface, but I did, tipping my head at the dirty plates. "I've got to clean up," I whispered.

"Leave it. I'll help you — in the *morning.*"

"It won't take long."

"Clare, are you —"

Cuckoo, cuckoo, cuckoo, cuckoo went the clock.

He pointed. "See, the bird agrees with me."

"Very funny."

That's when I heard the chain jingling. While we were kissing, Quinn had quietly closed his bottle-opening bracelet on my left wrist.

"Sorry, sweetheart, you're in my custody now."

"Mike, what are you —"

With a click, Quinn snapped the other handcuff on his own wrist. Then he gently tugged, and I was suddenly trailing him into the den and through the double parlor.

"Where are we going? Central Booking?"

"Up the stairs to the master suite. I'm a patient man, Cosi, but now it's time for bed."

"But, Mike, I'm not a bit sleepy."

His smile widened. "Who said anything about sleep?"

Twenty-One

Early the next morning, I heard it again, the manic drumming of fists pounding on a locked door. The desperate, insistent sound knocked me from my nap.

My eyes opened to stillness.

The pillow beside me was empty. The shower hissed in the master bath. Pink sunlight peeked through the curtains. On the antique night table, the digital clock read 6:05.

Was I dreaming, or had I experienced a flashback to the strange events in my coffeehouse?

Then the chimes rang, and I bolted upright, ripping away any lingering cobwebs. Someone was at the front door.

Up and out of bed, I threw on my white terry robe, vaguely aware of something stuck in the sleeve. By the time the chimes rang for the third time, I was hurrying down the carpeted staircase.

At the entryway, however, I paused, vowing not to make the same mistake I'd made last night.

"Hello?" I called through the closed door. "Who's there?"

"Sorry if I woke you, ma'am," replied a muffled female voice. "I'm here on official business."

Suddenly I was gripped by panic.

Did Sergeant Price see through my lies and send an underling to bring me in for questioning? Or is this the Secret Service? Maybe Abby never made it back to her dorm room, and they're here to pick me up for interrogation. Either way, I was in a boatload of trouble.

I opened the door, expecting to face a phalanx of official uniforms. Instead, my visitor was alone and out of uniform, despite the police ID dangling from a plastic necklace.

She was a young African American woman on the kinder side of thirty. Tall and angular with short-cropped black hair, she was also gorgeous — flawless mocha complexion; large, inquisitive brown eyes. Her bright yellow rain slicker was damp with morning fog, and she clutched an overstuffed envelope under one arm.

After registering surprise, she looked me up and down, lingered for a moment on my left wrist, and glanced past me, as if looking for someone else.

"Excuse me, I'm here to see Michael Ryan Francis Quinn —"

"I'm here!" Mike bellowed, thundering down the steps.

My eyes widened. *Is Quinn streaking?*

No. Though dripping wet, Mike had managed to wrap a towel around his hips after jumping out of the shower.

He might have at least grabbed a robe!

Apparently Quinn decided his Department of Justice shield was more important. With one hand he held the towel in place, while the other waved the DOJ ID.

When she caught her first glimpse of the man she came to see, the mystery woman smiled wide.

"Come in," Mike insisted.

As soon as she stepped over the threshold, he checked the street, then closed the door.

"You're alone?" he asked.

Glancing at me uneasily, the woman nodded.

Finally Quinn faced me. I expected an explanation, or at least an introduction. I got neither.

"Thanks, I'll take it from here," was all he said.

The implication was clear. It was time for

me to give them privacy.

"I'll make coffee," I announced.

On my way to the mansion's cavernous kitchen, I told myself that I was behaving quite rationally for a woman who'd been sent packing by her half-naked man so he could be alone with an incredibly attractive stranger, who appeared at my door with a mysterious purpose —

Hey, wait a minute!

Twenty-Two

I turned on my heel and marched back to the front entryway, where I stopped by the decorative column, close enough to eavesdrop without being seen.

"I got your text, but I wasn't expecting you this early," I heard Quinn say.

"Sorry, they want me at the precinct, after all," the stranger replied. "So I'm going straight back to Baltimore. Since the DA doesn't want anyone to deviate from their normal schedule, I had to make this delivery super early."

"That's okay," Quinn said, securing the towel around him. With both hands free, he accepted the parcel and shook it. "Are they all here?"

"If the theft was reported within your time frame, it's there," she replied.

He tore into the thick package, yanked out a cover sheet, and began to read. Within seconds he'd forgotten he had a guest.

"Those reports. That's all small-time stuff," the woman remarked.

"It only looks that way," said Quinn, still scanning the page.

Another uncomfortable moment passed. Finally, I decided it was time to intervene. After loudly clearing my throat, I reentered the hallway.

"I'm sorry, Ms. . . ."

I let the words hang, but the woman refused to fill in the blank.

"Detective," she gently corrected.

"Can you stay for coffee?"

"I have to go. Thanks anyway."

I opened the door, and she tossed me a friendly nod. Then she paused to make a final, frank appraisal of Quinn.

He absently combed back his shower-slicked hair with one hand, still immersed in his paperwork.

"You're one lucky woman," she told me. Then her gaze moved to my left wrist, and she lifted a smooth eyebrow in a kind of amused admiration.

When she vanished into the misty morning, I closed the door and finally *looked* at my wrist. Quinn's handcuffs were still locked on to it.

I would have died of embarrassment, but I was too curious.

"What was that about? . . . Mike? . . . Mike!"

Quinn finally looked up. "Oh, uh, it's just material I need for my work."

"That's not the first delivery to arrive at an odd hour," I pointed out. "Last week, there was that guy in a trench coat, and the Metro DC patrolman the week before."

"It's just work, Clare."

"And they couldn't be delivered to your office at the Robert F. Kennedy Building?"

Quinn stuffed the envelope into the attaché case he'd left beside the hall closet. Then he wrapped me in his arms. "I needed to see those reports outside of the office, that's all. I've been away for a week, and I want to get up to speed . . ."

The man's body was an island of warmth and comfort in the large, drafty foyer. I pressed my cheek against his damp chest and enjoyed the scent of his favorite soap, still clinging to his skin.

But I smelled something else, too . . .

"This is about Katerina, isn't it? You're making a case against her, behind her back."

"Try not to worry," he whispered. "I have to do this. I'm the only one who can. Do you understand?"

"I understand it's a terrible risk. Because if she catches you, and she's smart enough, then you're the one who's going to end up in handcuffs . . ."

That's when I remembered what was on my own left wrist.

Given the First Daughter's dangerous stunt, the collapsed State Department drunk, and my false statements to the DC police, I wondered how long I'd be able to stay out of them.

TWENTY-THREE

"Keep your eyes open, Clare. We need to find that address . . ."

In the glow of the Baltimore streetlights, I watched block after block of rundown brick row houses crawl by, most with bars on the windows, some with graffiti-tagged walls or boarded-up doors.

As for the sidewalks, they were eerily empty. No brightly lit bodegas or busy take-out joints — the kind you'd see peppering even the poorest sections of New York. I did catch sight of a dreary tavern with metal bars covering the windows. The door had blackened glass, and a dozen vehicles were double-parked outside, a disturbing mix of junkers, high-end SUVs, and pristine muscle cars.

"What part of Baltimore is this?"

"Not one of the nicer areas . . ."

"An unnecessary clarification."

We were on Jefferson Street, that much I

knew. A glowing light in the distance illuminated a small municipal park and basketball court. This late at night, there were no moms or dads or children playing; only dozens of teenagers, many sporting gang colors.

"One thing I know, we're not in Georgetown anymore."

"Better this than an interview room at the U.S. Custom House."

"Custom House?"

"The Department of Homeland Security's headquarters here in Baltimore."

"Point taken."

I called out the street at the next intersection, and Quinn made his turn. This road was narrower than the others with more row houses flanking us. Near the end of the block, the residential buildings ended with a string of empty lots — cracked concrete and neglected weeds.

The final lot on the corner held an old body shop with a pair of worn gas pumps out front. I saw no sign and the square cinder block building lacked any windows.

It didn't appear as if this crumbling edifice had been occupied since Jimmy Carter was President, but Quinn rolled right up to the graffiti-covered garage door and cut the engine.

"Mike, who exactly are we meeting here?"

Holding up his left hand to me, he reached his right into his jacket.

I thought he was going for his weapon, but instead he pulled out a phone and began to dial.

"Wait! Didn't you say our phones could be traced?"

"This is a prepaid phone, Clare. I picked it up in Union Station."

"Then, where's your smartphone?"

"In a FedEx box, on its way to my son in New York."

"You sent Jeremy your —"

Once again, Quinn's hand put me on pause. "It's me," his deep voice told the phone. "We're here."

Quinn listened a moment for the reply and quickly ended the call. Then he reached across me, flipped open the glove compartment, and placed the .45 on the dashboard between us.

"Why did you do that?"

"She told me we'd have to wait here about an hour —"

"She?"

"Yes. And like I said, this isn't one of the nicer areas of town. So let's just say if anyone takes an interest in us" — he tipped his head toward the cannon-sized handgun

136

— "I'm sending a signal."

The signal I understood — after all, I was a New Yorker. It was the "she" part of Quinn's reply that threw me.

"So who is —"

"You've met her," he said before I could finish asking.

A woman in Baltimore? Then it came to me.

"The *she* on the phone was that young, black detective, wasn't it? The woman who banged on our door at six in the morning? The young, *beautiful,* black woman," I amended.

Quinn raised an eyebrow. "Was she beautiful? I didn't notice."

"Well, she noticed you. That I remember."

"Really?"

I stared at him. "For a detective, you don't notice much."

He touched my cheek. "I notice what's important . . ."

Mike's sweet gesture was unexpected — unfortunately, so was the harsh clatter and screech of the garage door lifting, which effectively shattered our private little moment.

I tensed as the rising door revealed a large patch of oily concrete. The rest of the dimly lit interior was swathed in shadow.

Quinn started the engine and rolled in anyway.

Twenty-Four

The heavy metal door thundered down so quickly it nearly scraped our rear bumper. Quinn cut the engine again and our vehicle's interior lights dimmed.

For a breathless second we sat in total darkness. Then the garage lights flipped on and fluorescent glare burned into our retinas.

Blinking the white spots out of my eyes, I discovered our SUV was now surrounded by a half-dozen youths in identical black jackets, black work denims, and steel-toed boots. Two of them wore Baltimore Orioles caps — backward — and all had unfriendly expressions framed by dark, scruffy facial hair I can only describe as neo-conquistador.

Though no one wore a name tag, *gang-banger* was written all over them.

A heavyset young man stared through my passenger window. He had visible tattoos on his bull neck, and a gold tooth punctuating his sneer.

The big dude looked me over with a combination of snickering disdain and animal interest — until he spied the .45, which was no longer on the dash. Then his predatory smile vanished, and he met Quinn's eyes with a kind of grudging respect.

"You got business?" he asked.

Quinn cracked my window, just enough for his deep voice to carry: "I'm here to see Chan. He's on his way."

The big dude nodded, turned to his posse, and whirled his finger above his head. Immediately they backed off, and after a brief discussion in Spanish, the gang left through a clanging steel door — all but one.

A skinny, tattooed twenty-something moseyed over to a table and chairs set up across the room. He turned one of the chairs to face Quinn's car, presumably to keep an eye on us.

When he put his booted feet up on a crate and began to play a smartphone game, Quinn put the gun back on the dash, and I released a breath I didn't know I was holding.

"Take it easy, Clare. It'll be okay."

"Who's Chan?"

"He works with our detective friend. You'll see."

"You know I trust you, Mike?"

"I know."

"But I have to ask . . . what are we doing here? I thought that young detective was helping you build a case against your boss at Justice."

"You thought right."

"So what does that have to do with the mess I'm in? Is your boss involved in framing me?"

"I can't say for sure."

"Well, what can you say?"

Quinn shifted in his driver's seat.

"Mike, what are you keeping from me?"

Quinn met my eyes. "Katerina Lacey was the one who told me you were in trouble."

Wide-eyed, I was stunned I'd misjudged her so badly. "So she was trying to help?"

"In a way," Quinn said. "But not in a good way."

"I don't understand."

Quinn rubbed the back of his neck, clearly wrestling with how much to tell me.

"Please, Mike. I want to know everything."

Reluctantly, he nodded.

"This morning Katerina called me into her office and shut the door. I figured she was going to hit on me again, and I was ready for that. But I wasn't ready for what happened next . . ."

TWENTY-FIVE

"Sit down, Michael," Katerina said, tone somber. She rose and walked around her desk, fluffing her strawberry blond bangs with manicured fingers.

"What's up?" Quinn asked.

"We need to talk."

Lowering her slender form on the office sofa, she patted the cushion next to her.

At least she's not crossing her legs, Quinn thought. *So I won't have to put up with her pointy high heel bobbing up and down at me like a patent leather ice pick. Now, if she would only stop staring at me like I'm lunch . . .*

Quinn took the seat. "Well?"

Katerina reached into her jacket pocket, tugged out a sheet of folded paper, and held it up. "This is highly classified. I'm risking my career sharing it. But I respect you, Michael. And I like you. That's why I don't want to see your career destroyed."

As she handed over the paper, Quinn

caught a whiff of her *parfum.*

Eau de cloying, he thought, unfolding the sheet and scanning the photocopy, an official document with a simple list of names. A few of them, he recognized: *Gardner Evans, Sergeant Stanley McGuire (Ret.), Clare Cosi —*

"What the hell is this?"

Quinn immediately realized his mistake, but he couldn't keep the anger out of his voice. It was exactly the reaction Katerina wanted, and he saw it in her barely hidden smile.

"The FBI is planning to pick up these individuals for questioning . . ."

Katerina then revealed what the authorities were keeping from the public. The President's daughter, Abigail Parker, was discovered missing that morning and was believed to have been kidnapped sometime during the night. Even worse, the kidnapping was violent.

Blood was found in the course of tracing her movements through Glover-Archbold Park to Georgetown Waterfront Park. It was Abigail's type — and the authorities were now rushing DNA tests to determine whether or not it was really hers.

"I don't understand," Quinn said, forcing his tone to sound blandly professional.

"What does all that have to do with the people on this list?"

"They're suspected of involvement in the crime," Katerina explained, "providing information, setting Abigail up."

Quinn wanted to explode, but he kept himself in check. Sitting back, he rubbed his jaw, as if in thought. "How strong is their case?"

His change in demeanor helped the situation. Katerina began to relax and open up with more details.

"I shouldn't be telling you this, either, but I understand a known associate of Eastern Bloc organized crime and fringe terrorists has been tracked entering the back door of Ms. Cosi's jazz club several times, after hours. And that's not all. Metro DC police has been building a case against her."

"For what?"

"A Sergeant Price sees Ms. Cosi as the prime suspect in the suspicious death of a State Department employee." Katerina shrugged. "Mr. Jeevan Varma must have quarreled with Ms. Cosi or demanded a larger share of some kind of big payoff for helping the kidnappers. That's the current theory."

"I see," Quinn replied, clenching his jaw to keep from screaming.

"I'm sorry, Michael, but it looks like you've been played." With an almost gleeful condescension, she patted his shoulder. "You shouldn't feel bad. Men in higher positions than yours have been fooled by slick operators like Ms. Cosi."

Quinn took a breath, let it out. "All this is a shock, of course. But I'm not sure why you're telling me. Do you need my help?"

"Help?"

"Do you want me to assist in the apprehensions?"

"Oh, no. I simply wanted to warn you. You'll have to stay away from anyone on this list. Especially Clare Cosi."

"Yes, that's a given." Quinn frowned a moment, pretending he was thinking it through. "I have to say, I'm impressed with you, Katerina. I appreciate your taking this risk to warn me about these pending actions."

Katerina beamed, a look of triumph on her face. "It should all be over in twenty-four hours. Then that awful woman will be in custody and you can be rid of her and get on with your life."

"I'm certainly relieved to hear it will be over soon." Quinn shifted enough to allow his leg to make contact with hers.

Katerina reached out and gripped Quinn's

hand. Her touch made him queasy.

"Here," he said, pulling his hand away to offer up his smartphone instead. "Maybe you better hold this until she's apprehended. She might try to contact me."

"That's not necessary. You know I trust you. Just let her calls go to voice mail."

"Good idea," Quinn said, pocketing the mobile.

"I'm sure this is upsetting for you," Katerina purred. "Why don't I stop by tonight, say eight o'clock? We can order some dinner and —"

"That would be nice, but I'm afraid Clare Cosi might do the same thing. You know, drop in on me? That would be . . . problematic."

"If that woman spends the night with you, you could be taken into custody with her. You know that."

"Yes. And I know I'll have to answer questions for the FBI — but you've got my back, right?"

"Absolutely."

"So why don't I visit my kids in New York for a few days? Let's call it overdue personal time."

"I don't know —"

"And after Ms. Cosi is in custody, we can do that dinner. A nice long night for you to update me on what I missed while I was out. How about it?"

Katerina studied Quinn a moment before wetting her lips and leaning close to his ear. "I can see you're a survivor, too, Michael. Go ahead and take a few days; and if you need me — for anything — use that phone of yours to give me a call."

"Sure will," Quinn said, swallowing hard to keep his lunch down. Then he removed her hand from his thigh, went back to his office, and strapped on his Glock.

He also grabbed his .45, along with his extra magazines, tossed them into his gym bag, and locked his office door.

On the street, he hailed a taxi and loudly asked to be taken to Union Station, where he used his credit card to purchase an Amtrak ticket to New York.

Exiting through a back service door, he moved to a side street, hailed another cab, and took it to the nearest FedEx office, rerecording his voice mail message on the way:

"I'll be out of touch for a few days. Leave a message for me or contact Acting Director Katerina Lacey at the following number . . ."

He dropped the phone and its charger into a FedEx box and sent it rush overnight to his son, along with a hastily scrawled note:

Jeremy —
Do me a favor. Keep my phone safe.
Don't make any calls or answer any. Let
them go to voice mail. <u>But you can play
Dragon Whisperer all you want.</u> The
game app is loaded. Hug your sister for
me.
   I love you both.

                                    — Dad

*There you go, Katerina, and whoever the
hell you're working with. Feel free to ping my
phone ad nauseam.*
   Then he picked up Agent Ned Bastian's
SUV and took off for Wisconsin Avenue to
rescue the woman he loved.

TWENTY-SIX

"We can thank Katerina for one thing," Mike said in conclusion. "She may have alerted me to the situation for reasons of her own, but it helped us. We got clear of the Beltway, and we're free to do something about the situation besides rely on our defense attorneys."

"But what about Gardner and Stan?" I held my head. "Mike, I *never* would have left DC if you'd told me they were in trouble, too!"

Quinn took hold of my shoulders. "That's exactly why I didn't tell you. I needed you to come with me; and you know as well as I do that the best way to help your friends is uncovering the truth about Abby."

"But we're sitting in Baltimore, pursuing a case against your boss. How is that going to help us find out what happened to the President's daughter?"

"Add it up. Katerina conveyed facts to

warn me away from you. But none of those facts should have crossed her desk. She's an acting director of a marginal DOJ task force, Clare, one that primarily concerns itself with corporate and commercial malfeasance. She has nothing to do with advising the FBI on warrants, ethics, procedures, or anything else."

"But she could have a friend in that position at Justice, couldn't she?"

Quinn sat back, his hands curling into fists. "That woman always stinks of perfume, because somewhere down deep she knows she's dirty. Look, I honestly don't know whether she's involved in these crimes; working behind the scenes to help frame you; using the information to manipulate me; or all three. But she's got *something* to do with this. I can smell it."

"And you think the detective we're meeting tonight has a lead on untangling this mess?"

"Yes, I do. You just have to trust me a little longer."

"I'll try. But I've been adding things up myself."

"And?"

"I can't explain the blood, but I think I know what the President's daughter was doing in that park. She gave me the clue herself."

"When?"

"The day after you came back from Los Angeles. I'll never forget it — because it was the day she kidnapped *me.*"

"She what?"

"You heard me."

Quinn stared, astonished. "Okay, Cosi, I'm listening . . ."

Twenty-Seven

As I unlocked the front door of the Village Blend, DC, that Friday morning, my brain was fogged, my eyes half-closed. But duty called, so I took our morning bakery delivery, ground the coffee beans fresh, brewed up our morning selections, and filled the airpots. Finally, I calibrated the espresso machine, pulling the first oh-so-satisfying shots of the day.

As the caffeine kick-started my heart, I heard the banging of pots and peeked through the swinging kitchen doors. Chef Tad Hopkins had entered the building, through the door to the back alley — like our unwanted visitor last night.

Next on my to-do list: have that thing permanently bricked shut!

It was highly unusual for Tad to come in this early, but I didn't have a chance to quiz him. A gentle knock on the front door heralded the simultaneous arrival of two of my part-time baristas — Kimberly and Freddie, fresh-faced undergrads from nearby Georgetown University. As I unlocked the door for them, our first morning customers came in on their heels. Then the morning crush was on.

The volume was much heavier than normal for a Friday, including a seemingly endless stream of police officers.

"What's with all the cops?" Freddie wondered after the two-hour tsunami of blue uniforms.

"I don't know," Kim said. "Ms. Cosi, do you have any idea?"

Unfortunately, I did.

The memory of Officer Tom Landry's reaction to my coffee came back to me (*"Liked it? I'm in love . . ."*), along with his promise to spread the word — and his midnight pass, prompted by the misguided assumption that I was hot to jump his bones.

"Uh, no idea," I lied.

"Well, they seem to like it an awful lot," Kim said.

Her tone wasn't altogether happy. Though I'd trained her and Freddie personally, they were still fledgling baristas, and they had a difficult time keeping up with the morning's demand.

The constant crowd of cops attracted attention, and before we knew it, commuters and tourists were curious to try the coffee, too.

If business increased any more, I would be forced to add staff to the morning shift — *experienced* staff, which was nearly impossible to come by.

But, hey, increased business was good news. And by the time the AM crowd was ensconced in their government offices and university classrooms, I was feeling optimistic about the future.

The feeling didn't last.

During the lull before lunch rush, I heard a *tap-tap-tapping* behind me — no, not tiny footsteps, but the *tink* of Chef Hopkins's thumb rings rattling against his smartphone.

Exhibiting impressive dexterity, he filled a personalized *World's Greatest Chef* mug while simultaneously typing a text message. I noticed he'd chosen our *most expensive* offering in the process — the creamy-textured Sulawesi, which Matt (our coffee hunter) had sourced from the very old coffee trees of Indonesia's Toraja region.

I should have ignored the tinking and tapping. But since we worked together, I thought a civil greeting was common courtesy.

Friendly. Casual. Respectful. That's my motto.

"Good morning, Tad."

He snorted. "It kills you to address me as *Chef,* doesn't it?"

Oh, brother.

"Don't be defensive," I countered. "You don't hear me address Kimberly as *barista,* or our evening bartender, Tito, as *sommelier,* even though he's worked as one. And I'm certainly not *Master Roaster Clare.* We're all equals here."

Still thumbing his smartphone, the chef shook his blond head. "You must be exhausted."

"Excuse me?"

"Managing all this egalitarianism has to be really wearisome. And you do look tired . . . *Clare.*"

"Your insult is duly noted. But I'm not put off — and I remain determined to see some of Luther's dishes on tomorrow night's menu."

The chef sighed and shook his head. "Up to now, Clare, you've coasted along on the reputation of a century-old brand name. But truly, you're no more than hired help. You had nothing to do with starting the Village Blend, because you know nothing about starting a business from the ground up. Now you want me to cook to the tune of low-end customers by serving low-end crap."

He finally lowered his phone, to flash me a grim little grin.

"But I was hired by your boss to execute my cuisine. Sophisticated dishes for discerning tastes. Food for the kind of people who don't particularly care to fraternize with college kids and aging jazz junkies."

The volley of insults was too much to waste time swinging at, so I simply asked: "And how do you plan to pack the place with these rarefied big spenders?"

Tad shifted his gaze back to the smartphone screen.

"They'll come," he declared. "They'll come because I figured out how to get buzz even if you can't. In eleven months I'll be collecting my performance bonus from Madame DuBois, and you'll be running back to Manhattan with your tail between your legs, to your old job at the Village Blend — if they'll have you."

So angry I could steam milk, I was about to let loose on the deluded peacock when Tito came through the door, reporting for his barista shift.

Despite his youth, Tito had years of experience, having worked since childhood in his family's restaurant near Milan. Blond and blue-eyed, his Northern Italian good looks made him a favorite with the college coeds, but it was his work ethic that made him one with me. He was also the most experienced staff member I had here in DC, and I was glad to see him on this busy morning.

"Boss! You got a visitor," he called, Italian accent thick. "It's that piano girl. She's outside beeping her horn like crazy and yelling for you."

"Abby's alone?"

"*Solo?* Sure. Why not?"

I raced outside, and into a blast of chilly air that set me shivering.

There she was. The President's daughter, sitting behind the wheel of a red Ford Fusion, madly honking the horn. She looked more goth than usual this morning with her black-and-purple-striped tee over black leggings. Her window was rolled down and when she saw me she tossed back her beautiful dark curtain of hair and yelled —

"Get in, Ms. Cosi! Hurry!"

I looked down at my apron, while my hand reached for my fast-deconstructing ponytail. "Give me a minute to grab my purse and coat —"

"No!" Abby cried, her tone desperate.

"There's no time!"

At that moment a pair of identical black SUVs rolled onto Wisconsin Avenue. It wasn't hard to guess who was behind the wheel.

"Please," she begged, "before Agent Cage catches up!"

I ran to the door and climbed into the seat. Before I'd even settled in, Abby released the brake and hit the gas. I fumbled with the shoulder strap as we barreled down Wisconsin. Traffic was light, but Abby still did too much zigging and zagging around the few vehicles that were too slow for her mission.

"Why the hurry?"

Hunched over the wheel, she refused to meet my gaze. "I wanted to get to you before they did."

"They? Who's *they*?"

"The Secret Service."

"Abby, where are we going?"

"My mother wants to meet you. We're going to brunch at the White House."

TWENTY-EIGHT

"I can't go to the White House looking like this! I don't have my purse. I don't have makeup. I don't even have lipstick!"

"You look fine," Abby assured me as she swung the car onto M Street — without applying the brakes. The tires squealed as we made the turn, then she punched the gas, and I was pressed into my seat by the sudden acceleration.

But our speed was only one on a list of my concerns.

Topping it was my coffeehouse, which I'd unwittingly abandoned. At least Tito had arrived to man the espresso machine. I knew he was capable of handling the staff and customers until I returned. That boy was assistant manager material if ever I'd seen it, so I considered this a test. *If he can handle my freakish absence with reasonable aplomb, I swear I'll promote him.*

Next on my list of concerns — my appearance.

I glanced down at my black skirt, black tights, and thin, black V-neck sweater — all covered by a blueberry-hued Village Blend, DC, apron.

I twisted the ceiling rearview mirror to check my face. After the night I'd had, what I saw wasn't pretty —

"I'm going to need that!"

Abby tugged my hand away from the mirror as the sedan swerved into the opposite lane. This time someone else's tires screamed.

"Why are we going so fast?"

Abby glanced at the rearview. "They're catching up."

"This is the second time you've done this," I said. "Last night —"

Abby cut me off. "Last night I was staying at my friend's house. It's a beautiful home, with a private garden *right next to Glover-Archbold Park.*" As she spoke Abby put her index finger to her lips and then tapped her ear.

"Bugged?" I mouthed, incredulous, and she nodded.

The park she mentioned was a beautiful strip of land running from Northwest Washington all the way down to the Potomac. My GU baristas said students used it to jog or bike the worn dirt paths between Georgetown and American University.

With that one clue, I could easily see how she'd gotten away.

If Abby had insisted the Secret Service give her privacy in her friend's home, they probably stationed a few agents on the public street. She could have left her panic button and tracker in her guest bedroom, slipped out a window or back door, and moved through the home's private garden, or even over a low wall, right into the park.

Then it would be a straight shot, under the canopy of trees, away from closely observed streets, to Georgetown's campus, where she could easily blend in as a student and finally make a short walk to the Village Blend, DC.

The blare of the car radio brought my attention back to our Washington speedway. Abby had turned up the radio's volume to hide our conversation from the planted listening device. Waving me close, she spoke low into my ear.

"I wanted to have some time alone."

I studied her. "You mean alone with Stan, don't you?"

She nodded *yes*.

"You really care for him?"

She nodded again, with much more enthusiasm. "*Please* don't give me away, Ms. Cosi."

"Abby, I don't know what to say. What you did was a risk —"

"*Promise* me. Please? It will be hard on me if you rat me out."

She looked so desperate. "Okay," I found myself saying, "as long as you promise *never* to do that again."

"I won't," she said and smiled with relief.

We swerved right, onto Pennsylvania Avenue. I glanced over my shoulder to find one SUV closing fast. A dour Agent Cage sat in the passenger seat. Our eyes met and the agent telegraphed her disapproval.

"They're right behind us," I warned.

Abby's black leather boot hit the gas.

"It's clear you learned to drive at the Indy 500," I said, hands gripping the shoulder strap. "But where did you learn to ditch a security detail?"

"Easy," Abby replied. "I did my research."

TWENTY-NINE

"Research?"

"Of course!" Eyes on the road, Abby beamed with pride. "After the election, but before we moved to the White House, I wanted to know what I was getting into."

Abby passed a slow-moving car — no biggie, except she did it by swerving into a lane with oncoming traffic!

"I looked into the lives of other First Daughters to see how they survived living in a bell jar. It proved helpful." She grinned. "Jenna and Barbara Bush were free spirits. A lot of times, the Bush girls did what they wanted, and the Secret Service had to play catch-up."

A traffic light went from green to yellow, but Abby didn't stop. And the heavy flow of cross traffic left a brace of Secret Service agents behind at the red light, playing "catch-up."

"Chelsea Clinton was lucky," Abby continued. "The Secret Service gave her a lot of space while she was in college. Of course an agent lived in the room next door, and they installed bulletproof windows in her dorm, too. But at least she could open them when she wanted fresh air."

"You can't open your dorm windows?"

Abby shook her head. "My room is on the sixth floor and they sealed them . . ."

She didn't finish her thought, but I wondered, given those scars on her wrist. *Were they afraid Abby might lose it and jump?*

"I researched the Princess of Wales, too. Do you remember Lady Di, Ms. Cosi?"

Yes, I thought, *the memory is distant but it's still stored somewhere in my "older-lady" brain.*

"Lady Di did all kinds of things to bamboozle her security detail." Abby's grin widened. "She was so cool!"

Another wild ride through a fast-changing yellow light set the Fusion's tires to howling again.

"Abby, you *do* know that Lady Di tragically perished in a high-speed traffic accident?"

The First Daughter's reply was to pass another slow-moving car.

"Of course you do," I continued, "because you've done your research."

Fortunately I no longer had to worry about a deadly crash. Abby had entered the Washington Park traffic circle — and she couldn't seem to find her way out.

While she looped around a second and then a third time, a flock of black SUVs appeared. Expertly jockeying through traffic, two vehicles flanked us like hungry raptors while a third pulled up right behind, and a fourth zoomed in front of us.

Boxed in by the bigger vehicles, Abby was forced to slow to a reasonable speed. But by now, she'd given up the fight — and flight.

"You see, Ms. Cosi, there's no getting away," she said as we came out of the circle, onto Pennsylvania again. "Freedom is fun. But it's fleeting. And that's inevitable."

She glanced at me. "It's best to know what's inevitable, don't you think? Only crazy people get blindsided by life's little surprises. I never want to be crazy. Not ever again."

"Whoever said you were crazy?"

"Forget it," Abby said. "Helen said I should never, ever use that word."

"Helen? Is that a college friend?"

"No. She's on the White House staff."

Before I could ask more questions, Abby announced —

"We're here!"

She turned off the blaring radio, and I prayed my hearing would come back before I met the President's wife.

I noticed our escort vehicles came to a stop, allowing Abby enough room to drive her car through a narrow corridor between huge, traffic-blocking concrete-potted plants.

As we reached a tall iron gate beyond, guards appeared to open them. These members of the Secret Service Uniformed Division had obviously been expecting Abby. They immediately waved us through the gate, and we rolled deeper into the White House grounds.

Abby followed a narrow road that ran parallel to the lush lawn, until we reached the East Appointment Gate.

The gate opened automatically, and we were waved through.

Previous to this, I'd only admired the White House through books and strolled past as a curious pedestrian, gazing through the fence. It gave me chills to be on the other side.

We followed a gently curved driveway around a bubbling fountain, then Abby pulled right up to the two-story, colonnaded East Wing building, which I already knew served as the office of the First Lady and her staff.

More people were gathered outside the virgin white structure, all waiting for us. Things got more crowded when Agent Cage's SUV and two others parked behind ours.

I felt the door slam and realized Abby was already out of the cab and was racing for the entrance. I rolled my window down and called after her.

"You're leaving me?"

"The Secret Service will take care of you," Abby yelled back. "I'll see you inside."

That's when I saw a torn piece of sheet music lying in the driver's seat, my name scrawled on it.

I turned it over. In the same hand I saw eight words.

Watch out for my mother. She's onto us.

I didn't know what to do with the note. If I were in a spy movie I'd probably eat it. Instead I stuck it between the seat cushions — and just in time, too, because the frowning face of Agent Sharon Cage suddenly filled my window.

"Please step out of the vehicle, Ms. Cosi. You'll have to clear security before you meet the First Lady."

THIRTY

I entered the somber, wood-lined East Wing Lobby anticipating a security check along the lines of a TSA airport screening.

I got that — and a whole lot more.

The difference was: here in the People's House, under the watchful eyes of the Presidents and First Ladies, whose portraits hung on the walls, things were polite . . .

Exceedingly polite.

"Welcome to the White House, Ms. Cosi. My name is Carol. How nice of you to visit us today."

My greeter had a light Virginian drawl and a rosy, cherubic face like Mrs. Santa's on a vintage Coca-Cola poster. This jovial woman also possessed a tasteful bouffant of snow-white hair, and the most gracious and genuine smile I'd ever encountered.

I liked Carol instantly. I couldn't help myself, and her warm, wise sapphire eyes told me she liked me, too. That's when it struck me, looking at her rosy cheeks, white hair, and blue eyes.

Carol seemed to embody the best of America itself.

"May I take your wrap?" she asked. Without a hint of condescension or even levity, she relieved me of my Village Blend apron. Then she draped it over her forearm as if it were a full-length chinchilla coat.

"Come along with me, Ms. Cosi. We'll get the messy stuff out of the way as fast as we can so you can get on with your day."

Heels clicking, Carol ushered me along the East Colonnade, a long corridor with massive windows along one wall. We trod along a central gold rug that reminded me of the yellow brick road. In the February sun, the floors on either side of that rug were as slick and shiny as just-Zambonied ice before a Penguins hockey game.

(Sports analogy again. *Yes, I was that nervous.*)

Agent Cage silently followed, while Carol happily chatted away, informing me that these windows faced the Jacqueline Kennedy Garden.

"Trees, shrubs, and flowers all seem to thrive in the shelter of the south-facing White House," Carol noted. "The rays of the spring sun are reflected and magnified

170

by these white walls. The light helps everything in the garden grow, which is as it should be, I think."

Because it was late February, the view wasn't as colorful as it soon would be, but my guide regaled me with descriptions of the coming pink tulips and magnolias, and the bronze and gold spoon chrysanthemum Starlet in the fall. Carol pointed out the dedication plaque, then directed my attention to a white, cast-iron Rococo Revival garden bench that had been on the White House grounds since 1850.

"I like to think Abraham Lincoln rested there during our nation's most trying days," Carol said, eyes misty.

Next we arrived in the East Garden Room, a sunlit space with double doors that led to the Kennedy garden we'd passed. An enormous bronze bust of Lincoln by Gutzon Borglum occupied a niche on the west wall. The east wall was dominated by four massive presidential portraits.

"This room, I admit, is a bit austere. But I wish you could have seen it a few months ago," Carol said, beaming now. "Christmas decorations hung everywhere, and the official greeting cards the First Family received were displayed on the wall panels beside Lincoln."

Carol's holiday story was heartwarming, but there was little goodwill toward men in this room at the moment. I suddenly found myself flanked by officers of the Secret Service Uniformed Division, here to complete my screening process.

I was asked to remove my shoes, along with the claddagh ring Mike gave me, and a delicate gold cross on a long chain that was my confirmation gift from my nonna. But instead of dropping my stuff in a dirty plastic tray, Carol took them for safekeeping.

In another especially nice, extra personal touch, Agent Sharon Cage used the security wand on me herself.

"I didn't even have time to grab a coat," I told her. "So you can bet I'm not armed."

"We already know you don't have a *gun*," Agent Cage informed me. "Magnetometers scanned you when you drove through the gate, and again when you entered the lobby. Right now I'm checking for chemical or biological agents, as well as explosives."

I made my arms into angel wings. "Check away."

THIRTY-ONE

Sharon Cage seemed almost disappointed to find me free of anthrax, nuclear waste, and improvised explosive devices.

But all was not lost.

Cage stepped back and signaled a courteous but annoyingly thorough female member of the Uniformed Division, who began a pat-down of my person.

Cage took the opportunity to poke and prod me, as well — not with her hands but with questions and innuendo.

"I see you were previously screened to attend one of the DOJ's holiday parties."

"Yes, it was held at the Lincoln Cottage. A lovely affair —"

"Affair? Is that a Freudian slip?"

"Excuse me?"

"Were you on a real date or were you with a beard?"

"A beard?"

"Sometimes a prominent man's wife and

mistress both insist on attending a prestigious event. He escorts his wife, and finds a beard to take his —"

"My date was Michael Quinn," I said, cutting her off. Not only had I heard enough from this impertinent young woman, but the uniformed agent unexpectedly began probing a few tender spots.

"I don't know any Quinn at Justice," Agent Cage said suspiciously.

"He's an NYPD detective on special assignment with the DOJ. If you need to know more, I suggest you call — *Yikes!*"

The gloved hand that slipped inside my sweater and between my breasts caught me a little off guard.

"I'm so sorry," Cage said in a tone that was not at all apologetic. "After our high-speed chase over here, I asked the security screeners to be *particularly* thorough."

The hand withdrew and I adjusted my clothing.

"So how close are you to this New York cop?" Cage asked. "Are you sleeping with him, or simply stringing him along?"

I slapped a probing hand away from my ponytail and freed it for inspection myself. As my chestnut hair came tumbling down, I turned to face Agent Cage.

"Look, I understand you have to do your

job, but you'll find I don't intimidate easily."

"That's all I *am* doing, Ms. Cosi, my job."

"Is it your job to dislike me?"

"I dislike anyone who knowingly endangers the President's daughter."

"That's an unfair charge and you know it. And I'll tell you something else. I'm a mother, which means I know from hard experience that keeping kids in protective bubbles only works if the kids go along. If they want out, they always manage to find a way."

Cage stopped goading me after that. She stopped talking to me, too, but in her eyes, I could see that I'd made my point.

She knew as well as I did that Abby *wasn't* a kid. She was a twenty-year-old woman, smart enough to evade her security detail if that's what she was determined to do.

And yet, in that moment, I did seriously consider violating Abby's confidence and telling Cage about her escape to my coffeehouse the night before.

But there would be consequences to my speaking up.

For one thing, Abby would never trust me again. And I sensed she needed people in her life she could trust.

For another, there was my official statement to the DC Metro police. I'd lied to protect Abby, but they wouldn't see it that way, and I knew the First Family wouldn't want their daughter dragged into a messy situation like that.

Nevertheless, my internal struggle continued, right up until a male voice called out —

"Agent Cage, would you step over here, please?"

THIRTY-TWO

As Sharon Cage was called to a spot beside Honest Abe, a shiver went through me. For a few minutes there, I'd forgotten that President Abraham Lincoln had once lived on these grounds. That fact swung back on me with awesome force.

I thought about those years when our country was at war with itself — and the Underground Railroad was at work under my temporary home on N Street.

It was hardly the same, yet I couldn't help seeing the similarities in Abby's situation. From her point of view, she was waging her own little rebellion, complete with her own secret routes to freedom.

As the voices buzzed across the room, I tried to make out what they were saying. Two stern-looking men in three-piece suits were showing Agent Cage something on a tablet computer.

"Who are those guys?" I asked Carol as

she returned my jewelry.

"Oh, they're the fussbudgets from the Protective Intelligence squad." She waved a dismissive hand. "Seems they ran some background checks on you and hit a few snags."

"What sort of background checks?"

Carol tapped her ruddy cheek and turned her blue eyes skyward.

"Well, they surely went to the National Crime Information Center, and the National Law Enforcement Telecommunications System to see if you've ever been arrested. They likely ran your name through the LexisNexis Accurint for Law Enforcement, too. After that, they would have gone to the FBI, the DEA, the IRS, the NYPD . . . Oh, and did I mention Interpol?"

"With that kind of thoroughness I'll bet a security check on Mother Teresa would have 'hit a few snags,' too."

As Carol chuckled, I hung the cross back around my neck and tucked it into my sweater. Next my escort surprised me with the loan of a compact mirror and a hairbrush. In a few moments I did what I could to control my flyaway hair. I would have to go with the little makeup I had on.

As I handed back the mirror and brush, Agent Cage returned.

"Do you have your driver's license on you?"

Why? I thought, blinking at the woman. *Are my parking violations now a matter of national security?* But what I said was —

"Sorry. I don't have it."

"Sharon! I've got it!"

The Secret Service agent I mistook for a Saudi in my coffeehouse now hurried across the gleaming diamond-checkerboard floor, waving a piece of paper.

"Good work, Agent Sharpe."

I pointed. "Is that what I think it is?"

"It's a photocopy of your New York State driver's license," Agent Sharpe said as he passed the sheet to his boss.

"Would you mind telling me where you got that?"

"When you opened your club, you applied for a C license to serve liquor in DC. At that time, you were required to submit a copy of your ID." He flashed a self-satisfied grin. "I contacted the Alcohol Beverage Regulation Administration, and they e-mailed a copy over to us."

I shouldn't have been surprised. Quinn's own interdepartmental work in New York had taught me that government bureaucracy was one big happy family. With a very Big Brother.

"But why all the fuss for my license?"

"Your passport and your license both display your photo," Cage explained. "We need two visual IDs to confirm you are really you."

"Because you already have my passport photo, right?"

Agent Sharpe nodded. "And by the way, the State Department informed us that your passport has expired. If you plan to travel, you'll have to renew it." He paused. "*Do you* plan to travel outside of this country, Ms. Cosi?"

"No, I don't plan on leaving the country . . ." *And I'm not a foreign operative, I swear.* "But thanks for the advice on the passport —"

Just then, the staccato whip-cracks of snapping fingers echoed through the quiet space with all the comfort and joy of dry bones rattling in a midnight cemetery.

The sound was especially chilling because it was so familiar.

"Let's go, Lidia, I have another meeting to get to . . ."

And there she was, Quinn's boss at the U.S. Justice Department. Acting Director Katerina Lacey.

THIRTY-THREE

Katerina's assistant, an attractive young Latina, was working hard to balance herself on high heels while overburdened by a briefcase and a tall stack of legal-sized files.

Acting Director Lacey was hands-free, of course. All the better to snap those obnoxiously impatient fingers.

I had to admit the woman was striking, easily the most attractive person in the room. In contrast to her somber gray pinstripes and pointy leather pumps, Katerina's flawless alabaster skin seemed almost spectral. She was as tall as half the men in the room, which explained her assistant's attempt to rise to her level — at least in height. She wasn't shapely, but her slenderness was fashionable, and with her shiny, blunt-cut, strawberry blond hair perfectly framing her face, Katerina turned a few heads.

Despite the attention from the males in

her gravity, however, Katerina must have felt my gaze on her as well, because she looked right at me. Immediately my emerald eyes met her pea-greens. With a toss of her hair, Katerina lifted her perpetual pout into a smirk. Then, to my horror, she turned her kayak-shaped toes toward me.

"Clare, isn't it? What a place to meet!"

"Funny, huh?"

"What are you doing at the White House? Do tours begin this early?"

"I'm here on official business. And you?"

"The same." Katerina's pretty brow wrinkled. "But I wasn't aware of any catered events scheduled for today. And I certainly didn't know your little shop had the gravitas to be commissioned for such a function."

Oh, brother.

"My coffeehouse hasn't been commissioned for anything, Katerina. I'm —"

Carol reappeared. "I'm so sorry to interrupt, but the First Lady is quite anxious to receive Ms. Cosi. Shall we go?"

I expected Katerina to register shock, but she didn't raise one plucked eyebrow.

"Good luck," she said instead, in a tone that wished me anything but. Then she whirled on her low, pointy shoes and strutted to catch up with her still-tottering assistant.

After Mike's revelations, and my own misgivings about this woman, Katerina's lack of surprise came as something of a shock to me.

Perhaps it shouldn't have, for as Carol ushered me through the same doorway Katerina and her assistant had exited, my White House guide spoke in a suddenly hushed tone.

"We're in the presidential residence now. This is the main building of the White House. You should feel honored to be invited here."

I would, I thought. *Except that Katerina was just here, which means she likely met with the First Lady or a member of her staff.*

And the subject of that meeting?

After what happened last night, all the security I had to pass today, and those snags the intelligence wonks hit, I had a bad feeling about that.

THIRTY-FOUR

Once through the doors, we took a short stroll down a long carpeted hall with a dramatic vaulted ceiling. As we walked, Carol pointed out open doors to the White House Library, Map Room, and China Room.

Sharon Cage followed at a discreet distance. Like a well-behaved German shepherd, the agent knew when to fade into the background.

Carol paused at a closed door, her hand on the latch. "Through here you'll find the Diplomatic Reception Room, one of three oval rooms at the White House. It is here that ambassadors from all over the globe present their credentials to the Leader of the Free World . . ."

And given the way I'd been summoned, I was willing to lay heavy odds that I was here to do the same. "Is there a special protocol I should follow?" I asked. "I don't have to curtsy, do I?"

"Oh, heavens, no. Address the First Lady as 'Mrs. Parker.' The President's wife has many ceremonial duties, but she is a private citizen, like you or I."

Then Carol surprised me by leaning close.

"I'd also like to say that the First Lady is just regular folk," she whispered in my ear, "as down-to-earth as you or I, but Mrs. Elizabeth Noland Parker really isn't."

With that observation (or was it a warning?), Carol ushered me in, and two things immediately struck me: the majestic nature of the room, and how many people were in it.

On my right, four servers stood at attention beside a white-draped caddy holding china dishes and cups bearing the presidential seal. I also noticed a silver coffee service — and couldn't stop myself from wondering (a little jealously):

Whose coffee will we be drinking?

To the left, a stiff middle-aged woman in a stiffer suit of navy blue stood at attention beside a slim man in gray, sporting a silver-blue tie. A pretty, young intern stood between them. As we entered, Sharon Cage took a position beside the older woman in blue.

With sunlight shining through the vestibule facing the South Lawn, the Federal-era mahogany bookcase, and stunning grandfather clock, this magnificent oval room managed to feel stately yet opulent, the latter largely due to its Regency cut-glass chandelier dangling over our heads, and the matching sofa and wingback chairs upholstered in yellow damask.

As Carol whisked me across a thick carpet, I noticed the interweaving stars, a design that felt disturbing, like a spider's web spinning its way back to the commanding figure posed before an uncomfortably active fireplace.

"Clare Cosi, welcome," she said, enveloping my rough server's hands in her smooth manicured fingers.

"Mrs. Parker, it's an honor," I said, meeting her penetrating stare. I had to look up, of course. This First Lady was fashion-model five-nine. Her skin was flawless, her figure toned and athletic under a starched, formal coatdress.

"Call me Beth," the First Lady said after bending low for a hug and air kiss so swift I barely felt the golden brush of her crisp, over-sprayed hair.

"I'm Clare," I replied, self-conscious about my casual attire.

But if the First Lady disapproved, she

didn't show it. With a dazzling smile, she led me by hand to one of the armchairs covered in yellow silk damask, placed a little too close for comfort to the crackling fire.

"I thought a nice blaze would make the room comfy. By the way, did you know it was Franklin Roosevelt who had this chimney opened? He used this very hearth for his famous fireside chats."

The First Lady wiped her brow theatrically. "Thankfully, that was before both of our times!"

We laughed together.

"And who installed the wallpaper? It's breathtaking . . ."

"I confess that's my favorite part of this room. I understand Jackie Kennedy had it done during her renovations . . ."

The paper was printed not with a recurring pattern but a sweeping wall mural that circled the oval room with rustic scenes from early America: Boston Harbor, the Natural Bridge in Virginia, West Point, New York, Niagara alls, and many more.

"I understand it was printed in France, back in the 1830s," the First Lady noted. "Goodness knows where Mrs. Kennedy got the idea."

"A room with no windows can feel claustrophobic," I replied, admiring the mountains, trees, and sailing ships. "Our jazz club's greenroom had the same problem, but I solved it with the same approach — a panoramic mural with bucolic imagery. Of course, mine isn't anywhere near this ambitious, just a simple forest scene in acrylics."

"Oh, who was your decorator?"

"No decorator. I painted it myself."

For a brief second, a confused frown shaded Mrs. Parker's expression. *Painted the walls yourself? Good heavens, why?* But that utterly confounded moment was quickly dispatched by the polite reaction she knew she *should* be displaying.

"How perfectly lovely, Clare. You know I was told you *studied* fine art —"

"You were?"

"— but I wasn't aware of your own artistic abilities."

Leaning forward on her wingback chair, she lowered her voice.

"Abigail will be joining us shortly. But before she does, I wanted the two of us to share a private moment . . ."

THIRTY-FIVE

Private *moment*? I thought. *There are ten people in this room. I guess that's why they call it "a public life."*

Still leaning forward, the First Lady placed her hands on her knees. "If I may, I'd like to speak with you as one mother to another."

"Of course."

"Your daughter is older than Abigail, Clare, but I suspect she gave you headaches now and again. Goodness knows, all children do —"

Something tells me you more than "suspect," Mrs. Parker.

"In the end, you were fortunate. Your daughter weathered the trials of new adulthood to find her place in the world. She's apprenticing as a chef in Paris, isn't she?"

"She's back in New York City for the time being, helping her father run our Greenwich Village coffeehouse."

Mrs. Parker nodded. "A family business is a wonderful thing. And I understand your daughter is outgoing, gregarious, social. Like you. Like her father."

I suddenly felt like I was getting a headache. It might have been the heat radiating from the fireplace . . . or something else.

She leaned even closer, invading my space.

"Abigail is different from your daughter. She's vulnerable. And fragile. Did you know that six years ago, Abigail attempted suicide? That was a trying time for all of us, but we found our way through. Now we're moving Abigail along, toward a better life."

Moving her along? I thought. *More like controlling her every move.*

But, as Gardner advised me to do when I first relocated to DC, I held my frank opinion and spoke instead in bland generalities.

"I think Abby . . . Abigail is a unique young woman. She's smart, sensitive, and she possesses remarkable musical talent —"

"Which the President and I very much fear will be *exploited.*"

"Excuse me?"

"Oh, I'm not suggesting *you* are doing anything wrong, Clare. I know that Abigail enjoys her time at your little club above your coffeehouse, that she's been treating it like

190

a second home, which the President and I can accept."

The First Lady's piercing gaze was now practically impaling me.

"What is *not* acceptable is *publicity* — of *any kind.* If Abigail's musical dabbling became public knowledge . . ." She paused to shudder in a manner I hadn't seen since the cinema adaptations of early Stephen King. "I can't imagine the spectacle of the First Daughter playing honky-tonk piano in a Georgetown loft. It would be a circus. A freak show —"

I tried to hold my tongue. I really did. But —

"Mrs. Parker," I said, forcing my tone to remain respectful, "it is not honky-tonk piano. It is jazz, a modern American art form, some say America's only true art form, because it began here before becoming beloved around the world. Abby's passion for jazz is a beautiful thing to see — and hear. You should take the time to witness it —"

"Well, Clare, you'll excuse me if I take *your* evaluation of my daughter's musical ability with a grain of salt."

"You don't have to. Accomplished, professional musicians are impressed with how well she —"

"*Authoritative* music teachers have already judged my daughter to be mediocre at best —"

"Excuse me, but how many years ago was that judgment made?"

"I don't know . . ." She glanced at the grandfather clock a moment. "Six or seven years, I guess."

"That's a long time in the scheme of any young artist's development, and Abby herself told me she was playing *classical* piano at that time. Jazz is not the same as —"

"Enough, Clare. You simply do not understand. Music is Abigail's place to hide. But she cannot hide forever. She must grow up and face the world . . ."

I took a breath for patience. Either Elizabeth Noland Parker did not wish to understand her daughter or she was incapable of it.

Maybe that judgment was unfair, given my brief view of the pair. But I couldn't help my reaction. I'd seen far too many of these misunderstandings back in New York, where cultures clashed on a 24/7 basis, and extroverts continually labeled artists and introverts as "weird" or "antisocial" or "deficient" in social graces, never stopping to consider how introverts viewed them —

as unimaginative, condescending, and distressingly deficient in depth.

I couldn't help wondering where Abby's artistic genes came from. If not from her mother, then she must take after her father, which gave me a new respect for the President. I'd never met the man. But now I was curious to make his acquaintance.

"Clare, I did not bring you here to debate," Mrs. Parker insisted. "I brought you here to ask for your word that you will not exploit my daughter."

"I only want Abby to be happy."

"That's not good enough. We are the First Family. Not a reality TV stunt. Do you understand?"

"Of course, I understand, Mrs. Parker, and as long as your daughter chooses to perform under an assumed name, we will honor that. I've personally kept her secret from my friends, family, everyone — and it will always be safe with me."

"Your word?"

"You have it!" I even raised my hand, as if taking an oath.

The First Lady's expression immediately softened.

"You must understand. The President and I are pleased Abigail is enjoying her college years. We've decided it's best that she get this music bug out of her system now. College is the perfect place to indulge a frivolous fantasy."

She touched my hand. "But it will soon be time for Abigail to put aside childish things, even if those things make her *deeply happy.*"

Despite the blast furnace of a fire, and the perspiration trickling into my bra, I felt a shiver slither up the back of my neck.

The First Lady had deliberately echoed my words to Abby on the night the First Daughter and I met. My gaze automatically found Sharon Cage, standing at attention across the room — just as she had in our greenroom the night I'd said those words.

The knowing look in the First Lady's eyes told me this wasn't a coincidence. Either my conversation with Abby was reported back to the First Lady verbatim or *recorded* and played back.

Now, I was well aware that people with power and position had handlers whose job it was to feed them information about the people they encountered in a given day. But it was one thing to know this objectively; quite another to be the ant under their microscope.

Even worse, I suspected Agent Cage wasn't the only one telling tales.

Katerina Lacey had exited the very doorway that I walked into.

Given that Katerina was working within the executive branch — reporting to someone who reported to someone who reported directly to the President — I couldn't help suspecting the First Lady of asking her to investigate me.

I recalled Katerina's assistant, Lidia, juggling all those files. They couldn't all be on me, could they? And if they weren't, then whose were they?

Is Katerina doing political dirty work for the White House in addition to her Justice Department duties?

"The music industry is so . . . tawdry," the First Lady continued. "And Abigail has so many better things to look forward to. Her graduation, with honors. And her pending nuptials, which we're anticipating with great excitement."

I blinked. *Did I just hear the words "pending nuptials"?!*

"I ask you, Clare. Can anything be more delightful than a Rose Garden wedding in June? Abby will make such a lovely bride!"

THIRTY-SIX

I think my jaw may have bounced off that star-clustered carpet.

"Abby is engaged? She's getting married?"

"It hasn't been announced to the public yet, and I'd appreciate it if you kept that little secret under your cap."

"Of course."

"I think of President Parker as an actor on the world stage; and, like all great actors, he seeks those moments that define his presidency, and the nation . . ."

The First Lady's eyes seemed to stare into the distance. "This Rose Garden event will be one such moment. When the Commander in Chief strides down that aisle as father of the bride, he will be seen as the Father of the Nation."

Another chill went up my neck, and I couldn't help thinking: *Who's exploiting Abby now?*

"This is the second reason I asked you

here," Mrs. Parker continued. "Abigail has made a request. She wants your Village Blend, DC, to provide the coffee service for her wedding day."

My jaw struck the carpet again. "I'm honored, truly —"

"You know, Clare, I've always appreciated coffee. But my real love affair with the beverage began while I was living in Morocco."

"Morocco?"

"Oh, yes. Ever since high school, I enjoyed my morning cup, but when I got pregnant I had to give it up. I was amazed at how much I missed it, so after Abigail was born I went a little crazy. I visited my favorite stall in the souk every morning for that entire summer. I'd down five or six cups in a row. I savored some of the finest coffees in the world in that souk." The First Lady paused. "Which brings us to another dilemma."

"Dilemma?"

"The Village Blend is historic, and its reputation has long been esteemed. Yet your debut in Georgetown was . . . less than successful. I'm sorry to bring it up, but your reviews were not favorable."

There's not much you can do with a broken gas line and a no-show barista, I thought with embarrassment.

After that disastrous first day I'd replaced the gas line and tirelessly continued screening applicants until I found Tito. But there was no point in peddling excuses. The truth was the truth.

"Growing pains," I replied. "The Village Blend, DC, is now well past those problems."

"Good, because your reputation for coffee in New York is impeccable. That's why I asked our White House chef to brew some for our brunch. I'm anxious to see if it lives up to its reputation."

Speechless for a moment, I suddenly realized my question was finally answered: *Whose coffee will we be drinking?* Apparently, my own!

"I'm sure you won't be disappointed," I said with confidence.

"Let's hope not. And if I choose to humor Abigail in this request, we'll have to raise the Village Blend's profile — and yours, Clare."

"Mine? How?"

"The solution is simple. But first . . . I need to know what you know about the history of coffee."

"Excuse me?"

"Coffee, Clare. Do you know something about its history? Or is your knowledge of

198

the beverage limited simply to roasting and serving it?"

"Why? Is this some kind of test?"

"Don't think of it like that." She waved her hand. "Like most people, other than drinking it, I really don't think much about it." Her gaze pierced mine. "*Educate* me."

I smiled politely, guessing there was a reason for the First Lady's strange demand. And, despite her denial, I could see this *was* a test of some sort. The question was —

What happens if I fail?

THIRTY-SEVEN

"History of coffee? Okay . . ." I cleared my throat.

The First Lady folded her hands on her lap and waited expectantly.

"I doubt you want me to go all the way back to a flock of overactive goats in Ethiopia, so why don't I begin with coffee in America?"

"And what can you tell me about that?"

"Well, for starters, the Revolution was plotted by coffee drinkers in coffeehouses in Boston and Philadelphia."

The First Lady nodded approvingly.

"After the Boston Tea Party, Americans almost universally switched over to coffee. It became the beverage of patriots. There's a funny story about John Adams, who adored tea. He complained to his wife about having to embrace the bean, because tea drinking was considered unpatriotic, and he would be suspect if he continued to 'imbibe the leaf.' "

"Very good, Clare, go on . . ."

My mind raced. "Have you visited Monticello, in Virginia?"

"I know I should. But regretfully . . ."

"Well, if you do, be sure to look for Thomas Jefferson's silver coffee urn. It was purchased in France. Oh, and did you know Jefferson was known to present coffee urns as gifts to friends and fellow businessmen?"

"No, I didn't. What else can you tell me?"

I went on "educating" Mrs. Parker about coffee in America: cowboy coffee, coffee during the Civil War — the soldiers roasted their own green beans over open flames and used their guns to crush them up. This led to the custom of roasting at home, which gave way to small batch shops, which led to large batch, mass-market roasting, the general decline in quality, and the rise of a new generation of coffee professionals with a passion for sourcing, small-batch roasting, and re-creating the coffeehouse culture that first gave birth to our country.

I mentioned Teddy Roosevelt's love of coffee: "His custom cup was so big that one of his sons described it as 'more in nature of a bathtub.' " And I explained how his children contributed to coffeehouse culture with their chain of New York coffeehouses.

Finally, I glanced again at the room's magnificent wallpaper, which reminded me —

"Jacqueline Kennedy is famous for her White House restoration, but she changed more than the décor under this roof. The way she served coffee revolutionized the way men and women socialize here."

"Really? How is that exactly?"

"It was Jackie who began the practice of mixing the sexes after state dinners. Prior to that men retired to one room for their coffee while women were sent to another — which consequently cut off the women from some of the most important discussions of the day. Jackie put an end to the coffee service segregation."

"That's truly fascinating!"

"Coffee was also a vital part of John F. Kennedy's rise to the presidency. As a junior senator, he and Mrs. Kennedy invited influential people to coffees held in their Georgetown home. Those casual gatherings helped lift the young senator's profile with the Washington establishment."

The "sway of influence" story had further swayed the First Lady. She was more than impressed. She looked overjoyed.

As an afterthought, I told her that one of the coffee services Mrs. Kennedy used during that period was something I admired every day.

"Pardon me?" Mrs. Parker leaned forward. "What do you mean?"

"I'm living temporarily on Cox's Row, in Mrs. Bittmore-Black's Georgetown mansion. Mrs. Kennedy was a lifelong friend and gifted one of her silver services to the former ambassador. It sits beautifully in the dining room, on top of a sideboard that once served Abraham Lincoln."

"Outstanding, Clare!" Mrs. Parker clapped her hands. "Of course, *everyone* knows Mrs. Bittmore-Black. The former ambassador has impeccable taste! Oh, this is all going to work perfectly. Just perfectly!"

"Excuse me? What exactly is going to work perfectly?"

"The Smithsonian is mounting an exhibition on coffee in America. It seems to me that *you* would be the perfect expert advisor."

I blinked. "Mrs. Parker, I'm certainly honored" — *shocked was more like it* — "but I'm hardly a historian."

"You've proven your expertise *to me.* I'll have you work with the White House Curator on her end of the project: *Coffee and the Presidency.* You two can work together. What you don't know, Mrs. Trainer probably does. I can't wait to see what you and Helen come up with!" Her gaze speared me again. "How about a conference call with her early next week?"

"That will be fine," I said, surrendering to the unstoppable force that was Mrs. Elizabeth Noland Parker. "Whatever is convenient for the curator."

The First Lady waved a finger at her female assistant in navy blue, who began tapping into a computer tablet.

I sat there, feeling bowled over — or more like *steamrolled* over.

"I don't know what else to say."

"You've already said *yes,* so there's no need to talk anymore about it. Ah! I see Abigail has finally decided to join us . . ."

THIRTY-EIGHT

I was relieved to hear that Abby was joining us — and anxious to see her familiar, smiling face.

Except I didn't.

Entering the room was a frowning young woman in a starched white blouse, hair pulled into a tight, high ponytail, its black color nearly obliterated by a large pink bow that matched her knee-length skirt.

A friend of Abby's?

A second look and I realized this girl *was* Abby — or rather, Abigail Prudence Parker, First Daughter of the President of the United States.

Gone were the black leggings and boots, replaced with nude hose and low-heeled sling-backs. Her face looked different, too. The purple eyeliner had been wiped off. And clear gloss replaced the dark lipstick.

Gloss over darkness . . .

The phrase whispered through me as I

watched Abby robotically cross the room. With each step closer to her mother's roaring fire, the light inside Abby's eyes seemed to dim. Hands clutched in front of her, she bent low to kiss the First Lady's cheek. Then she turned to greet me with a limp handshake and a formal "Ms. Cosi."

Finally, as demurely as a choir girl, she positioned herself on a yellow damask wing chair between us. Hands on her knees in a perfect imitation of her mother, Abigail's bland smile had less life than a corpse.

As we began to talk, I could tell the *other* Abby — the one I'd seen onstage at the Village Blend, even in our wild ride to the White House — was replaced with some kind of Stepford Abby, complete with an engagement ring on her left hand.

That was the final shock. The diamond was as big as a Steinway, and just as loud.

More air-filling conversation ensued, then a stiff tour of the China Room, and we returned to find chairs and a table set for three had magically appeared in the center of the Diplomatic Reception Room.

The menu was very French, and everything was appetizing — the escargot in grass-fed garlic butter and the *poulet à l'estragon.* Dessert was a simple but elegant chocolate mousse served with thin, crisp chocolate-almond cookies reminiscent of the Kennedy White House *tuiles.*

When my Village Blend's coffee was served, the First Lady actually gushed.

And I complimented the White House chef, who'd picked our sultry, full-bodied Krakatoa blend of Matt's Sumatran- and Ethiopian-sourced beans (my own take on a Mocha-Java), with notes of cocoa, sweet dried cherry, and fresh-grated cinnamon that perfectly complemented the light chocolate dessert.

Through the entire meal, Abigail said hardly a word of her own. She answered her mother's queries perfectly appropriately, but it was strange to see the Abby I knew nodding dutifully about designer bridal gown fittings and Rose Garden guest lists.

Finally the First Lady excused herself, and I watched a stranger named Abigail follow her mother through the oval room's curved door.

She's trapped in a Washington loop, I thought. *Like those infernal traffic circles. And she can't find a way out . . .*

"There's a car waiting to take you home." Carol was at my shoulder, my apron once again draped over her arm. "I do hope you enjoyed your visit to the White House."

■ ■ ■ ■

The ride back to the Village Blend was excruciatingly slow and decidedly cool, my driver a brooding Agent Cage, who was no doubt lamenting the fact that we'd be seeing a lot more of each other.

"Don't forget your *apron,* Ms. Cosi," Agent Cage taunted as she dropped me at the curb.

Reentering my coffeehouse, I wished for just one familiar, smiling face.

Be careful what you wish for.

Officer Tom Landry met me as I came through the front door.

"Hey, Clare, what's up?"

In uniform and apparently on duty, Landry was not alone. Loitering near the door were a half-dozen other young cops — all watching us.

"We were wondering where you were," Landry continued. "You slipped out of my net."

"We?"

"I've been telling my boys how great your coffee is."

I looked over the young cop's shoulder.

From their whispers and elbowing, I doubted that was the only thing he'd been telling his boys.

"I *might* have also mentioned how hot the owner is." He grinned.

"I appreciate the compliments, Officer. But shouldn't you get back to policing? I'm certain there are still criminals out there, waiting to be caught."

Landry shook his head. "Not until we have some of that coffee of yours."

I yanked the folded apron off my shoulder and tied it into place. Then I beckoned the boys in blue to follow me to the coffee bar, where they lined up for me to serve them.

Tito eyed the police presence warily. "Everything *bene,* boss?"

"Yes, Tito, take a break — and *grazie* for covering."

"Anytime."

"By the way, you're now an assistant manager."

"I am?"

"*Sì,*" I said, and in Italian explained that the promotion came with a raise. "We'll talk more later, okay?"

"Okay!" He clapped his hands and rubbed them together. *"Grazie! Grazie!"*

Now Landry stepped up, and I waved him closer. "Have you heard any news about that poor man from the State Department?" I lowered my voice. "The man who collapsed upstairs last night?"

"Nothing came up in our morning briefing," Landry said with a shrug, "so I figure he's okay." He studied me. "Hey, don't worry, Clare, I'm sure all the guy really needed was a few pots of your coffee."

"Thanks," I said. But I *was* still worried.

The hospital wouldn't give me any news on Mr. Varma, so I planned to keep an eye out for the man. For one thing, I wanted to know why he'd come to our back door and what he meant about the truth and the President. Questioning Tito and my staff about serving him one too many was also on my to-do list.

In the meantime, I spent the next fifteen minutes filling coffee drink orders and ignoring grins and winks. Then Landry and his pals were on their way, and the shop was quiet at last.

A few customers were sipping lattes at tables near our front windows, but the counter was empty, so I began restocking and tidying up.

That's when I heard the ominous *tap-tapping* behind me.

Fearing another run-in with our thumb-ringed chef, I clenched my fists and whirled to find Four on the Floor's drummer, Stan McGuire.

Hoover cane in hand, the young vet stood at attention, waiting for mine.

"Hey, Stan, what can I get you?"

"A few minutes of your time, Ms. Cosi, if you can spare it."

"Is anything wrong?"

"I'd like to speak with you privately. It's about Abby . . ."

THIRTY-NINE

"You were right to do what you did last night," Stan blurted on a rapid-fire roll. "If the Secret Service found out that Abby gave them the slip, they'd come down so hard I would never see her again. That's what they're like . . ."

Stan and I were sitting at a quiet corner table.

With Kimberly back from her afternoon classes, I asked her to watch the counter so Stan and I wouldn't be interrupted. Then I poured us fresh, hot coffees and put a plate of our Big Chewy Oatmeal Cookies in front of him. (Two textures of oatmeal was the secret to their café-style crispy yet chewy perfection, along with generous pinches of nutmeg and cinnamon and extra vanilla, all of which made them extra popular with our customers.)

When we first sat down, Stan was jumpy. It took him a minute to settle into his chair.

He adjusted the Captain America eye patch he always wore, and tugged at his clothing. Finally, he leaned the cane against the table and opened up.

"If Abby's mother found out what we've been doing, she'd probably ship her off for psychiatric care. She's threatened Abby with that line before . . ."

The phrase *"what we've been doing"* echoed in my head. The words implied Abby and Stan had been slipping away from the Secret Service on a regular basis.

This alarmed me. But instead of hammering him on how many times they'd done it in the past, I decided it would be better for all of us to focus on the future.

"From now on, Stan, I know you'll be smart. You wouldn't want to lose the chance to have contact with Abby, right?"

"No, ma'am, I would not." He rubbed his pug nose. "Anyway, I wanted to say thanks. Thanks a lot. You saved us both from a major FUBAR."

During our exchange, his leg jerked back and forth. I knew from experience that if he were to catch himself and stop, he'd start to drum the table, because Stan was a compact bundle of raw energy. He reminded me of my ex-husband, Matt, both of whom were polar opposites to the tall, taciturn Mike Quinn.

The calm in Quinn — even in the most harrowing situations — astounded me. But it also confounded me. Most days I had to guess what the man was thinking. And over time, I'd learned that Quinn's calm sometimes masked a slowly building storm.

With Stan (and Matt), there was never any effort to hide the storm. Their passions were raw and open. And they usually shared what they thought the very moment they thought it.

Even without both eyes visible to me, Stan's lopsided yet likable face registered more emotion than most people I knew.

"What's going on between you and Abby?" I probed.

"We're close . . . I mean, we're *friends*," he said, too quickly. "She's a great musician, a real talent in the making."

"Seems to me there's more than music going on between you."

"Well, I care for her, if that's what you mean."

I sighed. It was not my place to tell Stan what I'd learned at the White House. The wedding was Abby's news to tell. Still, I felt I should warn him —

"Be careful, okay? Remember who Abby

is. She may be your friend, but she's also Abigail Prudence Parker, the daughter of the President and First Lady. Please don't forget or you could get hurt."

He slapped his bad leg. "Too late for that!"

FORTY

Stan laughed and so did I.

I couldn't help admiring the young vet's ability to make light of his terrible injuries. It was easy to see how Abby had come to care for him.

"So how did you get into music, anyway?" I had wondered about that since he'd joined Gardner's ensemble. "Soldier to jazz drummer seems an unlikely transition."

"I was a musician before I was a solider, Ms. Cosi. Piano. Guitar. A little bit of saxophone, along with the drumming."

"You studied?"

"I got plenty of lessons. Here and there. My dad made sure of that. I was an army brat. Every three years it was time to up and move. But no matter where I ended up, there was a school band, or someone was starting a band, or a student band at the base. That's how I made friends, no matter the country."

"Music is the universal language. That's what Gardner believes."

"And he's right. Music and good coffee . . ." He took a long sip. Then he dug into the oatmeal cookies and exclaimed: "Oh, man! *And* good food!"

Smiling in agreement, I snuck a cookie off his plate. "What made you choose drumming over piano and guitar?"

"After I was discharged, the docs told me it would be good physical therapy, and the shrinks thought drumming would be a 'socially acceptable outlet' for my anger."

He laughed it off, but it was clear Stan had a lot of anger. His forearms were developed; his biceps and pecs looked rock hard.

"Why did you enlist in the first place?"

"I got used to army life, I guess," he said between satisfying chews and swallows. "The only adults I knew were grunts. Both my parents were army docs, and I learned plenty about battlefield trauma, but I wasn't serious enough about the sciences to get into med school, so I became a combat medic. I figured I could work as a city paramedic after my tours, but then . . ." He pointed to his eye and leg and then shrugged.

"I take it you saw a lot of the 'combat'

part of your job description."

"Yes, ma'am . . ." was all he said. Like most veterans, Stan didn't like to talk about his military past — and I could guess why.

At twenty-five, he'd probably witnessed more horror and death than most people saw in their lifetimes, which meant he had little in common with civilians, including practically all of his peers. His bandmates, however, were on a different level for him. He clearly loved and trusted them.

One night, while Stan was having beers with Gardner in the third-floor greenroom, I overheard him opening up. I was quietly at work in the corner, painting a section of my mural, when he began talking about his second tour of duty in Afghanistan.

Sergeant McGuire was part of a combat medevac team sent on a rescue mission in the mountains. His helicopter was struck by a rocket-propelled grenade.

The device was a dud and didn't explode. If it had, Stan and his whole crew would have died. But the grenade did plenty of damage as it bounced around the interior of the chopper. Among the casualties were the muscle in Stan's left calf and the vision in his right eye, which is why he kept the patch on it.

But from his next remark, it was clear that

Stan had found a kind of truth in his personal darkness.

"There's something I learned over there that I wish I could teach Abby, Ms. Cosi."

"What's that?"

"Not to be afraid."

"What does Abby fear, do you think?"

Stan's whole body shrugged.

"Disappointing her parents. Failing. Going crazy. All of it and more, from what she's told me. She's so dynamic and determined when it comes to getting the music right. But the rest of her life . . ." Stan shook his head. "Abby lets her mother bully her about everything. She's scared to break away. But if she doesn't, who knows what her mother is going to push her into next?"

A marriage, I thought, *or so it seems.*

To be fair, I hadn't met Abby's fiancé. Maybe he was right for her and the marriage was something she truly wanted as much as her mother did. Then again, Stan had spent much more time with Abby than I had, and he clearly held my troubled view of the quiet daughter and outspoken mother.

"I hate bullies," he said simply. "And I can spot them a mile away. When I was growing up, some bully or other would come at me within the first week at any new

219

school. I was lucky, though. I learned how to deal with them. Abby didn't."

"Not everyone has your courage, Stan, especially when you have to live with a bully every day."

"Like you, Ms. Cosi?"

"Me?"

He nodded. "The situation you're in with that obnoxious chef of yours."

I blinked, speechless for a moment.

Stan leaned across the table. "Sometimes, ma'am, you don't have to stand up to them. Not when a bully is too damn big. Think tactically. That's what this country was founded on. When you can't win toe-to-toe, you flank them. Surprise them. Knock the legs out from under them." He spread his hands. "Hey, it worked for me. I'll bet it will work for you, too."

While Stan drained his cup and blithely began drumming the table to a tune in his head, I sat back to consider his words.

Chef Tad Hopkins *was* a bully. A bully with an ironclad contract. I'd been going toe-to-toe with him. But to beat him, I would have to outsmart him.

"You know, Stan, Gardner was right about you. For a near-blind guy, you see an awful lot."

"Thanks, Ms. Cosi," he said and popped the last cookie into his mouth.

FORTY-ONE

An hour later, I turned the floor over to Tito and Kimberly. Then I risked my neck by poking my head into the kitchen — praying Chef Hopkins wasn't around to chop it off.

"*Pssst* . . . hey," I whispered to the only person in the room. "Where is Hopkins?"

Luther Bell turned away from chopping vegetables to jerk his head in the direction of the chef's office.

Perfect.

I stepped through the doors and joined Luther at the counter.

"I want to get the chef out of that room in a hurry, quickly enough that he'll forget to lock the door behind him."

Luther turned his eyes toward the ceiling. Finally he snapped his fingers.

"I got it. A faulty microwave will put Chef Tad in a panic."

I made a face. "That says a lot about his cuisine. None of it good."

"I know," Luther said. "Practically all of tonight's menu comes wrapped in plastic, but that should help you." He leaned close. "The microwave acted up last week and I fixed it without telling him. I was afraid if the chef found out he'd throw one of his hissy fits."

"You know how to fix a microwave?"

"I know how to change a breaker. The problem was in the basement fuse box."

"Could you break it again? Pretty please?"

Luther grinned. "Anything for you, Clare Cosi."

A half an hour later, I was peeking through the swinging doors, waiting for my moment to pounce. Luther threw me a wink before rushing toward Chef Hopkins's closed office door at the back of the kitchen.

"Chef! Chef!" He knocked frantically.

"What do you want?" demanded the muffled voice behind the door.

"Bad news," Luther called. "The microwave is on the blink. I can't turn it on. It won't power —"

He didn't even finish his sentence before Chef Hopkins burst out of his office. "What do you mean it won't work? It was fine an hour ago. Show me!"

Luther led Tad to the microwave, where

the pair fretted over the machine for a few minutes. Finally, Luther suggested the problem might be the fuse box in the basement.

"Go fix it," Tad barked.

"Me?" Luther shrugged and spread his arms. "I wouldn't know where to start."

"Fine!"

A moment later Tad pushed through the swinging doors, the Village Blend's toolbox in hand. He was in such a panic that he didn't even notice me jumping clear. As Chef Hopkins descended the basement stairs, I slipped into the kitchen.

"You've got three minutes. Five, tops," Luther cautioned. "And I can't warn you because he sent me out to bus tables."

"That's not your job!"

"Just go!"

I nodded my thanks and hurried to the back of the kitchen. Inside Tad's office, I closed and locked the door. Suddenly I felt giddy. The fact that I didn't even know what to look for was thrust aside by the sheer triumph I felt at getting this far.

Now for the hunt!

The chef's office was cluttered and windowless, and the stark overhead light cast deep shadows. Like much of the newly renovated kitchen, the space smelled of fresh paint.

A printer was perched on the corner of Tad's desk, but most of its faux-cherrywood surface was buried beneath old Jazz Space menus, scribbled notes, and numbers on Post-its. I riffled through a stack of clips from the *Washington Post* and the *Georgetown Current,* a community newspaper. Tad collected ads for other restaurants, foodie reviews, even a few recipes.

I checked his laptop next, and found it locked. Apparently the chef's paranoia extended pretty far, which signaled to me he had something to hide.

I attempted to decipher the notes, but they were a jumble of meaningless scrawls and unidentified phone numbers. The desk drawers were unlocked, but contained only office supplies. I hunted up the trash can, but it was empty.

Heartsick, I realized I'd come up empty.

What did you expect, Clare? A cashier's check marked "profit from stolen sea trout"? A photograph of the mysterious Eastern European man with his name and address scrawled on it?

With time running out, my eyes drifted back to the printer. A quick glance at the control panel and I felt hopeful again.

A print memory!

I powered up the machine and found two jobs stored in the microchips. I selected them both and pressed *Print.*

The first page was a guest list, forty-plus people on it. Many of the names had a culinary restriction or food allergy noted in red ink.

The second page was the purloined letter, the Maltese Falcon, and the map to Treasure Island all rolled up in one little piece of paper. That print-out was my transit paper to Nirvana, and Tad Hopkins's one-way ticket to Palookaville.

My bliss ended when I heard the click of a key in the lock, and then the office door opened.

FORTY-TWO

I whirled to face a livid Tad Hopkins, his stocky frame filling the doorway. He clutched the toolbox in one hand, and waved a Phillips-head screwdriver in my face with the other.

"What the hell are you doing in *my* office?"

I was cornered in that tiny space, and I probably should have been scared. But I'd been intimidated one too many times by this gastronomic gadfly, and I was too angry to back down now.

"What am I doing here?" I flashed the catering menu I'd printed out. "I'm busting you. That's what I'm doing . . . *Chef.*"

"What is that you're waving around?"

"The menu for the event you catered — *with my sea trout!*"

The toolbox clattered to the floor.

"I may not be familiar with the DC penal code, but in New York, fifteen hundred dollars' worth of pilfered seafood qualifies as fourth-degree grand larceny."

Hopkins still gripped the screwdriver, which he used to drive home his point. "You're deluded!" he bellowed. "Prove I stole your precious fish! You can't."

"That's the beauty of it. I don't have to."

As he began to sputter, I knocked his arm aside and slipped around him. When I was through the door, he turned to face me again.

"You've got nothing, Cosi!"

"I've got this!" I pointed to the beautiful typeface at the bottom of the menu.

" 'Service provided by Tad Hopkins of Reston, Virginia,' " I read aloud. "And look at the date."

"Get out of my kitchen —"

"Contracts cut both ways, Hopkins. And you signed on for two years of exclusive service. *Exclusive.* This piece of paper proves you violated the exclusivity clause on your contract. That means you're fired."

"But —"

"There are no buts. Now" — I couldn't wait to say it — "*you* get out of *my* kitchen!"

"You are a total BITCH!" he shouted.

"And you are a CAUGHT FISH! *And* an embezzler. So get out!"

"Fine, I'm going. But you'll hear from my

lawyer!"

"Glad you have one," I shot back. "Because if you make any trouble for Madame or this business, I'll report the theft of my sea trout to the Metro DC police. It'll be easy. Half the force was in here for coffee this morning! So sure, you can sue us — from jail!"

Our civil war had drawn a crowd. Tito and Kimberly had poked their heads through the swinging doors, and Luther stood gawking in the middle of the kitchen, gripping a plastic tray full of dirty glasses.

As embarrassing as it was to have an audience, I was thankful for the witnesses. For one thing, it kept Chef Hopkins from taking a swing at me. I could see his fists clenching. Honestly, the man looked angry enough to kill.

Maybe my employees prevented my murder. Maybe not. But the presence of eyewitnesses didn't stop him from making more ugly threats.

When Hopkins was finally gone, I leaned against the wall. My knees were wobbly and I felt like a hundred bats were battering my chest, trying to get out.

"You okay, boss?" Luther asked.

"All in all, I feel pretty good, Chef."

"Chef?" Luther looked around. "I'm

sorry, but Hopkins is gone."

"I know. I'm addressing you." I faced him. "Because you are now in charge of our kitchen, Chef Bell."

He swallowed hard. "You're sure you're not confusing the CIA with the CIA?"

"Excuse me?"

"Tad Hopkins graduated from the Culinary Institute of America. My experience with the CIA was in its federal cafeteria."

"I know. And I can't wait to get rid of Tad's menu and put yours in its place. More importantly, our customers can't wait, either. We'll talk about your new work hours and salary in the morning."

FORTY-THREE

"Hello . . ." My eyes were still closed, my ears barely open.

"Clare, did you see it?"

"See what?" I rasped into the phone while glancing at the bedside clock. All I could make out were blurry numbers.

Last night, Mike and I celebrated the vanquishing of Hopkins the Horrible with a full bottle of champagne, my irresistibly festive Cherry and Port–Glazed Pork Tenderloin (wrapped in bacon), and my light and lovely Chocolate Kahlúa-Cream Whoopie Pies — not to mention a night of making whoopee. *(Okay, I mentioned it.)*

This decadence wasn't negligence on my part. I was supposed to have the morning off. Gardner had agreed to open the coffeehouse for me. Then he planned to crash until a few hours before our Jazz Space showtime.

So why is he calling at the crack of 7:15?

"Don't tell me we're having trouble with the gas lines again."

"No. I sent a link to your smartphone. You need to check it. *Now.*"

I sat up.

Whoa, too fast . . .

While the room spun, I vaguely registered Mike's big, warm body, softly snoring next to me. As quietly as I could, I threw off the covers, tied on a robe, and moved into the master suite's sitting room.

Tapping the phone screen, I followed Gard's hotlink to *The District,* a website devoted to the Washington, DC, social scene.

The news was right there on the home page:

FIRST DAUGHTER "ABBY LANE" JAZZES THINGS UP IN GEORGETOWN!

Suddenly my legs had all the strength of wet noodles. As I sank onto the sofa, Gard informed me —

"I heard the news on the radio. They claimed their source was *The District* website, and that's where I found the pics and video —"

"Video? They have video!"

I tapped the headline and up came the

smartphone snaps of Abby playing at last Wednesday's Open Mike, along with a short digital recording. The sound quality was poor, but I recognized a few bars of "Cool Reception."

The post claimed the Village Blend, DC, provided the "publicity" materials. It listed tonight's showtime and our address, making it look like we'd released the news ourselves.

"Who did this?!" Gardner wailed. "Do you think a fan figured out Abby's identity and thought they were helping us?"

"It's possible . . ." I played the video again and noticed a dark image flash into the frame. A quick rewind and pause revealed the guilty party's thumb — and his all-too-familiar *thumb ring.*

"That Son of a Bunny!"

"Clare?"

"Tad Hopkins did this!"

"Are you sure?"

I squeezed my eyes shut, recalling yesterday morning's argument at the espresso bar — right before Abby drove me to the White House, where I *promised* the First Lady that her daughter's identity would remain a secret.

"Hopkins boasted to me that he found a way to attract customers to our Jazz Space.

'They'll come,' he said, 'because I figured out how to get buzz even if you can't!' "

Gardner cursed. "How did he know about Abby's identity?"

"Maybe he overheard the band talking, maybe the two of us." I pounded the sofa cushion. "*That's* why he refused to serve Luther's specials tonight. He assumed once Abby's identity was out, we'd be packed, and he wanted to showcase his own food!"

"So what do we do? Kill the show?"

"That's up to Abby. We have to find out how she feels about all this. Sit tight. I'll be there in fifteen minutes . . ."

Cursing our former chef, Gardner and I ended our call.

Almost immediately, the phone went off again.

Between the bewildering news and last night's bottle of bubbly, I was feeling disoriented. But seeing the name on my caller ID did more to shock me awake than a quad espresso down my throat and a bucket of ice water in my face.

With a hard swallow, I lifted the phone.

"Hello, Agent Cage . . ."

FORTY-FOUR

"You're a real piece of work, Cosi. You know that?"

"I can explain —"

"The First Lady is not interested in excuses from you — or more lies."

"I swear I didn't want this to happen —"

"But it did."

"*Please* just hear me out. Will you meet me at the Village Blend?"

"I'll be there," Sharon Cage barked. "But not to hear explanations. And I'm not coming alone . . ."

What does that mean?

It sounded like she was planning to arrest me! But as ugly as this situation was from an ethical standpoint, what took place wasn't against the law. All of our Open Mike artists signed publicity releases.

Then she explained —

"I sent Agent Sharpe over to your java joint for an eyes-on. He says a small group of journalists and bloggers are already lining up for Abigail's show, which is *thirteen hours* away."

"Is *The District* website that big?"

"No, but the wire services picked it up. Then the *Drudge Report* posted it. You've heard of the *Drudge Report,* haven't you, Cosi? Two million visitors a day. Seven hundred million page views a month."

Give me strength. "Yes, I've heard of it."

"Believe me, we know how a story like this rolls out. Local radio has it now. Next the national morning cable shows will pick it up and then the networks. The White House Press Secretary is already scrambling for an official reaction."

"What should we do? Cancel Abby's show?"

"We *should* cancel. But Abby *insists* on performing, despite the publicity, and the higher level of risk, and do you know why? Because she doesn't want to *'let down'* her 'new friends,' which means *my* advance security team will be at *your* coffeehouse within the hour. I'll see you there."

When Cage broke our connection, I snatched fresh slacks and a blouse from the closet, and sat down on the edge of the bed to dress.

That's when I felt a strong arm wrap

around my waist.

"Hey!" I protested.

"Hey, yourself," Mike countered. "You've got the morning off. What are you doing?"

"Getting dressed."

Suddenly I was tugged backward onto the bed, and gently but forcibly pinned to the mattress. Mike's sandy hair was mussed from sleep, and his beard stubble sandpaper-rough as he nuzzled my neck. Then he lifted his head and gazed down, those cobalt eyes still able to cut the breath from my lungs.

"I thought we were going to have breakfast — *in bed.*"

"I'm sorry; I can't. Not now. How about a rain check for *tomorrow* morning?"

I moved to peck his cheek, but the wily detective made our lips meet instead and a heated kiss followed.

"Man," he growled, "I'm hungrier than I thought . . ."

With regret in my touch, I cupped his cheek. Then I squirmed out from under him.

Mike sighed. "Do I at least get an explanation?"

"There's an emergency at work. And I better tell you about it because I don't want you to be shocked when you find out."

"Shocked?" Rolling onto his side, he propped his head on one elbow. "This I've got to hear . . ."

As Quinn watched me dress, I boiled down the crazy events that had happened to the two major points: (1) The President's daughter had been playing anonymously at our Jazz Space Open Mikes since we opened and (2) The news got out about her headlining tonight.

(And, yes, I left out all the messy stuff about the White House, the First Lady, Abby's secret assignations with an army vet jazz drummer, my simmering feud with a female Secret Service agent, and my actionable lies to the DC Metro police!)

"It's all a complete FUBAR!" I cried, borrowing Stan McGuire's handy term. "Abby's identity was supposed to be kept secret — and we are in no way prepared to handle the publicity!"

When I finished, Quinn stared a moment. "You're right, Cosi, I am shocked. When did you get so good at keeping secrets?"

"A certain police detective taught me. A guy who's far better at it than I am."

"Touché."

Snatching my keys from the dresser, I blew him a final air kiss — mainly because the sight of Quinn's powerful body lying there, half-draped in Egyptian cotton, made me certain of one thing: any more physical contact between us and I'd leave Gardner, Cage, and her entire advance team hanging till noon.

"Give 'em hell, sweetheart!"

As Quinn's deep voice echoed down the mansion's staircase, I found myself smiling, despite the impossible situation. Then I put on my game face, pulled up my speed dial numbers, and hailed New York.

"Clare? What time is it? Did you butt-dial me again?"

"No, Matt. This is a real, actual, 'meant to call you' call."

A short pause followed as the sound of Matteo Allegro's groaning yawn traveled down the eastern seaboard.

"What's up? Is something wrong?"

"Very. And I'll explain everything. But first I need you to get *your* butt out of bed and do something."

"What?"

"SOS."

"Clare, did you just say —"

"Yes. Send Our Staff!"

FORTY-FIVE

"Listen up, Cosi, you will need to provide accommodations for my detail. That means a room on the ground floor where we can establish a command post. I'd get on that, first thing . . ."

Despite her youth and bouncy blond ponytail, Agent Cage spoke like a battle-hardened general preparing for combat. In her crisp navy blue pantsuit, athletic form erect, she stood like a military pillar in the middle of my relaxed, bohemian coffee-house.

Needless to say, the contrast was unnerving.

Flanking her were two members of her detail — the tall, dark, and irritated Agent Sharpe, and a bald, brawny guy in a dark blue vest with *SECRET SERVICE* emblazoned across the back.

Obviously not *one of the agents meant to blend in with the environment.*

When I first arrived, I found the "small group" of reporters and bloggers, which Agent Cage had described, was much bigger — and growing.

Up to now, our Jazz Space didn't take reservations, and these folks were clearly desperate to get in.

But it didn't mean all of them would.

Gard and I agreed to come up with a plan that would give Abby's loyal Open Mike fans the chance to see her headline tonight, while still allowing these early line squatters their earned entry.

Until then, Gard was happy to finally use those brass posts and velvet ropes that, sadly, we'd never needed before today. The deep blue color of the velvet matched our Jazz Space motif, adding panache to our exterior, and (honestly) seeing them put to use on our sidewalk gave me a little thrill.

Meanwhile, the Secret Service troops began to move in. Several of their large, black vehicles were parked along the street as more rolled down Wisconsin. Inside one of the windowless vans, I heard *barking.* Apparently, bomb-sniffing dogs would be searching our premises — and re-searching them all day.

Do they bring dog food for something like this? I wondered. *Or was I supposed to sup-*

ply the kibble?

Next, agents from the Uniformed Division began shifting tables and chairs by the front door.

"We need a screening area," one of the men announced.

With a sigh, I ducked behind the counter, pulled my first espresso of the day, and shot it back like a gunslinger getting the nerve up for a high-noon standoff.

Gardner was already back there, filling airpots.

"Matt's sending people down from New York," I informed him. "In the meantime, we need to call in every part-timer we have in DC. I've already phoned Luther and warned him . . ." I paused, getting an idea. "Be right back."

"Agent Cage," I called, dodging a few big males and one skyscraper of a female. "Your people can use my former chef's office. He won't be back today, or ever."

"Show me," Cage commanded.

Leaving her team behind, she followed me through the kitchen to the former large closet turned small office. She poked her head through the door and scanned the windowless room.

"This will do," she declared. "I'll get back to you on our security plan. And I'll need a list of your employee names and social security numbers."

"What are you going to do with them?"

"Standard background checks. If anything questionable comes up, I'll let you know."

"Can I allow customers to come in now? We've got coffee and pastries ready to sell."

"It shouldn't be too long. When the magnetometers are in place, Sharpe will give you the okay."

As I turned to go, she called me back. "Cosi . . ." The agent actually looked sheepish. "Would you mind . . ."

"What?" I tensed. "Do you need something else?"

"A triple espresso? And one of those muffins in your glass case?"

"Which?" I asked with relief. National security freaked me out, but coffee and pastries I could handle. "How about our Oatmeal Cookie Muffin? The oats are soaked in buttermilk to soften them, and the muffins are packed with the flavors of brown sugar, cinnamon, and raisins, so they taste just like a fresh-baked oatmeal cookie. Or maybe you're more of a Farmhouse Peach Muffin kind of girl? That one has sour cream in the batter and a beautiful peach glaze drizzled on top. Our Maple-Bacon Pancake Muffin is excellent with coffee, but so is our Charming Chocolate Chip. The crumb is delectable, and if you sip your espresso as you eat the muffin, the rich roasted flavor of the coffee mingles on the palate with the bits of chocolate in a mind-blowingly sensuous dance . . ."

Sharon Cage stared at me, speechless. Her lower jaw had gone slack and a tiny drop of saliva glistened at the corner of her mouth.

Obviously the woman skipped breakfast.

"I'll bring a selection!" I declared. "And I'll get an airpot of hot coffee for your team, too."

"Thanks," she managed.

I turned to leave but stopped and faced the woman again.

"Agent Cage, I want you to know, for the record, that our former chef was the one who released the news about Abby — without my knowledge. I've fired the man, and he won't be back. Please believe me. Gardner and I will do anything to keep Abby safe."

Cage refused to meet my eyes. "What I believe doesn't matter. The only thing that does is the safety of the President's daughter in the next twenty-four hours. I want to get Abigail through this without harm or inci-dent . . ."

As I turned to go, she added one last thing.

"Please remember, Ms. Cosi. I'm willing to stake my life on it."

FORTY-SIX

Sharon Cage's last words made me realize how serious the situation was.

As a quiet college student, Abigail Prudence Parker was nearly anonymous. Few people cared what she did. But all this publicity now made our "Abby Lane" a target — for crackpots, enemies of the President (foreign and domestic), maybe even terrorists. And over the next few hours, that publicity became overwhelming.

As Cage predicted, the news of the First Daughter's jazz show hit the twenty-four-hour TV cable cycle. Network vans pulled up with satellite dishes, and well-known correspondents started interviewing members of the public in front of our coffeehouse.

Our queue was alarmingly long now, *far* past the velvet ropes. It snaked all the way down to Blues Alley, where these sorts of lines were usually seen — *near showtime.*

But Abby's performance was still eight

hours away, and the mob of locals and tourists flowing into and out of our coffeehouse — excited to drink down our roasts and gobble up our pastries — was making me nervous.

All it takes is one nut with a bomb or a gun . . .

I tried not to think about that, but the idea made me view every single customer in a different light, and I began to get a clue why Sharon Cage was such a hard case.

When she came back out to the coffeehouse floor, I was on my third attempt to contact our freelance baker, but my calls kept going to voice mail, which meant she was probably busy with an on-site wedding cake assembly.

"Looks like we'll have to refill the pastry case ourselves," I told Gardner.

"How about those Best Blueberry Muffins you brought to our greenroom last week? They were fantastic."

(I called them "Best" not because they were the most elaborate, but because the recipe was one I used all the time. With little fuss and few ingredients, it produced amazing results — juicy berries packed into a vanilla-lemon crumb with the tender texture of scratch pound cake.)

"I'll give Chef Bell my recipe . . ."

"And what about those Honey-Glazed Donuts he makes for the staff? Can't he fry up a giant batch for the customers? Maybe with chocolate glaze, too?"

"Sounds like a foodie plan —"

"Cosi!"

Sharon Cage's barking voice continued to take a bite out of my central nervous system. After waving me to the side of the coffee bar, she began to share her plan, too, but it didn't involve fresh blueberries, and she was in no mood to honey glaze it.

As she rattled off her daunting to-do list, I could hear professional pride (and a little sadistic mirth) in her tone.

"At one o'clock sharp, Abigail will arrive with her Secret Service escorts. She plans to rehearse with her band and then rest in your greenroom before the show. Once she goes up there, we're sealing the second and third floors. Nobody but you and select members of your staff will be permitted upstairs until you're ready to seat the audience."

"Okay, got it."

"In the meantime, beginning at noon and continuing until everything is wrapped and our asset is safely off these premises, we'll be conducting constant security sweeps and perimeter checks around your building.

We've placed magnetometers at the front and back doors. And if warranted, we'll search anyone suspicious who wishes to come in. We might even check for shoe bombs."

I took a breath. "Look, I have an idea for you. One the NYPD uses for Times Square every New Year's Eve. I think it will work for our situation."

And maybe make our coffeehouse a little less intimidating than Checkpoint Charlie.

"I'm listening," she said.

FORTY-SEVEN

"The shops around us close early on Saturday," I began, "so why not seal off the entire block a few hours before the show? You can screen everyone who goes in, and once they're inside your controlled space, people can move freely. That will be far more comfortable for everyone."

"What about the line of customers you have now?"

"Gardner worked out a ticketing system. We've reserved fifty seats for the loyal customers who've already registered with us over the past few months, which means we can pass out seventy-five premium vouchers to people already in line — it's up to them to go to our website and fill out our membership registration. It costs five dollars, but it comes with a free drink and a year's access to the Jazz Space's live streaming. A good deal. Then they can pay for the show ticket with a credit card, show the voucher to get in, and we can check their photo ID and card against the registered, paid-up names."

"Seventy-five tickets isn't very many," Cage pointed out, "and you've got a very long line out there."

"That's why we're going to sell *second-tier* seating on this floor. We'll put speakers and a big-screen monitor down here in the coffeehouse and offer our full Jazz Space menu.

"Finally, our *third-tier* tickets won't be allowed to enter the building, but they can be part of the event by listening to the concert through outdoor speakers and buy drinks and snacks at a food stand we'll set up outside."

Cage fell silent a moment. "I like that everyone with a ticket has to register with a name, address, and credit card — and show a photo ID to enter the secure perimeter. That alone will help us eliminate most of the problematic people."

"Problematic people?"

"Criminals, troublemakers, crackpots."

"Don't they have addresses and credit cards, too?"

"They also have records, and we'll know that up front."

"What about the crackpots who don't have records?"

"*That's* why we have the magnetometers and bomb-sniffing dogs. But what I like most about your plan is the large perimeter. If we block off the street, we won't have to worry about random traffic passing through, and Abby will be as safe as we can make her."

Cage gave me a grudging half smile. "Yeah, Cosi, we're in agreement."

"On everything but the terminology."

"Excuse me?"

"Feel free to call it a secure perimeter. But I'm going to call it a *Village Blend Block Party.*"

"Call it what you like. Just be sure to reserve some of those upstairs tickets for the White House — ten seats."

I swallowed hard. "Are the President and First Lady coming?"

"No. They're committed to another engagement, but I'm sure they'll watch some of Abby's performance, like most everyone else, via the live stream on your website."

"Then who are the tickets for?"

"The deputy press secretary. She's bringing a press pool reporter and photographer, some White House staff, and a few media VIPs."

"Hey, Sharon!"

I turned to see Agent Sharpe striding up

to his boss.

"We have a problem at the front door." He spoke low. "The man claims he works here, but he's not on the employment roster, so we've detained him.

"Point him out," Cage demanded.

"It's that guy with the mop of dark hair and neo-pioneer beard. He won't let us search his backpack. Instead he made some crack about 'jackbooted fascists.' "

I followed Agent Sharpe's pointing finger, past a few women in the crowd whose heads had already been turned by the athletic, olive-skinned figure with shoulders broad enough to fill up most of the front doorway along with his torso-hugging *Cup of Excellence, Guatemala!* T-shirt.

His jeans were worn and his right wrist displayed a glittering Breitling chronometer; his left a multicolored tribal bracelet made from braided strips of Ecuadorian leather.

Nearly as tall as the two agents flanking him, he must have felt our stares, because his hairy head turned, and his expressive brown eyes caught mine. After a beat, he slung his leather jacket over one shoulder and, with a half-amused expression, cocked his head.

"The guy's backpack is covered with airport stickers from all over the Third

World," Agent Sharpe continued. "Hellholes like Rwanda, Colombia, and Indonesia. He's trouble, for sure. He even looks like an international terrorist —"

"Why, Agent Sharpe," I cut in, "I'm shocked, *shocked* at your prejudiced profiling."

Agent Cage frowned. "What are you talking about, Cosi?"

I pointed at the bearded, shaggy detainee. "That's no terrorist. That's my ex-husband!"

FORTY-EIGHT

After clearing Matt through security, I pulled him to a quieter section of the coffeehouse floor.

"I'm glad to see you, but what I said was SOS — as in send our *staff*!"

"Take it easy, Clare. Joy's here to assist Chef Bell."

"Where is she?"

"Getting her chef's jacket from the luggage. She and Mother took the bags straight to the N Street house where you're staying."

"Your mother came, too?"

"Are you kidding? After you yelled SOS, I couldn't keep her off the plane."

"Who else?"

"Tuck and Punch will help with service. They're driving my van down with Esther and Boris, and fifty-plus pounds of freshly roasted coffee beans —"

"Which beans?"

He studied the ceiling. "The Yirg, more Sumatra, that primo Toraja Sulawesi —"

"*Tell me* you remembered my warning on roasting that Sulawesi?"

"Sure, I remembered. My batch cupped beautifully."

"We'll see. What else?"

"The Guatemalan micro-lot, and I got you the Kona."

"Extra Fancy?"

"Of course."

"Really? Oh, Matt, I could kiss you!"

"Sounds good to me." He grinned. "Now? Or later?"

"Figure of speech, Allegro."

"Hey, you know me. I'm always ready to pucker up."

"And that's precisely why our marriage didn't last."

"You didn't get enough kisses?"

"No. You applied your philosophy *globally.*"

Just then, Agent Sharpe's deep, authoritative voice caught my attention as it rose above the crowd. "Yes, Ms. Cosi is here." He pointed. "There she is!"

"Mom!"

Sharpe stepped clear, and I saw my daughter.

Matt beamed, watching us race to each

other across the crowded shop. After our tight hug, I stepped back to get a better look at my baby. Okay, not exactly a baby anymore, but in my daughter's heart-shaped face, warm peach complexion, and lively green eyes, I'd always see that first baby smile and those first baby steps, even the first meal she made — a Mother's Day breakfast of ricotta pancakes and coffee — with a little help from her father.

After a few minutes catching up, she pulled her wavy chestnut hair into a work-ready ponytail and announced —

"I better get into that kitchen!"

"Go ahead, honey. I'll be right there."

And she was off again, striding through the swinging doors with the kind of confidence that comes only from experience.

Before I even knew my lips were moving, I heard myself saying, "I'm so proud of her . . ."

Joy may have inherited her father's height — and fearlessness — but from me she got her stubborn streak, which, I admit, made her hard to handle in her teen years, but it served her well in adulthood.

It was Joy's stubbornness that kept her from quitting after being expelled from her Manhattan culinary school. And when her grandmother arranged a lowly position in

Paris, she dug in, tirelessly working until she'd proven herself with that male-dominated kitchen brigade. She'd not only risen in their ranks, but earned their respect, contributing dishes to the menu that helped Les Deux Perroquets earn its first-ever Michelin star.

That star had become Joy's ultimate goal while in Paris, and I was relieved she'd achieved it before moving back to New York.

With my move to DC, she knew her family needed her, so she'd agreed to pitch in and help Matt run our busy Greenwich Village coffeehouse.

But the family business wasn't Joy's only reason for her return home. A certain young, streetwise NYPD detective had used his influence to entice her back, as well. His name was Emmanuel Franco and for reasons too numerous to mention, including Matt's animosity toward anyone with a badge, Joy's father couldn't stand the sight of him.

But that was another battle, for another day.

"I'm proud of her, too," Matt assured me. "And I'm glad we're working together . . ." He looked away a moment, gaze going inward. "I missed a lot of years . . . you know, as her father."

"I know."

"So it's been nice having this time with her. And I know she's enjoying the break."

"Break?"

"That Paris kitchen was a pressure cooker, Clare. She says compared to that, coming back to Greenwich Village has been a vacation . . ."

The revelation worried me. Matt made it sound like Joy was planning to return to Paris.

And there it was again — that familiar ripping down my middle, half of me wanting to give my daughter the freedom to do as she pleased; the other half desperately wanting her to stay close to home, close to me.

"Oh, and speaking of our New York shop," Matt blithely went on, "Tuck and Punch are bringing down a surprise."

"Surprise? What kind of surprise?"

"I don't know. Hence the word *surprise.* They said you and Gardner should be thrilled. Speaking of which, did you know Mother's putting the whole gang up at your temporary digs?"

"On N Street? Tell me you're kidding."

FORTY-NINE

"Don't worry. Mother brought her maid along so you won't have to deal with linens and towels and getting everyone settled into all those bedrooms —"

"Six," I pointed out. "There are six bedrooms — and eight guests, nine if you count me. Ten if you count Mike."

"Quinn?" Matt shook his shaggy head. "Tell the flatfoot to find another place to crash."

I felt awful kicking Quinn out — especially after promising the man a rain check on our ruined morning. "Does he really have to bunk back at his apartment? It's all the way across town."

"We're a full house tonight, Clare. Joy even recruited an old friend from culinary school. She's coming down in the van, too —"

"That's *more* than a full house!"

"I guess some of us will have to double

up." Matt arched a dark eyebrow. "How about it? You and me? For old times' sake?"

"The finished basement has a pullout couch," I informed him flatly. "And there's always a hastily purchased air bed. I suspect you have enough hot air to inflate it."

"Well, if you change your mind —"

"I won't."

"We'll see . . ." His brown eyes flashed with mirth as he checked his watch. "Tuck should be pulling in around three o'clock, long before the Jazz Space opens, and I'll help behind the bar."

"Thank you."

"So you're set."

"Not by a long shot. I can't keep our pastry case stocked. We have a limited time to prep our supper club menu, and we're stuck creating it from the food Tad Hopkins already bought . . ."

By now, Matt had heard an earful about Hopkins's shortchanging our customers to launch a catering business on the side. My anxiety must have shown on my face because he put a hand on my shoulder.

"Clare, you did the right thing. You shouldn't second-guess it."

"What I should have done is fire him *sooner*. Or found some other way to —"

"Stop! My mother has some things to say

about that, but I'll leave that for her to discuss with you."

Great. "I *really* didn't want her to find out this way."

"She's a tough old girl, you know that." He squeezed my shoulder. "And so are you."

"I'm a tough old girl?"

"No . . ." He stroked his beard. "You're more of a scrappy MILK."

"Milk? As in Harvey?"

"As in *Mother I'd Like to Kiss.*"

"You sure cleaned that up, didn't you?"

"Hey, no need to be vulgar. And there's no need for panic. We'll get through this like a family should. Together."

"I appreciate family. I really do. But to get through *this,* we'll need more."

"What?"

"Some of Gardner's musical talent."

"You want us to play jazz?"

"Absolutely. Today is the day the Village Blend learns how to improvise."

FIFTY

"That's an awful lot of cream cheese," Joy observed, twenty minutes later. "What do you suppose Hopkins planned to do with it?"

The three of us (my daughter, my new chef, and I) were standing in the walk-in, taking stock of what we had — and what we didn't.

Luther Bell shook his head. "I hesitate to share it with you ladies."

Joy and I exchanged glances.

"Come on, Chef Bell," she teased. "Now you *have* to tell us!"

Luther folded his big arms. "Japanese-Style Crepes . . ."

"That's not so bad," Joy said. "What did he plan to fill them with?"

"Flaked Halibut and . . ." He sighed. "Miso-Infused Cream Cheese."

Joy blanched. "For *this* club? Really?"

"Really."

"Farfelu!" she cried.

Luther tilted his head. "What is that, Ms. Allegro? A French recipe?"

"No, no!" She laughed. "It's what my brigade used to say to our chef when his menu suggestions became so pretentious they entered the realm of harebrained. *Usually* he would listen and wise up."

"Well, Ms. Allegro, not Tad Hopkins."

I nodded. "Now you see what I was up against, honey?"

"Mom, I feel for you. You, too, Chef Bell . . ."

Luther and I exchanged relieved glances. After the smug Chef Hopkins, Joy's positive energy and cooperative attitude were like a breath of fresh air in this kitchen. It energized us both.

"So what should *we* do with this cream cheese?" I asked them.

"Cream cheese with butter makes a nice smooth chocolate frosting," Luther suggested. He snapped his fingers. "How about we use it to frost my Black Magic Cake?"

"Awesome idea!" Joy nodded. "That will go fast."

"How many?" I asked.

"Eight slices per cake, one hundred servings," Luther calculated. "Make a baker's dozen . . ."

I nodded, jotting *13* down on my notepad. We'd already agreed to turn Mrs. B's catering kitchen into our own little bakery. It was up to pro code, and Luther would get us started (as the law required). Madame, her maid, and I would then work on the dessert menu while Luther and Joy prepped savories and main dishes in the Village Blend kitchen.

Now Joy snapped her fingers. "Mom, why don't you make your favorite cheesecake, too? The one you adapted from that old *New Yorker* recipe."

"The *New Yorker* may have published it, but the recipe came from the CUNY Graduate Center cafeteria . . ."

The light and creamy cheesecake became so popular with students that it continually sold out, becoming the talk of the town. I smiled, remembering the legendary Emilio, the cafeteria chef who'd created that recipe. He had a lot in common with our Luther Bell.

"That version bakes and chills fast, too," I noted. "Good idea, honey."

"You know, I like to use cream cheese in my Southern Pimento Cheese. It's my secret to getting it nice and smooth. How about we offer little plates with black pepper crackers and celery stalks — for the light eaters?"

"Pimento cheese has made a real comeback," I agreed, nodding happily. "We'll need a light main dish, too."

"What about the halibut?"

"We can grill it simply with lime butter," Luther suggested. "I did that for the U.S. Senate Dining Room and it sold out the first hour."

"Done!"

Joy's face lit up. "When did you work in the Senate Dining Room?"

"After the CIA cafeteria." He rubbed the back of his neck. "Boy, I was glad to get out of Langley. The security there was crazy!"

The sound of tramping boots made us all look up. Two Secret Service agents in combat vests were moving toward Agent Cage's command post in the back of the kitchen. Joy and I tensed at the sight of the huge rifles slung over their shoulders.

Chef Bell didn't bat an eye.

"Well," I said, "I'm glad at least one of us is used to cooking around live ammunition."

FIFTY-ONE

We continued going through ingredients: blue cheese, local honey, Vidalia onions, *lots* of heavy cream, day-old baguettes, apples, frozen puff pastry shells . . .

"Joy, what about your Mini Tarte Tatins? Madame and I can prep ramekins with caramel and apples — and since there's no time for scratch puff pastry, you can use the frozen shells and bake them to order."

"Good idea." Luther nodded. "And if they're tarte Tatins, I assume you flip them onto dessert plates?"

"You got it," Joy said. "They're foolproof, too, one fast flip out of the oven and they're ready for service. The caramel sauce looks amazing, flowing over the baked apples and pastry — as if you've sauced them with care."

"One problem . . ." I tapped my chin with the pencil. "*Individual tarte Tatin* doesn't fit with the Great American Food theme we've got going."

"Well, apple pie is about as American as you can get," Luther argued.

"A rose by any other name?"

"As long as the rose is something the customers enjoy. That's my motto."

"Mine, too."

"Mine, three!"

Like one of Gardner's Open Mike trios, we continued improvising what we could with what we had. Finally, I pointed to the flank steaks. "What was Hopkins going to do with those?"

"Stew them in a curry," Luther said, "with pecans, dried figs, and blueberries."

"Blueberries?!" Joy and I cried together.

"To be served on a bed of herbed polenta and topped with caramelized fennel foam."

"For a relaxed, coffeehouse jazz club?" Joy smacked her forehead. "Ahh! *Farfelu!*"

"How about my Bourbon Sugar Steak instead?" Chef Bell offered. "I'll slice it nice and tender, against the grain."

"Beautiful," I said. "Your Sugar Steak is one of my favorites."

"With shoestring fries, Chef Bell? *Pretty please?* I've been missing my steak *frites!*"

He laughed. "Okay, then."

"I know Mom's making good use of those blueberries. I can smell them baking in her muffins. What about the pecans and figs? Shall we use them for dessert?"

"I'll have a savory in mind for the figs," the chef promised. "As for the pecans, how about my pecan pie? Or we could do Pecan Sandies?"

"Your pecan pie makes my knees go weak," I confessed, "but let's make it in slab form and cut it into bars. We can make the sandies, too, and sell both at the outdoor stand tonight."

"I'm sorry, Mom," Joy whispered as Chef Bell stepped away. "I've been out of the country awhile. What exactly are 'Pecan Sandies'?"

"Sables," I whispered back.

"Oh!" She clapped her hands. "Give that job to Grandmother. She can make *sables* in her sleep!"

"Done," I said, and our menu was complete.

FIFTY-TWO

After sending Matt and Freddie out for last-minute supplies and ingredients, I called my music director to the kitchen.

"We've got it, Gard."

"Got what?"

"Your *new* Jazz Space menu . . ."

VILLAGE BLEND, DC
JAZZ SPACE

SWINGIN' HEADLINERS

Bourbon Sugar Steak, freshly seared and sliced, served with Crispy Shoestring Fries, Smoked Tomato Ketchup, Truffle Oil Mayo

Fresh Halibut, grilled simply with Lime Butter, served with a side of Roasted Vegetables, Lime-Garlic Bruschetta

Buttermilk Fried Chicken Wing Plate, dipping side of Alabama White BBQ Sauce, Cheddar-Corn Spoon Bread, Luther's Hard Cider Green Beans

California Cobb Salad with juicy Grilled Free-Range Chicken, sliced avocado, crumbled bacon, House-Made Garlic-Parm Croutons

BEBOP BITES

Trio of Steak Burger Sliders, topped with melted Cheddar, and slices of Seared Pork Belly

Southern Pimento Cheese served with black pepper crackers and celery stalks

Bacon-Wrapped Bourbon Figs stuffed with Iowa's Maytag Blue & Texas Pecans, drizzled with local honey

Pile of Crunchy Vidalia Onion Rings served with Smoky Chipotle Dip

DESSERT DUETS

Mini Caramel-Sauced Apple Pie with a scoop of No-Churn Vanilla Bean Ice

Cream and a pressed pot of
Hawaiian-Grown Kona

Birthplace of Jazz New Orleans Beignets
served with our dipping-sized cup of
café au lait

Luther's Black Magic Cake, a dense,
moist, coffee-kissed chocolate cake,
made *and* served with our famous
Village Blend espresso

The famous Light & Creamy *New Yorker*
Cheesecake, served with a shot of Fresh
Strawberry Sauce and a Clover Cup of
Toraja Sulawesi

Cookie Plate of Luther's Pecan Pie Bars
& Pecan Sandies made with
Honey-Gingered Texas Pecans, served
with a personal Chemex of Ethiopian
Yirgacheffe, or our special Ginger Tea
with local honey

TONIGHT'S DRINK SPECIALS

Bloody (Proud) Mary served with bacon
strips cooked down to crispy perfection in
an iron skillet with coffee, brown sugar,
and cayenne

Espresso Martini served with Dark Chocolate–Covered Espresso Beans exclusively made for the Village Blend by J. Chocolatier of Washington, DC

See our printed beverage menu (at your table) for our full range of hot and cold espresso drinks, pressed pots of our handcrafted coffee blends, wines, beers, and specialty cocktails.

Luther Bell, Executive Chef
Gardner Evans, Jazz Space Manager and Music Director
Clare Cosi, General Manager, Food & Beverage Director
Madame Dreyfus Allegro Dubois, Owner

Gard whistled loud as he read. "Y'all are going to sell out of *everything* on this baby!"

Chef Bell grinned. "How about we get some stationery especially for Abby's big night? Maybe something with red, white, and blue stripes across the top and bottom?"

"Where do we get something like that?" Gard asked.

"Groovy, DC," I told him. "It's a gift shop on Capitol Hill. They share the building with J. Chocolatier — we use her for our chocolate-covered espresso beans."

"I'm on it," Gard said, heading out.

"One last thing, ladies . . ." Chef Bell looked *very* serious all of a sudden. "And this is important to me."

Joy and I exchanged concerned glances and huddled up.

"In the heat of the action tonight, I'm afraid there might be a very big problem . . ."

"What?" we asked together.

"If you ladies call out, 'Chef Bell,' I'm afraid I won't know who you're talking to. Can we please go back to calling me *Luther*?

I could see that Joy, who was used to the French brigade system, didn't like the idea at all. But it was Luther's kitchen — his rules.

"All right," my daughter finally said. "I'll call you Luther. But no more *Ms. Allegro*. You will call me Joy —"

"And I will call you *Goddess*!"

We all turned to find Tito Bianchi gawking at my daughter's heart-shaped face. *"Bellissima,"* he murmured and kissed his pursed fingers. "Joy, you are a joy to look at."

"Excuse me," my daughter replied in Italian. "What is *your* name?"

"Tito."

"Well, I'm happy to meet you, Tito, but I'm *taken.*"

"Are you married?"

"No."

"Engaged?"

"No."

"Then you are *not* taken, and I have a chance!" He grinned with a gamer's gusto. Then he turned to me and spoke in English —

"We have sold the last of your muffins, boss. The glass case is empty again, but the customers are still hungry. This is my news. And now, back I return" — he winked at Joy — "to the battlefront!"

"Who was that idiot?"

"He's not an idiot. He's my new assistant manager. He's also a brilliant barista and bartender — with a sommelier's knowledge of wine — and he's a very hard worker."

"He's very fresh!"

"Not usually. But he is Italian. So if he pinches *any* part of your body, I want to hear about it."

"Fine, but you better not tell Manny Franco."

"Believe me, Joy, it took me ages to find Tito. I have no intention of seeing him murdered by your boyfriend."

Ding!

"Perfect timing," I said, hurrying to the oven.

Another giant batch of my Best Blueberry Muffins was ready for the empty pastry case!

FIFTY-THREE

An hour later, I was ready.

Matt had warned me that his mother had things to say about firing her "prodigy" chef, and I'd put it off long enough, so I plowed my way through our crowded coffeehouse, dodged the crazy traffic on Wisconsin (largely due to us), and trudged over to N Street.

Not that I was in a hurry to get there . . .

Deal with it, Clare, it's time to face the music . . .

Unfortunately, the musician I was about to face had eighty-plus years of crooning her undiluted opinions. In culinary terms, Madame Dreyfus Allegro Dubois didn't sugarcoat her words.

Oh, she had a beautiful heart, but it was well calloused by hard knocks. I admired her for that. But then, I'd been on her good side most of the time. We'd been through so much together — as mother- and daughter-in-law; as mentor and apprentice. It was because I loved and respected her that I dreaded the idea of disappointing her.

As I entered the Cox's Row mansion, I heard crashing noises from the gourmet kitchen. Girding myself for a chilly greeting, I moved through the elegant rooms and pushed through the swinging door.

Madame was not a petite woman. Like her son and granddaughter, she was blessed with height. But she looked small in this large space, amid all the spotless tiles and stainless steel. As she threw open the cupboards and chattered with her maid, however, it was clear her trademark energy had not diminished.

For a moment, her clothing threw me. Madame's usual attire ran to designer pantsuits and whimsically printed silk scarves. But *this* lady was dressed like a vagabond. And then it hit me: *dry-clean-only ensembles don't mix with flour, butter, eggs, and cream!*

The capri jeans and slip-on sneakers looked like Joy's. And the giant, faded T-shirt had to be my ex-husband's. The size of the shirt was a giveaway, but so was the phrase across the chest: *Extreme Kitesurfing ~ Kona, Hawaii!*

Not that Madame wasn't daring. Her

Midsummer Night Swing dance moves at Lincoln Center were proof of that. But surfing Hapuna Bay with a power kite strapped to her back? Nope, couldn't see it.

What I did see in the strong light of the afternoon sun was a determined octogenarian pulling out pans and measuring cups, shuffling recipes, and taking inventory on the ingredients she found in the kitchen versus the ones her beloved son was in the process of fetching.

At last, she noticed me. "Finally! I've been waiting for you!"

"Matt said you wanted to speak with me?"

For an awkward moment, Madame gawked at my tense expression. Then she plopped a long-fingered hand on her hip and began her lecture —

"Clare, what is *wrong* with you?"

I gritted my teeth, waiting for the rest.

But there was no lecture. Only a demand: "Come over here and give me a hug!"

"A hug?" I blinked. "You're not angry?"

"About what?"

"My firing Chef Hopkins."

"Oh, that! The truth is — I am angry. Very angry. At myself!"

I studied her gently wrinkled face. "I don't understand."

"Yes you do. Tad Hopkins is a brilliant

chef, but he's also a brilliant con artist." The hand on her hip waved in the air, as if swatting away an annoying bug. "Back in New York, he was all charm, telling me he was ready for a move. I thought I was lucky, securing a chef of his caliber for our DC kitchen. I assumed he'd be a great help to you, a burden off your shoulders. I envisioned you two as a dynamic duo — your sophisticated knowledge of coffees and beverages and his youthful energy and dazzling menus."

She shook her head, her silver pageboy shimmering in the sun. "I should have known better. *That's* why I'm angry!"

"But I'm responsible for the overall management here, and the only reason we're in a fix today is because I didn't fix the problem sooner." I looked away, embarrassed. "When we came down here, Gardner and I dreamed of success, of having Georgetown dance in the streets. But all we've done is cost you money."

"Clare, you did your best in a bad situation — and, frankly, with a bad man."

"Because he stole from us?"

"Because he accused *you* of stealing."

FIFTY-FOUR

"He did what?!"

"You heard me."

"He accused *me* of stealing?"

Madame nodded. "A few days ago, Hopkins rang me up, claiming he caught you embezzling from my business. You were incompetent, he said, and he simply couldn't work with you — oh, and he was about as generous with his comments when it came to Gardner, as well."

"What did you say?"

"Not a thing. I told him I'd have to think it over. Then I ended the call and immediately contacted my lawyer, asking him to review Hopkins's contract and find out what our options were for getting him the hell out of our business."

A wave of relief flowed through me. "So *you* were going to fire him?"

"My dear, I already knew about the poor reviews of the man's food. He could have tempered that ego and worked with you and Gardner to adapt his menu, make it work for this time and place. Instead, Hopkins played politics — and lost. I've been around a block or two, you know, and the moment he accused you of stealing, I knew *he* was. That's the game of the wrongdoer, look for a scapegoat, someone to blame or frame."

Then she smiled wide enough to deepen the gentle creases in her cheeks.

"I'm proud of you, Clare, not only for standing up to that awful man, but for finding a strategy to beat him. According to my lawyer, if we had fired him without cause, we would have had to pay him a fortune."

"I'm just glad I found cause before *he* caused me to jump in the Potomac. Some of those nights, I swear, I came close!"

"I promise you, I won't hire another employee for the Village Blend — in New York or Washington — without your vetting the person first."

"Please don't be so hard on yourself. The chef came with a fine pedigree."

"But he wanted to be the star, the *only* star, and our coffeehouse has always been an ensemble production. It's called Village *Blend* for a reason, you know?"

"I know."

Then Madame opened her arms, and we

finally shared that hug.

"Now, tell me, how do you feel about tonight?"

"I have confidence in our new chef, our dedicated staff, and in Gardner, who'll be managing the Jazz Space program. But there's a wildly unpredictable element in this mix . . ."

"Young Abigail?"

I nodded, unable to stop seeing the image of her tender pale wrist and those terrible vertical scars.

"Abby played well during our quiet Open Mike Nights," I said. "But this? Grand Central station has less traffic than our ground floor right now, and tonight the Jazz Space will be packed. Press will be there and we're streaming live on our website. She chose not to cancel tonight, but I have no idea how she's going to react to the pressure."

"You'll have to have faith, Clare. Walk forward, head high, as if everything will work out — and perhaps it will!"

"Maybe. But if things go wrong tonight, I'll never forgive myself . . ."

And by *wrong* I didn't simply mean Abigail Parker running off the stage in tears. I was thinking like Sharon Cage now, looking at every customer as a possible nut with a bomb or gun.

Maybe the President's daughter would play well tonight. Maybe she wouldn't. I just prayed nothing would blow up in our faces. Or worse — Abby's.

FIFTY-FIVE

"Good evening, ladies and gentlemen, and welcome to the Jazz Space at the Village Blend . . ."

Gardner's deep voice gave me a little thrill as it resonated through our packed house, adding voltage to the buzz of anticipation already in the air.

The human electricity alone could have powered our LED star field, which now actually *twinkled* against our twilight blue walls and ceiling — thanks to some theatrical tweaking by Tucker and Punch, both of whom were fixtures of New York's cabaret scene.

Together with the flickering votive candles, which Esther and I had placed on every table, those sparkling stars added to the enchantment of this already-magical night.

Downstairs, our coffeehouse was equally packed — and just as buzzy. Our big-screen monitor was streaming directly from the stage, and dinner service was going smoothly. Even our block party refreshment stand was doing swift business out on Wisconsin Avenue.

Now Gardner was warming up the audience with the ease of a seasoned professional, his deep, mellow voice sweet as melted chocolate as it flowed through our sound system.

At his mention of the "Jazz Space," applause broke out, the loudest coming from the tables up front, where we'd seated Abby's Open Mike fans, including one of her most loyal followers — the guy I thought of as "Ponytail Man."

When he'd first arrived, he even collared me to ask —

"How is Abby doing? Is she nervous?"

Ponytail Man had the kind of face I would have loved to paint, with a broad, slightly crooked nose and dusky coloring that made his trimmed gray beard appear almost white. Small scars and blemishes marked his craggy skin, suggesting he'd done some hard living, yet his nearly black eyes were alive with sharp intelligence, glistening like the dark oily beans of a New Orleans roast.

"I . . . ah . . . I haven't seen her today," I confessed, finding it hard to look away from those intense eyes. "Gardner spent most of the afternoon helping her rehearse with his band . . ." I waved him over.

"She's excited," Gard informed us. "And a little nervous. But as long as she remembers to *swing* up there, she'll be fine."

"Nice advice." Ponytail Man nodded his approval. "Wish her luck for me."

After settling him into a good seat, I tapped Gard's shoulder. "What's that gentleman's name? I'd like to greet him more personally next time."

"I don't know his name. I thought you did."

"I'll ask Abby after the show. He's probably one of her AU professors . . ."

After our Open Mike fans were seated, my co-manager moved to the stage's grand piano. Stan joined him on drums, Jackson on bass, Theo on sax, and together Four on the Floor serenaded the rest of the incoming audience with gorgeously played versions of American jazz standards.

When everyone was settled and the first round of food and drinks was under way, Gard ended his band's opening set and approached the standing mic to officially welcome the crowd to our Jazz Space.

"We are streaming *live,* as we do every

287

night," he announced, "but on this very special evening I'm told the President and First Lady will be watching. Let's give the First Couple a round of applause . . ."

More clapping followed, but this time the pumped-up volume came from the tables in the *center* of the room, where we'd seated the White House staff.

Two familiar faces stood out in that group — the White House chef and a fiftyish brunette, who'd been to our Jazz Space at least once before.

I could see the brunette was wearing Fen again tonight, just like me, but her outfit was *much* farther up the food chain, along with that five-hundred-dollar Fen bag I'd coveted.

I remembered one more thing about the well-heeled woman, and that was the impeccably dressed Indian man who'd gotten cozy with her last week at one of our Open Mike tables — Jeevan Varma.

FIFTY-SIX

I didn't see Mr. Varma here this evening, but I remembered him well enough. *How could I forget a man whose crazy behavior led to my telling lies to the DC Metro police?*

Now, at least, I understood Mr. Varma's connection to Abby. His girlfriend obviously brought him to this club so she could brag about knowing Abby Lane's true identity. But that failed to explain the man's actions two nights ago . . .

Why would a State Department employee, with a girlfriend in the White House, no less, come banging on my back door, drunk as a skunk, in the dead of night? And why would he rush the First Daughter, ranting to her about the President?

Part of me was hoping to see Jeevan Varma back here tonight so I could get some answers. Then again, part of me feared it.

Maybe the Secret Service kept him out . . .

If Mr. Varma worked for the State Department, I doubted there were things in his background that raised red flags. Then again, who knew what sort of trouble he may have gotten into before he showed up in that inebriated state at my coffeehouse?

For the first time, I was actually grateful to Sharon Cage for being a hard case. No doubt, Abby's parents were, too.

"Psst!" From behind the busy bar, Matt caught my eye. I moved closer.

"Did Gard announce that the President is watching tonight?"

I nodded.

"That sure ups the ante," Matt whispered, shaking up a fresh batch of Espresso Martinis.

"What worries me isn't the Commander in Chief. It's the man's chef . . ." I tilted my head in her direction. "Let's hope she doesn't get indigestion."

Matt's confident grin was dazzling. "Not with *our daughter* in the kitchen."

I mouthed a thank-you for that — and for trimming that bush of his (at my request). Gone was his "detainee" look. My ex-husband's strong jawline was now outlined by his closely cropped beard, his shaggy dark hair pulled into a short ponytail. His worn T-shirt and jeans were gone, too, exchanged for a nicely filled-out black shirt and slacks, which made us a match tonight — in color, that is.

After my quick shower, I'd applied makeup, pulled on black stockings, and zipped up my little black dress. I even added some soft curls to my chestnut hair because I knew very well that this evening wasn't only Abby's chance to impress Washington. It was ours.

"Before we bring out our lovely headliner," Gardner continued from the stage, "I have a question for y'all. By a show of hands, how many of you have never been to a jazz club before tonight? Wave your paw if this is your first time . . ."

At least 30 percent of the audience put hands up, many with drinks still in them. The sight was hilarious, like a massive toast.

"Well, look at that . . . I see some of y'all need refills!"

Everyone laughed and hooted — and some actually ordered refills.

"Okay," Gard continued, "how about I break jazz down for you newbies? It's like this: Here in Washington, you're experts at improvisation. You may have a point of view, but there's always someone with another, and a third, and a fourth. Well, the conversations you see on a jazz stage are like the conversations you have in your offices and agencies and on Capitol Hill.

"You may bring written notes with you to start your presentation — but what makes or breaks your argument is how well you perform *unscripted,* in the heat of the moment; how well you listen and respond. Jazz is the art of discovery, and the art of acceptance. In jazz, there are no wrong notes because they're part of the performance, part of the music, part of the flow . . ."

"That's right! You got it! Tell 'em, Gard," cried fellow musicians at the tables up front.

"More than any other musical form, jazz is the individual voice of the performer, coming through his or her instrument. That's the whole nut. In fact, we have a saying in jazz. You don't play your instrument —"

"YOU PLAY MUSIC!" shouted Stan, Jackson, and Theo behind him.

The crowd loved it. They clapped and cheered. They were on board.

"Tonight, the *music* you're about to hear Ms. Abigail Parker play is coming from her heart and soul. To respect that as an audience, all you have to do is listen. Not only with your ears but with *your* soul and with *your* heart." He paused and smiled. "If you do, I promise, you're about to fall in love . . ."

FIFTY-SEVEN

As Gard finished his intro, Abby entered the room and crossed to the stage. Tonight she'd abandoned her funereal look for a shimmering, sleeveless shift the color of our twilight blue walls. Her industrial eyewear was gone, and she'd changed her hairstyle, placing two metallic blue barrettes at the sides of her head, nipping back the dark curtain to let the world see her true identity.

While Abby looked beautiful, anyone could see that she was visibly tense and purposely avoiding eye contact with the audience.

As she settled herself on the piano bench, I remembered the name of her signature piece, "Cool Reception," and better understood what Abigail Parker believed about how the world saw her.

I felt for her in that moment, and I feared for her, too.

The public was quick to make judgments

these days, and snarky comments were the norm. Internet trolls could do more than provoke a cool reception to an artist like Abby — they could make her want to quit completely.

Gard noticed Abby's anxiety, too. Moving to her, he bent down and whispered in her ear. Abby nodded, her gaze immediately going to Stan at the drums.

As Gard left the stage, Stan picked up his brushes and began sweeping his snare with a slow, steady rhythm, his good eye fixed on Abby.

For quite a few bars, Abby nodded her head in time with Stan. It was longer than usual for an intro, and the audience began some uneasy murmuring. Finally, as if for luck, she rubbed the musical notes tattooed on her arm, lifted her hands, and began to play.

The quick, lively tune was recognizable, but not from anything she'd performed at our Open Mikes. This was the song Gard had promised us in his introduction —

"Let's Fall in Love."

The great American standard had been covered by countless jazz artists, but Abby chose Dave Brubeck's punchy approach. The brightness of the piece uplifted the room. It brought palpable relief, as well.

We all wanted Abby to succeed, and thanks to Gard and Stan she was off to a solid start, segueing almost immediately into a jazzy version of "Tonight," the classic from *West Side Story.*

Some brief cooperative improvisations in the middle of both pieces also gave Stan and Jackson a chance to shine. When they finished, warm applause followed.

At this point, headliners usually addressed the audience, as Gard had, striving to make a personal connection. They might talk about the next song, or introduce the band, or simply tell a joke.

Abby looked as though she were about to say something, but one glance at the packed house, and she froze, fixing her gaze on those black-and-white keys.

Once again, the audience mumbled uneasily.

And once again, Stan knew what to do.

"Abby," he whispered from behind his drum kit. When she looked up, he locked his gaze with hers, shot her a smile, and began to nod his head in a steady rhythm.

One, two, three . . . One, two, three . . .

Abby mimicked his head movements, feeling the rhythm flow through her as she nodded, then her fingers found the rhythm. Using the lower piano keys, she began to play.

Budum, budum, budum . . .

When her right hand joined in the higher range, she'd successfully launched "A Little Jazz Exercise," an unassuming name for one of the most challenging short pieces for a jazz pianist to master. No surprise, it was written by a master — Oscar Peterson, one of the most accomplished jazz artists of the twentieth century.

In lightning-fast stride, Abby's fingers raced up and down the ivories. There were fluid arpeggios, black note slide-offs, and demands for controlled changes of tempo and dynamics. Despite the complexity of the piece, Abby displayed no hesitation, not a moment's struggling.

She may have been unable to address the crowd, but her pleasure at playing this marvelous composition connected her with the audience more powerfully than any words could.

I considered it a minor miracle.

Earlier today, some of the TV cable shows presented Abigail Parker as a painfully shy prelaw student with questionable talent whose Georgetown show was nothing more than a political stunt to help her father's flagging poll numbers.

"Come on, how good can she be?" the pundits cracked.

This piece blew those assumptions out of the water, and when it was over, absolute silence fell over the room. Much of the audience didn't seem to trust what they'd witnessed.

But Gard's musician friends did — and so did Abby's loyal Open Mike fans, starting with Ponytail Man, who stood up and began to clap. Then everyone stood.

The applause went on for a solid minute.

Stan was grinning so widely, he had a hard time keeping his eye patch in place, and I could see Gard whistling and clapping in the front row.

Abby slowly stood, as if coming out of a trance. She bowed deeply, dark eyes glistening, and hurried out of the room. The band followed her up to the greenroom and the first set of the night was (thank goodness!) over.

"Looks like I was right," I told Gard a few minutes later at the bar.

"Right about what?"

"Given the pressure, I was dreading Abby might end up running off the stage in tears."

"Yeah . . ." He grunted. "Thank the Lord they were tears of joy. But the night's far from over, Clare. And she's got two more sets. Let's hope the joy continues . . ."

FIFTY-EIGHT

"To reach a level of mastery in jazz," Gard told the audience at the start of the second set, "you must understand that music is about something other than chord changes. A true artist uses the art form to express something, to communicate what he or she can't in any other way.

"Since most music is about a human condition, that's how it should be felt and played. Sad songs should make us cry. Up songs should make us want to dance. Romantic songs should make us want to . . . well, y'all know . . ."

The crowd laughed, and Gard flashed a playful smile.

"When that music is *jazz,* it has something more, what we call *swing.* Here at the Jazz Space, to swing with you again, is Ms. Abigail Parker . . ."

Abby seemed more relaxed for this set, smiling at her bandmates as she settled onto her bench. Then she shocked the heck out of me with her next move. Leaning toward the mic by her piano, she finally addressed the crowd with five words —

"This one's for Clare Cosi."

The band immediately swung into Johnny Costa's jazzy version of "Won't You Be My Neighbor," the classic theme song from the *Mister Rogers* children's show.

Now, I have no idea what possesses jazz artists to turn simple children's fare into nightclub tunes — "A-Tisket, A-Tasket," "Mary Had a Little Lamb," "Humpty Dumpty," "Little Brown Jug" — but Abby's musical joke went over big.

Behind the bar, Matt laughed himself silly, and so did my staff, who began singing along with the melody, prompting the entire audience to join in — and, given that we were streaming live on our website, I suspected I'd be hearing it crooned to me over and over for weeks (or possibly years) to come.

Next came "Black Coffee." The song, that is. Although at this point in the evening — having been up and down the stairs dozens of times to keep our food and beverage service on track — I was shooting double espressos.

By now, Theo and his sax had joined the

trio, adding a throaty fourth to the group, and the cooperative improvs continued through "Someday My Prince Will Come," going back and forth in a jam with true swinging.

One last song in the set prompted Abby to use her mic again.

"This one's for my Secret Service detail," she said sincerely. "*Especially* Special Agent in Charge, Sharon Cage . . ."

At the mention of her name, Cage's stoic expression faltered.

While she remained unmoving at her post near the stage, when Abby began to play a gorgeous version of "Someone to Watch Over Me," I could see the change come over her.

I doubted anyone else could. But after deciphering Mike Quinn's cryptic emotions for so long, I knew Sharon Cage was touched by the First Daughter's gesture.

For a fleeting moment there, the woman actually smiled.

By the start of her third and final set, it was clear to anyone paying attention that Abby was an accomplished jazz pianist, but not yet a comfortable stage performer. In our safe Jazz Space it didn't matter because Gardner was there, "watching over her" —

300

just as protectively as Cage.

And he wasn't the only one.

Stanley McGuire didn't take his good eye off Abby all evening.

"Ever felt love at first sight?" Gard asked the audience at the standing mic. "You meet someone and you instantly connect — you can talk to them all night long. You feel that person knows you better than a girlfriend or boyfriend you might have had for years. Well, it's the same thing in jam sessions. Two or more musicians can just click — even if they just met. It's a language you both understand; and if the chemistry's right, there's nothing like it . . ."

Gard turned and smiled. "That's how I met the three gentlemen you see behind me . . ."

He spoke briefly about Jackson on bass and Theo on sax. Finally, he came to Stan.

"The rhythm section has the most difficult job in a jazz band because you're providing accompaniment for unknown riffs and improvs. Because you can't plan for it, all you can do is react with a kind of prescient anticipation. Our drummer, Stan McGuire, spent time as an army medic. That might be why he understands improvisation on the most primal level of all —"

The crowd interrupted Gard to give the

young military vet a round of applause. Stan looked embarrassed, but I was so pleased!

"As for Abigail," Gard continued, "she once told me why playing is so important to her. 'If I'm confused about what I'm feeling,' she said, 'I sit down at my piano and sort out my emotions that way. I couldn't live without music, and I don't think I'd want to . . .' "

Gard continued talking, but my mind couldn't get past Abby's words.

I could see Gard took her statement as figurative. But given those old scars on Abby's wrist, I wasn't so sure.

FIFTY-NINE

For her final set, Abby couldn't wait to sit down at her piano bench. With a little smile for her attentive drummer, she moved to speak into her mic.

"This one is for Stan," she said, louder and more boldly than any of the dedications she'd made all night.

When she looked up at him again, he was gawking, as if dumbfounded.

Now everyone in the room was leaning forward, waiting to see what Abby would play. When she began "Our Love Is Here to Stay," I saw an uneasy reaction at the center of the room — the tables with White House staff.

When the number was over, Jackson and Theo quietly left the stage.

Stan was the only one who stayed, which made no sense, because the next few numbers were piano solos. There was nothing for him to do but sit quietly at his drum kit.

Abby obviously wanted him there because she continued looking to him for grounding before beginning.

The first was a moving version of a gorgeous song, "Love Ballade," composed once again by jazz legend Oscar Peterson.

She paused before playing her next number, sweetly touching the musical notes on her arm. "For my father," she said almost reverently and began to play "Over the Rainbow," evoking Keith Jarrett's moving performance of the song at La Scala.

Oddly, she dedicated the next one to her father, too, but this time she said it in a much more formal way: "To the President . . ."

When she began to play "America the Beautiful," the audience stirred. Abby's version, with lush, jazzy chord progressions and a soulful finish, left everyone glowing.

Finally, she played the most offbeat choice of the night: concert pianist Natalia Posnova's arrangement of "Who Wants to Live Forever," a moving ballad recorded by the rock group Queen, which Ms. Posnova had transformed into a virtuoso piece for piano.

With dramatically sustained chords and a flurry of flying fingers, Abby didn't need a band. The piano did everything. The piece itself, a melancholy meditation on love and free will, on having everything decided for you, brought back Gardner's words, about the music being more than notes — about it being a way for the artist to express herself, communicate what she couldn't in any other way.

When Abby finished, the meaning of the lyrics seemed to resonate through her emotional performance. Our future was inevitable, out of our hands. The end is always there, waiting for us, but we can have now, we can have today. *Who wants to live forever, anyway?*

I couldn't see how she could top that. In fact, I thought it was the end of the show, but she had one more piece to perform. And it was no solo.

This very special finale was something she'd planned with Stanley McGuire.

SIXTY

To begin this number, Stan made his way over to Abby's piano bench. With his weak leg, he was partially limping, and the audience whispered curiously, wondering why this injured vet was making such an awkward move.

Stan ignored the whispers and cheerfully sat next to Abby, but facing away from the piano.

Meanwhile, Jackson and Theo carried over two items for him: a single snare drum positioned in front of him and the hi-hat of two small cymbals beside it.

As the two band members found seats, Gardner gave up his and moved to stand next to me near the bar.

"What are they doing?" I whispered.

"You'll see . . ."

Stan lifted his sticks, and Abby spoke low to him. She looked anxious, but when he whispered in her ear, her tension broke and she actually laughed.

Then she nodded. The stage lights above them dimmed, and a single spot shined down on the pair like a ray of heavenly light.

Abby began to play a simple piano phrase, one I'd heard on FM radio.

"I know that song," I whispered in Gardner's ear. "What is it?"

" 'Fix You,' " he said, and I understood.

Instead of a typical jazz standard, Abby and Stan had selected a newer piece of music to adapt for their duet. The famous Coldplay tune about loss, failure, pain, and redemption was clearly meaningful to both of them.

Stan, head down, listened for a dozen bars. Then he began playing his snare. The duet became more intense before the two broke from the melody and began a musical conversation.

The playing was at a level I'd never heard before, not in this room — or any room. I noticed Gardner suddenly grin with a kind of cheeky anticipation.

"Why are you smiling?" I asked.

"Watch . . ."

Stan put down his sticks and swung himself around to face the piano's cabinet, which he began thumping like a drum with his bare hands.

"He learned that when his dad was stationed in Germany," Gard whispered. "Keith Jarrett's Köln concert recording is legendary over there — brilliant!"

Finally, Stan began playing the keys with Abby, commanding the bass notes while she danced along the treble. Soon their hands were crossing over in a fast and flawless stride.

Before long, the pace slowed to a melancholy finish, quiet, contemplative. Stan spun around to his drum again, quiet sticking, and then silence as he let Abby's final, sweetly haunting notes linger in the air.

The entire room sat stunned.

No one had seen — or heard — anything like it. And they absolutely loved it. The roar of applause, shouts, whistles that came next was deafening. The first floor was applauding, too, and then I heard the noise on Wisconsin Avenue. From the second-floor window, I saw the crowd clapping and shouting.

Abby grinned so widely I thought she would burst. Stan said something in her ear and she laughed, threw her arms around him, and kissed him on the mouth. He looked a little surprised, but he didn't hesitate. He kissed her right back!

The crowd went crazy.

Together they stood and bowed — and called Gardner's band members back to join them.

I thought the remarkable show was over.

But as the audience chanted "More, more, more . . ." the band looked to Gard, who had a surprise. First he waved to those musician friends at the front tables, and they quickly moved onto the stage — trumpets, trombones, and two more saxophones.

As Gard took his place as the conductor, he signaled to two people who'd been waiting for their cue. When I saw them, I nearly fell off my low heels.

Tucker and Punch strode into the room and onto the stage.

The two were no longer in their waiter's uniforms. Using their theatrical bag of tricks, they'd transformed themselves into Tony Bennett and Lady Gaga — an odd couple in the music world, who'd paired up to record jazz duets.

Tuck and Punch (as Tony and Gaga) each grabbed a mic. Then Gard faced his band and pointed to Stan, whose pulse-pounding drum solo opened a bold, brassy, brilliant performance of Duke Ellington's —

"It Don't Mean a Thing (If It Ain't Got That Swing)"!

Tuck and Punch were pitch-perfect as

they sang through the song's bouncy lyrics, having fun with each other and the audience, the same way they did in their New York cabaret shows. Then they stepped off the stage and the jam began. Abby's grin was cheek to cheek as she traded hoppin' solos with Stan and the rest of the band.

Some of the crowd clapped along, others stood up, arms waving.

Suddenly, I felt a hard tug and realized someone had hooked me at the waist and was spinning me around.

"Matt! What are you doing?"

"Just look," he demanded, dancing me to the window. "Look at our new neighborhood!"

When I did, I finally felt the tears well up. I couldn't help it. After all we'd been through, it felt like a dream. And it was, a dream come true.

Our Village Blend, DC, literally had Georgetown dancing in the streets.

SIXTY-ONE

"A toast!" Madame declared, raising a flute of chilled champagne.

For a brief moment, the backslaps and fist bumps ceased, as everyone in the greenroom turned their attention to our club's octogenarian owner.

In a flowing Fen pantsuit of electric blue, a whimsical silk scarf of musical notes draped around her regal neck, and her silver pageboy in an elegant twist, my former mother-in-law stood before the fireplace, her proud gaze sweeping the crowd. I knew that behind those vibrant violet eyes, a million memories lurked.

For more than half a century, the indomitable woman had kept the Allegro family's iconic Greenwich Village coffeehouse business going through recessions and riots; taxes and turmoil; greed and gentrification.

Through it all, she'd forged affectionate relationships with some of the most influential artists, writers, poets, and musicians of the twentieth century. And, in her toast on this very special evening, our beloved grande dame evoked an old memory while acknowledging this brand-new one —

"Tonight, my dear Abby, you brought back a treasured memory of my son's late father." She tipped the glass toward Matt. "Antonio and I were lucky witnesses to pianist Erroll Garner's performance of jazz at Carnegie Hall. A momentous night for music — and for America. I felt the same tonight, my dear. None of us will ever forget your brave and brilliant performance."

"Hear! Hear!" Gardner cheered.

"She is brave," Stan gushed, "and brilliant!"

"Brava," Jackson agreed.

Madame's gaze met Abby's tearful eyes. Then she hoisted her glass even higher and exclaimed, "To the brightest star in our nation's capital tonight, Abigail Parker!"

Grinning shyly, Abby only sampled her champagne. Already euphoric, she didn't need further stimulus. We all felt that same euphoria, and the boisterousness of our celebration threatened to burst my mural-covered greenroom's walls.

Gardner kept shaking his head as if he couldn't believe our good fortune, and

Stan's grin was so wide his upturned cheeks kept displacing his eye patch. (And I was pretty sure Stan's bliss had as much to do with Abby's kiss as it did with the success of their performance.)

For Abby it was a triumph she never imagined possible. And me? I was big on relief — happy to stand back and quietly watch iced bottles of Dom Pérignon passed around for refills. I clinked glasses quietly with Luther, too.

"The White House chef was here tonight," I informed him. "She complimented your menu."

"Our menu," he said, clinking my glass right back. "And, as you well know, we sold clean out of everything."

I gleefully nodded, having heard raves all night about our food — as well as our coffee and specialty drinks. But it was our improvised menu that I was sweating, and the success felt sweet.

When Abby saw us, she broke from her well-wishers — including a brace of journalists vetted by the White House press office — to take me by the hand. She grabbed Stan's hand next. Then she motioned for Madame, Luther Bell, Gardner, and the other members of Four on the Floor to join our circle.

"I'd like to propose my own toast," she declared. "To Clare Cosi, Gardner Evans, and my dear Stan. To Four on the Floor, and Chef Luther Bell. But especially to Madame DuBois, who had the faith to invest in this space. This has been — and still is — the happiest night of my life, and I owe that happiness to all of you! I can't ever thank you enough!"

Hugs, kisses, laughter, and another round of champagne were interrupted by the White House Deputy Press Secretary. With a tight smile, the woman reminded Abby that reporters were waiting to interview her.

She led Abby to two chairs in a quiet corner, near the room's fireplace. Abby sat down in one, waiting for the empty chair to be filled.

As the reporters in line were politely reminded that their interviews would be limited to five minutes each, I noticed a familiar face in the group — our enigmatic Ponytail Man with the trimmed gray beard and piercing dark eyes.

"Mystery solved," I said, sidling up to him.

He tensed. "Mystery?"

"I already knew you were a fan of Abby's. Now I see you're a journalist."

I extended my hand, and he took it.

"My name is Clare."

"Bernie Moore. I write for *Jazz Beat.*"

That intense gaze of his drifted back to the First Daughter, who was speaking with a woman from the *Washington Post.* Gard and the other band members quieted down their chatter, but their grinning continued. Like a band of big brothers, they were proud to see Abby finally getting some star treatment.

"Are you planning to write a feature about Abby?"

"Of course. It's clear she's been keeping her light under a bushel. Her gift should be shared with the world —"

"Please! One more question," the *Post* reporter begged after the press secretary announced her time was up.

"Abby, why did you decide to play in Georgetown, here at the Village Blend, DC?"

"The management sent me a personal invitation," she replied. "The week the club opened I received a little postcard advertising Open Mike Night."

We sent out invitations?

This was news to me.

SIXTY-TWO

"Did you send an invitation to Abby?" I whispered to Gardner, who looked equally confused.

"I sent out nothing."

"Then who did?"

I couldn't wrap my mind around this. Nobody at this club knew the President's daughter had an ability to play piano, let alone jazz piano.

Gardner didn't have any answers, either. He quietly asked his bandmates, but they were clueless. And since Abby believed *we* invited her to play at our Open Mike, she couldn't shed light on the mystery, so I simply let it go.

"I was thrilled to come," Abby continued. "I'd been practicing alone for years. That invitation is what got me out of my room. Gardner and Stan were so encouraging. I could never have done it without them!"

With the *Post* reporter's question answered, the deputy press secretary signaled Bernie Moore to take the vacated chair.

"I've got to go, Clare," Bernie said, "but it was nice to meet you."

"I'm sure we'll meet again."

When he introduced himself to Abby, the girl reacted strangely.

"I'm sorry to stare," she said after a pause. "It's just that you look familiar to me. Spooky familiar. Have we met?"

"I've been in your Open Mike audiences for weeks." Bernie smiled. "I guess you saw me out there applauding."

"No, that's not why you look familiar," Abby insisted. "I know! I saw you on campus — up at American University. You were on the steps outside Bender Library, right?"

"You're right," Bernie said. "I was chasing a story."

That's strange, I thought. *What story would a professional music industry magazine writer chase on a college campus? Unless that story was Abby . . .*

Bernie barely began his interview when they were interrupted by the deputy press secretary, ushering over a silver-haired older man in an open-collared sports shirt and custom-cut jacket.

"Abigail, you remember Grant Kingman,

CEO of Consolidated Television Network —"

The seriously tanned exec swept past the woman and took Abby's hand. "We met during your father's first Presidential campaign!"

"Yes, I remember —"

"I was mighty impressed by your performance, Abigail. Fantastic! Our network would be honored if you'd play something on *The Good Day Show*."

Abby's eyes went wide. Stan and Gardner beamed like proud parents, and Jackson and Theo made noises that sounded a lot like "Whoo!"

But the happiest reaction seemed to come from the forgotten man sitting across from Abbie. Bernie Moore's grin was wider than Alice's Cheshire Cat.

"*The Good Day Show* is the top morning broadcast in America," Kingman continued. "And I think all of America would appreciate hearing you play."

Abby exchanged a giddy glance with Stan.

"Thank you, Mr. Kingman," she said. "I think I speak for every member of the band when I say we would be delighted to perform on your show."

Kingman's CEO suave melted into perplexity. "Oh, no. You misunderstand. A *solo* piano appearance is what we'd like from you, Abigail. I spoke with the First Lady by phone earlier, and she's agreed to make the appearance with you, so —"

Abby stood up. "I'm sorry, Mr. Kingman, but I performed with *this* band tonight." She gestured to her friends. "I won't play without them."

SIXTY-THREE

Kingman's perplexed expression deteriorated even further, into naked annoyance. "My dear, don't you know? You mother is planning to —"

Before he could say another word, the deputy press secretary surged forward. "Mr. Kingman, please don't trouble yourself with these mundane details. Arrangements like these will be finalized through the White House. Doesn't that make good sense?" Wrapping the executive's arm around hers, she deftly herded the high-powered CEO away from the First Daughter.

Meanwhile, Abby and Stan put their heads together — a position they clearly enjoyed. Stan rested his carved forearms happily on Abby's shoulders and she smiled widely.

Jackson bumped fists with Gardner and Theo. "Imagine us on *The Good Day Show*?" Jackson gushed. "Between our mothers and aunties, we're gonna have all of Baltimore watching!"

"We should play something brand-new," Abby told them, her eyes radiating excitement. "Why don't we come up with — oh, wait!"

Suddenly, she remembered the journalist, waiting quietly in his chair.

"I'm so sorry, Mr. . . . ?"

"My last name's Moore, Abby."

As she sat down again, his smile for her was genuine, without a trace of impatience.

She nodded. "Why don't you ask me those questions now?"

Before Bernie could speak, the press secretary reappeared, sans CEO.

"Time's up, Mr. Moore."

Abby objected, and the press secretary apologized, but insisted that Abby stick to the schedule. Bernie Moore's shoulders slumped, his smile disappearing, but he vacated his chair without protest.

"We'll see one another on campus, Mr. Moore," Abby earnestly promised. "Then you can ask me all the questions you like!"

The next journalist swept Bernie aside in his lunge for the hot seat, and immediately began firing questions at Abby. She was so focused on her answers that she didn't notice the commotion on the stairs.

"Come on, guys, make way, make way!" Agent Sharpe's deep voice called. Then he burst into the greenroom with a smile on his face and a handsome blond man by his side.

Though he looked no older than twenty-five, the newcomer projected self-assurance worthy of a junior senator — with a wardrobe to match. The blue blazer was custom cut, the gray slacks beautifully tailored.

I recalled seeing him in the audience tonight, sitting with the White House staff, and it was clear the Secret Service detail knew him well. Calling many agents by their first names, he traded lively banter. But it was a facile confidence, a smooth, traveling-salesman sort of charm.

Finally, he broke from the pack. Following Agent Sharpe, he moved behind Abby, who was still preoccupied in her interview chair.

"Look who came to see you on your big night!" Sharpe interrupted.

When Abby glanced up, the young man flashed a dazzling smile, and all the euphoric joy, which had radiated in Abby's face since her performance, melted away.

"I didn't know you were in town," she said.

Her voice had changed, the tone no longer

full of life and certainty. It was the voice she'd used in the presence of her mother, the Stepford Abby voice.

"I came back early so I wouldn't miss the show!" Bending down, he pecked her cheek. She accepted the gesture with less ease than a cornered cat.

"You were surprisingly good," the young man went on, sweeping back his golden hair. "And you only froze up a few times — I don't think that many people noticed. Anyway, the way you played your instrument was great."

"Preston . . ." she said quietly. "We don't play our *instruments.*"

"Is that so? What do you play, then?"

"We play *music!*" Gardner, Jackson, and Theo all answered with her.

The members of Four on the Floor all laughed and bumped fists.

Everyone but Stan.

Preston smirked at the band. "The truth is, I'm not really into *that* kind of music —"

"Oh?" Gardner said. "What kind of music do you like?"

"I don't know." He shrugged the question off. "I came to support Abigail. And from all the applause she got, I'd say she made a fifty-yard touchdown in the last quarter of her final game!" He patted her shoulder.

"Nice job. It's great that you got that out of your system, isn't it? Think of the story you can tell our children one day."

Stan stood watching this exchange in a state of profound confusion.

Then Preston noticed Abby's hands. "Why aren't you wearing my ring?"

The words made the situation clear enough. But Stan looked to his bandmates, unable to believe his own ears.

"What did that guy say?"

My stomach clenched at the question, because now I knew. Abby had never shared the truth about her engagement. And I knew one more thing —

The best night of Stanley McGuire's life was about to become the worst.

Sixty-Four

"Tell me you didn't lose my diamond," Preston teased with a smile.

"I don't wear your ring when I perform," Abby quietly told him. Then she dared to meet Stan's shocked gaze. Her next words were louder. "It restricts my ability to play."

We all watched Stan go stiller than stone. With his one good eye, he cast a long, hard look at the golden-haired boy in the blue blazer. Then he shifted his gaze to Abby.

"Do you want to explain to me *who* this guy is?"

"Preston Emory," the stranger cut in, offering Stan his hand. As they clasped, he jerked the musician close, careful to keep the tight smile in place for the onlookers. "Abigail and I are engaged to be married. No public announcement yet, but that's mere days away."

Then he invaded Stan's space further, hissing into his ear. "That was a cute scene between you two on that piano bench. Stuff happens onstage, I know, so we'll call it a stage kiss. But if it happens again, I won't be happy."

Preston released Stan and he stumbled backward on his game leg. Still wobbly, he faced Abby.

"You're not serious about this clown!"

"I'm so sorry," she whispered, eyes pleading. "I tried to tell you a few times. I did say my life was complicated. That it's not a normal life —"

"We really should *go,* Abigail," Preston loudly cut in. "I spoke with your mother and she and the President are waiting up at the White House to congratulate you. The staff has champagne on ice and everything!"

"But I don't want to go!" She stood up from her interview chair, the fight in her finally rallying. "My friends are *here.*"

Preston gently took Abby by the shoulders and gazed into her eyes.

"Honey-bunny, don't be selfish. You should consider all these Secret Service people. They've been here, guarding you, since morning. Now it's nearly one in the AM. Don't you want to be fair to them?"

Abby's bolstered expression melted to confusion, then completely crumbled. "I guess you're right," she mumbled. "I wasn't thinking . . ."

I glanced at Agent Cage. Though she continued to hold her posture stiff as a statue, her expression was no longer stone. Preston's ploy angered her. But she held her tongue.

Stanley McGuire didn't.

"Don't let this guy guilt-trip you!" he cried. "You don't have to leave!"

Preston turned on him. "Stay out of this, Cyclops."

That did it.

Stan wasn't a tall guy, but his drummer's physique was lean and tough. As he balled one of his powerful hands into a fist and drew back his strong arm, Jackson put aside his drink and Gardner stepped forward.

But it was Abby who intervened, jumping between the two young men.

Cupping Stan's cheek, she whispered, "Calm down. You and I are still friends. And I'll see you soon."

One touch from Abby and Stan's whole body relaxed.

"Remember the TV appearance on Monday?" she said hopefully. "We'll have to rehearse, right?"

"So we'll see each other tomorrow?"

"I'm sure we will," she said, but anyone could see she wasn't so sure.

"Time to *go,* Abigail."

Stan's wiry form tensed again, but he kept his gaze locked on Abby's. "This clown will *never* trade fours with you. You know that, don't you?"

Abby's lips moved, but before any sound could come out, Preston wrapped a possessive arm around her and propelled her toward the exit.

Shaking with emotion, poor Stan watched Abby being swept away, a small army of Secret Service agents blocking his last view of her.

"He'll never trade fours with her," he repeated to his bandmates, his gaze lost in the empty space where she had been. "He'll never trade fours . . ."

SIXTY-FIVE

Mike Quinn rubbed the back of his neck. "Trading fours? What does that mean exactly?"

"Trading fours is something that happens in jazz. Each member takes four bars to play a short solo. They can trade two or eight or sixteen, or as many as they like. It's a back-and-forth thing."

"So why did Stan say that about Preston Emory?"

"Trading fours is about cooperation and chemistry within the band. That night in our greenroom, Stan was trying to warn Abby that Preston was not the kind of guy who'd step back and let her play her own solo, express her own voice. Abby's fiancé was condescending, self-satisfied, and controlling. We all saw it!"

Emotional now, I pounded the SUV's dashboard to make my point — a mistake. For the first time since we'd pulled the vehicle into this dank garage in "not the nicest part" of Baltimore, the gangbanger watching from a folding chair put aside his smartphone game.

From across the empty space, he fired off an unfriendly stare. I returned his gaze with a *friendly* smile, and he returned to the animated action on his tiny screen.

Behind the steering wheel, Mike completely ignored the punk. "You sound very sure that the relationship between Abby and Stan went beyond friendship, beyond a shared love of music."

"When I first found them alone in our Jazz Space, after hours, I suspected something was going on beyond practicing. When I saw them onstage together that night, I knew they were in love. Now that I'm considering all the details of their story, I have to say — I believe Abby is a runaway bride."

"Okay, I get it. But I don't know if I agree."

"Why not?"

"Because your story makes it sound like the President's daughter was trapped in some sort of arranged engagement —"

"You think she wasn't?"

"I think that's how *you* see it."

"What about Stan? He saw it that way, too."

Now he gave me that Quinn look — the one I'm sure he uses on unreliable perps. "Stan is not exactly an impartial observer."

"I can't believe what you're saying."

"Look, you've painted a vivid picture of an emotionally fragile young woman with behavioral issues —"

"But —"

"Add it up. Abby attempted suicide in her past. She even took you on a high-speed chase through crowded streets, running from the very people who are supposed to protect her. Does that sound *rational*?"

"She's a young woman, Mike. In case you hadn't noticed, young women aren't always rational."

"By your own description she showed Jekyll and Hyde dissonance. Face it. Abigail Parker has issues. It sounds to me like her parents and fiancé were just trying to help her deal with them, keep her on track, help her cope. Wasn't Preston showing mature judgment in making Abby see that her parents deserved time with her, and her security detail should have time off?"

"I was there, Mike. I saw that boy's slick transitions, working Abby until he got what he wanted. She was a star, feeling worthy and powerful. And Preston didn't like it, so he dragged her back down to earth. What I witnessed was not an act of maturity, it was an exercise in manipulation and control. Preston knew how to press Abby's buttons, just like her mother. He guilt-tripped the girl into leaving her friends on the happiest night of her life. It was wrong."

Quinn fell silent a moment. "What do you know about this guy?"

"Plenty . . ."

After that display in the greenroom, I'd made it my business to find out more about Preston Emory.

SIXTY-SIX

"Abby's fiancé came from a family like hers."

"They're politicians?" Quinn assumed.

"His mother is. She's a congresswoman from the President's home state. They're political allies. And Preston has political ambitions. He went to American University because of its strong tradition in educating students for public service. In his case, his goal is to follow his mother's footsteps into elected office . . ."

From what I'd learned, Preston socialized wisely and well during his freshman and sophomore years. He dated a governor's daughter and joined the same fraternity as Abby's famously popular older brother, Kent, aka "Kip" Parker. That friendship with Kip was how Preston was introduced to the soon-to-be First Family. He became a fixture at holiday gatherings and at their vacation home.

When Abby enrolled at American, Preston was at her side to help her through orientation — and keep other potential suitors away. At that point he'd broken up with the governor's daughter, to focus on a bigger prize.

Step one was to join Parker's presidential campaign, another smart move because Preston and Abby saw a lot of each other on the campaign trail, and it was Preston who escorted Abby to President Parker's inaugural ball.

After his graduation, Preston became a junior member of the White House staff, where he continued to see Abby. It helped that the First Lady seated him with her daughter at every White House function.

"Preston may have grown to care for Abby," I finally admitted to Quinn. "But from what I've learned, his engagement to her is more of an arrangement than a true romance. I mean, ask yourself: Would a boy like Preston really fall passionately in love with a girl like Abby — without a strong motive? To put it another way, the guy's got big plans for himself; and if Abby had been some anonymous, slightly odd wallflower at AU, instead of the President's only daughter, would he have given her the time of day?

"Anyway, the plans were set. Right after

Abby's graduation in May, she was scheduled to get married to Preston in June and leave for a monthlong European honeymoon. Then the 'happy couple' was supposed to move out of Washington and back to Preston's home state. He already bought a McMansion in some tony area, where Abby was expected to join the Junior League and start a family while he started his bid for political office."

Quinn stared at me a moment, a little dumbfounded. "How in the world do you know all this?"

"After that night in the greenroom, Abby knew Stan was wrecked. When she called him the next day to apologize, she told him *everything* about her relationship with Preston. And when I saw Stan the next day, I grilled him — and not only about Preston Emory. He and Abby kept on talking, not face-to-face, only over the phone, but they spoke every night, sometimes for hours. Given what we know about Abby's disappearance, aren't you convinced yet that she'd want to be a runaway bride?"

"The only thing I'm convinced of is *why* Abby was in that park. And the reason I'm convinced is because she herself told you. It was clever, using that park to evade her security detail."

"Like I said, the park runs all the way down to the Potomac River so it could get her to Georgetown without using any streets."

"I'm sure the FBI used dogs to trace her movements from her girlfriend's home. And that's what led them to the blood — which does *not* support your runaway bride theory, I'm sorry to say."

"It does if she ran away to meet Stan and something went wrong. Maybe someone was watching her, waiting for her, and they took that opportunity to snatch her. Or maybe she simply tripped on a rock and fell! We need more information. We need to know if Stan is missing, too!"

Quinn nodded. "I'll ask Danica if she can find a way to help us with that."

"Danica?"

"The detective we're here to meet. That's her name, Danica Hatch."

"I see."

Quinn studied my tight expression. "Don't tell me you're jealous?"

"I'm not jealous. But I am wondering why she's helping us tonight. It's a huge risk for her to take."

"She has her reasons. You'll have to trust me on that. Like I trusted you with your ex-husband that night."

"What are you talking about?"

Quinn folded his arms. "By your own admission, you were dancing with Allegro the night of Abby's show. And wasn't he the same guy who threw me out of N Street and suggested you two 'double up' for the night?"

"Oh, come on. You know Matt."

"Yes, unfortunately, I do. And that's why I don't trust him. So where exactly did you sleep that night?"

"Why is that important?"

Quinn gawked at the guilty look on my face. "Clare, you *didn't*. Are you telling me you went to bed with Allegro?"

"No!"

"So you didn't sleep with your ex-husband?"

"To be totally honest, I did sleep with him. But not in a bed."

"Oh, I can't wait to hear this."

"Good, because what happened between me and Matt that night was nothing compared to the shock I got the next morning. And you should hear about that, too."

"Fine. But do me a favor and start with you and Allegro. I want to know *exactly* what the two of you did that night."

"What we usually do — argue . . ."

SIXTY-SEVEN

"Clare, will you get off your feet before you fall off?"

"Take it easy, Matt, I still have a few more things to check."

My ex-husband threw up his hands. "You said that an hour ago!"

I ignored him.

The President's daughter and her massive security detail were gone, but the night was far from over. There was still cleaning, restocking, and after-hours management.

Gardner and his musician friends were back on stage for an all-night jam. Luther and our staff took a load off, listening as they sipped drinks and unwound. Some die-hard jazz fans hung out, too. Then a few people mentioned they were hungry, and Luther went right back to his kitchen.

Our cupboards were bare, but I scrounged a few packages of wieners.

Luther sliced them up and threw them in

a skillet with some brown sugar, ketchup, dry mustard, and a generous splash of bourbon. Then Joy insisted we all use little bar pretzel sticks to spear the Bourbon Hot Dogs Bites, another ingenious improvisation. The combo of salty crunch with tangy-sweet barbecue sauce made it a fine and folksy foodie finale for the Village Blend's big night.

At last, Gard and his friends played " 'Round Midnight" with Punch re-creating Ella Fitzgerald's moving vocals. Then everyone called it a night, although by now it was 'round *four* in the *morning.*

As my New York staff headed for our Cox's Row crash pad, their raucous descent echoed down our staircase . . .

"Esther, why are you complaining?" Joy asked. "At least you've got Boris to cuddle up with. I wish my boyfriend were here."

"Franco's not here because he values his life," Esther pointed out, "and if he tried to 'cuddle up' with you on N Street, your father would *end* him."

"Don't remind me!" Joy cried. "I've been fighting the good fight for months now. If you ask me, my dad and Franco have *too much* in common. Anyway, Mrs. B.'s mansion is beautiful. And we'll all be together — one big happy Blend family!"

"You make us sound like the Brady Bunch. Or worse, the Waltons!"

"What's wrong with the Waltons?" Tuck called on the steps behind them. "It's a great old American TV show. And it was set in Virginia — right next door."

"Oh, yes!" Punch agreed, still in silver sequins. "I'd adore being part of the Waltons. Can I be John-Boy?"

"If anybody's John-Boy, it's Tuck," Esther returned. "In that Gaga getup, you've got more in common with Mary Ellen."

"And with that attitude, you're already the grouchy grandma." Punch snapped his fingers. "As I recall, her name was Esther, too."

"Why you little —"

"Whoa there, Granny!" Joy grabbed Esther's arm before she went for Punch's blond-bombshell wig. "Time to hit the road. Boris is waiting, remember? Good night, Daddy! Good night, Mama!"

Esther waggled her fingers. "Good night, Mary Ellen. Goodnight, Tuck-Boy!"

And the girls were gone.

I thought Tuck and Punch would follow, at least to get in a few more verbal jabs, but instead they approached me and Matt at the coffee bar.

"We have news!" Tuck announced.

"A surprise!" Punch added.

"Another surprise?" I threw a worried glance Matt's way. "Your last one nearly knocked me over."

"You better lean on something, then, because this one's even bigger . . ." Tuck pointed to Punch. "Drumroll, please."

Punch pounded two barstools as though they were bongos.

Matt caught my eye. "Everything's theater with these two."

"Exactly!" Tuck said. "We know how to attract an audience and keep them coming back. That's why Gardner is on board for our big idea, which is . . ."

"Torch Song Thursdays!" Punch announced.

"Okay," I said, "you've got my attention . . ."

According to Tucker, they had set up the whole thing with Gardner, who happened to mention that our Thursdays were pathetically slow.

"So we'll come down from New York once a week to create a cabaret show for the Jazz Space. Punch is going to impersonate legendary divas: Billie, Ella, Sarah, Nina, Aretha, Diana, and, of course, Gaga!"

"And, we're going to reach out to gay DC. It will be fabulous!"

"I promise, CC, when we get through with our social media outreach, your Thursday nights are going to be packed!"

"Not bad." Matt lifted an eyebrow. "And I thought your idea was going to be a drag."

"Oh, sweetie, it will! The hottest drag on the eastern seaboard . . ." Punch pinched his cheek. "Still so cute."

"And still so straight."

Punch shrugged. "Nobody's perfect."

Apparently, the upstairs brainstorming wasn't limited to diva impersonations. Gard's group lobbied for "Funky Fridays" with guest sets that focused on a broader spectrum of the jazz world — rhythm and blues, soul, and danceable retro covers of artists like Stevie Wonder, Ray Charles, and the Motown songbook.

"You'll get a bigger sampling of bands and the general public coming in with that mix," Tuck promised.

Matt shot me a glance. "And with our new chef and menu that public might actually *enjoy* the table minimums."

I checked my watch and smiled. *Yep. It really is a new day . . .*

Though I invited them both to sit down for coffee, Tuck and Punch were ready to hit the hay.

"Oh, I almost forgot," Tuck said, turning

around. "I have something for you —"

"Another surprise?"

"You wish. But it's just a boring old flash drive."

I took the small red rectangle from him. It looked like a standard memory drive that held computer files. But why give it to me?

"Punch and I found it upstairs," Tuck said. "We thought it might be digital music — you know, the kind you plug into an electronic keyboard. But when we looked at it, the only thing on there were government text files."

"Did they list an owner?"

Tuck shook his head. "There's only one folder. It's labeled *U.S. Senate E-mails.* We read a few — they look like correspondence involving the President, back when he was a senator."

I stifled a yawn. "I'm supposed to meet with the White House Curator this week. I'll give it to her. I'm sure she can find out who it belongs to —"

"Fine, but you should also know —"

"Come on, Tuck-Boy!" Punch called from the door. "This little Walton is bushed."

"Keep your panties on, Mary Ellen!" Tucker cried.

"It's okay, Tuck, go on. I'll see you later this morning."

Nodding, he headed out, pausing at the door to throw a special wink our way. "Good night, Mama! Good night, Daddy! Sleep tight . . ."

SIXTY-EIGHT

"That flash drive," Quinn interrupted. "You told me all about that before Abby went missing."

"I did. But when Tuck handed it to me, I didn't think anything of it."

"Well, it can't help us now, so there's no use trying to dodge the rest of the story."

"You don't want to talk about the flash drive?"

"No. I'm waiting for details on the other part — the part about sleeping with your ex."

"Oh, that."

Quinn folded his arms. "Let me help jog that memory of yours: Tucker and Punch leave; and the musicians leave; and there you are, all alone in the closed shop with Mr. Java Hunter. Is that about right?"

"Yes," I said. "Believe me, I did tell Matt to hit the road — and the sack. But he refused to go . . ."

"Drunks are still out there, wandering the neighborhood," Matt argued. "I am not leaving you here alone."

"Suit yourself," I said, "but my decision's made. I'm pulling an all-nighter . . ."

"Because?"

"The whole staff is exhausted, and I need to make sure this *relaunched* shop *reopens* at seven AM, without a hitch. All the beds are taken at N Street, anyway, and Quinn's across town."

"Are you sure you won't reconsider?" Matt pressed. "My offer to share a bed still stands. I'll wake you up in time — and I'll keep my hands to myself. *Promise.*"

"Promise?" I nearly laughed. "And you expect me to believe you?"

"Well . . . we *are* in Washington."

Shaking my head, I headed for the kitchen with zombielike determination.

With Abby's performance hitting the morning news, we were sure to be swamped again. And while my baker agreed to increase our order, she wouldn't deliver till eight.

The empty pastry case needed a solution.

We were out of blueberries, so I checked our cornmeal supply. We'd eighty-sixed the herbed polenta on the old Hopkins menu, but Luther's Cheddar-Corn Spoon Bread had been a heavenly hit, and — *yes!* — there was just enough cornmeal left for a big batch of my Breakfast Corn Muffins!

Feeling relieved, I returned to the front and found Matt behind the counter.

"What are you doing?"

"If you refuse to get some shut-eye, at least get off your feet for thirty minutes together." He guided me to the banquette on the far side of the room and gently pushed me down —

"Sit. Rest."

This time, I didn't argue. The cushions felt like clouds under my tired bones, and my aching feet were thrilled I'd gotten off them. Matt was right, it was nice to sit still in the quiet shop.

"What's that?" I asked, as he approached with a tray bearing cups and a French press.

"*This* is the Sulawesi that we brought down today. I followed your roasting instructions, and I think it's perfect. But you never took time to sample it."

"I'm sure it's fine."

"Oh, better than fine. But if it's not, I'm sure you'll tell me."

"That's my job, isn't it?"

"Yes, it is. Which is why you deserve

this . . ." From out of nowhere, Matt produced a single long-stemmed rose. "Abby wasn't the only one who gave a virtuoso performance last night."

"Thanks, but our success was a product of *cooperative* improv."

"Every band needs someone to form them, inspire them. And every successful business needs someone to care. This week, partner, that someone was you."

He dipped the flower to my nose. Like our newfound success, the fragrance was sweet — with a nod, I accepted it. Then Matt poured our coffees and we toasted the turning point for our DC shop.

Matt was right about something else. His Sulawesi was excellent.

One of the best coffees on the planet, it had a clean brightness yet unusual depth and complexity. Layers of flavors delighted the senses, from the tantalizing tingle on the tongue to the floral sweetness in the rising aroma. He handled the roast superbly, protecting the almost supernaturally low acidity. There wasn't a trace of bitterness.

I wish I could say the same about this evening . . .

Unlike the Sulawesi, however, some bitterness lingered. And Matt knew it.

"So . . . are you going to talk to me?"

"About what?"

"Clare, I know you. You're not running around just to prep the place for morning business. You're upset."

"It's nothing."

"Tell me anyway. What could it hurt? It might even help."

"Okay," I said, too tired argue. "Two things are bothering me. And the first is the worst: Tad Hopkins."

SIXTY-NINE

"Hopkins? The man who accused you of stealing? That ass of a chef is gone. Why waste brain cells worrying about him?"

"Because it was Hopkins who released the truth about Abby. And the result was more success than Gardner and I dreamed possible."

"So?"

"So wouldn't you feel terrible if you saw all this success as a result of your actions? Yet you didn't earn a dime from it? Or receive one bit of credit?"

"Clare, Hopkins released that information without Abby's permission. He didn't deserve to benefit from what came of it. And, anyway, some member of the press or public would have recognized Abby eventually. The news was bound to get out. Hopkins simply speeded up the process — for his own selfish benefit."

"I didn't think of it that way . . ."

"See?"

"The problem is — Hopkins won't, either."

"What do you mean?"

"I mean that Hopkins is arrogant and spiteful. The *least* he's going to do is sue us."

"Mother's lawyer will handle that, don't worry."

"I'm not worried about a day in court. I'm worried about the kind of person who doesn't care about court . . . or the law . . . or what's right. I'm worried about a person who sees himself as wronged and fixates on revenge. And I'm not just worried about what Hopkins might do to us. What if he decides to take his rage out on Abby?"

"Abby is protected by an army of Secret Service agents."

"So was JFK."

"You actually think Hopkins will try to *kill* her? That's a ridiculous leap."

"Is it? Agent Cage and her detail have a job for a reason. What if Hopkins turns out to be one of those crackpots? What if this Abby situation pushes him over the edge?"

"*What-ifs* will drive you crazy, especially at this hour of the morning. Look, I know you're tired. Admit it, will you? Why don't you lean against me, just for a little while?

Close your eyes and try not to worry so much . . ."

I didn't argue. Matt's body was warm and strong. I sidled a little closer, he put his arm around me, and I tucked in.

"What's the other thing?" he murmured against my hair.

"What other thing?"

"You said two things were bothering you. One was Hopkins. What was the other?"

"Stan. I feel for that boy. Seeing him hurt so badly tonight was awful."

"Ah, young love."

"That's easy to say — and far too dismissive. Abby and Stan truly belong together."

"I don't disagree. Seeing them on that stage, playing their music together, with the light coming down from above . . . it reminded me of the *tongkonan* . . ."

"The what?"

"It's a word the Toraja use, the people who grow this beautiful coffee. They build these structures in their villages with soaring roofs. According to legend, they were first built in heaven. That's what Abby and Stan created in that moment. Something higher than the earth. Something transcendent."

"That's lovely, but I guarantee Abby's mother and fiancé didn't see it that way. They seem blind to her gifts. But not Stan.

I spoke with him after Abby left. We're both afraid she's being railroaded into a marriage that will make her miserable. She'll go through the motions like she does with her mother, walk down a Rose Garden aisle, and end up surrounded by people who don't respect what matters most to her."

"All that may be true. But you're not her mother, Clare. You're just her neighbor. Remember?" Matt actually began singing the theme from *Mister Rogers' Neighborhood.*

"Okay, enough!" I covered his mouth with my hand. "I'm more than just a neighbor. I'm Abby's friend. And friends don't let friends throw away a chance to be deeply happy for the rest of their lives . . ."

As I dropped my hand, Matt caught it.

"Then it's up to Stan to do something about it . . . or he'll lose the woman he truly loves. And that's a loss he'll always, *always* regret . . ."

With a sad smile, Matt kissed my fingers, his brown eyes melting into liquid pools. Those irresistibly dark depths weren't easy to emerge from, but I had once, and I did again.

"That's touching," I managed, voice not quite there. "And I believe you. But please remember, I love Mike Quinn . . ."

Just the thought of Quinn snoring softly across town made me smile, and I closed my eyes, tucking back into my ex for a few minutes of shut-eye.

I couldn't be sure, but before drifting off, the lips pressed against my hair seemed to send the whisper of a thought through my mind, one I couldn't argue with . . .

You love Quinn. But you love me, too. And you always will.

Seventy

Bzz. *Bzz-bzz-bzz* . . .

An annoying bug had entered my dream, buzzing like crazy around my head. I wanted to swat it away, as Madame would, with an elegant wave. But it defied me completely. *Bzz! Bzz-bzz-bzz!*

I opened my eyes — and immediately squinted.

The coffeehouse was flooded with morning light. I was still sitting on the banquette, leaning against Matt, who was sleeping soundly, eyes closed, arms encircling me.

The buzzing began again. But this was no bug. My mobile phone was vibrating on the café table. I picked it up and heard a deep male voice —

"Good morning, Ms. Cosi."

"Who is this?"

"Sergeant Price. Metro PD."

Oh, God. "I'm sorry, Sergeant, but this isn't a good time."

"Yes, I can see that. Who's your friend?"

"Excuse me?"

"The man whose arms are around you. He doesn't look like a fed. Aren't you supposed to have a boyfriend working at Justice?"

"Sergeant, *where* are you?"

"Right here."

"Right where?"

A very loud knock shook one of our large front windows. I followed the sound to the figure of a heavyset African American man in a blue police uniform, waving grimly.

"Matt! Wake up!"

"Huh? What?"

"You have to leave. *Now.*"

"Are you kidding?" He yawned big. "I'm not leaving. Not without a *doppio* . . ."

As Matt dragged himself to the espresso bar, I adjusted the hiked-up skirt of my little black dress, rubbed my sore neck, and hurried to unlock the door.

"Sergeant Price," I said, forcing a smile. "What brings you back to my coffeehouse?"

"My officers were assisting the Secret Service last night. I volunteered to check the area, make sure the street barricades were collected, but that's not why I came."

I stifled a yawn. "Then it must be for the coffee."

"There's that," he said with a nod.

"Come in, then, we can talk at the espresso bar."

Matt pulled us all sustenance then he headed for the restroom.

"Who was that?" Price asked.

"My business partner."

"Do you two spend many nights like that?"

I felt the heat blooming on my cheeks. "We were up late, that's all. It was perfectly innocent. We just nodded off . . ."

The sergeant sipped his double, studying me for a minute before he changed the subject.

"I don't mean to be the bearer of bad tidings, especially on a Sunday morning. But I came to ask if you knew about your friend?"

"My friend?"

The sergeant nodded. "Mr. Varma of the State Department? That fellow you claim rushed in through your back door three nights ago — he passed away late last night, without regaining consciousness."

The sergeant's use of the word *claim* didn't get by me. But I was far more concerned with the terrible news.

"Mr. Varma is dead? I don't understand. He was still breathing when they took him away in the ambulance. On Friday morning, I asked Officer Landry about him. He said he thought Varma would be fine once the alcohol wore off."

"Officer Landry should refrain from practicing medicine without a license," Price said, eyebrow raised.

"How did he die?"

The sergeant replied with a gallows chuckle. "That alcohol never did wear off, Ms. Cosi. Varma succumbed to acute alcohol poisoning. But that's not the end of it. The autopsy uncovered irregularities."

"What sort of irregularities?"

"Most victims of alcohol poisoning regurgitate while unconscious, and then suffocate. The doctors were ready for that, but it didn't happen. Not in Mr. Varma's case."

"I already asked my staff about serving Mr. Varma. They said there was mostly a college crowd Thursday night. They don't remember serving anyone matching his description. I checked my credit card receipts, too. The last time Mr. Varma came here as a customer was Open Mike Night well over a week ago."

The sergeant tapped the back of his own neck. "Varma also had a puncture wound right about here. Would you know anything about that?"

"Punctured how? From a knife?"

"Not a stab wound, Ms. Cosi. Medical

technicians call it a needlestick injury, like when doctors or nurses accidentally prick themselves with scalpels or hypodermics."

"Varma stabbed himself with a needle?"

"From the angle of entry, it's unlikely the injury was self-inflicted." Price folded his big arms. "And in Mr. Varma's case, it was more of an injection than a jab."

"He was injected? With what?"

"Alcohol, Ms. Cosi."

"Just alcohol. Then why did he die?"

"When you drink, a war breaks out between your stomach and your liver," Price explained. "It takes twenty minutes for the stomach to pump alcohol into the blood, while the liver filters it out. That time lag gives your body a cushion to prevent alcohol poisoning. But an injection puts the alcohol right into the bloodstream, too fast for the liver to cope. In Mr. Varma's case, the alcohol overwhelmed his system, but not before it produced the manic behavior you witnessed."

The sergeant paused. "Of course, it would make my job a lot easier if that wound was inflicted by a meat cleaver."

I blinked. *Meat cleaver?*

"Like the meat cleaver with your fingerprints on it," Price stated flatly. "The one I impounded out of your restaurant's kitchen that night."

"I don't think I like where you're going with this, Sergeant."

"You know what, Ms. Cosi? I don't like it, either. Not one bit. Because there's something *wrong* about that night. And there's something wrong about your story. I think you're holding information back."

"I have nothing to hide. I stand by my sworn statement."

I did my best to mean it because, now that Varma was dead, I had no intention of involving Abby or Stan. Furthermore, Price was a uniformed sergeant, not a homicide detective. Though he was *trying* to make a case here, he clearly didn't have one.

I had no relationship with Varma. No reason to kill him.

Just stand firm, I told myself, *and Price will give up.*

The sergeant drained his demitasse and set the cup aside, but not because he was giving up.

"I'm going to keep looking until I can make it right," he vowed. "Mr. Varma's family wants answers, Ms. Cosi. And so do I."

Price rose and sauntered to the front door. But before he left, he turned to face me. "Your espresso is excellent, by the way. I look forward to sampling it again . . . and very soon."

SEVENTY-ONE

"It's obvious Sergeant Price thought I was in some kind of secret relationship with Jeevan Varma," I told Quinn as I leaned back in the car seat. "You should have seen his face when he caught me huddled there in the closed coffeehouse with Matt, wearing my wrinkled clothes from the night before."

I threw up my hands. "And don't forget Tom Landry! That young officer totally misunderstood my friendliness the night I met him. I can't imagine what he told his buddies in blue about me — no, I *can* imagine it: 'She's a MILK in heat!' I'm sure that's the gossip he spread about me. *Hot MILK.* It's scandalous!"

"Why is hot milk scandalous? I thought it helped you sleep."

"Not that kind of milk. I meant —"

"Excuse me, sweetheart, but I'm still trying to process the part about your ex-husband sleeping with you."

"Then you *missed* the part about it being *totally innocent* with no bed and absolutely no hanky-panky. Don't you have an opinion on Price?"

"Calm down. You're upset, and you have a right to be, but the sergeant's visit that morning was a fishing expedition. He's a good cop with a rumbly gut that tells him when someone's lying. And you were lying. You hid the truth about Abby and Stan."

"But that had nothing to do with the incident itself."

"You're sure of that, are you?"

I collapsed against the car seat. "I can't be sure of anything. Not anymore."

"Well, I can't, either. But somehow you became a primary suspect in Varma's murder."

"How could that happen?"

"Varma's real killer could have framed you for his murder."

"How?"

"Oh, I don't know — planting the murder weapon in the Village Blend and tipping off police."

I held my head. "You know what makes this even worse? As bad as I feel about Abby being missing, I'm finally realizing . . . she's a witness to my innocence. If Stan is gone, too, I'll have no one left to back up my version of events."

Quinn frowned. "I hadn't thought of that."

"What?"

"The connection between these cases seemed tenuous, but I think you found it."

"What?"

Quinn aimed his finger my way.

"Me?"

"With Abby and Stan gone, no one would be able to corroborate what really happened that night in your coffeehouse. No one could get in the way of your being framed for Varma's murder —"

"Stop. I know you're tired and on edge, but that theory is off the rails. No one would kidnap or kill the President's daughter just to cover up a frame job on a murder . . . would they?"

Just then, a metal door clanged somewhere inside the cavernous building. The punk lowered his smartphone and raised a very large gun.

Quinn was about to reach for his weapon, too, but paused when an attractive, young African American woman stepped out of the darkness and signaled the *all clear* to the gangbanger.

This woman was the detective we'd been waiting for, the same early riser who'd come to Mrs. B.'s mansion with papers for Mike.

"That's her," Quinn said. "That's Danica Hatch."

Following Danica out of the shadows was a hard-faced Asian man in his late twenties, maybe early thirties. He sported a neck tattoo made up of Chinese symbols and wore an overstuffed pack strapped to his back.

"Is that the man you told those gangbangers you had business with?"

Quinn nodded. "That's Chan."

"What in the world is he carrying in that giant backpack?"

"If we're lucky . . . the proof we need to keep you out of prison."

SEVENTY-TWO

Quinn followed Chan and the gangbanger guarding us — who turned out to be an undercover cop — to an island of fluorescent brightness in a corner of the gloomy garage. Scattered on a battered workbench in front of them were tools, a jeweler's magnifying glass, and dozens of smartphones intact and dismantled.

The rest of the space was in shadow, but not silence. I heard the occasional wet *plop* of water leaking through the roof, and the patter of rats scurrying about in the darkest recesses of the nearly deserted building.

Detective Danica Hatch called me away from the men. We sat on rickety folding chairs, a stained card table between us.

"Detective, may I ask you a question?"

"Sure," she said, eyes still riveted to the men.

"You don't know Quinn and you don't know me. Why are you willing to stick your neck out to help a couple of potential candidates for *America's Most Wanted*?"

Danica swung her long legs under the table and faced me.

"Actually, I know Detective Quinn better than you think."

I leaned forward. "But he seemed a stranger to you that morning in DC, or was that some kind of a ruse?"

"No ruse. I never met Detective Quinn face-to-face until the morning I met you. But I've known him for several years, and I owe him a debt . . ."

She paused to fill her paper cup and mine with coffee from her thermos. I quickly downed half my cup. It was weak and lukewarm, but I didn't care. At this point, I was simply grateful for the caffeine.

"I still don't understand. What sort of debt would you owe Mike?"

"Sorry. But it's personal. You don't really need to know."

"Yes. I do."

Danica lifted an eyebrow. "You don't trust me?"

"No offense, but I've only seen you once before."

The detective glanced at the men again, who were still intensely conversing. She leaned toward me. "Mike Quinn helped someone in my family, okay? That's why I owe him a debt."

"What did he do, help your brother join the NYPD? Something like that?"

Danica almost laughed. "Not even close. My brother used to despise the police. When I joined the Baltimore force, he turned on me."

I nodded, not surprised. After years of serving coffee to police officers in New York City, I'd heard plenty of similar stories.

"How old was your brother when you joined up?" I asked.

"Devon was eighteen — with a chip on his shoulder, and a lot of bad friends. Suddenly I wasn't 'Danny' anymore. I was 'the man' . . ."

"Go on, I'd like to hear."

"Well . . . the recession hit Baltimore hard. Dev couldn't find a part-time job. But all of his brothers were flush with cash, because they were dealing for a local gang. One day Mom calls to tell me Devon's missing. Five days later, he turns up in New York. Dev's friends had convinced him to take a ride to the Bronx to pick up some new product. They got to sampling their stash in some dive hotel, but this wasn't the stepped-on crap they were used to, and when they shot up . . ."

Danica's cheek quivered, but she quickly covered her reaction by dumping a packet of Splenda into her cup. "By the time the housekeeper found them, only Devon was alive — barely — and facing Class B felony charges for possession of a large amount of heroin with intent to deal."

"Oh, now I see. You know Mike from his work on the OD Squad."

She nodded. "Detective Quinn found Dev handcuffed to a bed at a New York City hospital. He got the cuffs removed, and he was there when Dev came out of his coma."

Danica drained her cup, and I poured us each another.

"My brother was lucky, in a way. There was something wrong with the smack, and the OD Squad was tasked with getting it off the street. I think any other cop — and that includes me — would have tossed Dev in a cell and forgotten about him. But Quinn was different.

"He offered Devon a plea deal. As long as my brother cooperated with the prosecution, he'd be treated as a material witness, not a suspect. Because of Devon's testimony, the OD Squad made a half-dozen arrests and got the poison off the street. And Quinn was as good as his word.

"Before my brother got home, Quinn arranged treatment for him at a facility here in Baltimore. Now Dev's a sophomore at Morgan State with a three-point-five average in computer science." Danica smiled for the first time since she began her story. "He'll be making more money than me someday."

She locked eyes with me. "*Now* you see why I'd go to bat for Detective Quinn anytime he needs me, anywhere he needs me."

"Are you telling me that through all that, you never met Mike face-to-face?"

"There's irony there," Danica said. "I was working undercover on a drug sting in this very neighborhood while this all went down in New York. My mother and I exchanged a lot of e-mails, and a couple of phone calls with Quinn, and when it was finally over I called to thank him, personally."

She laughed.

"I imagined Quinn as this bald Irish guy with a beer belly. If I'd known how hot the man was, I would have driven up to New York to express my appreciation *in person.*"

I laughed, too. "You know I might have had something to say about that?"

"I know . . . and from that bracelet I saw you wearing the morning I brought over those reports, I'd say you two have something pretty special going on. I'd never mess with that . . . Anyway . . ." She held my gaze. "I'll say it again. You are one lucky lady."

All those hours of tension must have caught up to me, because I was suddenly misty-eyed.

"Can I tell you something?" I asked her. "It's not anything Mike would want you to know, but it's been weighing on me . . ."

"You can trust me, Clare."

I glanced across the gloomy room, making sure the men were still occupied. All three were in a huddle around the magnifying glass, so I lowered my voice and confided the embarrassing truth.

"Katerina Lacey has been sexually harassing Mike."

Seventy-Three

As I described the situation — and Katerina's behavior — an emotion that I could describe only as deep revulsion passed over Danica's face.

"I didn't know," she whispered.

I studied my murky cup. "Part of me wishes Mike would have simply quit. Just walked away."

"I understand why you feel that way, but I know why he didn't."

"Because he's a cop?"

"Because he's a *good* cop. When a guy like Mike Quinn sees someone like Katerina, he's not thinking about what she's doing to him. What concerns him are the other people she's victimizing — even fellow workers who might fall under her future authority."

"It's still hard to swallow."

"Then let me break it down for you. The reason Quinn didn't walk away is because he hates bullies. And he knows a bully with authority, like Katerina, is the most dangerous kind. So he's determined to take her out — and not to dinner."

"I knew what you meant, Detective." Ignoring the posse of skinny rats scampering across the room, I swiped at my wet eyes. "I just doubt very much he can do it. Katerina Lacey is smart. And ruthless. She's been careful not to incriminate herself on the sexual harassment, which is why he wouldn't go to human resources. And even if he had, she has friends in high places, very high places —"

I paused, remembering the superior look on her face when I saw her that day in the White House. "Whatever Mike planned to charge her with at Justice, I doubt very much she would have gotten more than a slap on the wrists. And now she's in a position to sink us both."

"Listen to me . . ." Danica surprised me by reaching across the table to squeeze my hand. "Alone he might not have been able to — but together you two can beat that woman."

"You don't think she's going to end us?"

"No. Because you're going to end her, and I'm going to help."

"How?"

"There's an old saying: *Everything in Washington comes with a history, and so does everyone.* Well, it's true of Katerina Lacey, too. She's been playing dirty for years."

"How do you know?"

"Because Ms. Lacey began her career right here in Baltimore, in the DA's office."

"That must have been more than ten years ago . . ." I studied Danny's baby-smooth mocha skin, the full, pretty cheeks. "You're so young. How much could you know about that?"

She admitted that after Mike contacted her, she was inspired to do some snooping on her own. "I was caught riffling through Katerina's case files by the new district attorney. She's a real up-and-comer who was already concerned about Ms. Lacey's past work for the Baltimore DA's office . . ."

According to Danica, many of the high-profile cases Katerina had handled were falling apart on appeal — mostly because "confidential informants" who'd provided the most damning evidence were never named in the indictments, or vanished off the face of the earth after the first trial. Without full disclosure, the defense prevailed, and those setbacks sullied the entire Baltimore office. And really pissed off the new DA.

"I hooked her up with Detective Quinn, and since then, the DA has been feeding Quinn evidence. At first, some of the stuff Quinn asked for didn't make a lot of sense — reports on stolen phones and perps who specialize in Apple picking —"

"Apple picking?" I stared in confusion. "Why would Quinn care about fruit theft?"

"Fruit theft?" Danny blinked. "No, no! Apple picking is slang for stealing expensive phones and laptops. It started with iPhones and iPads, but now any mobile phone or tablet is game."

"And what does that have to do with my situation?"

Danica looked away when she heard the confab breaking up. Chan the Phone Man left with the undercover detective, and Quinn approached us, a high-end smartphone in his hand.

She lowered her voice. "Ask him later. He'll tell you."

"Chan said you prepped a safe house for us. Is that right?" Quinn asked.

Danica nodded. "It's a short drive —"

"You mean we're not staying here?" I said, the relief so obvious on my face that Danny laughed.

"Don't worry, Clare. I think you'll be pleased with your overnight accommoda-

08"I hooked her up with Detective Quinn, and since then, the DA has been feeding Quinn evidence. At first, some of the stuff Quinn asked for didn't make a lot of sense — reports on stolen phones and perps who specialize in Apple picking —"11

"Apple picking?" I stared in confusion. "Why would Quinn care about fruit theft?"

"Fruit theft?" Danny blinked. "No, no! Apple picking is slang for stealing expensive phones and laptops. It started with iPhones and iPads, but now any mobile phone or tablet is game."

"And what does that have to do with my situation?"

Danica looked away when she heard the confab breaking up. Chan the Phone Man left with the undercover detective, and Quinn approached us, a high-end smartphone in his hand.

She lowered her voice. "Ask him later. He'll tell you."

"Chan said you prepped a safe house for us. Is that right?" Quinn asked.

Danica nodded. "It's a short drive —"

"You mean we're not staying here?" I said, the relief so obvious on my face that Danny laughed.

"Don't worry, Clare. I think you'll be pleased with your overnight accommodations . . ."

As she led the way out, I couldn't follow her fast enough.

To borrow a phrase from *The Godfather,* sleeping with the fishes was something Quinn and I might be doing before this mess was done.

But tonight, at least, we wouldn't have to sleep with the rats!

Seventy-Four

Danica led us through the clanging steel door to the area behind the garage, an expanse of broken concrete strewn with old tires and empty booze bottles.

The detective's shiny silver SUV stood out like a UFO in a rusty junkyard. As odd as that sounded, the comparison was apt, because inside of fifteen minutes that sleek vehicle transported us to another world.

While I stretched out in the backseat, Danny got behind the wheel, and Quinn rode shotgun, tuning in an all-news radio station. Eyes closed, I listened to sports scores, celebrity news, human interest, and absolutely nothing on the First Daughter's disappearance.

"The feds are keeping a tight lid on this," said Danica, watching the road.

"They must still have strong threads to follow," Quinn noted.

"What happens when they run out of

leads?" I called from the backseat.

"Then they'll turn to the public," Quinn said.

"Unless a sharp reporter gets wind of the scoop sooner," Danny added.

"Some members of the press may already know," Quinn said. "My guess is the White House is asking them to hold back the story for the safety of Abigail . . ."

As the two continued their discussion, I dozed off. When I opened my eyes again, we'd landed on Planet Prosperous — or so it seemed.

Gone were the rundown buildings and cracked concrete. Around us now was an überaffluent neighborhood of exclusive shops and magnificently restored Federal-style houses.

"We're here," Danica called to me.

"Are we still in Baltimore?"

"Yes, ma'am. Federal Hill."

The evening was warm, so I cracked my window. The tang of the waterfront drifted in with fresh night air.

Danny hung a right, passing a luxurious catering hall and a chic restaurant. Then she swung left, onto a private driveway beside a tastefully lit sign.

Danica flashed her badge, and we were waved through a gate by a clean-cut uniformed guard.

From the parking lot I could see over a hundred boats gleaming in the moonlight, masts and antennae swaying in the stiff breeze. Like a black canvas, the dark waters of Patapsco River stretched beyond, dotted here and there with the golden glow of slow-moving ships.

"Am I dreaming?"

"What you see is what you get," said Danny. "You don't mind sleeping aboard a luxury yacht, do you?"

"I think I can adjust. Who's the lucky owner?"

"The City of Baltimore. The yacht was seized by the BPD in a raid last month. The former owner is in jail, but since the harbor fee is paid until the end of this month, nobody is going to mess with the boat until then."

"I don't suppose the luxury interior includes a fully stocked galley?"

"Great question," said Quinn.

Danny rolled her eyes. "You two are always on the same page, aren't you? Don't panic. I got you takeout, dessert, and some locally roasted whole-bean coffee, too."

"Give that woman a medal!" I cried.

Quinn nodded. "I concur."

Ten minutes later we were strolling along Pier K, a floating dock with a line of boats moored on one side, and the lapping waters of the river on the other. This was the farthest point from shore, but it wasn't exactly secluded.

A Tiki Barge, packed with revelers, was moored on the pier's river side, and a fifty-foot yacht was now motoring into its slip, four berths away. Fortunately, the bar was far enough away not to pose a threat, and the crew on the other boat paid no attention to us.

Our "hideout" turned out to be a forty-foot yacht in metallic white with mauve highlights, complete with a roof sundeck.

"Desperate Measures?" I read across the boat's stern.

"Yeah," Danny said. "Among other things, the owner sold cocaine."

"Were the *measures* grams or kilos?" Quinn asked.

"Mostly kilos, which is why this baby is yours for the night . . ."

The ship interior was tight but cozy, with

dark wood walls and sterling silver fixtures. Mirrors and recessed lighting made the space seem larger, and the upholstered furnishing continued the exterior's mauve motif. There was a bedroom, a small living space with satellite TV, and a galley. Best of all, the bathroom had a working shower!

Before Quinn jumped in, Danny wished him a good night, promising to return in the morning. I expected the detective to leave. Instead, she waved me into the ship's kitchen, pointing out the location of the food and coffee.

She had one last thing to point out, but it had nothing to do with dinner.

SEVENTY-FIVE

"Mike's pretty wound up," she said, leaning against the counter.

"Considering our situation, that's not surprising."

"No. But you know what you've got to do, right?"

"Excuse me?"

Danny folded her arms. "You need to help him get some sleep — some *good* sleep. That means no alcohol. And no sleeping pills."

When I didn't reply, she gave me a long stare. "Do I have to spell it out? Find *another* way to get the man's mind off your situation. Help him *unwind.* Are we on the same page?"

Oh, for heaven's sake. "Yes. Message received," I said, cutting off the discussion.

The young detective's advice was getting far too personal, but given the stakes involved, propriety was the least of my worries. Quinn and I owed her for sticking her neck out — boy, did we — so the last thing I was going to do was give her grief over something I agreed with anyway.

"I'm going," she said, squeezing my shoulder before heading out. "I'll be back, first thing. Just keep your heads down around here, and you'll be okay . . ."

Keep our heads down? I thought, watching her climb up to the deck and onto the dock. *What else would we do? Go to the Tiki Barge and party all night?*

With Mike still in the shower, I started a pot of coffee, and hoped for the best on dinner. Danny said takeout was in the oven, and I expected burgers and fries, maybe a lukewarm pizza, but when I pulled open the door, two thick Outback steaks with fixings met my hungry gaze.

The dessert in the cupboard turned out to be a local favorite — a package of Berger Cookies. Famished, I ripped open the plastic to mountains of fudgy frosting heaped on cakelike vanilla cookies . . . *ahhhh* . . . right in my mouth!

The Bergers reminded me of New York's famous black-and-whites, but there was no white in Baltimore's version, and no restraint on the fudgy icing. The cookies were heavy with it, dreamy, ridiculous dollops.

Layers so thick your first bite left teeth marks.

I handed one to Quinn in the shower. He inhaled it and put out his hand for another. I gave it up. Then I moved back to the galley through the bedroom, where I saw Danica had left us new clothes.

Jeans and a white sweater for me with a pair of slip-on sneakers. For Mike, a pair of high-tops with a shimmering velour jogging suit — the kind a semisleazy yacht owner might wear. Perfect camo for a square-jawed, suit-wearing fed attempting to hide from his own kind.

She'd thrown in two oversize Orioles tees along with underthings, not that Mike bothered. He returned from his shower shirtless, sandy hair darkly wet. His dinner attire — a thick mauve towel wrapped around his hips, another hanging on his neck.

Too hungry for words, we ate the thick New York strip steaks, butter-slathered baked potatoes, and steamed green beans in silence. As Quinn cleared the dishes, I poured us both fresh mugs of coffee. Then I set the rest of the fudge-frosted cookies on the table between us and settled in for what I hoped would be some clarity.

"Okay," I said, "I'm ready to hear good

news. Did you get what you needed from Chan?"

Mouth full of Berger Cookie, Quinn nodded, retrieved the phone Chan had given him, and set it on the table between us.

"Do you recognize that device?" he asked between chews and swallows.

It looked like a typical smartphone, powered down so I couldn't read the screen. Other than that, it meant nothing to me.

"I don't understand," I said. "Why do you think I would recognize it?"

"Because it belonged to the man you're accused of killing — the late Jeevan Varma."

SEVENTY-SIX

As a harbor foghorn wailed in the distance, my mind went back to the night Varma collapsed in my coffeehouse . . .

I knelt beside the well-dressed man, checking vital signs and thinking there was nothing more I could do for him. Since I didn't know his name, I went through his clothes.

The man's pockets held little: a half-empty pack of cigarettes; a few after-dinner chocolate mints from J. Chocolatier; and a fine leather wallet, which contained loose bills, credit cards, and a U.S. State Department ID.

I found nothing else on him . . .

I sat back, slightly stunned by the realization.

"I didn't find *a phone* on Varma that night. And what State Department employee wouldn't have a phone on him?!" My gaze locked on to Quinn's. "The person who killed Mr. Varma must have taken this phone!"

Quinn nodded.

"Then, Chan killed him? Or he knows who did?"

"I wish it were that simple. But Chan 'the phone man' is only the receiver of stolen goods."

"Like a fence?"

"Yeah, that's the old-school name for it. But he doesn't care about gemstones and watches. He's a fence for the digital age. He's also an informant for the Baltimore PD because he's been dealing in stolen smartphones for the last few years. The phones are delivered as is — unwiped — because the data can be mined before the phone is restored to factory default and resold. He bought Varma's phone in a consignment of devices stolen in and around DC."

"But how did you know he'd have Varma's phone?"

"I didn't. I just went fishing. When Katerina told me you were the prime suspect in Varma's murder, I got word to Danica, asked her to look for any hits on Varma. She came up with this — *his phone*."

"And Danica doesn't know who stole it, either?"

"No. Like I said, Varma's phone was part of a purchased lot — the way a fence might go to a pawnshop owner with a bag of hot jewelry. The consignment Chan purchased matched phones that were reported stolen in a robbery at a catering hall in Reston, and one from a robbery in a bistro on Connecticut Avenue —"

"I remember that Connecticut Avenue robbery. I was worried the same thing would happen at our supper club. There were two men, weren't there? They stole wallets, smartphones, and jewelry at gunpoint."

"That's not the whole story . . ."

According to Quinn, "The stickup was a panic move to cover up their real business."

"Which was?"

"Cloning those phones. These thieves weren't simply pickpockets, they were smart and skilled. Their game was to grab devices, take them into a secluded area, and clone them, but something went wrong this time. A woman noticed the man's hand in her bag and she screamed. That's when it turned into an armed robbery to cover up the cloning."

"Cloning . . . that's making a copy, right? But what exactly is a *cloned phone*?"

"It acts like a mirror image of the original. When the first one rings, so does the clone.

All communications go to both phones, all text messages, pictures, and videos stored in the original are accessible on the clone, as well. There's only one bill, and it goes to the original owner. So whoever owns the clone can make calls free of charge, but that's not why someone would want a clone. The real value is in the information."

"So it's the ultimate wiretap?"

Mike nodded. "It's what the NSA and CIA call tradecraft."

"Spies use it?"

"And criminals. And blackmailers."

My mind raced on the blackmailing angle. People stored their whole lives in their devices, including things they shouldn't: naughty pictures; sexting; communications they wanted to keep off their public office computers . . .

"Mike, if we have Varma's phone, then we can find out who he was planning to meet with on the night he was killed, right? It's a real lead!"

"It *would* have been. But all texts and voice mails in the forty-eight-hour period prior to the phone being stolen — and presumably Varma being attacked and killed — have been erased."

"Can't you use some kind of forensics to un-erase them?"

"If I had my full powers, I would get a warrant to access his cloud drive, but we're not exactly in the position to do that."

"Then this phone is of no use to us?"

"The phone itself is evidence because whoever holds the clone is guilty of one murder at least. And we got lucky with one more thing . . ."

He turned on the phone and showed me its contact list. The list was long, but there was one name on it that we both recognized — *Katerina Lacey.*

SEVENTY-SEVEN

I stared at Katerina's name, feeling numb for a moment, then angry, and finally frustrated.

"This *proves* they knew each other."

"But little else."

"So what do we do?"

"For now, we hold it."

I pounded the tabletop. "This may not prove Katerina did anything to Varma, but it's proof enough to me that she's involved in this mess."

"Me too. The bad news is — there's nothing else. When Danica told me she had a connection to your case, she was right, but . . ."

Mike sat back.

"I get it. If Mr. Varma's recent voice mails and texts were wiped, we can't prove he met with Katerina the night he was murdered." I shook my head. "Maybe he didn't even meet with her. Maybe she sent someone to do her dirty work . . ."

I thought of Lidia, that pretty, young Latina assistant I saw by her side in the White House, teetering on those stilts, trying to measure up to her boss. *I'll bet she'd do anything Katerina asked . . .*

"We're stuck, Clare. We're out of leads."

"We can't be . . . we just *can't* . . . Let me think . . ."

And to fuel my little gray cells, I intended to eat.

Yes, I know I just inhaled a steak dinner, but those fudgy Berger Cookies were calling out to me, and I was going to answer — *with* a fresh, hot cup of joe. Chocolate and coffee were too good a pairing to pass up, especially after dinner . . .

Hey, wait a minute. I froze, my mind racing. *Chocolate and coffee . . . after dinner . . .*

"Mike," I cried. "Chocolate and coffee!"

"Excuse me?"

"Give me your prepaid phone. I need to make a call . . ."

When I took a minute to explain my plan, Quinn was all for it.

"Keep the call short," he warned. "Speak in Italian as much as possible, and do not use any real names. Use code."

"Got it . . ."

■ ■ ■ ■

"Hello, Tito, *cosa c'è di nuovo?*" I asked. (What's new?)

"Chi sei?" he demanded. (Who are you?)

"Your old friend," I replied in Italian. "*Signora* Rogers. Remember? From *Signor* Rogers' neighborhood?"

"Holy Mother!" Tito cried. "Where are you?!"

"Speak in Italian," I advised — in Italian. "And I can't tell you where I am. You understand?"

Tito paused, then his voice was much calmer. "I understand . . ."

I asked him about the drummer boy. "Have you seen him?"

"No. He's gone. Disappeared."

"And what about the piano man. The one who has an office on the third floor. Is he around?"

"No! Men in suits came and took him away. Now he's gone, too!"

"Tito, I need your help."

"Anything. What can I do?"

"I want you to call the woman who runs J. Chocolatier and ask her for the names of the locations she supplies with chocolates. Narrow the area to twenty blocks around our Village Blend's address. Do you understand?"

"I understand. I don't know why you're asking such a thing, but I understand."

"Don't worry about why. Get the information, and I'll be grateful . . ."

"Okay. I'll do it."

"I'll call again, Tito. Thank you. Don't tell anyone about our talk. And try not to worry. *Buona sera.*"

"*Buona Sera, Signora* Rogers."

I handed Quinn back the prepaid phone. "Enough code for you?"

"Good job."

"We'll see," I said. "But those J. Chocolatier chocolates in Varma's pocket should have been a dead giveaway — excuse the pun. The man was impeccably dressed. It made no sense for him to be carrying around after-dinner chocolates unless he'd gotten them at a restaurant the same night."

"Did Tito understand what you asked?"

"Absolutely . . . and once we know who serves J. Chocolatier chocolates in our area, we'll have Danica check their security cameras. If we're lucky, we'll see Katerina's bony ass sashaying in on the same night as Mr. Varma."

"You missed your calling, Cosi. You should

have been a cop."

"Thanks, but guns and I don't get along," I said, going for a refill. "I'm better with coffee."

SEVENTY-EIGHT

Feeling more positive, I finally took my shower. The warm water felt heavenly sluicing over my naked curves. I washed my hair, too, and used the blow-dryer to fluff it up prettily. Then I wrapped myself in a mauve towel, took a deep breath, and sashayed into the bedroom.

Oh, shoot. No Quinn . . .

I could hear the TV in the other room. And I could guess why.

Down deep, the man was a romantic. Back in Greenwich Village, he loved lighting the fire in my bedroom's hearth. A bottle of wine, soft music, and he was putty in my antique four-poster.

Unfortunately, *this* boudoir had all the charm of a 1970s pimpmobile.

It didn't even have the tasteful 1890s "Mauve Decade" palette going for it like the rest of the boat. The few pieces of furniture were upholstered in either purple or pink, or purple *and* pink — and every-thing was fuzzy, very fuzzy. The fuzziness extended to the pink and purple animal-print carpeting.

Illumination was provided by a pair of lava lamps — naturally, one was purple, the other pink — positioned between the pil-lows on purple acrylic nightstands.

In between the lamps was the water bed. A terribly underinflated water bed. And it was circular.

Dropping the towel, I got in.

While oozing bubbles rose and sank beside my head, I felt the sloshy mattress under me, rocking me back and forth like a rud-derless lifeboat in a storm-force gale.

"Mike, this bed is crazy!" I called loudly. "I'm getting seasick, and this yacht's never left its dock. Why don't you come in here and throw me a line?"

"Just shut your eyes, sweetheart," he called from the couch. "You'll be asleep in no time."

"What about you?"

"I can't sleep right now. I'll be in soon . . ."

Lying there in the pink and purple gloom, I sighed the sigh of a woman ignored.

I'd been down this road before. Anyone involved with a cop knew The Job was always there. In Mike's case, when the stress of his work wasn't eating at him, his mind was working overtime on cases — and in *this* case, we were on the hook for our very lives.

Now I was worried. And I knew Danny was, too, which is why she put me on the spot earlier in the galley.

If Mike didn't get some good rest tonight, he wouldn't be at his best tomorrow. And a guy packing a Glock, a .45, and a gym bag of extra ammo needed to be at his best.

Drinking was a bad idea. I agreed with Danny on that. And a sleeping pill could put him out for too long. Which meant we were down to two choices: *Hot milk. Or hot MILK.*

Peeved at the thought of lukewarm moo juice trumping my "older lady" sex appeal, I rose from the drowning pool, tossed on one of the oversize Orioles T-shirts, and peeked into the yacht's small living room.

Mike's big body was folded on the couch, watching cable TV news, one knee bouncing anxiously. I was about to launch my plan when he rose abruptly and crossed to the stocked bar, but not for a glass of warm anything.

He poured himself a few fingers of straight scotch.

Crap.

He sat back down, knee bouncing again. But before he could start sipping the alcohol, I moved into the living room, blocking his view of the big screen.

"Sweetheart, what are you doing?"

"I'm sorry, but" — I threw up my hands — "I lost an earring!"

"You what?"

Bending at the waist, I began to scan the carpet.

"Darn, no luck . . ."

When I moved to my hands and knees, Mike's knee stopped bouncing.

"It's a shame," I said, moving ever so slowly across the floor. "This *could* go on all night."

"Clare?"

"Yes?"

"You didn't wear earrings today."

"Didn't I?"

Mike put down his drink. "And I see something else . . ."

"Oh? What's that?"

"You forgot to put on underwear."

"Did I?"

That was all it took.

One minute later we were back among the lava lamps, making waves.

Seventy-Nine

A short time later, Mike was in dreamland, and I followed him there. His strong arms were around me, lovingly possessive, the sweet sensation of his lovemaking lingering in my limbs, making everything good again.

Even this ridiculous water bed felt different.

Gone was the seasick sensation of riding out a rocky gale. With Mike's warm body next to mine, the undulating mattress sent me to an island paradise where gentle waves lapped pristine sand, until —

Glaring light and a thunderous racket ripped me from my beautiful beach.

I hardly opened my eyes before I was dragged out of floating tranquillity and onto the hard, fuzzy floor. As Mike blanketed me with his own body, I glimpsed a shocking sight through the portholes — beams of white light stabbing the dark.

"Mike! What's happening?"

My cry was drowned out by the rolling throb of engines overhead. A helicopter was flying so low its downdrafts rocked our boat. Shouted commands and the bark of a dog added to the clamor. Then came the bouncing stomp of running boots along the wooden pier.

Mike pulled me closer, whispered through my hair.

"It's a raid, Clare. They're coming for us. Helicopters, boats, SWAT teams, dogs —"

Oh, God, I thought. *It was my phone call to Tito. They must have traced us!*

A motorboat roared by, its wake slamming the yacht against the pier. Flashing scarlet lights and the scream of a siren added to the kaleidoscope of chaos.

"Mike, what's going to happen?"

"They'll rip through this cabin like a tornado. When they get to the bedroom door there'll be no warning. They'll crash it down."

Arcs of stark halogen light bathed the night in brightness, piercing the shadows, and bleaching the walls in a colorless white glare.

"They'll lead with flash grenades," Mike warned. "They're meant to stun, not kill, but close your eyes and cover your ears so you won't get hurt."

The wake of a second boat battered the yacht. Meanwhile the thundering boots were getting closer.

"When they come through the door, stay on the floor but raise your hands so they can see them." Mike spoke faster, his tone urgent. "We'll be separated for interrogation, Clare. I won't be able to help you. Keep demanding a lawyer and say nothing; eventually they will have to give in."

Mike shifted his body so I could cover my ears. Before I did, he whispered one more thing.

"If I never see you again, please remember . . . I love you."

I began to pray while the pounding beat of racing feet got louder and louder as they reached our yacht — and then receded as the men kept right on going.

On the water, the sirens faded as the twin motorboats raced to the far end of Pier K. Finally, the helicopter veered away, too.

"What the hell?"

Mike sounded as bewildered as I felt. And then we got curious.

In seconds, we were on our feet and through the door. We moved through the darkened yacht to an enclosed part of the upper deck and cautiously peeked through the window blinds.

The beam of a hovering helicopter shone down on the fifty-foot yacht that had pulled in when we'd first arrived at the marina. FBI agents in Kevlar vests and helmets surrounded the boat; and, in the middle of the pier, three people in pajamas were on their knees, hands behind their heads, half a dozen guns trained on them.

More boot-stomps approached.

"A drug raid?" Mike whispered.

"No," I said, recognizing the figures jogging past our yacht, toward the commotion. "Those three are Secret Service . . ."

One was the bald guy in the vest who'd set up the front door checkpoint at my Village Blend. Next to him was Agent Sharpe, an automatic weapon in his hands. The third figure was clad in black from the tips of her boots to the helmet on her blond head.

"That woman is Agent Sharon Cage. They must be looking for Abby."

Mike still looked confounded. "Could they have gotten the wrong boat?"

I watched as Agent Cage boarded the fifty-footer, and went belowdecks. A few moments later she reappeared, and strolled to the bow of the boat.

Mike studied their actions, trying to fathom why *that* yacht was raided, and not ours. "They're not making any moves to search the other vessels, so we're in luck. But I wish I knew what was really going on."

Me too, I thought. *But the party isn't here. It's four berths away, at that other boat.*

Without waiting to consult with Mike, I slipped through the door, to the edge of the boat. Taking a deep breath, I dived over the side and into the dark water.

EIGHTY

Son of a bunny! This river is freezing!

No surprise. It was late March, not early July. But did it have to be *this* cold?

There were two ways to warm up, and since I wasn't getting back aboard *Desperate Measures* until I knew what was going on, I took my own desperate measures and swam toward the chaos.

I soon discovered I wasn't alone in the water. A pair of U.S. Coast Guard motorboats were cruising around, so I ducked out of sight.

Sucking in a breath, I dived under a section of the floating pier. Visibility was murky to nil, with only the dull glow of the pier's lights to guide me. But I used the same long strokes I'd used for years at the 14th Street Y, which kept me going in a straight line toward the yacht under siege.

As I approached, someone on the dock waved off the helicopter, and much of the noise pollution and blinding glare was alleviated. Finally, I heard harsh voices, arguing a few feet above my head.

"You have no right to do this —" The speaker was a young woman, on the verge of tears.

"Why were you on the Potomac this morning?" This time it was a man's voice, deep, authoritative, and used to giving commands.

"No reason! We were just cruising," a frightened male voice replied. "Testing her out for the summer."

"You didn't stop along the Georgetown Waterfront Park, to pick up someone onshore?"

"What? No! I've never even heard of —"

A dog snarled, then barked.

"Hold up. Is this about that weed in the galley?" the nervous man continued. "It's legal in DC but I forgot to dump it when we left, that's all —"

"I'm asking the questions."

They didn't raid the wrong boat, I thought with relief. *And they aren't asking about me or Mike. They're simply following a lead on Abby . . .*

I circled around to the bow of the yacht, moving toward the lone figure on deck, telephone to her ear. I stuck close enough to the hull so Sharon Cage couldn't see me, even if she looked down. Unfortunately, I couldn't see her, either, and when I positioned myself below the spot where I thought she was standing, I heard only the lapping of waves.

Finally Agent Cage spoke, her voice a defeated monotone.

"Bottom line, she's not here. It's the right yacht. The satellite photos match, and the owner admits they were on the Potomac. But this may be a dead end. I'll get back to you after a more extensive search is conducted."

That set off alarms. *A boat-to-boat search will surely ferret us out . . .*

A heavy pair of booted feet thumped on the yacht's wooden deck.

"Agent Cage?" It was the harsh interrogator from the pier.

"What is it, Karpinski?"

"Your package was *never* here."

His tone was impatient and irritated, and not much different from the one he'd used to intimidate the victims of this misguided raid.

"You don't know that," Cage replied. "There are a lot of boats moored at this marina."

"But this is the only vessel from *this port*

that sailed the Potomac in the last twenty-four hours. It's the only boat we're legally permitted to search at this location, and the dogs found no scent. Ms. Parker was never aboard. She's not here."

A pause, and the man spoke again.

"There's been another development. The forensic lab at Quantico has finished the rushed analysis on the blood and hair found on that scarf from Georgetown Waterfront Park. The DNA from the hair is definitely Ms. Parker's, no doubt. And the cane we found beside it was Sergeant McGuire's."

I think Agent Cage and I felt the same horror and dread at that moment, and it only got worse.

"There's concern about the amount of blood."

"It's not that much," Cage insisted. "One splatter on the trail. A thin stream leading along the river steps, down to the Potomac. No more than a nosebleed or a gash would cause —"

"If she went into the water, we don't know how much she bled out. And if she slashed her own wrist and McGuire went into the river after her —"

"No one is talking suicide, Karpinski. Abigail has a lot to live for. She was glowing at the bridal shower her friend from college threw for her. She was happier than I'd seen her in weeks."

"If she was taken, let's hope the kidnappers know first aid. As for the other theory, we've had divers in the river already, and we're going to start dragging the water in the morning."

"Before we do that, let's go backward," Cage pleaded, desperation in her tone. "Let's return to the park, the spot where her trail went cold, maybe —"

"That's not going to happen. You lost her, Agent Cage. Now the FBI is going to find her — or her body. And not by chasing our tails in Georgetown."

"You're not going to continue this search without me."

"Yes, we are," he said. "The word came down from the Oval Office. You are relieved. Go home, Agent Cage. And pray she turns up *alive* by morning."

The heavy boots stomped off. A moment later, Sharon Cage's defeated footsteps followed.

A few minutes later, I hauled myself back aboard *Desperate Measures.* I entered the cabin dripping wet, my tears mingling with the river water pooling on the carpet.

"Clare! Where the hell did you go? I turned around and you were gone —"

Shivering, I broke down.

"I should have told Sharon Cage about the park, how Abby was using it to slip away from her security detail." I gasped. "Now Cage has been relieved. Her career is over and Abby is gone. And that blood trail leading to the river . . . They think she was either kidnapped or slashed her own wrists and went into the water. And, Mike, they found Stan's Hoover cane —"

"Easy, Clare. You're shaking, and your lips are blue."

Mike grabbed a blanket off the bed and wrapped me in it.

"I heard them talking . . . If Abby went into the water, I know Stan would have gone in after her, tried to save her. But with his bad leg and the river's current . . ." I shook my head, choking up. Despite the blanket around me, I couldn't stop quaking.

"They're going to drag the river in the morning for their bodies. And it's all my fault! It's all my fault!"

EIGHTY-ONE

"Calm down, Clare. We're in this together. Take a breath and tell me everything you learned . . ."

Quinn guided my damp, shivering form to the galley and sat me down at the table. While I recounted what I'd seen and heard, he replaced the wet blanket with dry towels. Then he brewed coffee to warm up my insides, too.

By the time I got my story out, I'd downed a hot cup of joe and I wasn't shivering anymore. But I was still inconsolably upset.

"Was Abby kidnapped? Did she kill herself?" I said, emotion welling up again. "I don't know what to believe. Not anymore."

Quinn locked his gaze on mine. "Do you think Sharon Cage is a good cop?"

"Yes, of course I do."

"Tell me what Agent Cage thinks."

"That Abby's alive. That she didn't kill herself — despite the blood they found in the park."

"Remember Sergeant Price from DC Metro? Remember his internal lie detector? What does your own rumbly gut tell you?"

I closed my eyes and considered what I knew to be true.

"I believe Abby is a runaway bride. That she ran away to elope with Stan. I'm sure that's why she was so happy at her bridal shower — because she knew Stan would be meeting her that night in the park."

"Let's start with that assumption and ignore everything else. Abby and Stan ran away together. What then?"

"They escaped Washington. Maybe they're on their way to Vegas right now for a quick wedding."

Quinn shook his head. "Trains, planes, and automobiles are out. They're photographing everyone who pays a toll or drives through a tunnel. And you know firsthand they're checking boats, too."

"We managed to get out of DC when they were looking for us."

"Because I'm a law enforcement professional and knew what to avoid. We stayed off highways and toll roads. I knew all the ways they could track us, and we were driving another man's vehicle. We also had help from Danica. I promise you, the FBI is looking at every friend and associate of Stan's and Abby's. If they borrowed a car, they would have been discovered. If they rented a car, a credit card would have given them away."

I nodded, a lump growing in my throat.

"The White House is using every resource they have. That means every law enforcement agency on a federal, state, and local level. The TSA is looking for them at the airports, the police at train stations. The Coast Guard is watching the ports. Every security camera feed is being reviewed. And you heard Agent Cage mention satellite surveillance. That's probably the NSA. On top of that, the First Daughter is a minor celebrity who might be recognized, and with an eye patch and a limp, Stan doesn't exactly blend in, either . . ."

Quinn shrugged. "There is no way Abby and Stan got out of DC."

Now came the tears. "Then we have nowhere to go, no lead we can follow."

"Every detective hits a wall at some point." He took my hand and squeezed it. "I've seen veteran officers tear up in frustration over cases, especially when they become emotionally involved. Clare, I know you care a great deal about Abby and Stan, but try not to let emotion get in the way. Look at your evidence from a different angle, and do it as objectively as you can."

"Okay . . ." I closed my eyes again and played back those voices on the pier. "I remember Agent Cage saying she wanted to go back to Georgetown."

"Why?"

"She wanted to recheck the riverside spot where the dogs lost Abby's scent . . ."

I thought about that idea — losing the scent.

"If you cross water, can you throw off bloodhounds?" I asked hopefully. "There's a rowing club in that area. Maybe they used a small boat and crossed the river that way."

"The bloodhounds would have picked up the scent again on the other side. And anyway . . . wouldn't crossing the Potomac like that have been a pretty desperate plan?"

"But Abby *was* desperate. She was being railroaded into a marriage, and . . ." My voice trailed off as a memory came back to me.

"Clare, what's wrong?"

"Railroad . . . Railroad! Oh, my God, Mike, I know where they might have gone!"

"I told you the trains are being watched."

"Not that railroad."

"There's another?"

I nodded. "A very old one . . ."

Quinn scratched his head. "I don't get it."

"That's because you don't know everything yet. Some of what I'm about to tell you I was asked *never* to divulge to anyone. But I'm going to reveal it now because you were right, Mike. Details matter . . ."

EIGHTY-TWO

After Abby's stunning performance, nothing returned to normal at the Village Blend, DC — which was a good thing.

The publicity sent our walk-in coffee business through the roof. Our Jazz Space made nightly use of the blue velvet rope we'd never needed before, and our new, revised menu continued to impress customers and local food critics, which meant our prestige grew along with our popularity.

And it got better . . .

A few days after Abby's performance, the First Lady sent a stunning bouquet of dark pink roses to me, expressing appreciation for "doing for Abigail what we never could . . . Our daughter is now a star, thanks to you and everyone at the Village Blend, DC."

In that same note, Mrs. Parker reiterated Abigail's wish that we provide the coffee service for her Rose Garden wedding. The

First Lady also requested that Chef Luther Bell and the Village Blend cater the Smithsonian's three-hundred-guest party celebrating the opening of its *Coffee in America* exhibition at the Museum of American History.

With little more than two weeks to plan and execute the request, Luther and Joy went into a paroxysm of advance preparations.

A week later, I was scheduled to meet Mrs. Helen Hargood Trainer, Curator of the White House.

By this time, the curator and I had made contact by phone and traded dozens of e-mails about the White House contribution to the exhibition. But we had yet to meet face-to-face, so Helen Trainer graciously invited me to the White House to view the collection of artifacts being lent to the Smithsonian, largely based on the work we'd done together.

The day of my scheduled visit, Madame and I were in the mansion's kitchen, preparing to pack up Mrs. Bittmore-Black's contribution to the show — the exquisite silver coffee service gifted to her by Jacqueline Kennedy. It was still sitting in its glass case, on the kitchen counter, when the doorbell rang.

"I hope that's not Helen's people," I said, checking my watch. "If it is, they're two hours early!"

Instead of a White House courier, I found a bedraggled Stan McGuire on the front porch. His usual ramrod-straight military bearing was gone, and he'd forgotten to comb his unruly brown hair.

"I'd like to talk, Ms. Cosi. It's about Abby."

Madame took charge, leading Stan to the kitchen, where she sat him down at the center island. As I poured him a cup of our Smooth Jazz blend, Madame split a fresh blueberry muffin, slathered it with Joy's favorite high-fat, European butter, and set it in front of him.

"Eat that right up," she said, taming his wayward locks with a gentle touch.

"What's happening with Abby?" I asked.

"I was hoping you could tell me. Gard mentioned you're going to the White House today. Would you please talk to Abby, Ms. Cosi? I need to know if she's okay."

"But you talk to her every day, don't you?"

"We talk. But I haven't *seen* her for ten days, not since the show at the Jazz Space." He paused. "I assume you know what happened on *The Good Day Show* last week?"

The whole world knew. Millions of Americans watched Abby's meltdown live, and the video went viral after that. Stan blamed it on the First Lady.

"Abby's mother made sure our band wouldn't appear — which forced Abby to play cold, without support or backup. And what her mother did next was just sadistic . . ."

The First Lady had gone on the show with Abby, and right before her solo performance, Mrs. Parker announced Abigail's secret engagement and the Rose Garden wedding in June.

"There Abby sat, on that piano bench, waiting for her cue," Stan recounted, "and all of a sudden her mother was telling the world about the history of her relationship with her fiancé . . ."

And that wasn't the worst of it. While Abby managed to hide her shock over the unexpected wedding announcement, she was openly gob-smacked by what happened next.

"Abby was going to play a solo version of 'Fix You,' " Stan explained. "But nobody warned her she was supposed to re-create, you know, the part when she kissed me."

"Oh, I remember that," Madame said.

"*Everyone* does!"

"Except this time Abby was supposed to lock lips with Preston Emory."

EIGHTY-THREE

When Abby's fiancé walked onto *The Good Day Show* set as a "surprise guest" and sat down beside her on the piano bench, she displayed the same disturbed reaction she'd had in our greenroom after her big performance. Only this uncomfortable scene was telecast live, to the whole world.

Stan grimaced at the memory.

"You could hear the director cueing her, but Abby froze," he said bitterly. "If I had been there, I could have snapped her out of it."

"How?" I asked — and not skeptically.

I marveled at how Stan had bonded with Abby musically, and I was honestly curious how he'd gotten her through her big headliner debut.

"Abby is a true artist, Ms. Cosi. She doesn't just bang notes on a cabinet with internal strings . . ." Stan paused and studied the ceiling. "You know how we say,

'You don't play your instrument. You play music.'? The reason is because the music isn't in the instrument. That's not where it comes from. It comes from inside the musician. Abby needs to *hear* the music. Only then can she play."

"And you help her hear it?"

Stan nodded. "Once you've grounded yourself in the rudiments, the work is internal. To do it right, you have to stop criticizing yourself."

"So you're saying Abby is afraid of making a mistake?"

He leaned forward. "In jazz, there are no mistakes. There's just you — and the music. If you can understand that and accept yourself, when you *swing,* you'll sweep that audience right along with you."

"And you remind Abby of that?"

"I remind Abby to love every sound she makes."

But that morning, in front of the TV cameras, Stanley McGuire wasn't there to remind Abby to love every sound she made. And after too many seconds of embarrassing silence, what viewers heard was Preston Emory harshly command —

"Just play it, Abby!"

What she finally played was a slamming rendition of "Chopsticks," followed by a key sweep and dead silence.

The network jumped to a commercial after a final shot of Abby glaring at Preston. And Preston blinking at the camera.

"Mrs. Parker is using that television fail against her now. She claims what happened on TV proves Abby doesn't have what it takes to perform. She keeps pressuring her to 'be rational,' 'stick to the plan,' and 'put aside her pipe dream.' "

Stan's finger quotes slashed the air.

"Abby's supposed to 'do the *sane* thing': Marry Emory. Start a family. Be happy." Stan dropped his hands to clutch his coffee cup. "Meanwhile her mom won't let her out of the White House. She insists Abby's celebrity has become a 'security risk.' "

"Have you asked if you can see her?"

"More than once. She says I'll never be approved as a guest."

For a moment Stan sat in silence.

"You want to know the scary part, Ms. Cosi? Abby herself. She's so confused. I'll convince her to break it off with that clown and stick to her music, and she promises she will. Then I talk to her the next night and it's like she doesn't remember the first conversation. They've got her on meds again. And I know why she needs them. She can't hear the music anymore. All she can hear is their criticism."

EIGHTY-FOUR

My heart went out to Stan, who shook his head in despair.

"If you ask me, the problem isn't Abby and her music," he declared. "It never was. It's the truth that girl represents —"

"What do you mean?" I asked, but Stan was on a rolling rant.

"You know what I think? Her own mother *set her up to fail* on that damn morning show so she'd have an excuse to take complete control of her daughter's life again. Even Abby thinks it was payback for dedicating 'Somewhere Over the Rainbow' to her father."

Madame frowned in confusion. "Why would the First Lady be bothered by a tribute to the President?"

"She wouldn't. But President Parker isn't Abby's real father."

On the checkerboard patio, a pair of songbirds got into a chirping argument. I noticed only because in the kitchen there was stunned silence.

"How do you know this, Stan? Did Abby tell you?"

He nodded. "Her biological father died when she was eight. Do you know that tattoo of musical notes on Abby's arm? It's the opening phrase to 'Somewhere Over the Rainbow,' the song her dad always sang to her." Stan drained his cup. "She said his playing was transcendent, and I'm not surprised. He was the one who taught her to play."

"Who was her father?" Madame asked.

"His name was Andy A. Ferro. Beyond that and his birth date, Abby knows very little. She was told that he worked overseas for the government, and I thought he might be military, so I reached out to a friend, but the search he did of government and military personnel came up with nothing. And I mean a big, fat donut, no records of the guy anywhere. If he really did work for 'the government' — and I have my doubts — his records are wiped."

"Does Abby know how he died?" I asked.

"Only that it happened in Morocco."

Morocco? I thought. The First Lady had mentioned something about Morocco and her coffee obsession —

". . . after Abigail was born I went a little crazy," she'd told me. *"I must have visited my favorite stall in the souk every morning that summer . . ."*

Abby's mother must have met her father while she was in Morocco, or maybe he was working there and she visited him for a period of time.

"How does the world *not* know about this?" I asked.

"Because Abby's father and mother never married. Her mother even refused to put down her real father's name on Abby's birth certificate. That made it pretty easy to cover up Abby's true history — reinvent her story for the public."

"Reinvent how?"

"According to Abby, her mom worked for President Parker back when he was a senator. That's how the two fell in love. Parker's wife died shortly after giving birth to Kip, which made the senator a widower for years. Everyone assumes he had an affair with Abby's mother during those years he was alone, and Abby was the result — their love child. They think he only married Abby's mom when he began to consider running for President. He knew he needed a First Lady, not a First Mistress, and it made sense to make everything legit."

"Then very few people know the truth about Abby's late father?"

Stan shrugged. "It only matters to me because it matters to Abby . . ." He ran both hands through his thick, brown hair, wrecking it again.

"Ms. Cosi, can you *please* talk to Abby today when you go to the White House? I'm worried about her."

More than worried, I thought. Stan looked like a drowning man who'd been denied his lifeline.

"I will talk to Abby," I promised. "But I can do more . . . for both of you. The Village Blend has been asked to cater an upcoming Smithsonian party. That means I can pick my staff. How would you like to play a waiter next Saturday night?"

Stan's head shot up, happy excitement in his face. "Ms. Cosi, if I get to see Abby, I'll play a rodeo clown!"

"I'll tell her about it when I see her today."

"If she knows I'm going, she'll be there. I know she will!"

"Well, there won't be an exhibition if I don't box up these things before the courier arrives to pick them up. You'll have to excuse me . . ."

While I went to work, Madame played the indulgent grandmother with Stan, plying him with more muffins and coffee. Already heartened by the possibility of seeing Abby, he began happily drumming the table.

Meanwhile, I took the computer flash drive, which Tuck and Punch had found in our Jazz Space, and slipped it into a plain, white envelope. No one had stopped by looking for it, and I'd been too busy to send it. This was my first opportunity to get it back to its owner, and I was confident the curator could help.

On the envelope, I wrote —

Helen Hargood Trainer,
Office of the Curator of the White House.
I'll explain this when I arrive.
— Clare Cosi

I placed the envelope with the flash drive in the box.

Next I opened the glass case and lifted out the historic sterling silver coffeepot. I felt a thrill knowing that John F. Kennedy and First Lady Jacqueline imbibed the brew that poured out of this very spout.

I upended it, to see if I could find the manufacturer's mark. When I did, the attached lid flipped open, and a piece of yellowed paper flittered onto the floor.

"Ms. Cosi, you dropped something," Stan

said, scooping it up.

He unfolded the paper and scanned it. "What is this?"

Madame glanced over his shoulder and suddenly went white. "Perhaps we shouldn't look at that, young man."

But Stan was already grinning in boyish wonderment. "This is a treasure map! There are riddles here, places to look inside this house . . ."

I glanced at Madame. "Didn't you tell me Mrs. Bittmore-Black was famous for her Washington power parties — and the legendary treasure hunts she staged to break the ice with her guests?"

"Yes," Madame admitted. "Tenacious liked to put 'teams' of people together who, as she put it, '*should* be working together to solve problems, but are not.' "

"Cool," Stan said. "We should follow this!"

"Perhaps not," Madame demurred.

I looked over the clues with Stan. The note was handwritten in a delicate script, but clear and legible. A woman's handwriting.

Tenacious Bittmore-Black herself?

"This looks like fun," I said.

Stan nodded. "Maybe there really is a treasure."

But Madame kept shaking her head; so,

with a lame excuse to Stan, I tugged her into the next room.

"What's wrong with an innocent treasure hunt?" I asked. "At least poor Stan is smiling now."

Madame's violet eyes narrowed. "Not so innocent, I fear. A few years ago my old friend came to New York to talk to a publisher about writing her memoirs. Nothing came of it, but we had a two-hour brunch at the Four Seasons, and far too many mimosas. Over dessert she confessed something she shouldn't have."

Madame glanced over her shoulder, and then lowered her voice.

"You know Tenacious Bittmore served four years as an ambassador. And her husband, Edward Black, worked most of his life for the State Department."

"I've seen his pictures on the wall."

"Well, a different kind of diplomacy went on at the Bittmore-Black parties. Influential people came from the U.S. government and the many foreign embassies here in Washington, along with members of the press. Some of those people used this house as a dead drop."

"Dead drop?"

"It's a place where spies and counterspies leave information for one another." Madame crooked a finger and I leaned closer. "During the Cold War and afterward, information was passed. The people making the actual exchange were never at the same party. They were never even seen in the same building with the people who received their information. It was Tenacious's husband who made sure the right guests got the right treasure map, and that's how state secrets were safely passed to the CIA by foreign nationals, without anyone being the wiser."

"That's insidiously clever," I said. "But it's the past. There is no evidence that this particular map leads to secret CIA intelligence. It's probably one of many —"

"Did I hear you say this map leads to secret CIA intelligence?"

We turned to find Stan had crept up on us.

"If that's true, then we've *got* to follow the clues," he insisted. "There could be a national security secret buried somewhere in this very house."

Madame faced him. "If it's decades old, why would it have any value?"

"Because truth matters, Mrs. Dubois . . . and a truth about our past can alter how we look at the present, and move forward in the future."

Madame and I exchanged glances, and she threw up her hands.

"Very well. But if we find the corpse of Jimmy Hoffa, don't say I didn't warn you!"

Stan blinked. "Who?"

Madame rolled her eyes. "I do adore the vitality and optimism of youth, but really? How soon before they forget the Lindbergh kidnapping?"

"The what?" Stan asked, but this time I noticed his mischievous grin.

EIGHTY-FIVE

"The game's afoot!" Madame declared, convinced at last to follow the treasure map. "You may read the first clue, Stanley."

" 'On the top floor there is a circus, if you know where to look. Find the number on the Big Top, then open the book.' "

"To the top floor!" Madame cried, leading the way.

As part of our "Walton family" living situation, the upper bedrooms had been occupied and then vacated.

"I have to get these extra air mattresses to the basement," I said absently.

"There it is," Stan cried, pointing to an original framed poster for a "Broadway Bonanza" called *Pixie at the Circus.* It starred "the singing-est, dancing-est, cutest-est little girl in the whole wide world, Teenie Bittmore!"

"These mementoes date back to when Tenacious was known as Teenie," Madame explained, "child star of stage and screen."

I scanned the poster. Under Teenie Bittmore's dimpled twelve-year-old face, a circus-tent silhouette displayed the words *Opens May 3.*

"There is your number three," Madame declared. "Now where is the book?"

One of the bookshelves was filled with bound Broadway and movie scripts. Another shelf was packed with hundreds of black vinyl records — 78s, 33s, and 45 RPMs.

"Don't show them to Stanley," Madame warned, this time with her own mischievous smile. "He'll mistake them for dinner plates."

"There it is!" I reached for one book among a battered old *Encyclopaedia Britannica* set. "Volume three. Balt to Brai."

The book had been hollowed out, and there was a *key* inside!

Madame clapped her hands. "Oh, how exciting! What's the next clue?"

Stan checked the map. " 'In the library there is a chest of steel, unlock its heart for the next reveal. Shaken, not stirred.' "

Stan looked up. "Maybe James Bond is locked up there."

"A chest of steel with a heart," Madame mused. "Is there a metal chest of some kind? A heart-shaped jewelry or music box?"

"I don't remember any. I don't recall any hearts, either — Hold on, it must be that suit of armor. It has a breastplate of steel —"

"Protecting the heart of the knight!" Stan cried.

We thundered down the stairs to the first floor, found the library, and gathered in front of the suit of medieval armor. The breastplate was inlaid with an elaborate pattern of silver and gold, but there was nowhere to insert a key.

"Dead end," I said.

"Perhaps the armor was too obvious," Madame replied. "Let's look around."

The room was a treasure trove, as cluttered as a Victorian drawing room, with a Tiffany floor lamp beside a colossal, hand-painted floor globe depicting the nineteenth-century world. There was an antique rolltop desk — locked, but the key we'd found didn't fit. In the corner a Willard longcase clock measured the hours.

"I don't get the 'shaken, not stirred' part," Stan said. "Unless the next clue is hidden in an Ian Fleming novel. Only I don't remember the word *heart* in any of his titles, just *eyes* and a *finger.*"

"Look," Madame said, standing next to a side table that was also a replica of a knight's breastplate, with a keyhole left of center, where the heart would be.

I inserted the key, turned it — and was rewarded with a satisfying *click.*

"Open it, Ms. Cosi!"

The "breastplate" was really two doors that opened in the center, to reveal all the makings of a fine bar — a variety of glasses, mixers, jiggers, cocktail strainers, a muddler, and a shaker made of sterling silver.

"Shaken, not stirred," I said. Inside the silver shaker I found another key, this one ancient and rusty.

I grabbed the second key and locked up the cocktail server.

"What's next?" Madame asked.

Stan squinted at the map. " 'In the cellar you might feel all alone, but beyond the hearth you'll find a home.' "

Down we went, to the basement. This was the only part of the mansion that lacked style and grace, but to be fair, there was not much one could do to glam a laundry room, three hot water heaters, and a giant industrial furnace.

There was a finished room with a television and radio, along with ironing boards, clothing trees, and a sewing machine.

There was also a subbasement, a few steps down from the main section. It lacked overhead lighting and was swathed in shadows. Stan found the fuse box, with a working flashlight set on top. He grabbed it and led the way.

The ceiling was low enough to make things feel claustrophobic. A few cautious steps took us through a doorway to an old coal bin and an ancient fireplace mounted in the wall.

"There's your hearth," I said.

The mantel held only dust. The fireplace itself was ancient, and constructed of crumbling sandstone. No fire had graced this hearth in years, though the back wall was still carbon black — or was it?

I took the flashlight, got down on my knees, and looked closer. What I thought was a trace of light stone peeking through the carbonized layers was actually a keyhole — a very old keyhole!

I inserted the key and tried to turn it, but the lock was too rusty. Since Stan's hands were much stronger, he took over; and when he finally managed it, the click sounded like a lock in some ancient dungeon.

Stan pushed the heavy door aside, and a gush of cool, damp air rushed out of a hidden room.

"What is this?" Stan whispered. "A top secret root cellar?"

"It's a railroad station," Madame declared. "An *Underground* Railroad station!"

EIGHTY-SIX

Stan cleared away cobwebs with his walking stick, then played the flashlight beam through the opening. It barely pierced the darkness beyond.

"I think there's more than one room," he announced excitedly.

He scrambled through, then turned and helped me cross the threshold. Madame wouldn't be kept out, even though the only way through the hearth's secret door was to crawl.

"I kissed the Blarney stone. I think I can handle this!" she insisted with a huff.

Once through, we realized the ceiling was much higher here than in the subbasement, and we all stood up. Stan moved the flashlight around and we saw wood-framed beds, their straw mattresses long since rotted away.

Names, dates, and symbols were scratched or carved into the rough stone walls. An antique lantern hung from a railroad spike embedded in a rough wooden support beam in the center of the space.

" 'Joshua from Ken-took-ee, Year of our Lord 1859,' " Stan read in a reverent whisper.

"That was probably etched by an abolitionist," Madame observed. "It was illegal to teach a slave to read or write. And because escaped slaves couldn't read, they used symbols and picture codes, even elaborately sewn quilts to trace their secret route to freedom."

Madame nodded her silver head.

"Thousands of slaves escaped before the Civil War," she said. "Some of them were hidden right here in this chamber. If only these walls could speak . . ."

From the expression on her face and emotion in her voice, I knew Madame was thinking of her own history — a young child forced to flee her home to escape slavery in a labor camp, or worse, when the Nazis invaded Paris, her beloved birthplace.

Using the flashlight's glow, Stan located the next chamber, and another room beyond that.

"I'm going deeper," he announced.

"Maybe you shouldn't," I warned. "It might be dangerous."

Madame and I noticed a scrabbling sound that made us both nervous. "Do I hear a mouse?"

"More likely a rat," Stan replied, unfazed. "And close."

It took Madame and me about ten seconds to scramble through the hearth door again. Amazing how the word *rat* can motivate!

Stan insisted on exploring a little longer, and we indulged him.

"I do hope the boy's careful," Madame said as he and his flashlight beam vanished around a dark corner.

"Do you really think this was used as a CIA dead drop?"

"It's more Ann Radcliffe than John le Carré, but, yes, I do."

We returned to the comfort of the finished area of the basement and waited almost fifteen minutes for Stan to return.

"I couldn't get the key to work again," he reported. "A little WD-40 should do the trick."

"What did you find, my boy? A long-lost copy of the Pentagon Papers?"

"Seven thousand pages would have been pretty obvious, Mrs. Dubois."

"Ah! I see the boy knows *some* history." She threw me a wink.

"Not just a boy, ma'am, a former soldier.

And every soldier knows *that* history — or should. Anyway, it's pretty elaborate down there. Three rooms that connect to an old tunnel, which leads to a city storm drain. I could see light at the end . . ."

"So it does go to the river!" Madame's eyes brightened. "That verifies the legend!"

"That also explains the rats," I said with a shiver.

"You should see those rooms," Stan gushed. "Old rotting beds and lanterns, broken shelves. It's like something in a museum."

"Museum!" I checked my watch. "Thanks for the reminder. The White House courier is going to be here any minute to pick up that package. Then I'm supposed to meet the Curator of the White House later this afternoon. I better hop to it . . ."

EIGHTY-SEVEN

"Well, what do you think?" I asked Quinn. "Could Abby and Stan have gone into the river and climbed into the storm drain?"

"It's extreme," Quinn replied. "But it's possible."

"Not so extreme," I said, rubbing my wet hair with one of the yacht's thick towels.

"This from a woman who just jumped into the Patapsco River."

"Exactly. I did it because I was desperate. And so were Abby and Stan. Think about it — Stan is ex-army and he's very strong, despite his weak leg and blind eye. He could have prepared for it, too, hid a rope or whatever he needed to make it easy for Abby."

"But why would Abby do it?" Quinn rose to make us another pot of coffee. "From what you told me, it sounds like she saw Stan as a friend — not serious husband material. After all, she remained engaged to her fiancé, and the Rose Garden wedding was still on. That doesn't sound like a young woman ready to run away with a lover."

"That's because you haven't heard the rest of the story."

"Okay, then tell me. Did you see Abby at the White House?"

"I did, but something else happened first. Something disturbing. And you need to hear that, too . . ."

EIGHTY-EIGHT

My second trip to the White House was (thank goodness) much calmer than my first. No race down Pennsylvania Avenue. No peeved Secret Service agents prodding me with high-tech scanners and innuendo. Not even a lengthy background review.

But one thing was the same — I was still worried about Abby.

A brief security check-in earned me a green guest badge, allowing me to move through the White House complex un-escorted. Nevertheless, I was glad to see Carol's rosy cheeks, blue eyes, and tasteful white bouffant greeting me once again at the East Wing entrance.

"No apron today," I said with a smile. This visit I'd had time to don my tailored blue suit with matching heels and sheer hose. I'd even tamed my bad-hair-day frizz into a neat and sleek, preppy-DC ponytail.

I asked Carol if she wouldn't mind escorting me to the curator's office. Part of me feared a wrong-turn collision with a wall of frowning Secret Service agents, but I also needed to ask a favor . . .

"Would you mind telling Abigail Parker that I'm here?"

"I don't mind in the least," she said in her gracious Virginia drawl. "Ms. Parker is looking forward to your coffee service at her upcoming wedding. We're all excited about the happy event . . ."

Once again, Carol and I traveled the yellow brick road rug, paralleling the Jacqueline Kennedy Garden. This led to the ground floor of the main building, where we strolled down the wide center hall with its dramatically vaulted ceiling.

I glimpsed the library and China Room through opened doors and recognized the closed door to the Diplomatic Reception Room, where I'd had lunch more than a week ago with Abby and the First Lady.

Finally, Carol gestured to the half-open doorway of the curator's office.

"Enjoy your time at the People's House, Ms. Cosi."

As Carol departed, I knocked lightly.

"Come in!" called a bespectacled young man. "Don't be shy. We won't bite — unless, of course, we've skipped lunch."

The windowless room was large but cramped with white bookcases covering nearly every inch of wall space. From the carpeted floor to the vaulted ceiling, volumes of all sizes were packed into the shelves.

The young man read my badge and smiled. "I'm Pete and that's Beatrice, Ms. Cosi." He gestured to an older woman, also wearing glasses, who briefly waved from her lighted workstation.

"Nice to meet you both."

"Helen stepped out for a minute," Pete explained, "but she left a file. She said she was anxious for you to review it." He pointed to a large wooden desk at the far end of the room.

"What does the curator want me to do?"

"You've been helping her with the White House contribution to the temporary Smithsonian exhibition, right?"

I nodded. "*Coffee and the Presidency* — the sidebar for the larger *Coffee in America* show."

"That's the problem. There's too much content for a sidebar. I believe she wants your opinion on what to keep and what to cut. The file should have instructions."

"Okay. I'll get right on that . . ."

I moved to the curator's desk, settling into

her comfortable swivel chair. Books of all sizes were stacked high, their pages flagged with colorful Post-it notes. But Pete didn't mention books. He said Helen Trainer was *anxious* for me to *review a file.*

Only one sat on her desktop, but it wasn't marked *Coffee* or *Smithsonian* or even *Presidential Joe.* This lone file was marked with one word, which was also a name. An ancient female name —

Bathsheba.

The file contained printed e-mail messages. I riffled through the short stack, but there was no mention of coffee. The e-mails documented a conversation that took place more than ten years ago between President Parker — when he was Senator Parker — and a deputy secretary of the State Department.

The two men were talking about a third man who'd died in Casablanca, Morocco. One particular paragraph caught my eye.

. . . I'm also thinking of Beth Noland and her young daughter. Why put them through a prolonged investigation? My friend, I need your help and support to put an end to this now, for everyone's benefit. I'll handle the President. It's important that we keep this between us. If the

details ever got out, it could be a PR
disaster . . .

"Beth Noland" had to be Elizabeth Noland Parker, now the First Lady. Her daughter was obviously Abby.

The senator (and soon-to-be President)
was trying to persuade a highly placed official at the State Department to help and
support him on ending an investigation.

What investigation? I had no idea.

Some of the conversation was in bureau-
cratic and diplomatic short-hand. Terms like
casus belli, D.C.M., demarche, SFOD-D, and
GS-15s.

To understand it, I would need time to
research the references they made, but one
thing rang clearer than the Liberty Bell —

There's a secret here, a scandal . . .

These e-mails would cause a public rela-
tions "disaster" if they ever got out, at least
that's how our current President saw it.

So why am I reading them?!

That's when I noticed the handbag. The
gorgeous leather purse sat on the chair next
to the desk. I'd seen this Fen Pouch three
times in my life. Once in the Manhattan
shop window where its high price forced
me to pass it by — and twice more in my
own coffeehouse, carried by the impeccably

dressed woman I'd seen dining with the late Jeevan Varma.

As a shiver went through me, a soft commotion at the office door was followed by Pete's voice —

"Yes, ma'am, Ms. Cosi's arrived. She's sitting at your desk . . ."

"Very good, Peter. Now I'd like you and Beatrice to start that cataloging work we talked about. All of the items for our sidebar are collected in the China Room. I want them photographed for our records before they're lent to the Smithsonian. Take your time . . ."

After Pete and Beatrice left, the White House Curator shut and locked the door. Then she went to Pete's workstation and activated a media file with a C-SPAN program on the historical significance of presidential nicknames.

If anyone stood listening at that closed door, they would hear the lighthearted lecture rather than any low conversation taking place farther inside the room.

Finally, the middle-aged brunette made her way over to me.

I'd been conversing with this woman by e-mail. We'd spoken a few times on the phone, but this was the first time I'd met her in person, and nothing prepared me for the shock.

Helen Hargood Trainer, Curator of the White House, was the late Jeevan Varma's girlfriend.

EIGHTY-NINE

My heart was pounding as Helen Trainer removed her pricey pouch from the chair, placed her posh posterior in it, and fixed me with a withering glare.

"Ms. Cosi, I want the truth from you. The whole truth. Right now."

"What truth?"

"You're obviously working with Jeevan Varma. And this is a shakedown of some kind. Did he put you up to this? Or was it the other way around? And who are you to him? A girlfriend?"

"Me? I thought *you* were his girlfriend!"

"I am no such thing! *You're* the one who sent me this computer flash drive." She reached into her bag, pulled it out, and tossed it onto the desk. "The printed e-mails you've been looking through were the whole of its contents. So explain yourself."

"Wait a minute," I said with some righteous indignation of my own. "That flash drive is not mine. A member of my staff found it in my coffeehouse. I assumed someone from the White House dropped it on the night of Abby's performance."

Helen sat back, her heated anger cooling to wariness. "Do you *trust* the staff member who found it?"

"I'd trust Tucker Burton with my life!"

"Where exactly did he find it?"

"I don't know."

"You need to ask him. Right now. Where's your phone?"

I pulled out my cell and gave Tuck a call. Thank goodness he picked up right away. I put him on speaker so Helen could hear him.

According to Tuck, he and Punch had been adjusting the lights in the star field on the wall, replacing the steady bulbs with ones that would subtly flicker. As he worked, he found a missing bulb. Taped to the socket was this flash drive.

"It was hidden there?" I asked. "Behind the stars?"

"Yes. Punch and I didn't know what to make of it, so we handed it to you . . ."

I ended the call and Helen's eyes glazed over. "If the flash drive was found *before* Abby's performance, then it was already there when the White House staff came in.

And, remember, you seated us all in the center of the room, nowhere near the star field on the wall."

"But you sat next to that wall on another night," I pointed out. "Do you remember? It was the night I saw you with Jeevan Varma. That's why I thought you were his girlfriend. I was going table to table asking about the menu, and —"

"You're right! Mr. Varma and I were sitting against the wall with the star field." Helen shook her head, astonished with her private revelation. "Jeevan Varma had these e-mails all along! He obviously hid the flash drive in your light fixtures. Wait till I get ahold of him. Ms. Cosi, I'm so angry. I could kill that man!"

Now I sat back in confusion, until I studied her face and realized —

"You don't know, do you?"

"Know what?"

"Jeevan Varma is already dead."

Helen listened in mild shock as I explained what happened the night Mr. Varma was (apparently) attacked.

"When he rushed into my back door, he smelled of alcohol, and I assumed he was drunk. But the sergeant who responded to my 911 call believes he was murdered. The autopsy found a needlestick in the back of his neck . . ."

Now at least I knew why Mr. Varma had rushed up to our Jazz Space. He hadn't come to the coffeehouse to confront the First Daughter. He'd come to retrieve the small computer flash drive that he'd hidden in the light fixtures. Seeing Abby in our club after hours was as much a surprise to him as it was to me.

But why hide the flash drive in our coffeehouse in the first place?

"Did he say anything?" Helen asked.

"Yes," I said, recalling his slurred statements to me at the back door — and then to Abigail Parker on the second floor.

"Well?" Helen said, leaning forward. "What did he say?"

I shifted, uneasy about revealing another word to this woman. For one thing, I was determined to shield Abby and Stan from this mess. Telling her more felt like a risk.

"Look, this case is in police hands," I said. "*You're* the one who needs to do some explaining. I'm sorry, but I don't know if I can trust you."

Helen's frown deepened. "Do you think I trust you?"

For a long moment, we sat in stalemate, staring at each other. The C-SPAN presidential lecture continued in the background,

456

the audience's occasional outbursts of laughter making us even edgier. Still, we stubbornly sat, neither of us willing to give up a word or clear up a thing, and then —

Knock, knock . . .

A light hand at the door was followed by a small voice.

"Hello? . . . It's me . . ."

The voice was Abigail Parker's.

NINETY

Helen unlocked the door, and the President's daughter hurried in, closed the door behind her, and stepped out of the way for Helen to relock it.

The silent choreography was done with such swift ease it appeared they'd done this many times before. *But why?*

A few minutes of explanation made things clearer. After Abby sat down and assured Helen and me that we could trust each other, the mood in the room changed. Then I learned a great deal, including the fact that Helen's position wasn't attached to any particular administration. She'd served for fourteen years, under three Presidents, which is why it wasn't until after President Parker took office that Helen and Abby had become friends.

"But what exactly brought you two together?" I asked.

"The piano," Abby said, exchanging a

glance with Helen, who went on to explain how the Steinway & Sons company had donated two special pianos to the United States of America. One ended up in the Smithsonian. The other remained on display in the White House's majestic Entrance Hall.

"The first time I saw Abby, she was gazing at that Steinway with a look of wonder on her face."

"And it's no wonder," Abby quipped with a shy smile. "It's a magnificent concert grand."

"The design is streamlined deco," Helen told me, "with carved eagles supporting the cabinet. When I saw Abby circling it, I asked her if she played. And she said . . . *A little.* So I invited her to try it out. Frankly, I expected 'Chopsticks.'" Helen closed her eyes. "Abby played an exquisite version of Mozart's Piano Sonata in A Major. It gave me chills. You know, President Harry Truman played that same piece on that very piano. It was one of his favorites . . ."

According to Helen, President Truman had dreamed of becoming a concert pianist, too. By fifteen, however, he decided that he would never be good enough. So he quit.

"Like our Abby here," Helen said, shaking her head. "She never played that beautiful

Steinway again, for fear of being overheard, even though I pleaded with her to share her gift. She preferred the privacy of her digital piano in the small music room upstairs. She always wore headphones so no one would know what she sounded like."

I turned to Abby. "How did you get interested in playing jazz?"

"That started a year ago," she confessed. "We had a guest performer in the White House, Mr. Wynton Marsalis. He spoke with such passion about musicianship that it stayed with me. I looked up his public talks on the Internet. After that, I was hooked. Helen suggested an online master class series from pianist Chick Corea, which I took. Then Helen suggested I work on replicating some of the solos of the great jazz pianists: Oscar Peterson, Bill Evans, Keith Jarrett —"

"Abby understands what true practice is," Helen declared. "Not simply playing but working on the sections that are difficult, working until you get them right." She paused. "My late husband was a concert pianist, Ms. Cosi, so Abby immediately captured my heart."

"Then it was you," I said, gawking at Helen. "You were the one who sent her the invitation to our Jazz Space Open Mike Night."

"Me?" Helen looked confused. "Heavens, no. I assumed Abby wanted to keep her music private, and I respected that . . ."

I sat back, still bothered by the mystery of that first invitation. Somebody wanted her to play at our coffeehouse. The question of *who* remained unanswered. But I was finding answers to other questions; and as the two friends continued to talk, I finally learned why Helen first contacted Jeevan Varma.

"Abby asked me to use my expertise as a historian to find out what happened to her father — her real father."

NINETY-ONE

"You have to understand, Ms. Cosi. My dad died overseas in a bombing. That's all I was ever told. He didn't marry my mother, and she never wants to talk about him, not even to me . . ."

She leaned forward. "Then a few months ago, my mother finally let something slip. She said if the truth ever got out about my father, it would be a terrible scandal. I had no idea what she meant — and when I pressed her, she refused to say anything more. That's when I went to Helen and asked her to research the truth about him."

Abby paused and looked down at her hands in her lap. "I still remember the day . . . right after my dad died, going into my room and finding all of his photos missing. I was only eight years old. I cried and cried . . ."

"That's so cruel . . ." I whispered. *How could anyone do that to a little girl?*

"I can barely recall what my dad looked like, sounded like. But I remember that he was a loving man and a very good musician. He taught me to play the piano. Do you know the first song I learned?"

" 'Somewhere Over the Rainbow'?"

A sad smile came over her. "That was the second song. The first was 'Chopsticks.' "

I studied her a moment. "Is that why you played 'Chopsticks' on national television?"

She nodded. "I was furious with my mother for forcing me to perform alone on that show. Then she announced my wedding. And out marched Preston! I didn't see any of it coming." She wrung her hands. "It was my own little rebellion, playing 'Chopsticks' like that. And I let loose on my mother, too. But it cost me."

"Cost you?" I frowned. "How did it cost you, Abby?"

"My mother said my behavior proved that I was 'unstable' again. She decided that all the publicity I got because of my performance was now a security risk. So I'm not allowed to go back to class. I attend from the White House, using Skype, and I'll be taking my final exams here, too. My mother even hired a nurse."

"For what?"

"Medications. I take them three times a

day, like clockwork. If I don't, Mother's threatened to send me back to the hospital — the one that took care of me after I . . ." She held up her wrist, the one with the terrible scars.

I leaned toward her. "Stan is worried about you, Abby. He wants to see you."

"I know, but Stan can't come here. Preston works in the West Wing. If he saw Stan's name on the daily guest list, it would be a disaster. I've tried to tell my mother about my feelings for Stan, but she says I'm talking crazy. She says, 'You don't marry boys like Stan. You *play* with them, sure, but you don't marry them.' She says Preston is devoted to me, but Stan is just infatuated with the idea of being with a President's daughter. She says I'll be very sorry if I betray Preston and throw him out for some 'drummer boy.' She says musicians aren't interested in being saddled with a wife and kids — and the truth is, Ms. Cosi, I do want to be married and have children. I want a family of my own."

"Whoa, hold on," I said. "How do you know Stanley McGuire isn't interested in those things, too?"

"He never talks to me about things like that. I mean, he says he wants me to be happy. But *everyone* says that, and . . ."

Once again, she stared at the scars on her wrist. "I'm not sure I even know how."

"Of course you know how. You're happy when you play music. I've seen it. And you looked *very* happy onstage with Stan ten days ago. When you kissed him, you were beaming."

"That's because I love him. But I love my family, too, and I have a duty to them . . ."

There it is again, the Stepford Abby voice.

"I understand what you're saying," I assured her, "and it's noble of you to think of your family. But I believe they're taking advantage of you. I also know how difficult it is to watch your child make her own decisions. But that's what adulthood is, Abby, making choices for yourself, standing up for who you truly are, not what others bully or manipulate or guilt you into being. Adulthood is filled with trials and burdens and hard decisions. But you'll never find peace and happiness, you'll never meet your true self or free your full potential if you're hobbled by what people think, or define your limits by what others prescribe for you."

Tears welled in Abby's eyes. "I know you're right, Ms. Cosi . . . but with my past . . . and my mother . . . and the army of security . . . and the medications . . . you don't understand what I'm up against . . . I'm feeling so confused . . ."

I took her hand, the one attached to that scarred wrist, and held it in both of mine. "Would it help you to sort out your feelings if you could see Stan again, face-to-face? Spend a little time with him?"

"Are you kidding?" Her foggy eyes instantly brightened. "I would die to see Stan!"

"Then come to the Smithsonian party next Saturday night. He'll be there."

"Really?"

"Really."

"Then I'll be there, too. I won't miss it!"

A loud *KNOCK, KNOCK, KNOCK* made us all jump.

"Ms. Parker? Are you in there?"

The tone was deep and authoritative. Even through the thick door and the drone of the C-SPAN lecture, I recognized the voice of Agent Sharpe of the United States Secret Service.

NINETY-TWO

Like a rabbit caught in the hunter's sights, Abby froze, dark eyes wide.

Helen moved to answer the door, but Abby grabbed her arm.

"I'll go," she said.

A few steps later, the President's daughter turned and whispered, "Thank you, Ms. Cosi, for helping me and Stan. Thank you . . ."

"It's almost time for your next class, Ms. Parker," Agent Sharpe informed her in the doorway. "And Mr. Emory has been looking for you —"

"Honey-bunny, there you are!"

Preston Emory's golden good looks moved into the frame. He hooked Abby's waist, pulled her close, and kissed her cheek. She smiled blandly.

"What are you up to in there, my darling?" He peeked in at us.

Abby quickly pulled him away. "You know

I enjoy visiting with Mrs. Trainer," she said, voice diminishing as they moved down the majestic hall. "She knows so much about history. I *always* learn something when I stop by her office . . ."

Helen rose to reclose the door, jumping slightly when she found Agent Sharpe still lurking there.

Like Preston, the Secret Service agent peered into the room, but his gaze was more than curious. He looked openly suspicious.

"Hello again, Ms. Cosi," Sharpe said. "What are you up to in there?"

"We're working on a contribution to a Smithsonian exhibition," Helen quickly replied, frozen smile in place. "And we must get back to it. Thank you, Agent Sharpe!"

Helen closed the door, practically in his face. Then she stood, ear against wood, until Sharpe's steps receded.

With a frustrated shake of her head, she went to Pete's computer and selected another online lecture —

The Oval Office is the official office of the President of the United States. Located in the White House's West Wing, the office has a unique elliptical shape. Join us now, as we will explore the history and meaning of that shape . . ."

Helen's frozen smile melted as she strode back to me and sat down.

"Get this flash drive out of here," she rasped.

I picked up the small, plastic rectangle and moved it toward the jacket of my little blue suit.

"Not in your pocket," she whispered. "Somewhere safer."

My eyebrows rose as she pointed down her neckline.

"You want me to hide it in my . . . ?"

She nodded.

With a shrug, I did as she asked. Then I asked her to tell me everything she knew about Abby's father and Jeevan Varma —

Two dead men.

NINETY-THREE

"Andy Aamir Ferro, that was the name of Abby's real father," Helen began. "She remembered her mother calling him Andy in this country and Aamir when they visited him in Morocco."

"What was he doing over there?"

"From what I've been able to dig up, he was a young professor at a local university. His own mother was an American who taught at several schools in France, including the Sorbonne. His father was a French national of Arabic descent. Both are deceased. Andy/Aamir was born in Virginia, making him a U.S. citizen. But he quickly became interested in world music, and he studied in France, Spain, and Morocco, as well as here in DC."

"How did he die?"

"He was killed in the 2003 bombings in Casablanca, the worst act of terrorism in Morocco's history. There was a hearing about the death of Andy/Amir and I reviewed some redacted testimony by a deputy secretary of the State Department —"

"Redacted? You mean . . ."

"Anything deemed classified was blacked out."

"I see."

"But what bothered me was the terseness of the deputy secretary's testimony. It was in such shorthand that I knew he'd had off-line discussions before he'd come to the hearing room. So I decided to review his e-mail correspondence with the head of the committee — Senator Parker. I used an FOIA request to look up the deputy secretary's archived e-mails for the entire month before the hearing —"

"FOIA?"

"Freedom of Information Act — it's used by journalists, historians, and citizens to request documents from the government and review the work of our public officials. I wanted to learn more about the deputy secretary's testimony, but guess what? When the archived e-mails arrived, there was a black hole, a terribly suspicious one. Rose Mary Woods suspicious . . ."

"Rose Mary Woods? President Nixon's secretary? You think someone deleted the e-mails?"

"Yes. As I said, classified documents are redacted when they're released, the sensitive information blacked out. But these e-mails weren't redacted. They were missing completely."

"What did you do next?"

"I contacted the Office of the CIO at the State Department with my concerns about the missing e-mails, and Mr. Jeevan Varma got back to me. For years, he's worked in IT for State, and I was sure he could help me locate the e-mails. But he did not want to meet at the White House — he was emphatic about it. So I suggested meeting at the Village Blend on the night of one of Abby's Open Mike performances. I thought, *If this man has information, I'll call Abby over and we can all quietly talk.* But he claimed to know nothing of Abby's father *or* why the e-mails were missing!"

"Why do you think he lied to you? And why meet in the first place?"

"Now that I know he was hiding that computer flash drive, I think Mr. Varma must have thought one of two things: Either I was planning to offer him money for the missing e-mails. Or I was setting up a sting to have him arrested for deleting them. Either way, he had to play it safe. And that was very smart. He didn't want the evidence on him. But he wanted it close by. I remember he was already sitting at that table near the wall when I arrived."

"Why do you think he kept it there? Why not take it with him?"

"When our meeting was over, I didn't leave. I told him I was waiting to say hello to the President's daughter before her Secret Service detail escorted her back to college. After that, he left very quickly. Either he was planning to come back to retrieve it, or he was planning another meeting. Perhaps with a journalist to sell the information. Or with someone else who would pay him handsomely for it — a rival of the President, for instance, who would use it to harm him politically."

"Helen, how secret are these e-mails, really? I mean, if this digital discussion took place between Senator Parker and the deputy secretary of State, then why didn't you simply request to review the missing e-mails among Parker's archives?"

"Because they don't exist."

"What?"

"For years, officials have been conducting business using private accounts, which means there is no transparency, no answering to the public, and no record for historians."

She frowned in frustration. "Rose Mary Woods is infamous for erasing eighteen minutes of a crucial Watergate tape — 'the eighteen-minute gap.' What much of the American public doesn't realize is that there is a *thirty-year gap* when it comes to archiving government e-mails. And Senator Parker was part of that. The deputy secretary, on the other hand, followed the law, clearly stated in the Federal Records Act, and used the government servers, which allowed his e-mails to be archived. As a result, the *only* historic record of the e-mail discussion about Abby's father is right here, in this file, and, well —"

She pointed to my bra.

"Clare, we don't yet know who killed Mr. Varma, so *do not* hand that flash drive to anyone in the federal government. Only give it to the Metro DC detective assigned to Mr. Varma's murder case."

"There is no detective assigned. But I trust Sergeant Price. He's been questioning me and talking to Mr. Varma's family."

"Good. Very good."

"What about this secret file you've labeled *Bathsheba*? Can you decipher what the two men are discussing and why?"

"I recognize a name in these e-mails from my years here at the White House — the

474

previous President's chief of staff. He lives in Virginia now, and I'm going to reach out to him to see if he'll speak with me. It will all be off the record, of course, but I can and will do the research I'm trained to do as a historian to put the pieces of this story together. Then I'm going to tell Abigail. This is the People's House, not the Parkers' or any one President's, and I am the custodian of its history. That girl is an adult. She came to me in search of answers about her own history, and she deserves to know the truth."

"But, Helen, from what you're telling me, that truth got Mr. Varma killed."

"That's why we have to be careful, you and I."

"Then I'll take this flash drive right to the police precinct."

"No, Clare, don't do that."

"Why not?"

"Because you may be under surveillance. We don't yet know who murdered Mr. Varma, and we don't want this evidence to 'disappear' once it's in police hands. Just go about your business, as usual, and ask Sergeant Price to come to the coffeehouse. There's nothing suspicious about a police officer stopping for coffee."

"No, I guess —"

"Shhh. I hear voices . . ."

. . . and over the years, Presidents have decorated the Oval Office to suit their personal tastes . . .

Beyond the online lecture, I heard voices, too — a man and a woman. When we realized it was simply Pete and Beatrice returning to their desks, we sat back with relief.

Helen shoved *Bathsheba* into a desk drawer and quickly flipped open books. "Let's get on with our other work, Clare."

"Fine," I whispered as Helen's staff burst into the room, "just tell me how long you think it will take to get some answers?"

"I don't know. But I'll be sure to see you at the Smithsonian party. I'll update you then . . ."

. . . and because of its closed elliptical shape, all sound is sent to that focal point in the room. By design, then, the President can sit at his desk and hear whatever anyone in his office is saying, even when whispering . . .

NINETY-FOUR

The doors to the Smithsonian's National Museum of American History opened at eight o'clock sharp. By eight thirty, most of the invited guests had passed through security. Now, at nine, the party was in full swing, and I was nervously watching and waiting for the First Family to arrive.

The venue was Flag Hall, located at the entrance to the Star-Spangled Banner gallery, home to the flag that inspired our national anthem. The walls of this vast space were magically illuminated with shifting colors — electric blue to ivory white to dramatic rose red. Laser lights projected giant stars onto this changing canvas, as well as the ceiling and running balconies, where guests could view the festivities below.

On the far end of the room, an eighteen-piece orchestra played beneath a shimmering replica of our U.S. flag, built from hundreds of reflective tiles.

As for the Village Blend's contribution, I'd set up a wine and spirits bar, an espresso bar, and a *drinkable* exhibit I called *Good to the Last American Drop,* where guests could enjoy four-ounce sample cups of Matt's specially sourced coffees from Hawaii as well as Central and South America.

Tonight's guests would also have access to all four levels of "America's Attic," including a first look at the museum's *Coffee in America* exhibition and the *Coffee and the Presidency* sidebar that Helen and I had worked on.

Among our star artifacts were Teddy Roosevelt's "bathtub"-sized coffee cup; Jacqueline Kennedy's sterling silver coffee service; the last cup Abe Lincoln drank coffee from before leaving for Ford's Theatre; and the coffee urn, on loan from its home at Monticello, an exquisite example of Parisian silversmithing, purchased by Thomas Jefferson in 1789.

I'd even found a *working* replica of Jefferson's urn to serve our Great Americas blend, which I'd created expressly for this event.

Finally, the pièce de résistance: on the courtesy table next to the urn, we'd placed three hundred personalized Thomas Jefferson coffee mugs, each inscribed with a guest's name and the Founding Father's famous quote —

Coffee, the favorite drink of the civilized world.

It was certainly true tonight. So many famous faces were here from politics and pop culture, it was hard not to be starstruck. And so many approached me to compliment the coffee that I felt like Dorothy opening her eyes to find the world in Technicolor.

Despite the glitter of the room and the glamour of party dresses and evening jackets, I was still struggling to keep one ferocious worry at bay.

I thought by tonight all my anxieties over Mr. Varma's secret flash drive would have been "uploaded" to the possession of Sergeant Price of the DC Metro PD. Unfortunately, that never happened, and I'd found out why only a few hours ago . . .

It was early afternoon when the Village Blend's van pulled up to the museum's loading dock. The Secret Service advance team was already conducting sweeps in anticipation of the presidential visit, and I was helping Tito and Freddie unload dollies of our fresh-baked Double-Chocolate Espresso Cupcakes and thermal containers

479

of our No-Churn Coffee Ice Cream.

As the two young men pushed the goodies into the depths of the museum, I stepped outside for a breath of cool spring air. Releasing my messy ponytail, I was happy to spot a familiar face —

"Officer Landry!" I waved. "Over here."

Patrolman Landry and another young uniformed cop had been wrestling police barricades into place. Landry signaled his buddy that he was taking five. Boyish dimples flashing, he hustled over to greet me.

"Hey there, Ms. Cosi . . ." He pointed to my bulky chef jacket. "I hardly recognized you without those curves."

Oh, brother, here we go. "Sorry to disappoint you, but nobody works on a loading dock wearing a Fen halter dress . . ."

Actually, I couldn't wait to put it on. Made of a luxurious deep blue silk, the garment's V neckline flowed to a fitted waist with a full skirt that skimmed flatteringly over my full hips (hiding a multitude of sins, including one too many "samples" of Luther's brownies). The beautiful draping continued into an offbeat yet elegant asymmetrical hem. Sheer, nude hose finished the outfit, along with that simple string of pearls my daughter gave me — and my new strappy heels were killer, too.

Landry grinned. "Is that what you'll be wearing later? Because I'm going to be on external security all night. I'd like a look at that!"

"Okay, now you're just fishing for free coffee."

"Hey, I wouldn't say no to a cup, especially if *you're* pouring. Like I told you already, I love older ladies. You know what you want and you go for it —"

"And here's what I want from you, Officer: *information.* I've left several messages for Sergeant Price, asking him to stop by my coffeehouse, but he hasn't come by or returned my calls."

Landry rubbed the back of his neck. "Sorry, Ms. Cosi, I'll be honest. I'm not sure I should tell you why . . ."

"I think you'd better. I have new evidence concerning the Jeevan Varma case . . ."

NINETY-FIVE

Landry scratched his head. "What sort of evidence?"

I glanced around the loading dock. A few Secret Service agents were loitering nearby, but none were paying attention to us. Still, I stepped closer to Landry and lowered my voice.

"I'm holding Mr. Varma's flash drive with e-mails he deleted from the State Department servers. The White House Curator, Helen Trainer, is willing to make a statement explaining why that's important. If the sergeant is scheduled for external security, we can get this over with tonight."

"Sorry. Price isn't scheduled to be here. But if it's any help, I can file the evidence and ask the detectives to follow up."

"Detectives?"

"Yes, Ms. Cosi, the sergeant . . . well, he . . ."

The young officer hesitated again.

"Come on, spill it," I pressed, and then, though I hated doing it, I flashed Landry that smile I'd used on him the first night we met. "Please . . ."

"Oh, all right . . ." Landry lowered his voice. "Price mentioned that cook of yours. The one who used to work for you? The guy must be holding one terrible grudge. I'm sure that's why he gave the statement he did."

"What statement?"

Landry paused again. "Did you say something about free coffee?"

"Of course! You and the other officers are more than welcome to enjoy my coffee tonight."

"Good deal. Okay, here's the scoop. Your ex-cook told Price that you're a liar and a thief. He said not to trust what you say. He said you've been stealing from the business and he caught you, which is why you fired him . . ."

That son of a . . . "Chef Tad Hopkins is the liar. And the thief. I need to explain that. And I have witnesses."

"You'll get your chance. Sergeant Price turned the case over to the detective squad. They'll be following up on his leads."

"How do I contact these detectives?"

"The case has to be assigned. Then they'll

come to you. You better warn your witnesses. They shouldn't leave town."

"Don't worry, my people will be available whenever the detectives want to speak with them. And Helen Trainer works in the White House. She's not going anywhere."

Just then, Landry's partner whistled and waved him over.

"Got to go," he said.

"Thank you," I said sincerely. "And tell your fellow officers that I'll have a coffee urn set up for self service. Go in through this dock, use the stairs or elevator, slip into the hall, and you'll see it."

"Okay, I'll spread the word." Landry paused and gave me that look again, that hot MILK look. "How about I give you a ride home? After the party?"

"I appreciate the offer, but I have a ride — and a boyfriend."

"Hey, it was worth a try . . ." Dimpled smile still flashing, he strode away.

I kept smiling, too, but I wasn't happy.

With homicide detectives about to be assigned to Jeevan Varma's case, things were getting serious. Chef Hopkins was out to get me, and Helen Trainer was the only witness to my version of these strange events.

Along with Abby and Stan, a little voice reminded me.

I didn't want to involve the President's daughter, and I vowed to keep her out of this for as long as I could. But if it came down to defending myself in a real murder charge, I might have no choice.

NINETY-SIX

A few hours later, Flag Hall was lit up and so was my ex-husband.

"Great party," Matt said, sidling up to me.

My Coffee Hunter business partner looked exceedingly sharp in his designer evening jacket, black beard trimmed, hair-bush slicked into a neat ponytail.

Although the buffet table wouldn't open until the First Family arrived, the aromas now emanating from the area piqued every-one's appetite, including mine.

In addition to selections from our popular Jazz Space menu, Luther and Joy were preparing to serve succulent sliders of my Cherry and Port–Glazed Pork Tenderloin on fresh-baked Parker House Rolls; Breaded Chicken Tenders with Luther's Carolina Sweet Mustard BBQ Dipping Sauce; Creamy Casserole Cups of Pennsylvania Dutch Noodles with Diced Pieces of Smoked Virginia Ham; and my own secret recipe of Coffee-Glazed Barbecued Chicken Drumsticks.

In the meantime, my waitstaff moved among dozens of tall tables draped with white cloths, offering guests canapés and champagne as well as sweets and espresso shots from silver trays.

Matt nabbed one of Luther's Bourbon Street Brownies — rich chocolate, good Kentucky bourbon, and a kiss of French roast to deepen the flavor of the gourmet chocolate.

"Oh, baby, these are sinful," he murmured, mouth half-full. "And speaking of things that give me pleasure, I'm lovin' that new dress of yours, Clare, especially the neckline."

"Then perhaps you should try looking *at* it, and not *down* it."

"Hey, don't knock therapy."

"Therapy?!"

"Looking at a woman's cleavage prolongs a man's life. It's a scientific fact."

"Have you been drinking? I mean, something other than coffee?"

"I'm not kidding. The report was published by the *New England Journal of Medicine* from research conducted in Germany."

"And it sounds like something thought up in a beer hall."

"I'm proud to say I was way ahead of those scientists. My study of cleavage began at a tender age, and I'd rate yours in the top ten percentile."

"Okay, enough . . ."

I really wasn't bothered by my ex-husband. It was just Matt being Matt. But right now, his attention to that particular part of my anatomy reminded me all too abundantly that I was catering a party full of politicians, pundits, and press, not to mention the President himself, with a flash drive full of stolen state secrets pinned to my lace-trimmed Victoria's Secret.

For days, I'd been looking over my shoulder, wondering if I was being watched. I looked twice at every customer and three times at loitering pedestrians with sunglasses.

What next? Deep Throat?

Then the preparations for the party went into high gear, including a three-day roasting trip back up to New York, and I'd put the paranoia aside. But now I was back, anxious again, the flash drive still cozied up to my private parts.

"So what about it?" Matt waggled his eyebrows. "Don't you want to prolong my life?"

"Will you stop already? What would you

say if I walked up to you and announced that looking at *your* private parts would prolong *my* life . . . Wait! Don't answer that!"

"Are you sure? Because I'm happy to drop drawers in the name of preventive medicine."

"Please, Allegro, keep your pants on. And the next time you have an espresso-tini, leave out the *tini*."

"I swear, I haven't touched a drop. I'm drunk with *happiness*."

"Hum."

"It's true! Tonight the President and First Lady will drink coffee I sourced, made from beans you roasted in my family's landmark shop. My amazing daughter is preparing food for Washington's elite. My mother is across the room charming the Speaker of the House *and* the Chief Justice of the Supreme Court, and our new Jazz Space is the talk of DC."

"Yet your gaze appears to be missing the big picture."

Matt leaned in again. "Not from this perspective."

Shaking my head, I waved over a familiar face — an intelligent man with an air of gentility whose decorum and sensitivity might give Matt an example to follow.

NINETY-SEVEN

"Hello, Ms. Cosi. Excellent service tonight."

A smiling Bernie Moore raised his personalized coffee mug. "And this blend is outstanding. Some of the best coffee I've ever tasted."

Matt's ego, sufficiently inflated, flashed the man a friendly grin. "Who is your incredibly discerning friend, Clare?"

After quick introductions, I faced the music critic. Beneath his black suit, he wore an open-collared black shirt à la Johnny Cash, his white ponytail and trimmed beard a striking yet attractive contrast.

"So how did you wrangle an invitation to this?" I asked. "Are you a big donor to the museum or President Parker's reelection campaign?" Dozens of the latter were here tonight.

"I'm with the band . . ."

He paused to pick up a goodie from a passing tray — one of my "Hawaiian"

Chocolate Chip Cookies, loaded with macadamia nuts and sprinkled with hand-chopped, chocolate-covered Kona coffee beans. Then he tipped his head to the museum's resident ensemble, the Jazz Masterworks Orchestra.

"Did you know the U.S. Congress funds those guys?"

"Why is that?"

"Because they're a living museum, charged with 'presenting and perpetuating the legacy of jazz in American culture.' They're a tight group, too, and . . ." Bernie's grin widened after he sampled my cookie. "Oh, man, this is incredibly good. Anyway," he said between more contented bites, "I promised the band if they got me in, I'd write about the gig."

As the room's shifting light changed from ivory to electric blue, Bernie's white beard and ponytail seemed to glow in contrast. His olive complexion appeared darker, too, and I noticed small white scars along his hairline.

"I was hoping to see you, Ms. Cosi," Bernie admitted. "Do you know if Abby's coming tonight? Is she going to perform?"

"Please, call me Clare. I know Abby's on the guest list, and I'm hoping she comes, but I doubt she'll play."

He nodded, smile disappearing. "I suspected as much, after that debacle on television —"

Before he could say more, we were interrupted by a high-spirited call.

"Clare! I didn't know you liked men with beards! And here you are, with *two* of them!"

It was Helen Hargood Trainer, waving at me from ten yards away. Lifting a sloshing champagne glass over her head, she wended her way through the crowd.

Helen looked chic tonight in a midnight black designer gown with silver trim. Her hair was done up in a sleek chignon, silver hair comb and earrings shimmering against her dark locks.

"Oh, I just love men with beards!" Her gaze ping-ponged from Matt to Bernie, who seemed especially entertained by the attention.

"Did you know that only five Presidents wore beards?" Helen asked after I made quick introductions. "Four of them were veterans of the Civil War. But Lincoln was the first to enter the White House with a beard — and it wasn't even his idea! While he was running for the presidency, a young girl wrote to him. She's the one who suggested the craggy lines of his face needed facial hair."

"A beard *can* hide more than a few flaws," Bernie agreed.

"And you *can't* shave in the tropics," Matt added.

"That's true in the desert, too," Bernie said. "In the wild areas of the world, beards are not a fashion statement."

"Ulysses 'Unconditional Surrender' Grant was the second President with a beard."

"Is that so?" Bernie said, snagging one of our Boston Cream Pie Cupcakes (for tonight's theme, I'd kissed the chocolate glaze with a hint of espresso).

Once again, Bernie made yummy sounds.

Helen pointed to the dessert. "Did you know the Boston Cream Pie was invented at the very hotel where Jack Kennedy proposed to Jackie? The Parker House restaurant — they invented the famous rolls, too. Table 40 is where he asked her. He got down on one knee to present her with the ring, a custom-made emerald and diamond of nearly three carats each with baguette cut diamond accents."

Bernie smiled as he finished his cupcake. "You must be a historian, Mrs. Trainer. Or do you harbor a secret ambition to appear on *Jeopardy!*?"

Helen's light mood changed. She drained

her champagne glass. "I'm the curator of the White House, but I don't know how much longer I want the job."

Helen signaled Freddie and grabbed a replacement bubbly from his tray.

"I probably shouldn't mention this, but you have to hear it, Clare." Helen leaned close. "I came into work this morning and found my office had been searched. Nothing extreme, but I noticed little things had been tampered with. My computer was on, too, and I always shut it down."

Helen sipped her champagne, looking at me over her glass. "Only *one file* was missing."

I touched my heart, and Helen nodded.

She got the message. I still have the flash drive . . .

"There's something funny going on in the People's House, and it started with the current administration," Helen continued, eyes glassy. "What's next, a Secret Service escort out the door? All because I tried to help Abby."

She took a final gulp that finished the bubbly.

Bernie leaned close. "If I may ask, how did you help Abby?"

"I found out the truth about her father," she replied.

494

"Helen," I warned, "we shouldn't talk about this here."

"You're right. Why ruin the evening?" She looked at Bernie. "But I do love this man's beard. It reminds me so much of my late husband's —" Then Helen surprised us all by reaching out and touching his cheek.

Blinking in surprise at her own bold gesture, she glanced down at her still-empty glass. "I need another drink. Something stronger!"

Bernie chivalrously offered his arm. "Let's find the bar together."

"Helen, wait," I pleaded. "We have to talk. It's important."

I have to tell her about Sergeant Price turning the case over to detectives!

But Helen waved me off as she and Bernie melted into the crowd. "Catch me later, Clare. I'm not going anywhere until I sample that buffet . . ."

"She was fun," Matt quipped. Then he patted my shoulder. "I'll check on Joy in the kitchen, see if she needs any help."

"Thanks . . ."

I was about to recheck the Jefferson urn when I noticed a contingent of Secret Service agents enter Flag Hall and spread out all over the room, covering every door and exit.

Among them I spied Agent Sharpe, exhibiting a rare smile at his post as a svelte woman flirted with him. Her strawberry blond hair was pinned up, the better to show off her long neck and stunning scarlet gown with its sexy plunging back. Her silhouette looked familiar and when she turned in profile, I realized it was Mike's boss, Katerina Lacey.

Curious, I observed her easy banter with Agent Sharpe. It was more than friendly. You didn't invade personal space that closely unless you wanted to flirt — or intimidate.

And then I felt the presence of my own personal space invader.

A young woman in a pink party dress had moved out of the crowd to hover at my shoulder. For a moment I wondered if this perky, young Latina was shyly attempting to compliment my coffee, because she held her personalized gift cup to her lips for a long moment, long enough for me to read the name printed there — *Lidia Herrera*.

Lidia? That's when I remembered where I'd seen her before. The White House. This was Katerina's eager assistant, the one who'd followed her boss out of the First Family residence, overburdened by a tall stack of legal-sized files, tottering on too-high heels.

I watched Lidia's eyes drift toward Katerina and Agent Sharpe. She smiled crookedly as she lowered her cup.

"My boss loves men with guns," she announced. "I think she collects them."

"Men?" I asked. "Or guns? Or both?"

"That's why she likes *your* man," said Lidia, ignoring my question. "And by the way, *where is Michael Quinn* tonight?"

I couldn't stop my frown, but I remained silent as stone.

"*Baltimore,* right? With that cute, young detective . . ." Lidia Herrera cocked her head and put one hand on her hip. "Word up, girlfriend. Michael likes brown sugar, and they have a *thang* goin' on."

"So you're here to bait me? Or pump me for information? Or both?"

She snorted and looked away.

"I assume your boss put you up to this?" I pressed, and one glance in Katerina's direction told me I was right. She was practically salivating in anticipation of my reaction. "Do you actually *like* working for that female python?"

"Ms. Lacey gets things done, and she's going places. Someday she's going to be attorney general."

I shook my head. *Do creatures like Katerina*

attract other creatures? Or does she create them? Or both?

Lidia Herrera touched my gift cup to her lips again and made a face.

"This coffee's grown stale," she said with a smirk. "I think I need something fresher. But I suspect you've heard *that* complaint before."

"You know what, Lidia? I'd suggest a new pour, but it won't help you."

"Why is that?"

"Because you haven't lived long enough to understand that everything has a freshness date. And if you keep twisting the good in you to get what you want, one day you'll wake up to find everything in your cup's gone bad."

"Hmph" was her only reply before she spun on her spikey heels and toddled away.

NINETY-EIGHT

Mere moments after Katerina 2.0 lit up my life, the band struck up a rousing rendition of "Hail to the Chief."

Despite my increasing list of anxieties, a shiver of excitement went through me as the explosion of applause greeted the President and First Lady. Entering arm in arm, they were followed by their son, Kip Parker, and his escort for the evening, a willowy blonde in yellow with a dazzling smile.

I breathed a sigh of relief when Abigail, in her favorite color — black — made an entrance, unsmiling and uncomfortable, Preston Emory at her side. I knew I wasn't the only one relieved to see her. I'd placed Stan behind our sampling bar. Now, when I tried to catch his attention, he only had eyes for Abby.

The arrival of the President meant the food service could begin. Though this was not a sit-down meal for guests, a table was reserved for the First Family. They weren't expected to line up for their food, either. The experienced White House waitstaff was here to serve them.

But before they could eat, the presidential couple had to make it across this crowded room filled with fawning supporters — no mean feat, even for the Leader of the Free World.

There was much shaking of hands, air kissing, and even a few backslaps, so it took an inordinate amount of time just to navigate. As they approached our coffee bar, I hurried over and tugged Stan's sleeve.

"Okay, you're on. Time to ditch the apron and put on the jacket. You know the plan."

Stan did his quick change, then paused. "I don't have a mirror, Ms. Cosi. How do I look?"

I grinned at the new Stan. His sharp-pressed pants, shiny Oxfords, and black evening jacket made the man, but it was the black satin eye patch that made him over-the-top *dashing*.

"It looks to me like this party lost a humble waiter, and gained a gallant guest." I squeezed his rock-solid shoulder. "All right, James Bond. You're on."

Stan grabbed the single, bright red rose he'd stashed among the supplies.

"One more stop," he said and made his way over to the band.

Now the President and Mrs. Parker were only a few feet away from me. As they passed, I greeted the First Lady with a welcoming nod, and received a cool smile in return.

Then I called to Abby.

"Hello, Ms. Cosi," she said, extending a polite hand.

"We've missed you so much at the Village Blend," I cried, opening my arms like a loving Italian nonna. Before Abby could react, I wrapped the surprised First Daughter in an embrace, squeezed her close, and whispered in her ear.

"Find the ruby slippers. Someone is waiting to take you over the rainbow."

I stepped back. The smile on Abby's face told me she'd gotten the coded message. Following the First Daughter closely, Sharon Cage, in a crisp blue suit, raised a suspicious blond eyebrow at me as she passed.

Finally the members of the First Family were seated and served. Kip and Preston seemed more interested in glad-handing and networking than they were in their meals — or their dates. After a few bites of food, the young men excused themselves to "mingle," leaving Abby and Kip's date to fend for themselves.

The President and First Lady were too engrossed in each other to notice. They touched at every opportunity, they laughed at their own banter, and shared food from each other's forks. They weren't just a loving couple, they were still demonstrably in love with each other, despite the whirlwind of Washington elite around them. Seeing them in person made me realize just how much the President treasured his First Lady, despite the shadows he'd seen in her past.

After a few minutes, Abby excused herself. I couldn't hear what she told her family, but I knew where she was headed.

I silently crossed my fingers for Abby and Stan, and was going to grant them privacy — until I spotted Sharon Cage following Abby out of Flag Hall and into the American Stories area of the museum.

Now I was worried.

If the overzealous Secret Service agent interfered with this young couple, it could ruin everything.

But I was relieved to see Cage hanging back, lurking out of sight as she watched Abby approach Stan, who was waiting in front of those sparkling red slippers.

I stayed back, too, and separately Cage and I witnessed Abby's first meeting with Stan in more than two weeks.

I couldn't hear their words, but I didn't need to. Their body language told their story: two people who needed each other the way the rest of us needed food to eat and air to breathe.

When Stan offered her the red rose, their hands touched. Suddenly Abby's arms were around Stan's neck and he was holding her as if she were the most precious thing in the whole wide world.

At that moment, the orchestra in Flag Hall struck up the first phrase from "Somewhere Over the Rainbow," and Abby's eyes began to tear. Stan whispered something to her, and she nodded, fat drops raining down her cheeks, onto her shining smile. Then Stan kissed her and she was there with him, over the rainbow.

The music swelled and they began to dance, Stan leading, Abby's dark head resting against his sturdy shoulder, oblivious to the history around them.

When the song ended, the couple strolled away, still clinging to each other. Agent Cage stepped back, letting them pass into the Documents Gallery next door.

And then, instead of following her charge,

Sharon Cage shocked me by moving with interest toward the display case — the one holding the most famous shoes in the country.

NINETY-NINE

I quietly approached the Secret Service agent, who seemed momentarily mesmerized by Dorothy's glittering slippers.

"I know you're there, Cosi," she said, her eyes never leaving the display. "No need to creep up on me."

"I'm surprised you didn't follow them."

"It's killing me not to. But I know that boy would never hurt Abby, and they deserve their privacy. I also know the museum is secure. Agents are posted at every exit . . ."

She glanced at me. "It's still hard to let go."

"*Now* you know what it's like to be a mother."

I smiled as I followed her gaze back to the scarlet pumps.

"I've wanted to see these shoes since I was a little girl," she confessed. "I'd been meaning to come here. After five years in DC, tonight was my first chance."

"Are you a Judy Garland fan? I have a barista with a partner who does an uncanny impression. Stop by our coffeehouse Thursday nights."

"My interest in the shoes comes from Oz. I read all the Frank Baum books — and I'm actually *from* Kansas."

"I see. For you, there really is no place like home."

Cage finally smiled, and informed me Dorothy's shoes weren't red in the book. They were silver.

"The filmmakers changed it because of Technicolor. Red stood out better when Garland skipped down the yellow brick road." She gazed down at her own thick-soled flats. "Unfortunately, there's no clicking these hoofers for a ride back to Lawrence."

"Lawrence?"

"Technically, I'm from a tiny farming community *outside* of Lawrence."

"I'll bet your family is proud of you. And proud of the job you do."

"I suppose they are. But I'm sure the families of JFK's Secret Service detail were proud of them, too, right up to November 22, 1963."

I didn't know what to make of Sharon

Cage's sudden turn to the dark side. Maybe it was all this history around us. After all, this exhibition sought to present the story of America through one hundred touchstones of its history . . . light and dark —

A fragment of Plymouth Rock; Benjamin Franklin's walking stick; Eli Whitney's cotton gin; shackles worn by Abraham Lincoln's assassination conspirators; Alexander Graham Bell's box telephone; Bob Dylan's leather jacket; John Coltrane's tenor sax; an Apple II computer; Kermit the Frog; and, of course, the most visited item in the museum, Dorothy's ruby slippers from *The Wizard of Oz*. These objects, and many more, were displayed on the walls, or in freestanding glass cases. But Cage was only interested in discussing the red shoes. And, apparently, presidential history through homicide.

"Do you know when the Secret Service was created, Ms. Cosi? The day Abraham Lincoln was assassinated. He signed our formation into law before he took a bullet to the head. Then three more Presidents were murdered over the next century."

"And Ronald Reagan was shot in 1981," I pointed out, "but his Secret Service detail saved his life."

"Exactly. History provides my lessons: I

cannot slip up. Not once. And I have to be ready."

"Ready to spot the next nutcase with a gun?"

"Ready to lay down my life to save Abigail Parker." She paused, still looking at the slippers. "The truth is: Dying for her doesn't bother me. What I couldn't live with is something bad happening to that girl. That's my worst nightmare."

I touched her arm. "Agent Cage, if anyone could protect the President's daughter from the wicked of this world — and bring her home safely — it would be you, with or without magic slippers."

She shot me a glance. "There's no place like home, eh, Cosi?"

"As long as home is where the heart is . . ."

As my voice trailed off, I felt a presence at my shoulder. Sharon looked up, eyes narrowing with concern, which instantly worried me. Turning, I found a wall of mocha-skinned muscle in Italian wool.

"Is there a problem, Agent Dimas?" Sharon asked.

"It's the President," the giant said, voice deeper than Darth Vader's. "The Commander in Chief would like to speak with Ms. Cosi, as soon as possible."

Good heavens, are they onto me?

If they were, my goose was cooked. Pinning a secret flash drive to your bra works only if your interrogation isn't preceded by a federally authorized strip search!

"Come with me, ma'am," the Wall commanded.

With nowhere to run, I had little choice.

ONE HUNDRED

As we left the American Stories area, another giant Secret Service agent joined us and suddenly I was flanked. As the two Walls moved me through Flag Hall, a third agent arrived, boxing me up from the rear.

A bit of overkill, don't you think, boys? I'm a master roaster, not a terrorist mastermind!

Passing the beverage area, I spotted Helen Trainer, looking rather the worse for wear. She was still on Bernie Moore's arm, as much for support as camaraderie — though hopefully she was not still babbling state secrets to the music reporter. It was even more distressing to see her clutching a martini glass instead of a coffee mug.

Behind the urn, peeking through the open doors to the kitchen, I spotted some Metro DC policemen, Landry among them, winking at my blue halter dress. I just prayed they were there to take advantage of my free coffee offer, and not to assist with my arrest!

Matt shot me a puzzled look, and Madame raised a curious eyebrow.

I shrugged, as if I were clueless. Meanwhile my insides were roiling like a Turkish *ibrik* over a flame. Did they have a warrant? I envisioned a quick discussion, then the Mirandizing, and finally the click of handcuffs — which (this time) would not be engaged for recreational use!

My heart pounded as I was escorted to the First Family's table, where the President's wife was busy chatting up the Speaker of the House. It was President Benjamin Rittenhouse Parker himself who rose to his full commanding height — which was plenty tall, considering he'd been a college basketball star — and circled the table to confront me.

I'd never been so close to a U.S. President.

I had to admit, Parker was striking, with iron gray hair and eyes to match. Despite his midsixties age, he radiated a youthful dynamism yet still managed to project a friendly, avuncular persona.

Unexpectedly, he thrust out his hand. Robotically I extended mine and he gripped it.

"Wonderful occasion, Ms. Cosi," the President declared. "The food is delicious! And your coffee is *superb*!"

He leaned close for a theatrical whisper. "I insist you give up your secrets now . . ."

"Secrets?" My heart stopped, right next to that hidden flash drive, until the President replied —

"The ingredients for those Coffee-Glazed Barbecued Drumsticks. I'm a coffee fiend, Ms. Cosi. You *must* share the recipe with our White House chef."

Everyone around us laughed. Only then did I notice the cameras and realized this was a photo op, not a felony capture.

I *would* have breathed a sigh of relief, but I was afraid if I inhaled too deeply the hidden contraband in my neckline would pop out.

Gritting my teeth, I kept on smiling while I answered the President's questions about the exhibition.

Luckily, I'd done my research. I knew Ben Parker's favorite U.S. President was Teddy Roosevelt, so I kept my focus on Theodore, and their shared love of coffee.

"Did you know Teddy downed up to a gallon of joe a day?"

I quickly explained how the habit evolved from his days of drinking it to relieve his childhood asthma. "The caffeine is similar to theophylline, a bronchodilator, so the coffee helped open up Teddy's airways and relieve his wheezing and breathlessness."

"Take it from me, Ms. Cosi, *anything* that helps a President breathe easier on the job is much appreciated!"

Again, everyone laughed.

"And, as you probably know already, Roosevelt was famously credited with coining the iconic Maxwell House Coffee phrase —"

"Good to the last drop!" President Parker and I recited together, and we both laughed.

Finally, I likened Matt's worldwide sourcing trips to Theodore Roosevelt's own global adventures, including the former President's last great expedition in 1913, in a country well known for its coffee growing — Brazil.

"Roosevelt helped lead the first group of explorers to document an area of the Amazon basin, along the thousand-mile —"

"River of Doubt," President Parker finished for me. "The Brazilians call it Rio Roosevelt now. Did you know his expedition was partly sponsored by New York's natural history museum?"

"I do now."

"River of Doubt," he repeated. "I read TR's own account of the trip. Malaria, starvation, impenetrable jungle, white-water rapids, a drowning, and a murder. It was brutal. And beautiful. And I understand why he undertook it."

"Why is that, sir?"

"Roosevelt was a man of action and energy, Ms. Cosi, and he'd just lost his reelection bid for a third term . . ." A melancholy look crossed Ben Parker's face. "You know, that river is the perfect metaphor for what national leaders go through . . ."

"Impenetrable jungle? Or having doubts?"

The President smiled. "The American public doesn't want us to be fallible, and we do our very best, but the shape of the Oval Office is more than a physical design. So many times, we go around and around on big decisions, wondering if our choices are the right ones: Will they help? Will they hurt? Will history show us to be brilliant . . . or blinded?" He paused. "Well . . . at least TR and I agree on one thing that helps immensely when making historic decisions —"

"Consulting your spouse?"

"That, too. But I was going to say — a bottomless cup of coffee!"

We both laughed once more. Then, after expressing sincere delight at speaking with me, the President excused himself. As he walked away, the hyper focus in the room went with him, including the Walls in worsted, and I nearly collapsed with relief.

Abby's stepfather seemed like a nice enough guy, but I could practically feel the power radiating from the man, a fiery, sun-like energy impossible to outshine, and dangerous to cross.

Abby's mother was the same.

I recalled the uncomfortable heat of the *actual* fire she had roaring during our lunch in the Diplomatic Reception Room. I remember how it made me sweat. And the way she pressed me to say *yes* to her ideas by force of personality — and position.

But that was politics, wasn't it?

I understood Abby's predicament much better now. She was a shadow child trapped on an inescapable planet with blinding twin suns.

Blinded, I thought. That idea of being blinded had come up in my discussion with the President. Parker said history would judge him to be brilliant . . . or blinded.

But blinded by what? I wondered.

I didn't wonder long, because I hadn't forgotten about Helen Trainer.

Somewhere near the bar was a tipsy White House Curator. It was time I pumped some good strong coffee into the happy-hour historian, and got the truth out of her.

I'd been keeping state secrets close to my

heart for more than a week — and that was long enough!

ONE HUNDRED ONE

Unfortunately, I couldn't find Helen near the bar or *anywhere* in Flag Hall.

She and Bernie Moore weren't on the swirling dance floor, or at the buffet tables, or the coffee bars (where she *should* have been). When I finally did locate her, she was alone, slowly weaving her way to the exit.

"Helen, have you forgotten? We have to speak!"

She faced me. "I'm not leaving the party, Clare. I'm simply heading upstairs to the Hall of Music."

"Fine," I said. "Let's go up together. But wait for me to grab us coffees."

And for you, I thought, *maybe two coffees . . .*

Tito had just refilled the urn with a fresh batch of my Great Americas blend. I grabbed a pair of disposable eight-ounce cups — then I had a better idea.

Helen hadn't yet picked up her personalized Jefferson quote mug. It was one of the few still remaining on the courtesy table.

That cup's sixteen-ounce capacity was just what this barista ordered, so I went to the communal urn and filled Helen's mug to the brim with the hot, sobering brew. Then I poured a disposable cup for myself.

On the way to the stairs, I noticed Katerina's assistant, Lidia, lingering nearby. When she saw me, she tossed her hair and gave me her shapely back.

I see that girl is still working her Katerina 2.0 "thang."

Helen and I climbed to the third floor. The Hall of Music was in the west wing of the museum. No guests were around because there wasn't anything to see in this area, just an empty concert space.

Helen, however, had a reason to be here, and refused to speak of anything else until she satisfied her curiosity.

She led me through the doors of the dimly lit hall. Excited now, she hurried down the aisle, climbed onto the stage, and flipped on a few lights.

That's when I saw it — the famous "Gold Grand."

This magnificent piano stood on gold-leafed legs carved into American eagles. As we sipped our sobering brews, we walked around the Steinway, taking in its many, many — perhaps too many? — details. Most impressive to me was the painting on the lid, depicting ten women in pink, gray, and mauve centennial revival ball gowns against a vivid green background.

"This instrument was built to celebrate Steinway's fiftieth anniversary in 1903," Helen explained. "Here in the museum it's usually displayed in the First Ladies Hall, but Valentina Ysenko is going to play here tomorrow afternoon, and she specifically requested the use of this piano. Given her Ukrainian background, it's a brilliant symbol for her — music and freedom."

Helen sank down on the bench. "So here it is, tuned and ready, and in a worthy acoustical space for the first time since it was moved from the East Wing of FDR's White House!"

She tapped the keys, spread her delicate fingers over the keyboard, and began to play. It sounded like a snippet from Debussy's Nocturnes. After a minute, Helen abruptly stopped.

"I'm no good at this," she declared. "I never was."

Her inebriated exuberance had turned maudlin, but she showed little signs of sobering up. I sat beside her on the ornamental bench.

"Helen, please tell me. What did you find out about Abby's father, Andy/Aamir Ferro?"

She shook her head and muttered under her breath. "Andy Ferro is Aamir Tuli Abdal, that's what I found out, and I can't talk about the rest."

"What do you mean?! Why was he Aamir Tuli Abdal? Was that his alias?" I added it up fast and came to a clear conclusion. "Was he a terrorist, Helen? Did he die in those Casablanca bombings because he set off one of them?"

She looked at me through unfocused eyes. "I'm tired."

I urged her to drink more coffee, but she took only a few sips.

"Please, Helen, tell me what you found in those e-mails."

"I can't," she said with finality. "My source swore me to secrecy, asked that I only tell Abby and no one else. Better you don't know. Look what happened to me . . . to my office."

She shook her head. "Fourteen years at the White House. Three administrations. Now suddenly I'm living in George Orwell's universe and I'm angry."

"Do you have any idea who's responsible?

520

Was it the Secret Service? Someone else on the White House staff? The FBI?"

"I don't know who did it."

"What about your meeting with Jeevan Varma. Was anyone else aware of it?"

She shook her head. "I told no one, not even Abby. Why would anyone know? Wait a minute . . ."

"What? Tell me."

"The day after the meeting, one of the First Lady's acquaintances asked me if Mr. Varma had been helpful to me."

"Who was it?"

"A lawyer. I think she works at Justice. Katerina something —"

"Katerina Lacey?"

"That's her. I assumed she was friends with Mr. Varma, and that's how she heard about our meeting. But it was my private business, and I told her as much — civilly, of course."

I didn't like this revelation. Not one bit. "Was there anyone else who may have known about your meeting?"

"Mr. Varma might have told others. I don't know. And I don't know what's next. Maybe a security escort out of the building, which would be fine. Frankly, I don't even want to work in that . . . that *place* anymore."

Helen's weary eyes scanned the concert hall and then appeared to glaze over.

"Did you know this museum's music program coordinator is retiring? The director asked me to take the position."

"Is that a good thing?"

"It would be a step down. On the other hand, it would be so very enjoyable." She sighed. "You know, after my husband died, my passion for music history died with him. But helping Abby blossom . . . it's connected me to that again. Working here, in this new Hall of Music, *would* be an invigorating change. Perhaps it's time . . . but I fear what it will look like, that step down. What do you think, Clare?"

My gaze drifted to the black-and-white keys. " 'I dream a world . . . where every man is free . . . And joy, like a pearl, attends the needs of all mankind . . .' "

"That's beautiful. Is it from a poem?"

I nodded. "Langston Hughes, my co-manager's favorite jazz poet . . . and it seems to me, Helen, what I told Abby in your office applies to you, too. Freeing yourself from what others think, being true to who you are and what makes you happy . . . that's the only path I know to real joy."

" 'Like a pearl,' " she whispered, touching

the string my daughter gave me. "Thank you," she said after a moment and met my gaze. "I'm so sorry I can't share what I found out —"

"I understand — I think. Anyway, I hope the e-mails helped, before your file was stolen, that is."

"They helped. But not entirely. When I reached out to the former White House chief of staff, he told me what he knew, in confidence, and it finally connected the last few dots."

She stared straight ahead. "I sat Abby down yesterday and told her the entire *true* story of her father. It was the hardest thing I ever had to do . . ."

"Oh, Helen. Is the truth that terrible? Was her father really a murderer?"

Her eyes grew hard. "I can't tell you, Clare, I really can't. It's a question of Abby's safety. Please try to understand."

"Fine," I said, despite my exasperation. Then I pointed down my neckline. "So what am I supposed to do with this?"

"Place it in the hands of the Metro DC detectives." She stared at me a moment. "You *are* talking about the flash drive, aren't you?"

Oh, for pity's sake. "Yes, Helen! Drink some more coffee!"

She did. "All kidding aside. Someone *must* pay for what happened to Jeevan Varma."

"I agree," I said, and silently added, *I just hope it won't be me.*

Glancing at my watch, I rose from the bench. "I've got to get back to the party. Are you coming with me?"

She shook her head and leaned against the Steinway.

"I'm going to stay here awhile, think about that job change . . . then I'll finish the coffee and take a cab home." She touched my hand. "I really am sorry I can't tell you more."

"It's all right. Get home safely, okay?"

"Clare!" she called before I left the stage. "Remember, I can't tell the Metro detectives what the e-mails mean, but I *can* and *will* tell them everything I know about Mr. Varma and the apparent blackmail scheme that got him killed. Don't worry. I'm determined to set the record straight on *that* part of the story."

ONE HUNDRED TWO

"What happened next?"

In the yacht's galley, Mike Quinn lifted the French press and poured the last drops into my cup.

"This story has come full circle," I told him, "like the Oval Office, and the DC Beltway, and those infernal Washington traffic circles. Two days after the Smithsonian party, you were pulling up to the front of my coffeehouse, asking me to trust you, and pushing me into an SUV."

"Then you didn't see Helen again, after that night?"

"No. My catering work took over. I was so tired that I went into autopilot. We packed up and went home. Then you came home from Baltimore Sunday evening, and I finally told you about the flash drive."

"I remember . . ." Quinn nodded. "I advised you to hand it over to Sergeant Price on Monday."

"And I agreed. But Price was a night-beat cop. So I saw no harm in putting in a solid workday. I planned to find him at the precinct in the evening and tell him the whole story."

"But I showed up first."

"Which brings us back to Abby. You know I still have that flash drive. It's in the bedroom, pinned to my bra. I know we talked about it before we met Danica. But now that you've heard the whole story, do you *still* feel the same? That it can't help us?"

"It's useless, Clare. That information isn't a secret to President Parker and his wife. If it could have helped determine who kidnapped — or killed — Abigail, then the FBI has it already because the Parkers would have told them. So we're back to three theories: Abby was kidnapped or killed. Abby committed suicide —"

"Or Abby is a runaway bride," I finished for him.

"And with all the conspiracies swirling around her, you still believe the latter? That Stanley McGuire proposed to her in front of the ruby slippers? That she ran away with him to elope? And they're hiding in the old Underground Railroad bunker beneath the Georgetown mansion on Cox's Row?"

"Look, given the blood trail to the river, the scarf with Abby's hair, and Stan's Hoover cane, it's clear something went wrong. But I believe the Underground Railroad was part of their original plan. And if it was, we may find evidence that they were there, which could give us a new lead . . . or they *could* still be hiding under the house now."

"Then let's get some rest. In the morning, we'll have to go there and see for ourselves."

"I agree. It's too risky to involve anyone else. If there's heat to be taken, you and I should be the ones who take it."

"And . . . I hate to say it, but, given the blood in the park, whoever opens that sub-basement door might find the bodies of Romeo and Juliet."

"Oh, God, Mike, please don't think that."

"We have to consider all the possibilities, Clare, even the dark ones."

"I'm not giving up hope."

"Neither am I. When Danica comes back in the morning, we'll make a plan."

ONE HUNDRED THREE

After a short sleep fraught with disturbing dreams of blood and black water, I rose to a hot cup of coffee and instructions — both from Mike.

"Drink up. Danica will be here in thirty and we have to be ready to move."

Half an hour later, we met up with Danica in the parking lot. The detective greeted us with a nod as we piled into her familiar silver SUV, Quinn in front, me in the back, a big floppy hat and sunglasses masking my features.

"We've got a drive ahead of us, but we'll make the rendezvous on time."

Though the water was serene, and the docks much more quiet than they had been during last night's frenzy of official activity, I was not sorry to leave the yacht club behind.

"Did you bring it?" Quinn asked. "And is it clean?"

"As soap," she replied. "It's under Clare's seat."

The laptop was there, along with a variety of useful items, like a truncheon, a switchblade knife, and boxes of ammunition.

"You guys got lucky last night," Danica said as we left Federal Hill's traffic behind. "The local police made a fuss, so the FBI cut the raid short. They might have searched each boat if they'd stayed longer."

"What's going on at the Village Blend, DC?" I asked, suddenly missing my old routine.

"The FBI has set up shop outside your coffeehouse, and Mrs. Bittmore-Black's Georgetown mansion, too. They've been in and out of both places, so they're probably bugged. Your telephone lines are definitely tapped, and federal agents took all the files in your office, your smartphone, and your computer — I hope you didn't store nasty stuff on your hard drive . . ."

"*Food* porn. That's still legal, isn't it?"

Danica met my eyes in the rearview mirror. "There's more. Metro DC and the feds are now actively searching for you, Clare Cosi. My precinct got the BOLO this morning. We're going to have to be very clever to get you both inside that Georgetown mansion."

"Our plan will work," Quinn assured her.

We drove for forty minutes, until houses became as sparse as the traffic.

Finally, in the parking lot of a shuttered diner, I saw the Village Blend's van. Luther was there, opening the back doors. There wasn't another vehicle in sight as Danica pulled up.

Laptop under my arm, Quinn and I hopped into the windowless back of the vehicle and settled in among the boxes. Luther closed the doors, and we were off.

The van's interior was heady with the smells of roasted coffees, and once again I felt a painful longing for the lost comfort of routine. Opening the coffeehouse, the morning sun burnishing the polished floor, pulling that first espresso of the day . . .

Were those sweet moments, which I too often took for granted, gone forever?

Would I be spending the rest of my years in prison, separated from my daughter, from Mike, Madame, Matt, everyone I loved? Would I be drinking prison coffee for the rest of my natural life?!

"Welcome aboard the fugitive express," Luther called from the driver's seat. He made a U-turn and rolled onto the road. Then he reached into his chef's jacket and handed me an envelope.

"It's from Tito."

In the Italian boy's gracefully flowing cursive, Tito revealed that only two establishments served J. Chocolatier chocolates within a twenty-block radius of the Village Blend, DC. One was By George, a tony restaurant six blocks away from our coffeehouse. The other was Tillie's, a gastropub around the corner from our back alley.

I showed the note to Quinn and he immediately phoned Danica, who was following us. He asked her to go straight to those restaurants and review their security footage from the night Varma ran into the Village Blend and collapsed.

"With luck you'll find out who the dead man had dinner with that night."

When Danica replied, Quinn listened for a long time. I watched his jaw working, and his shoulders grow rigid with tension.

"Are you sure about this?" he asked.

Quinn didn't appear to like the answer. He grunted before ending the call.

"What is it, Mike? What's wrong?"

"It's bad, Clare. Danica reached out for an update from a friend at DC Metro. The reply came five minutes ago. They're after you for more than Varma's death. And this time the victim named you as the perpetrator."

ONE HUNDRED FOUR

"A victim named me as a perp?!"

Quinn nodded.

"Well, what in heaven's name did I perpetrate? And who is this victim?"

"According to Danica's source, a janitor at the Museum of American History found Helen Hargood Trainer collapsed on a piano bench, the personalized gift coffee cup still clutched in her hand."

"Helen! Oh, God, Mike. Is she alive?"

"Apparently it was touch and go, but this morning Helen was able to provide a statement to police from her hospital bed."

"A statement about what?"

"Clare, a single drop of coffee was left in her cup. Poison was found in it."

"Poison!"

A shadow crossed Quinn's face. "Helen Trainer told the authorities that *you* handed her the cup with the coffee already in it. That she watched you fill the cup and no one else touched it. She also told them you were in possession of sensitive information involving the First Family."

Panic welled up inside me, until I couldn't breathe. Quinn saw my distress and he held me until the initial shock passed.

Still in his arms, I looked up at his face, but found no comfort there. His expression looked beaten — as beaten as I felt.

No, I thought. *We are not beaten. Not yet!*

Pulling away from comfort, I locked a firm gaze onto him. "We have to find Abby and deliver the real killer. We have to!"

With a nod, Mike pulled himself together, and we began to brainstorm a loose list of suspects. As we talked, the list grew. Even worse, it was crowded with power players.

We both knew Katerina Lacey had to be involved. Her skill at opposition research made her perfect for the job of rooting out dirty secrets and deleting them. *But did she delete witnesses, too?*

Then there was Agent Sharpe.

Sharpe had been at my coffeehouse many times for Abby's Open Mike Nights. The evening Jeevan Varma broke in, Sharpe could have been the reason. He seemed awfully suspicious of Helen and me before the *Bathsheba* file went missing, *and* he and Katerina were particularly friendly. Lidia

Herrera even told me her boss had a thing for "men with guns."

Come to think of it, Katerina's ambitious young assistant had the same access to the White House as her boss, along with the same demagnetized moral compass.

And there were others.

What about the former chief of staff from the previous administration? Helen shared information with him about Abby along with the contents of that flash drive.

Could the President himself be involved? Maybe he decided his stepdaughter's past had become too dark a threat to his shining bid for reelection and sent in "cleaners" to get rid of the mess for good. Or could it be — God forbid — Abby's own mother who ordered her daughter and Helen gone? With her position and prestige threatened by her daughter's perceived "instability," perhaps she took action.

"What about the Ponytail Man?" Luther Bell chimed in. "Maybe he's involved."

"Who?"

"The guy with the white hair and beard who always came to see Abby perform."

"Bernie Moore? He's a jazz critic. How could he be involved?"

"Is that what he told you?" Luther shook his head. "Clare, that man works at the

CIA, and I'm not talking about the Culinary Institute of America."

Another round of panic took hold of me. "Are you sure?"

"No doubt about it," Luther replied. "I recognize him from a long talk we had at the Central Intelligence Agency's headquarters in Langley, Virginia, right before I moved to the Senate Dining Room. He complained about the 'Moroccan Stew' the cafeteria served, said it was too bland to be authentic."

Luther shrugged. "I agreed with the man, but it wasn't my recipe. I remember that talk because, right after that, I transferred out. That damn stew was the last straw. Their culinary standards were too low and their security hurdles too high. I was glad to get out of there!"

I'd stopped listening after Luther mentioned yet another Moroccan connection. It couldn't be a coincidence.

Abby's father died in Morocco and the First Lady spoke of living there for a short time after Abby was born. And then there was Helen Trainer, so unwilling to reveal the only truth possible — that Abby's father was a violent terrorist.

But what about Bernie Moore?

He was at our coffeehouse every time

Abby played. Abby said she noticed him on campus, too.

And the next thing you know, Abby's missing!

Bernie was also at the Smithsonian event, and took a real interest in Helen when she started talking too much about Abby and her father.

Did Bernie find a way to poison poor Helen? That has to be the answer!

"It's Bernie Moore," I declared. "He's some kind of black ops guy for the executive office or a double agent with ties to terrorism or a hostile government. Or he simply sold her out for an astronomical payday. He might have snatched Abby himself and turned her over to some group out to use her."

"Use her?"

"Think about it, Mike. They could brainwash Abby, the way heiress Patty Hearst was turned. The spectacle of America's First Daughter spouting revolutionary propaganda would be the greatest tool any terrorist could ever have."

I faced him. "I'm not even sure we should risk going back to the mansion now. It's a dead end. We have to find Bernie Moore, or discover the truth about him. That's the only way we can resolve this mess."

"No. We're going to the mansion first. This notion of a CIA mole is a solid line of logic, but it's not what your gut told you, Clare, and we're going to follow your Underground Railroad theory. That's the track your instinct gave us, and we're staying on it, all the way to the end of the line."

ONE HUNDRED FIVE

When Luther reached the mansion's Georgetown block, Danica distracted the FBI's stakeout team by pulling up to their car and flashing her badge. She told the two feds she just got the BOLO on Clare and asked for an update.

While the agents chatted with her, Luther steered the van down the narrow service lane behind Cox's Row and backed it up as close as he could to Mrs. Bittmore-Black's kitchen door. Mike and I donned ball caps and carried boxes on our shoulders to hide our faces.

As Quinn and I entered the mansion's sunlit kitchen, Madame brandished a rolling pin.

"I'll have no more armed fascists in this house!" she cried. "Warrant or not, you're leaving *now!*"

I lowered the cardboard box to reveal myself.

"It's me," I said in a whisper. "Don't say my —"

"Clare!" Madame cried.

I cringed and Quinn quickly found a radio and turned it up to drown out our voices.

Meanwhile Madame dropped the baker's tool and hugged me tightly, tears welling in her violet eyes. "Oh, dear, I was so frightened —"

I put my index finger to my lips, and Madame lowered her voice to a whisper.

"— The FBI has been here twice," she said. "And someone broke in last night. I heard noises. Maria heard them, too; but when we came downstairs, they were gone."

"They may have left microphones behind," Quinn said.

"Where's your maid now?" I asked, breaking our embrace and wiping away my own tears.

"Maria's gone sightseeing. The jackboots have the poor woman terrified!"

"Listen, Madame. We have to check something downstairs. I'll explain later."

"You won't have to, dear. I'm not letting you out of my sight."

Luther agreed to stand guard upstairs, while the rest of us hit the steps. In the sub-basement, I located the flashlight, and hoped the key was still in place.

It was, so on my knees, with Madame looking over my shoulder and an armed Quinn beside me, I gripped the key with both hands and turned. The lock clicked easily, *too easily,* as if it had been oiled since the last time.

Quinn placed his shoulder against the carbonized wood and pushed. The door flew open — and struck something or *someone*!

We both heard a grunt of pain.

Alarmed by the human sound, Quinn surged through the opening. I quickly followed, scuffing my elbow in my haste.

We didn't need a flashlight. The secret rooms were lit by battery-operated lanterns. The air mattresses we'd used for the Walton crowd were now inflated. A card table was set up with folding chairs, and the shelves held food pilfered from the mansion's kitchen.

Meanwhile, on the far side of the room, Quinn was pointing his gun at a man standing with his head tilted back, hands covering a bleeding nose. When the man raised his hands in surrender, I recognized his snow-white ponytail.

"Don't hurt him! Don't hurt my father!"

Abigail Parker charged out of the adjacent room and threw herself in front of Bernie Moore, arms spread.

Stan appeared next, clutching a rusty crowbar. When he saw me, his shoulders relaxed in grateful relief.

In the stunned silence that followed, Madame crawled through the door and rose to her full height. Hands on hips, she regarded everyone. Then she focused her sharp gaze on Stanley McGuire.

"Young man!" she said sternly. "You have *a lot* of explaining to do!"

ONE HUNDRED SIX

"Okay, it wasn't the smartest plan in the world," Stan admitted. "But Abby and I were desperate, and it was our only chance to be together."

The Fugitive Club had moved out of the Underground Railroad and up to the finished portion of the mansion's basement. I sat with Stan on the couch. Quinn paced the wooden floor. And at the lounge chair, Madame and Abby were fussing over Bernie as they iced his swollen nose.

"How did Abby escape?" Quinn asked.

"Her friend threw her a bridal shower," Stan replied, "and the First Lady agreed to let Abby stay overnight. When the party ended and the house went to sleep, Abby slipped away the same way she always did. Only this time I met her in the park."

Stan lowered his gaze. "I'm sorry to say, Ms. Cosi, we were going to borrow your van without asking. I'd already copied the key from Gardner's key ring, and I had a blanket for Abby to hide under, a change of clothes, even a wig."

"Where did you think you were going?" Quinn asked.

"Las Vegas. We were going to get married."

Quinn shook his head. "You wouldn't have made it out of DC. I doubt you would have made it out of Georgetown."

"That's what I told him," Bernie said, clutching a cloth to his nose. Underneath it appeared he was *grinning*. "You've got to admire the boy's spunk, though."

Quinn groaned. "Stan's *spunk* launched a million-dollar manhunt."

"That's right, and they *still* couldn't find him," Bernie said, sounding like a proud parent.

"We weren't going to leave right away," Stan countered. "We were going to wait it out in the Underground Railroad, then leave when the heat was off."

Quinn rubbed his eyes. "Son, when you help the First Daughter of the United States evade her security detail, the longer she stays missing, the hotter 'the heat' gets."

"I didn't say he was a mastermind at subterfuge," Bernie amended. "Only that he had spunk."

"So what went wrong?" I asked.

"Me," said Bernie. "I knew their plan, and I was trying to stop them. But upon reflection, I might have approached them differently. I rushed up to them in the dark park, and Stan mistook me for a mugger. Along with spunk, Stan has a great right hook. That was the *first* time I got a bloody nose in this misadventure."

"Then it was *your* blood they found in the park," I realized. "Along with Abby's scarf and her hair."

Bernie nodded. "I had to prove to Abby that I was her father, right there on the trail with my nose still leaking."

"And he did," Abby said. "He knew why I had the notes from 'Somewhere Over the Rainbow' tattooed on my arm. He remembered he taught me 'Chopsticks.' He described things in my childhood bedroom, what our house looked like, until I had no doubts."

"What happened next?" Quinn pressed.

"We agreed to go forward with part of Stan's plan," said Bernie. "I advised them to leave Abby's bloodied scarf and Stan's Hoover cane by the riverbank to throw off the dogs. Then we went into the river and climbed into the storm drain. Stan had a rope rigged already, and we helped Abby up into it. We followed the drain here, to your

Underground Railroad station, and camped out the last thirty hours or so. I took the time to let Abby get to know me a little better, and all three of us have been talking about options."

Quinn frowned. "Options?"

"It's clear these two will never get away with elopement. Even if we did get them to Vegas, the second they file for the license, the authorities will snatch them. Stan will be charged with kidnapping, never mind the circumstances. Sure, he'll be cleared, but there's no getting around the mess —"

"I can't walk out of here without a plan," Abby said, becoming emotional. "My mother will say my behavior was a 'cry for help.' I'll be back on medications and under even stricter security, right up to the moment she pressures me into taking a zombie walk to the altar with Preston!"

Tears welled in her eyes, and Stan crossed the room to comfort her.

"Let's all stay calm," I urged. "Gathered in this room we've got an intelligence officer, a combat veteran, an NYPD detective, and a woman who survived sixty years of running a small business in New York City. I *think* we can come up with something!"

One Hundred Seven

Thirty minutes later, Luther and Quinn went through the mansion, pulling down blinds, closing curtains, and turning on every radio or television they could find to thwart potential listening devices. Then we moved Abby and Stan upstairs, into the comfort of the double parlor.

In the kitchen, Madame made a large pot of my freshly roasted Wake Up Washington blend to the raucous sounds of BIG 100.3 — DC's classic rock station. It wasn't until she served the coffee that I noticed she was wearing earplugs.

Finally, Quinn, Bernie, and I took our coffee into the stately dining room for a serious discussion around the Walton family–sized table.

"You could talk to the First Lady," I suggested to Bernie. "Try to reason with her."

"That would accomplish nothing," he assured me.

"What makes you so certain?"

"Let's just say I know Beth Noland better than you do."

"You and the future Mrs. Parker shared a relationship once," I pointed out. "And you had a child together. Is there no hope?"

"Our history was a tad rocky, Clare, and today it's ancient. She wouldn't listen to me then, and she won't now."

"A comment like that makes me wonder how you two got together in the first place."

"Do tell," Madame said, removing her earplugs.

"I guess I should start at the beginning . . ."

In the next ten minutes, Bernie quietly revealed his true background, some of which I'd learned already from Helen Trainer: He'd been born Andy Aamir Ferro here in the USA, right across the border in Virginia. His father was an American university professor; his mother a French national of Arabic descent; and he'd studied world music here in DC, as well as in France, Spain, and Morocco. His love of travel and adventure and facility for languages reminded me of Matteo Allegro.

Then he revealed something I hadn't heard before . . .

"My uncle worked at the CIA. It was

through him that I was recruited to act as an asset, and inform on terrorist activity abroad. Intel I supplied prevented the bombing of a Paris concert, and I realized that saving those people who didn't even know they were in danger was as big a kick as the music . . . so I decided to become a CIA officer like my uncle. I returned to DC for training at the agency's headquarters, and that's when I met Abby's mother."

He paused to taste the coffee, and give Madame a thumbs-up.

"Beth Noland was already a seasoned CIA analyst at Langley, five years older than I was, and happy with her Washington career path. From the start, we were physically attracted to each other, and Abby happened. Beth had been told she couldn't have children, so when she got pregnant she was overjoyed, despite the complications it brought to her life."

"In matters of the heart, there are always complications," Madame pointed out.

"Not like these. I was being trained for a special assignment, and it was too late to back out. I asked Beth to give me five years in the field, then I'd return to DC and we'd marry. She was very unhappy with my decision. She left the CIA and took a job on Capitol Hill. But she did allow me a relationship with my daughter when I visited Washington. Beth even brought Abby on a few extended trips overseas to see me, and at one point she did consider a move to Casablanca."

"But she never did move, did she?" I said.

"No. Because of 9/11. After that, everything changed. The world, my outlook, and my relationship with Beth. She decided it would be too dangerous for her and little Abby to move. She tried to persuade me to come back, but my work was never more important, so I refused."

Bernie sighed. "By 2002, Beth had begun her affair with Senator Parker. Because no one knew of me inside the Beltway, everyone began to assume Abby was Senator Parker's love child.

"Then came the Casablanca bombings of 2003, the worst terror attack in Morocco's history. Two thousand suspected terrorists were arrested, convicted, and sent to the most brutal prisons you can imagine."

Sweat appeared on Bernie's brow. "I was one of them. My cover was so good I'd fooled the Moroccan authorities. My fellow inmates immediately began talking about a plan to escape. I believed they could do it, so I kept my cover and played my role to the hilt. I did terrible things, but I earned

549

respect in that prison, and trust."

Quinn rose from the table. When he returned, he had a shot glass and a decanter of very fine scotch.

He poured, and Bernie nodded his thanks.

"Moroccan authorities admitted nine terrorists tunneled out of that cesspool of a prison. In truth, there were more than twenty of us, and my fellow fugitives made me part of their new terrorist network. They trusted me completely now. It wasn't until I got to Pakistan that I finally managed to hook up with the CIA again."

Bernie drained his glass. "The gold I handed the agency after that, you wouldn't believe. I was living in the heart of the beast. I helped stop bombings of hotels in North Africa, an embassy and nightclub in Europe, a girls' school in the Middle East, an assassination of a world leader, and targeted attacks against our troops. I was also able to identify active terrorist cells for our military. Then a drone strike hit a meeting I was attending, and I was badly wounded, but officially I died in that attack, with everyone else —"

"You mean Aamir Tuli Abdal died."

Bernie was astonished at my intelligence gathering. "Stan said you would figure out we were here, and you did. But I had no idea you were so adept at my game. You may have missed your calling, Clare Cosi."

"Thanks, but after the last twenty-four hours, the only thing I've missed is the calm, cozy comfort of my coffeehouse."

Quinn poured again. This time Bernie actually tasted the scotch, and approved.

"Anyway, Navy SEALs extracted me. I've been in Washington about two years, healing up, getting plastic surgery in the process. Now I've got this new identity and a lecturing job at CIA headquarters, training case officers. In the meantime, I learned Senator Parker became President Parker, and my wonderful daughter became America's First Daughter."

Bernie set his empty glass aside. "Being an intelligence officer, I couldn't help using my skills to check up on Abby, and what I discovered, I didn't like: An attempted suicide. Confinement in a psychiatric hospital. I knew something had gone wrong in my daughter's life, so I decided to lurk on the fringes — watch over her."

He met my gaze. "I sent Abby an invitation to your Open Mike Night, making it appear as if the invitation came from your club. I was hoping she'd come, and she did. After that, it was easy for me to see her."

Finally, I asked the question that had been

bugging me for hours.

"How did you *know* Abby was going to elope?"

Quinn made a guess from his own work on Katerina's case. "You cloned her phone, didn't you?"

Bernie nodded sheepishly. "I'm not proud of it, but, yes, I did. This was long before she became a celebrity. The Secret Service kept its distance then to give her some semblance of freedom. I forged a faculty ID so I could move around. Abby was at the library one day with friends, and I was able to snatch the phone and return it."

Bernie's expression became more serious. "As I listened to Abby's conversations and read her texts, I became even more concerned for her future. The situation she was in with Stan and Preston gave me the chance to take the measure of both young men."

"And what did you conclude?" Madame asked.

"Preston talked down to Abby, treated her like a child. Called her 'the total package.' But it wasn't a compliment. It was a definition. He knew Abby had the kind of connections that could help him get ahead. And that's all he ever wanted to talk about — his political aspirations, his 'networking,' and what he needed from her."

Bernie glanced at me. "Abby's love of music so threatened Preston that he tried to make her believe you folks at the Village Blend were using her for her connections."

"Blatant hypocrisy!" Madame cried.

"Yes, the Prestons of the world are good at charging rivals with exactly what they're guilty of. And in her heart, Abby knew the boy was lying, that you had befriended her without ulterior motives."

"What about Stan?" I asked. "What did you think of him?"

"Stanley McGuire never talked about Abby's connections, only about how amazing my daughter is, how talented, and how much he cares for her. But I think it was Stan's philosophy about jazz that really endeared him to Abby."

I already knew what Bernie was going to say —

"Stan told Abby that she had to stop criticizing herself, and learn how to love every note she played."

"That's a beautiful metaphor, one that goes well beyond music," Madame observed. "No wonder you chose Stanley."

"My daughter chose Stanley," Bernie clarified. "She chose him freely. And I wanted to protect her right to make that

553

choice."

"Everyone at this table wants to do that," I said. "But how? We're a bunch of fugitive plotters in hiding. How can we thwart the wishes of a President and his recalcitrant First Lady?"

"We could go to the press," Madame suggested.

"No good," said Bernie.

I quickly agreed. Too much of what we'd discussed, including the truth about Abby's parentage and Bernie's real identity, was top secret —

Wait a minute! I thought. *Top secret. Just like that flash drive . . .*

"Mike, where's the clean laptop Danica brought you?"

"In the kitchen. Why?"

"Because Abby's father needs to see this!" Without thinking, I pointed to my cleavage. And Bernie Moore nearly fell off his chair.

ONE HUNDRED EIGHT

Twenty minutes later, Abby's father was still sitting in front of Danica's laptop, poring over the top secret e-mails about his own disappearance after the bombings in Morocco.

"Clare, when you handed me this flash drive, you said Helen Trainer kept printouts in a file that was stolen from her office?"

I nodded. "For some reason, she named the file *Bathsheba.*"

Bernie lifted an eyebrow. "Poetic, but true. Do you know the story?"

"I do," said Luther Bell, who'd joined us at the dining room table. "King David had the hots for a soldier's wife, so he sent her husband to the front lines to die, which left him free to dally with the missus."

"That's it, in a nutshell," Bernie said, "but you left out a few important details. Like the part about King David doing more than dallying with Uriah's wife. After her husband died in battle, David married Bathsheba and made her his queen."

Bernie finally closed the laptop. "It's the perfect parallel to my story, and even better, it's a story millions of voters will understand, which is why I'm going to use this against the First Lady."

"Use what, exactly?" I asked. "I know there's a scandal here, something that makes the President look bad. But I still don't know the specifics."

"They cut me loose," Bernie said. Though his voice was calm, I could see the cold rage in his gaze. "Right after the Casablanca bombings, my people at the CIA wanted an investigation. They wanted *confirmation* of my death. Or proof of life. But President Parker, then Senator Parker, worked behind the scenes with his crony at the State Department to kill the investigation. He was in love with Beth Noland by then, I'm sure of it. And he wanted me out of the picture. So he got his friend to testify that it would be a diplomatic disaster with the country of Morocco if they went looking for me. As a result, I was cut loose, declared dead."

Bernie swiped his hand across his throat. "These e-mails make it clear enough. The future President of the United States ended me."

"No wonder the administration tried to keep this secret," Quinn said. "A lot of military families would not be too keen on reelecting a President who left a man behind . . ."

Bernie nodded at Quinn's observation. Then, oddly, his craggy face split into a smile.

Now, I'd seen Bernie smile before. But never like this. It wasn't a fatherly smile, or a charming one, or even one that conveyed amusement.

It was the kind of smile that revealed who he really was — a ruthless, canny chess player who had finally found the strategic move for checkmate.

"*This* is how we're going to help Abby," he said.

I leaned forward. "How?"

He rubbed his hands together. "For this strategy to work, we need to wait until the world knows Abby is missing. Once the announcement is made, the White House won't be able to tell their version of the truth. They'll have to provide real answers to a curious press. Where did Abby go? Why did she run away? Who was she with?"

Bernie unplugged the flash drive and held it up.

"With *this* little piece of history, I can

make things very difficult for the First Lady unless she does what I ask. And all I want is for her to stop making Abby's choices for her. I want her to give Abby the freedom to make her own choices. And if she doesn't, I will go public and ruin her husband."

I exchanged a glance with Mike. "Do you think it will work?"

"Oh, yeah," said Quinn. "It's brilliant."

"Thanks," said Bernie. "The moment Abby's disappearance goes public, I'll place the call to the First Lady myself."

Quinn grunted. "As a fellow divorcé, I'm sure you're dying to make *that* call. But remember, the White House controls the FBI, the Secret Service, and the CIA. How are you going to bring in the authorities without losing control of the situation?"

"I know a way," I said. "Agent Sharon Cage knows Abby's story and she's become sympathetic to Abby's feelings for Stan."

"But how do we bring her here without bringing an FBI SWAT team down on our heads, too?"

It was my turn to display a chess master's smile. "Code. I can send Sharon Cage a text in a code only she'll understand. It's a phrase we privately shared. She'll remember, and I guarantee she'll figure it out."

Bernie looked skeptical. "What's to stop

her from alerting the FBI?"

"Embarrassment. Sharon was the head of Abby's security detail. Hours after Abby went missing, she was relieved of her duties. I witnessed it myself."

Madame frowned. "That poor girl. It's so unjust."

"But good for us," I said. "With Cage on the outs with the FBI and the Oval Office, she'll check things out for herself before sounding an alarm based on a coded message. When she arrives, Bernie can explain everything the way he explained it to us. With the press out front, Sharon Cage can be the one who brings Abby and Stan out of the mansion. A happy ending for everyone."

"That's wonderful," Madame said. "The woman will look like a hero."

I smiled, recalling my talk with Sharon in front of those ruby slippers. "Believe me, if anyone can get Abby and Stan safely over that rainbow, it's the agent from Kansas."

ONE HUNDRED NINE

There was a celebration in the dining room once the young lovers' dilemma was finally solved. Luther cooked up a quick snack, and Abby and Stan joined us at the table.

It was Bernie who noticed that Quinn and I weren't feeling the joy.

"What's the problem?" he asked. "Can I help?"

Quinn informed him that I was still wanted for the murder of Jeevan Varma, and that I was also the prime suspect in the poisoning of Helen Trainer.

"That's unacceptable!" Bernie said. He was fuming. "Who would do that to such a lovely woman? You know, Abby told me all about Helen, how supportive and helpful she's been. Personally, I found the woman very charming . . . and I was hoping we'd meet again."

I began to pace. "I just can't understand how she was poisoned . . . I filled her cup from the communal coffee urn myself. Everyone else drank the coffee from that urn, including me. And Helen's cup was empty when I filled it —"

"But it had Helen's name on it," Bernie pointed out. "The poisoner must have used a residue, something invisible when it dries. An eyedropper could have been used to deposit the toxin on the bottom of the cup. When the hot coffee went in, the residue dissolved and contaminated the drink."

"That's possible?" Madame said, amazed.

"It's simple tradecraft," Bernie replied. "It worked for me."

We all stared at him.

He shrugged. "I poisoned a sadistic Moroccan guard using strychnine I distilled from the rat poison scattered around the prison. I put it in his teacup. He didn't die from it. But the residue was enough to send him to the hospital. And he never came back to torture us prisoners again."

I stared at this man who, just two days ago, I thought of as a genteel jazz critic who could give my ex-husband lessons in sensitivity. *Maybe not.*

"Well," I said, "at least Helen recovered."

"From what I remember about the Smithsonian party," said Bernie, "too much champagne is what saved her life."

"Are you kidding?"

"No. It's called the Rasputin effect."

Madame blinked. "The Russian mystic?"

"As the story goes, a group of Russian nobles, threatened by Rasputin's political sway with the czar, invited him to dinner. They plied him with wine and poison-laced pastries. But because he got very drunk, the poison didn't kill him."

"Why is that?"

"Excessive alcohol can cause a temporary condition of malabsorption, in which the stomach can't digest certain nutrients. So the poison doesn't enter the system fast enough to overwhelm it."

"That's interesting," Quinn said. "But let's get back to the part about Helen's cup sitting in plain sight for the entire party. A defense lawyer could argue access by any number of people, which creates reasonable doubt for Clare."

"Thanks, but I'd rather deliver the guilty party," I said. "And I think I know who's behind it — Katerina Lacey. The strategy is sickeningly clever. Helen is poisoned and it looks like I did it. Two rival birds taken out with one deadly cup."

Bernie leaned forward. "Tell me everything you know about this Katerina person and why you think she hurt Helen . . ."

Quinn joined me in explaining the many faces of Katerina Lacey — politically appointed acting director of a Justice Department task force and sometime advisor to the First Lady.

"For years she's been advancing her career with 'fruit of the poisoned tree' evidence," Quinn continued. "I've been running my own investigation on her past in Baltimore — with the help of a detective there. Here in Washington, I've been helping her run stings with shady evidence that I strongly suspect was gathered illegally."

"You suspect," said Bernie, "but do you have any proof?"

"Only a theory and a small stack of police reports on lost, stolen, and returned mobile phones from the subjects of her Justice Department prosecutions."

"Where does Helen fit into all this?"

I jumped in. "Helen was a key witness to events surrounding the murder of a State Department employee, a man named Jeevan Varma who was trying to sell that flash drive to the highest bidder. We have reason to believe Katerina was involved in Mr. Varma's murder. We don't know if she was helping him with his blackmailing plan or trying to stop him, but we know she had access to the White House — where Helen's printouts of those e-mails were stolen. Helen even told me Katerina asked her about her meeting with Mr. Varma. How could she know if she wasn't involved? And, of course, Katerina was at the party the night Helen was poisoned."

"But who do you think poisoned Helen's coffee?" Madame asked. "Katerina herself or an accomplice?"

I faced Bernie. "Would members of the Secret Service know about residue poisoning?"

He nodded. "It's something they have to watch for."

"Then if Katerina didn't do it, she could have had someone else do it for her: Agent Sharpe, who I saw her flirting with on Saturday night. Or her assistant, Lidia." I snapped my fingers. "That girl actually made a crack about her boss liking 'men with guns.' Agent Sharpe certainly fits that profile."

"Does this woman just bend the law or is she truly corrupt? How dirty is Katerina Lacey?" Bernie asked.

"Very," said Quinn.

"And in more ways than one," I added. "Much to the delight of the men she pulls into her web. She's been trying to pull Mike in for some time."

Quinn shrugged. "As it happens, I'm allergic to female spiders."

"But who knows who else Katerina has seduced? We need to learn the identity of her accomplice, too."

Bernie turned to Quinn. "Do you have any physical evidence against her?"

"This." Quinn displayed Varma's cloned phone and explained how it came into his hands. "Not much of a connection. But it's a brick we can build on."

"Let's not forget Danica," I added. "She's looking for a hit on that security camera footage. If she gets one, then I have an idea that might catch Katerina in her own web."

"Your ideas have been good so far," said Quinn.

"Actually, it's half Stan's idea. We had a talk once about beating bullies with strategy instead of force. How's this for a strategy?"

I laid out the whole gambit, including the roles Quinn, Danica, and I would play. When I finished, Bernie nodded his approval.

"Out of curiosity, Clare, where did the *other* half of that idea come from?"

"Simple geography."

"How's that?"

"Katerina's luxury apartment building is in Maryland. According to the map, it's not far from Wisconsin Avenue, which means we can take Wisconsin all the way up to her home."

"So?"

"So do you know what Wisconsin was before it became a tony shopping district or a rolling road for Georgetown's tobacco port?"

"Haven't got a clue."

"An ancient *buffalo* trail."

Quinn laughed so loud I was worried the FBI might hear, but he wouldn't stop. The man was positively gleeful at the prospect of buffaloing his awful boss.

"You really do have a mind for tradecraft, Clare. If you ever want to lecture at Langley, give me a shout."

"Thanks, but from now on, the only CIA people I want to deal with are the ones in chef jackets."

Quinn clapped his hands.

"Okay, we've got a plan. All we need is an arrest warrant and a bouquet of flowers."

ONE HUNDRED TEN

Mike Quinn waited until the elevator doors closed. Alone in the silent, carpeted hall, he counted the doors until he reached 6D.

Five minutes, Mike told himself. *That's all the time I need. Keep her off-balance for five minutes. And make nice, even if it makes you sick.*

He knocked, waited, knocked again. Finally the door opened.

Katerina Lacey frowned in surprise. Her hair was sleep mussed and her slender frame was wrapped in a silk robe. Without makeup her face looked pale as a specter.

"Michael? What are you doing here?"

He put on the wounded-boyfriend pout. "Aren't you glad to see me?"

"Of course, but I thought you were in New York with your kids."

"It was time to come back. I found myself needing some . . . *adult* company."

"But this is so . . . unexpected."

He sensed her wariness. *Don't push,* he thought.

"I know it's late. But I was anxious for an update. And I wanted to hear it in person. From you."

"You should have called me," she gently chided, noticing the flowers. "I would have been ready . . ."

"I couldn't call. My son was playing *Dragon Whisperer* and broke my smartphone. I'm going to need a new one."

Katerina lingered at the threshold. Her eyes narrowed as she tried to read him.

She isn't sure she should invite me in. But she has to . . . or we're sunk.

He took a step back. "Look, I can see I'm intruding. I don't know what I was thinking, coming here so late. I should go."

It was the longest five seconds in his life, and then Katerina reached out and curled her fingers around his.

"No. It's all right. Come in," she said, leading him by the hand.

Katerina Lacey lived in a luxury apartment building in suburban Maryland, just thirty minutes from the White House. The emphasis was on luxury, with a sunken living room, a wall of windows, and a balcony view. But for a personal space, Mike could see it had no character. It felt as cold and impersonal as a hotel lobby.

"How did you get past the security desk?" Katerina asked.

"I told the night guard the truth," he replied smoothly. "I couldn't wait to see you, but I wanted it to be a surprise. Honestly, I think the bouquet did it. The guy must be a sucker for romance — of course, flashing my federal ID helped, too."

Katerina drew her index finger down his cheek. He fought to keep from shuddering. Then she took the flowers and moved away to find a vase. As she went to the bar to fill it, he gritted his teeth and glanced at his watch.

Hang in there. One more minute . . .

Back turned, Katerina spoke. "There's not much to update you on, Michael. They're still looking for your friend, Clare Cosi. The Metro police, the Secret Service, the FBI. She probably escaped with the gang who snatched the President's daughter."

He frowned. "You were right to tell me about her, Katerina. Your actions changed everything for me here in Washington." He paused, dropped his voice. "Tonight, I want to show you how I really feel . . ."

Katerina faced him again, drinks in hand. "If I remember right, you're a scotch man."

She passed the glass, her touch lingering.

She'd opened the silky robe. He hated to admit it, but the display of pink flesh was . . . well, diverting.

"To us," she said, and together they drained their glasses.

"You're probably right about Clare escaping." He regarded his tumbler. "The last time I took off without telling her, she staked out my apartment and stalked me. But tonight, when I dropped off luggage at my place, there was no sign of her."

"Forget that awful woman," Katerina said, moving closer. "She's a million miles away, while you and I . . . we're right here, alone together —"

The banging on the door startled them both.

Quinn made a show of cursing. "That must be your building's security. I told the night guard I'd have you phone down to make it clear I'm your guest and you're okay. I forgot to mention it."

"I'll get rid of him . . ." Katerina poked his chest. *"You* stay *here."*

Still holding the glass, Quinn held his breath, waiting for the fireworks to start. It didn't take long.

ONE HUNDRED ELEVEN

Katerina was so shocked at the sight of *me* standing on her doorstep, hands on hips, ready to strangle her, she took two steps back.

My role tonight was the "jealous and angry girlfriend," so I continued my pretense of glaring at the lady lawyer — until I caught sight of Mike standing in her living room, holding an empty glass.

In five short minutes with my man, Katerina managed to serve drinks and get half-naked in that obscenely gaping kimono?

Pretend I'm angry? Ha! No acting necessary!

"YOU WITCH!" I shrieked, lunging at her.

Katerina actually ran backward to get away from me. (Most impressive, I'd never seen *that* before.)

"Calm down," Katerina said evenly. "We can talk this through."

"Clare! What are you doing here?"

That was Mike, crying out in mock surprise. Then, in order to "flee from me," he ran deeper into Katerina's apartment — as per the plan.

Katerina didn't notice Quinn's retreat. She didn't notice that I left her front door open, either. Her attention was focused on one thing only — the crazy-mad, insanely jealous, Italian American woman currently *in her face*!

To honor my heritage, I launched into a string of Italian invectives that would have scorched my beloved nonna's ears, most of which I'd learned from my ex-husband, though I tossed in a few zingers I'd picked up from Tito.

Mother tongue exhausted, I switched to English.

"I knew you and Mike had some sicko thing going on. All those trips to the West Coast. The late nights at work. It was all a ruse so he could sleep with his hussy boss! Well, not anymore! I'm back, and this ends tonight!"

Unexpectedly, Katerina lifted her phone and hit speed dial.

"Calling the cops?" I chuckled menacingly. "They won't get here quick enough to save your bony butt-cakes!"

But they might get here soon enough to ruin our plan . . .

Katerina moved behind the couch. "Stay back," she commanded, one hand waving me off, the other clutching a phone to her ear.

"I need help. Code Red. Now!" she cried.

Desk security, I thought. *But he's already clued in, and won't butt in.*

I rushed around the couch, and Katerina hightailed it behind her bar. She and I locked eyes across the polished top.

"The authorities are after you, Clare. Do you know what that means?"

"I know what *this* means."

It was Quinn. He'd returned to the living room, displaying a jangling phone in his hand and a mirthless grin on his face.

"I found this in your bedroom." The phone sounded again. "Hear that Bollywood ringtone, Katerina? Enjoy it, because it's your swan song."

She narrowed her eyes into slits. "I don't know what you have —"

"Then I'll tell you. I have the cloned phone of a State Department employee named Jeevan Varma. The man you murdered. You used the clone of the man's phone to illegally surveil him."

"Really?" Katerina smirked. "You have *that*

573

cold, do you?"

"I do."

"Well, I have to say, I don't care, because I have *this.*" From behind the bar, she pulled up a gun and pointed the barrel directly at Mike's chest.

I gasped at the sight of it, and she told me to shut the hell up. "And don't move a muscle, you little bitch, or I'll put a bullet in your head *after* I blow his heart out."

Then she addressed Quinn again. "You *should* have had your gun on me, Michael, but then I always knew you were weak. And I assure you, I'm not. Now toss your weapon onto the couch."

Quinn folded his arms.

"She's a wanted woman," Katerina pressed, unnerved by his confidence. "Clearly, you helped her, which makes you a criminal, too. I could kill you both where you stand, and let my position at the DOJ do the explaining."

"That might work," declared a new voice. "Or I could shoot *you,* Ms. Lacey."

Danica Hatch strode through the open apartment door. She had a gun, too, and aimed it directly at the creature.

The distraction gave Quinn time to draw. Now it was two on one.

With a disgusted sigh, Katerina set the

Glock onto the bar. I snatched it and stepped back. Unbelievably, the woman was still smirking.

"Sit down," Quinn barked. "I want you to see this."

Katerina held Mike's gaze as she slowly wrapped the open kimono around her slender form, belted it, and sank down onto the couch.

"I heard you like electronic devices," Danica said. "Check this one out."

Black-and-white images passed across the policewoman's smartphone screen. Danica knew exactly where to freeze the picture.

"That's you, Ms. Lacey, entering Tillie's gastropub minutes after Jeevan Varma. A few hours later, Mr. Varma was in a coma. A day later the man was dead. You killed him."

Katerina's smirking gaze was still unbearably superior, almost triumphant.

She's unfazed. Why?

"Mr. Varma had something you wanted," Danica pressed. "Information that could hurt the President you work for. So you lulled him into thinking you were going to pay him for it, but you didn't pay for it. You murdered him instead."

"I didn't kill anyone," Katerina replied, unbowed. "I admit I met Varma that night.

He wanted to meet at the Village Blend, but I knew I would be recognized there, so he set the meeting around the corner instead, at Tillie's."

Quinn loomed over her. "Why the meet?"

"I was there to pay the man off. Look, a few years ago, when President Parker was a senator, planning to run for the big job, his people hired me to dig up incriminating evidence of potential scandals. They wanted to know about any dirt in Parker's past that the press — or his political opponents — could use against him. They did not want to know how I did my digging, they just wanted results, and any messes cleaned up. So when I found those incriminating e-mails, I paid Varma to erase them from the government servers. But the jerk kept copies, and with Parker up for reelection this year, he used those copies to blackmail me."

She shrugged. "So I paid him. I handed him the blackmail money that night. Two hundred thousand, cash. But Varma never delivered the goods. He handed me a flash drive with a document promising he would dead drop the material. Then *he* ended up dead."

Katerina met Quinn's stare. "But I *did not*

kill him, and you have no evidence that I did."

The smug smirk never left the woman's face, and I finally realized why: "You believe the President is going to protect you."

Katerina's nonchalant shrug told me I was right. It was Danica who finally shook her up.

"We're not here to arrest you for Mr. Varma."

Katerina blinked. "Excuse me?"

"With the help of a dedicated whistle-blower" — Danica tipped her head toward Quinn — "we have evidence that you've engaged in judicial misconduct, that you've conducted unlawful searches and seizures, that you have used your position to selectively prosecute the President's political rivals, not only in your current position at Justice, but during your time as an ADA *in Baltimore.*"

"Baltimore?"

Quinn stepped closer. "I told you I found Mr. Varma's phone. Guess I should have mentioned it was one among dozens of cloned phones and other devices I found hidden in your bedroom, devices that I'm going to connect to the illegally obtained intel you gave me to run stings against the President's political opponents, some of whom reside in Maryland."

For the first time, Katerina looked upset.

"Are you crazy?" she cried. "If you do this, you'll blow apart every case we prosecuted!"

"Illegally prosecuted. For political purposes."

Mouth gaping, she stared at Quinn, unable to believe anyone would burn his Washington career ladder in such a righteous bonfire.

But Quinn was doing exactly that — and dousing it with gasoline.

Danica smiled sweetly. "As much as I'd like to slap the cuffs on you myself, you're being arrested on federal charges, and being brought to a Maryland U.S. attorney working with my Baltimore DA, and that requires a federal officer." She tipped her head to Quinn once more. "Federal jurisdiction. Federal warrant. But we're booking you in Baltimore, honey, where your friends are few; and once you're there, we're not letting you go."

With pure rage, Katerina glared at Danica, who had trouble containing her glee. With a spring in her step, Danny went to the front closet to find her prisoner a coat.

"I'll beat this. Just watch me," Katerina bit out as Quinn pulled her up.

"The most you can hope for is a presidential pardon," he said. "But I promise you one thing, you will *never* wield the power of the law again. And that's good enough for me."

"You're a fool, Michael," she hissed, tugging on the trench that Danny tossed her. "We could have gone far, you and I. After this, no one at Justice will trust you again. Your Washington career is over."

"Fine with me," he said, clicking the cuffs on her. "Because after working for you, Katerina, I cannot wait to get back to policing New York."

Then Quinn advised his boss of her rights, including (thank goodness) the right to remain *silent*.

ONE HUNDRED TWELVE

"This is the best way, Clare. Forty minutes on the highways, and we're in Baltimore. Once Katerina is in federal custody, you, me, and Danica will go back and present our evidence to the Metro DC police. With that *and* Abby and Stan as your witnesses to these events, any charges pending against you will be dropped. I'm sure of it."

"I just wish we were driving *together.*"

It was the dead of night now, and chilly out here in the Maryland suburbs.

"Better I ride shotgun," he replied. "It's too much to expect Danica to drive and watch the prisoner, too. And with all the electronic paperwork flying back and forth across county lines, I might have to flash my warrant and my ID if a trooper or local cop pulls us over. It's the law."

Quinn glanced at the little silver SUV in the high-rise parking lot. Katerina was in the back, in handcuffs, her features steely in a frame of blunt-cut hair.

"Frankly, I doubt you want to spend forty minutes in the same vehicle with Katerina, anyway."

"Okay. You convinced me."

"Make a right out of the parking lot. After a mile or so through town, you'll see the sign for the interstate. The turn comes at a stoplight, then a few lonely miles to the on-ramp. Once we're on the highway, just follow the signs to Baltimore."

I couldn't shake a sense of unease as I climbed into the Village Blend van. It felt like an itch in my mind that I couldn't scratch.

Did I miss something?

When I started the engine, the radio came on, and I was distracted for a minute by the announcer's excited tone.

". . . and mere hours after she was declared missing, a solo member of Abigail Parker's Secret Service detail has located the First Daughter safe and sound, just minutes from her dorm room at American University . . ."

Sharon got my message. Way to go, Cage, now you're a hero. But then, you always were . . .

My happy excitement turned to concern as I realized how fast Danica had driven away. I pulled the van out of the lot and headed in the same direction.

The road I was on led out of town. Traffic was light, which is why I noticed the dark sedan. It passed Danica's silver SUV and made a slow U-turn to follow.

This was the direction to the interstate, so having other cars move this way wasn't all that suspicious. But I fumbled for my phone anyway. Quinn answered on the first ring.

"There's a car behind you. Do you see it?"

"Yes . . . and?"

"And back at Katerina's apartment, before you and Danica got the drop on her, she phoned someone, asking for help. I thought she was calling the guard at the front desk . . . but what if she wasn't?"

"Katerina has an accomplice, Clare. I have no doubt. Someone had to deal with the criminal element to steal phones and clone them. But Katerina is in custody. Only a good lawyer can help her now."

"Well, that car behind you has been following for half a mile."

"Take it easy. I know you've been through a lot, but Detective Hatch and I are well armed. So stop worrying and keep your eyes on the road. It's going to get very dark ahead."

Quinn ended the call, and I watched my driving, but I couldn't stop worrying.

At a crossroads, the yellow light turned to red and I got stuck waiting for a dump truck to clear the intersection. By the time the light turned green again, Danica and Quinn had made that sharp right turn he warned me about.

I knew what was ahead of them, an empty, twisting, three-mile stretch that eventually forked into the interstate's on-ramp. If that sedan was going to mess with them, it would happen now. So before I made the turn, I gave in to my need to test my hunch.

I cut my headlights and slowed the van.

Trees and brush were now on both sides of me, with streetlamps far apart. Most of the road ahead was in shadow. The dark sedan was far ahead by now. With my headlights out, there was little chance its driver could see me.

Suddenly an arm came out of the driver's window and slapped a portable magnetic bubble onto the roof. A pair of siren bursts shrieked and a speaker boomed —

"County Sheriff's Office. Pull over."

I sat back, relieved.

Quinn told me this might happen. Because he was taking a prisoner across county lines, he and Danica would have to speak to any local police that stopped them. The sheriff probably saw an electronic notice. But Danny had the e-warrant ready to show him.

As the silver SUV pulled over, the black sedan rolled onto the shoulder a few yards behind it.

Cutting my own engine, I came to a stop, too, more than twenty yards behind the sheriff. The road was empty and quiet, the trees and brush black, chirping insects the only sound. But I didn't feel much peace.

For justice to be done, someone else needed to be sitting next to Katerina in that backseat. Quinn believed his boss had an accomplice. And so did I.

But who?

I closed my eyes and pretended I was back painting my greenroom mural, the picture frustratingly incomplete, like a puzzle almost done yet still lacking that final piece.

Remember, Clare, details matter . . .

My mind raced back through all the events that brought us here, the situations and people, tragedies and triumphs, frustrations and fears.

Someone in this story had the perfect edges to slip into place . . .

And then it hit me —

Who was at the Smithsonian the night Helen

was poisoned?

The same man who was near the Village Blend the night Mr. Varma was killed. The same man who could easily make deals with lowlifes skilled at "Apple picking" and phone cloning.

The very same man who treated me like a MILK, making it look like I had an affair with Varma. And, while he was at it, making sure half the men on the DC Metro force knew what I looked like, so it would be easy to apprehend me after he framed me for his crimes!

Sure enough, the man who stepped out of his unmarked "sheriff's" sedan was exactly who I thought it would be — Tom Landry.

No wonder the guy liked "older ladies." No doubt, Katerina Lacey was sleeping with him on top of paying him handsomely for a few simple "favors."

Landry was not in uniform tonight. His car was unmarked and so was he. In his dark pants and black T-shirt, he looked like the criminal he was, and I'd bet silver dollars to warm donuts the gun tucked into the back of his belt was not his authorized police weapon.

I popped the glove compartment and grabbed Quinn's .45.

He'd taught me to shoot it. But I was no marksman. In a situation like this, I could hit Danica or Mike. Nevertheless, gun in hand, I climbed out of the coffee van.

As Landry approached Danica's car, he reached for his gun. There were floodlights on his vehicle and he was blasting them directly ahead, effectively blinding Mike and Danny to his approach. When he stopped, far short of the driver's window, and raised his weapon, I knew —

He was going to execute Mike and Danny, bullets to the head, in cold blood.

You son of a bitch!

I fired into the air.

The explosive sound bounced around in the trees like a nuclear blast. And because I fired over my head, the noise bounced around inside my skull, as well.

Landry turned.

I ran forward, firing over my head again. (You'd think you'd be ready for the noise after the first time. FYI: you're not.) Now my ears were ringing like Stan's cymbals after a jam session. Even my own voice sounded muffled as I shouted with all my strength —

"I know who you are, Tom Landry! I'm a witness to what you've done! You're a *murderer!*"

My ears were shell-shocked, but not Landry's. He heard me just fine. I knew because by now he was aiming his gun at me.

I froze, waiting for the shot.

When it came, it was Landry who spun in a circle, then crashed to the ground.

Danica was immediately out of the car and standing over him. Shouting for him to freeze, she stepped on Landry's right arm as he frantically groped for his fallen weapon. She had to press the barrel of her gun to his head before he finally raised his hands in surrender.

As Danica cuffed a bleeding Landry, I realized she wasn't the one who fired. That man was Michael Ryan Francis Quinn. He was standing on the other side of the hood, still gripping his service weapon.

His hand was steady, his aim true.

One Hundred Thirteen

I was back at the Village Blend, DC, savoring every moment of a daily routine that seemed forever lost just two short weeks ago. My joy was transcendent — so intense that the April sun streaming through the windows sparkled with a special magic. Food tasted better, desserts seemed sweeter, and the coffee I sipped was more comforting than I imagined possible.

My taste buds were so happy and honed that I used them to create my brand new Big Bold Beltway Blend. I couldn't wait to try it out on a certain NYPD detective.

Still, when his SUV swiftly pulled up to my shop, I felt a sudden panic — a post-traumatic reaction to the events of the past few weeks. But my fears rapidly receded when Mike Quinn strolled through the front door with that smile meant only for me.

Of course, it wasn't just my company he was anticipating. I'd promised the man a special treat, so I quickly ducked behind the counter to snag the last slice left in the display case, the one I'd set aside for him. Then I French pressed a pot of my new quadruple-B.

Five minutes later, Mike was sitting in the chair opposite mine, his long legs stretched out in front of him. His warm smile had morphed into an expression of sheer ecstasy after his first bite of Luther's Black Magic Cake, followed by a Big Bold Beltway Blend chaser.

"You weren't exaggerating, Clare," he said between chews. "I don't know what's better, Luther's outstanding chocolate cake or your amazing coffee."

"I was sorry you missed the food when you skipped Abby's performance, but at least you can sample the dessert."

Mike, still in the throes of a food trance, wasn't listening. "Upon consideration, the winner today is the cake. A sweet this satisfying is the perfect complement to sweet news."

I leaned across the table. "Sweet news? As in . . . ?"

"Tom Landry was indicted this morning, on all counts, including the murder of Jeevan Varma and the attempted murder of Helen Trainer."

"That is sweet news."

"And it's all thanks to you, Clare. If it wasn't for your quick thinking, Danica and I would be six feet under your Underground Railroad."

I shuddered at the terrible memory of that moment. The image of Landry's gun barrel pointed at the heads of Mike and Danny still gave me nightmares.

"In the end, though, it wasn't me who got Landry. It was that last drop in Helen's cup . . ."

The same drop that incriminated me ironically proved my innocence.

A forensic team found the same poison used on Helen in Landry's apartment, along with twenty thousand dollars cash, hypodermic needles, and the same grain alcohol that killed Jeevan Varma. After that, young Tom sang like one of those little bluebirds over the rainbow, telling the police all about his partner in crime, Katerina Lacey, in hopes of lessening his sentence.

"Landry's going to spend a lot of time in the Lee County Federal Pen," Mike declared, and he speared another delectable morsel of frosted chocolate cake with his fork.

"It's a tragedy," I replied. "I'm guessing Landry never intended to kill Varma."

"Good guess. The plan was to knock the man out after his meeting with Katerina and steal back the two-hundred thousand in blackmail money," Mike explained. "Landry got back the cash, but Varma tricked his killer. To ensure his safety, he gave Katerina a flash drive without the e-mails. When she opened it, all she found was the promise of a dead drop at a later date."

He shook his head. "By the time Katerina realized she didn't have the e-mails, Varma had broken into your coffeehouse, collapsed, and landed in the hospital, where he never recovered."

"But why did Landry return to the crime scene?"

"After he took out Varma, he heard the report of your 911 call on his police radio," Mike explained. "His goal was to influence the investigation and learn what Sergeant Price thought, while pretending to be a clueless young officer impressed by hot MILK."

"Don't remind me. All those cops staring. Goodness knows what they thought."

"I have a clue, sweetheart. But Landry was doing more than slandering your morals. By then, he'd reported back to Katerina, and they worked out a scheme to put a frame around you for Varma's murder. Then Abby went missing and it opened a window for Katerina to shove you through. She knew about your friendship with the First Daughter, and her acquaintance with the First Lady and perch at the DOJ put her in the perfect position to implicate you in a conspiracy."

"Funny how Katerina never once considered that Abby was in love with Stan, or that she eloped. But something tells me the word *love* isn't in that woman's vocabulary."

"No. Her favorite words were *sex* and *power* . . ."

Mike was right, especially when I considered what Danica had told us about how she and Landry got together. To borrow a phrase from a jazz standard, she'd put young Tom in her spell the day he pulled her BMW over for a traffic violation.

According to Danica, Metro DC's version of Internal Affairs had put together a background file on Landry. It appeared he always wanted to be a spy, but after a short stint in the military, Landry failed the Central Intelligence Agency's psychological screening.

"He settled for a local career and got through the Metro DC police department's psych screening, which isn't nearly as rigorous," Danny had told us. "The job was not as thrilling as he expected, but the uniform and gun gave him the trappings of power, and an air of danger."

When a young, eager, and armed Landry stopped Katerina on a traffic violation, she took him to bed. Pillow talk about his CIA dreams ensued, and Katerina gained a useful drone by offering Landry "another way to serve his nation."

Mike lifted his cup in a mock toast. "And once again, a big criminal mess comes down to unscrupulous underlings trying to get ahead by cleaning up a President's past."

Katerina's fate was predetermined. With pressure to contain the damage to the Justice Department's public image, lawyers convinced her to plead guilty. Now she was facing a twenty-year sentence in a medium security facility, with a presidential pardon unlikely, not with her story breaking in the press.

One of the President's aides was forced to admit he'd hired Katerina to "dust bust" (aka dig up dirt and neutralize it), during the President's first run for office. The man credibly swore that he knew *nothing* of Katerina's political targets or her phone cloning — a trick she learned, along with "parallel construction," from an ex-Drug Enforcement Agency boyfriend who routinely used those tactics to secure Federal convictions.

"Katerina was like a cocktail party girl who became an ugly lush," Mike said. "She abused a classic technique of law enforcement until it no longer resembled anything having to do with the law, and the word *justice* no longer had meaning beyond a tool for her own advancement."

"So how do we prevent people like Katerina from doing the same thing again?"

"We don't."

Mike was right, I realized, thinking of pretty-in-pink Lidia with her demagnetized moral compass — another Katerina in the making.

"I guess the only thing this country can hope for is that men and women like you and Danica have the courage to blow the whistle."

"It takes more than that," Mike said with a little smile.

"What else? A bottomless cup of coffee?"

"That . . . and citizens like Clare Cosi, who care enough to demand the truth."

Unfortunately, like Emerald City with its Great and Powerful Wizard, there would always be truths in Washington that the American people would never know.

"The Bathsheba Incident" would remain

behind the curtain, part of our government's thirty year e-mail archiving gap.

The flash drive I'd kept so close to my heart would stay in the possession of CIA officer Bernie Moore, who promised to keep it close to his vest as long as Abby's mother agreed to stay off the girl's back.

Madame put it all in perspective. "My dear," she said one night at dinner, "when you think about it, this whole story comes down to a family drama. It's simply the First Family!"

"Mail for you, boss," Tito interrupted, dropping a stack in front of me. I quickly saw the reason for his wide grin. On top of the pile sat an elegant envelope with "The White House" embossed in gold as the return address.

I opened it and read.

"I just received an invitation!" Now my grin was wider than Tito's. "And this is one memento I can't wait to frame and mount on our Village Blend wall."

I showed him the embossed card.

THE WHITE HOUSE
WASHINGTON, DC

The President and Mrs. Elizabeth Parker
&
Captain Harris McGuire, MD,
United States Army, and
Captain Grace McGuire, MD,
United States Army
request the pleasure of your company
at the marriage of their children

Abigail Prudence Parker
to
Sergeant Stanley Malcolm McGuire,
United States Army, Retired

Saturday at four o'clock
White House Rose Garden
Reception to follow in the East Room

Now Mike was grinning, too. "So," he said, "do you need a date?"

Before I could answer, he added —

"An even better question: Are you ready to set one?"

Epilogue

The sky over Washington was cloudless that day, the temperature kind. The only wet drops present were on the cheeks of the wedding guests at the sight of the retired young army sergeant in full dress uniform with a deep blue eye patch, awaiting his bride. Standing beside him was his best man, Gardner Evans, unable to suppress his grin.

Four hundred guests and two hundred staff were assembled in the West Wing's garden that June, and (unbelievably) I was one of them.

Abby, no longer in black, walked down the aisle to her own solo organ arrangement of "Fix You." And when the reverend pronounced them husband and wife, the Jazz Masterworks Orchestra struck up the joyous end to that song, now and forever their personal duet.

As for Bernie Moore, he was present to

witness the happy union, but he almost wasn't . . .

The First Lady had objected strongly to Abby's real father attending the ceremony, but Abby countered with a strategic invitation to her good friend, former White House Curator, Helen Hargood Trainer, who brought Bernie as her "plus one."

"Now, Mother, we can't be ungracious . . ." she'd cooed when the First Lady discovered she'd been trumped.

Yes, it seemed after four years studying political science, Abigail Prudence was finally learning how to win the game of politics in her own family — ironically from her lessons in jazz.

"Swing is about letting go of fears and inhibitions, of prewritten scripts and limiting strictures," she remembered Gardner telling her. "But it's also about balance and equilibrium in the face of very difficult rhythms . . . It's about the elegant way you negotiate your way through . . ."

Of course, the President was a seasoned veteran of political swing, and as the nation watched, he looked suitably fatherly, escorting the young bride down the garden aisle; and, later, sharing a father-daughter waltz on the polished floor of the East Room.

But Abby had something special planned

for Bernie, too.

Amid the crowd of couples, none but a handful of people knew why Abby had requested the band play, "Someone to Watch Over Me," before tapping the music critic's shoulder for a special dance.

Mr. and Mrs. Stanley McGuire shared their first dance of married life on that historic floor, as well, with the band playing a song Abby once again publicly dedicated to him: "Our Love Is Here to Stay."

As for their life after wedlock, Stan and Abby had a plan for public service born of their love of music and their own healing experiences from it. They were starting an outreach program of music therapy for wounded veterans. Their musical tour of VA hospitals was scheduled to start right after their two-week New Orleans honeymoon.

At Abby's insistence, Agent Sharon Cage would accompany them as the head of their traveling Secret Service detail.

My own contribution to the happy couple's day was culinary. I'd handcrafted a Village Blend coffee especially for them, which would forever be called Over the Rainbow.

Two single-origin beans made up the blend: an earthy Sumatra and a transcendent Sulawesi. Like Stan, the Sumatra provided the grounding beat, a stable, solid-bodied platform for the fragrant, colorful notes of the rarer coffee.

It was in my roasting room that I'd learned the secrets of Sulawesi.

Unlike other beans, when the heat was on, it didn't show a uniform color, which is why it was easy to look at the mottled little thing and misjudge it. As a result, this special and beautiful coffee was too often mishandled, over-roasted to ruin by those unfamiliar with its potential. But masters of the process learned how to see with more than eyes.

It all came down to a universal lesson: *Appearances can fool you. You must focus instead on what you get in the cup.*

Which brings me to the likes of Katerina Lacey, an intelligent, capable woman who'd stirred increasing spoonfuls of corruption into her work and life until it all became toxic, right down to the last drop.

No evidence was ever found that the President or his First Lady knew anything of Katerina's criminal actions. Now that the public knew the truth, however, they would have to decide for themselves whether to hold the man accountable.

Would Benjamin Rittenhouse Parker be reelected come fall?

That was up to the American people.

Personally, I was looking forward to an election in the far future. President Stanley Malcolm McGuire had a nice ring to it; and, it seemed to me this country could use a First Couple whose favorite song was titled "Fix You."

As for Mike Quinn, Katerina wasn't wrong about his Washington career. Oh, sure, when the story broke about her crimes, the attorney general himself shook Mike's hand for the cameras. But the man's smile was plastic and when the cameras stopped rolling, it melted off.

As a whistle-blower in a political town, Mike knew his career in DC was over. But he didn't care. Over the next few months he wrapped things up at the Kennedy Building and I officially hired the new food and beverage director for the Village Blend, DC — my daughter, Joy, who was excited about the new challenge. Happily, her longtime boyfriend, Sergeant Franco of the NYPD, was more than willing to commute to DC for visits — and thrilled she'd given up all plans to return to Paris. Joy was back in America to stay.

My ex-husband, on the other hand, was restless to get away, ready to go back to his global hunt for new coffees. As for me, I was looking forward to returning to my cozy, cluttered duplex above my beloved landmark coffeehouse in Greenwich Village.

While Washington offered prestige and glamor, breathless trips to the White House, and a sumptuous home in a historic mansion, leaving it all would not be difficult.

The reason came down to a moment Mike and I shared at Abby and Stan's wedding.

As the reception wound down, the newly minted husband and wife played a farewell duet for their guests, a song that told of a place they'd arrived at last — "Somewhere Over the Rainbow."

"I have a question for you," Mike said, his arms around me as the couple's sweet performance came to a lyrical end. "What *was* that secret code you texted to Agent Cage?"

"A profound little phrase," I replied, "one you can't help thinking when you're standing in the American Stories room of the Smithsonian, gazing at Dorothy's red shoes."

Mike got it. Pulling me closer, he whispered words that were more than a solution to a mystery. They were a promise for our future.

"There's no place like home."

No matter how dreary and gray our homes are, we people of flesh and blood would rather live there than in any other country, be it ever so beautiful. There is no place like home.

— L. FRANK BAUM,
THE WONDERFUL WIZARD OF OZ

COFFEE AND THE PRESIDENCY

A Country Made by Coffee

Only the United States of America can cite a dispute over a hot beverage as the reason for its founding. When the Sons of Liberty tossed imported tea into the harbor during the Boston Tea Party of December 1773, the harsh British response led to the American Revolution, and ultimately, to American independence.

John Adams — Changing Habits

After the Boston Tea Party, coffee became the patriotic drink, while tea was spurned as a "Tory's brew." John Adams, the nation's second President, was taught a lesson in patriotism when he asked a Maine innkeeper to bring him "a Dish of Tea provided it has been honestly smuggled." He was informed — harshly — that they served only coffee. In a 1774 letter to wife, Abigail, Adams wrote that the incident forced him to change his habits. "I have drank Coffee every Afternoon since, and have borne it very well. Tea must be universally renounced. I must be weaned, and the sooner, the better."

George Washington — Coffee Importer

The first President of the United States enjoyed coffee before it was fashionable among patriots. Washington was importing coffee for personal consumption as early as 1770. In his final years, he became something of a gourmet. In 1799 our Founding Father was searching for coffee beans from the "port of Mocha," then considered the finest beans in the world.

Thomas Jefferson — The Coffee Urn

Thomas Jefferson's love of coffee was legendary. He called it "the favorite drink of the civilized world." Like Washington, Jefferson was an importer, preferring beans from the East and West Indies. He gifted silver coffee urns made in Paris to close friends and political allies. One of those historic urns is on permanent display at Jefferson's home at Monticello. This exquisite example of Parisian silversmithing was purchased by Thomas Jefferson in 1789.

Andrew Jackson — Hooked on Caffeine

"Old Hickory" was the nation's seventh President, a tough former military leader who won the love and admiration of his troops. Jackson was also the first Chief Executive to cop to an addiction to coffee, as well as another all-American product. "Doctor," he told his physician, "I can do anything you think proper, except give up coffee and tobacco."

Abraham Lincoln — The Last Cup

The President who preserved the union in the nation's most tragic time was indifferent to well-prepared food and drink, which could be attributed to his frontier upbringing. A man of simple tastes, Lincoln was said to prefer "apples and hot coffee" to everything else. His well-known quote about his favorite beverage may be apocryphal: When served an unsatisfactory brew, Lincoln remarked, "If this is coffee, please bring me some tea; but if this is tea, please bring me some coffee." A solemn symbol of Lincoln's love of coffee is a gold embossed White House china cup from which he took his final sip. On Good Friday, April 14, 1865, as Lincoln was dressing for an evening at Ford's Theatre, he left that cup on a windowsill. Hours later the sixteenth Presi-

dent was fatally shot, and a servant preserved the cup as a relic of that tragic night.
The cup was passed on to Lincoln's eldest
son, and preserved as a family heirloom. In
1952 it was gifted to the Smithsonian.

Rutherford B. Hayes — Absence Makes a President Fonder

The nineteenth President of the United
States learned to love coffee during the
American Civil War, when the Ohio native
fought for the Union and was wounded five
times. At one particularly low point during
the conflict, Colonel Rutherford B. Hayes
and his troops had only bad water to drink,
and no food at all. Finally a supply sergeant
delivered hot coffee and a warm meal to his
troops. From that day forward, America's
nineteenth President always cherished and
appreciated his daily brew.

Theodore Roosevelt — "Good to the Last Drop"

America's twenty-sixth President was served
Maxwell House coffee at The Hermitage,
home of Andrew Jackson, in Nashville, and
was said to declare the brew "good to the
last drop," a pithy phrase that has remained
the product's tagline to this day. For a short
time, Roosevelt's face even decorated the

can. And why not? Teddy Roosevelt loved coffee and drank up to a gallon a day. His cup was "more in the nature of a bathtub" according to his sons, and he put up to seven lumps of sugar in each cup. Theodore Roosevelt's affection for coffee was passed on to his sons Kermit, Ted, and Archie, and his daughter Ethel. Together these siblings brought fresh-roasted beans and European coffeehouse culture to America, through a chain of coffeehouses all over New York City — more than half a century before anyone heard the name "Starbucks."

Franklin Delano Roosevelt — Do It Yourself

FDR was particularly fussy about his coffee. The White House kitchen actually roasted fresh beans for the President, and a coffeemaker was placed on the President's breakfast tray "so he could regulate the brewing to his satisfaction." During World War II, when coffee was rationed, Franklin Delano Roosevelt tried to stretch his allotment by reusing the grinds. The results were so unsatisfactory that the thirty-second President gave up coffee altogether.

Dwight D. Eisenhower — D-Day and Beyond

On June 6, 1944, during the D-Day invasion of Nazi-occupied Europe, General Dwight D. Eisenhower spent the day "drinking endless cups of coffee" while waiting for battlefield reports. The burden of leadership was heavy. A casualty rate of 75 percent was predicted, and Winston Churchill was convinced the invasion would fail. To cope with the stress, Eisenhower drank fifteen to twenty cups of coffee and smoked four packs of cigarettes each day. Despite high blood pressure, insomnia, and migraines, Eisenhower continued his caffeine and nicotine habit after he became the nation's thirty-fourth President. In 1954, alarmed by a spike in coffee prices, President Eisenhower ordered a Federal Trade Commission probe.

John F. Kennedy — Coffee with a Kennedy

During his U.S. Senate campaign, John F. Kennedy's mother, Rose, started "Coffee with the Kennedys," a chance to meet and greet the future President. The handsome young politician targeted women voters, and with the help of the prominent women in his family, coffee klatches were staged across

Massachusetts. As a junior senator living in Georgetown, those same coffee klatches, now orchestrated by Jacqueline Bouvier Kennedy, raised JFK's profile inside the Beltway, which ultimately led to his election as the nation's thirty-fifth President. After she became First Lady, Mrs. Kennedy revolutionized the way men and women socialized at the White House. Before Jackie, men retired to one room for their coffee while women were sent to another — which cut women off from important discussions of the day. Mrs. Kennedy put an end to that coffee service segregation forever.

Lyndon Baines Johnson — One Finger on the Button

Famously, Lyndon Baines Johnson had four buttons installed on his desk in the Oval Office. The buttons were marked *Coffee, Tea, Coke,* and *Fresca.* Historians agree that he pressed the button marked *Fresca* more than any other. Finally, a soda dispenser was installed in the Oval Office to satisfy the thirty-sixth President's cravings.

George H. W. Bush — Use It or Lose It

The forty-first President consumed at least ten cups of coffee a day for most of his adult life. Barbara Bush said he brewed the morning coffee himself until his duties as the Commander in Chief took precedence over domestic chores. When President Bush was diagnosed with an irregular heartbeat in 1991, he was forced to give up caffeine. "He's not happy with that decaf," reported a White House spokesman, and soon the doctors allowed Bush to enjoy regular coffee again. After he left office, Bush resumed his normal routine. But Barbara Bush revealed during an interview with Oprah Winfrey that the former President had not made his own coffee for so long, he'd forgotten how.

ABBY LANE'S PLAYLIST
THE JAZZ SPACE ★ VILLAGE BLEND, DC

Would you like to hear some of the music that inspired Abigail Parker's headliner concert at the Village Blend's Jazz Space or find out where Cleo Coyle watches jazz, streaming online every night, directly from New York's Greenwich Village? Visit Cleo's new online Jazz Space to learn more at coffeehousemystery.com.

Set One
"Let's Fall in Love"
"Tonight"
"A Little Jazz Exercise"

Set Two
"Won't You Be My Neighbor"
"Black Coffee"
"Someday My Prince Will Come"
"Someone to Watch Over Me"

Set Three
"Our Love Is Here to Stay"
"Love Ballade"
"Over the Rainbow"
"America the Beautiful"
"Who Wants to Live Forever"
"Fix You"
"It Don't Mean a Thing (If It Ain't Got That
    Swing)"

Jazz Resources
Learn more about jazz the way Abby did . . .

Visit jazz legends online:
Wynton Marsalis — wyntonmarsalis.org
Chick Corea — chickcorea.com

See Live Jazz in DC's Georgetown

Blues Alley
1073 Wisconsin Avenue, NW
Washington, DC
bluesalley.com/index.cfm

See Live Jazz in New York City

Jazz at Lincoln Center — jazz.org
The Blue Note — bluenote.net/newyork/
    index.shtml
Smalls — smallsjazzclub.com

FREEDOM OF INFORMATION ACT RESOURCES

Because truth matters, Mrs. Dubois . . . and a truth about our past can alter how we look at the present and move forward in the future.
— SERGEANT STANLEY "STICKS" MCGUIRE, USA, RETIRED

What is FOIA? Enacted on July 4, 1966, and taking effect one year later, the Freedom of Information Act (FOIA) "provides that any person has a right, enforceable in court, to obtain access to federal agency records, except to the extent that such records (or portions of them) are protected from public disclosure . . ."

Frequently Asked Questions About the FOIA:
foia.gov/faq.html

National Archives:
archives.gov/open/

Electronic Records Archives:
archives.gov/era/index.html

The National Security Archive:
nsarchive.gwu.edu/nsa/the_archive.html
    According to the National Security Archive's website, it was founded in 1985 by journalists and scholars to check "rising government secrecy." The organization serves as an investigative journalism center, a research institute on international affairs, and a library and archive of declassified U.S. documents — "the world's largest nongovernmental collection" according to the *Los Angeles Times.* The National Security Archive is also "the leading non-profit user of the U.S. Freedom of Information Act."

Open Government at the National Archives:
archives.gov/open/

RECIPES AND TIPS FROM THE VILLAGE BLEND

Visit Cleo Coyle's virtual Village Blend at coffeehousemystery.com for even more recipes, including:

* Luther's Great American Glazed Donuts
* Luther's Bourbon Street Brownies
* Clare's "Hawaiian" Chocolate Chip Cookies
* Madame's Pecan Sandies (*Sables!*)
* Clare's Oatmeal Cookie Muffins
* Clare's Farmhouse Peach Muffins
* Boston Cream Pie Cupcakes
* Parker House Rolls
* Luther's Honey-Chili Chicken
* Easy Smoky Chipotle Dip
* Luther's Mini Meat Loaves with Smashed Baby Reds and Roasted Garlic Gravy
* Luther's No-Churn Ice Cream (Vanilla, Cinnamon, and Coffee)
and more . . .

RECIPES

Music, food, and coffee are universal languages.

— CLARE COSI

CLARE COSI'S BEST BLUEBERRY MUFFINS

The humble yet beautiful blueberry, native to North America, is beloved across the USA. From Maine to California, nearly every diner, coffee shop, and bake shop has a version of the blueberry muffin. Now the Village Blend does, too. When a rush of new customers left Clare with a sold-out pastry case, she swung into action, creating this instant classic.

So why does Clare call these her Best Blueberry Muffins? Because this recipe produces impressive results with little fuss and few ingredients. It's the best not because it's the most elaborate, but because it's the kind of recipe she uses again and again. These are not cupcakes pretending to be muffins —

with more sugary cake than berries. Blueberries are a healthful superfood, and they are packed into these muffins. The muffins will bake up beautifully, too. No gray batter. And the crumb is tender with a taste like pound cake, yet you don't need to drag out your mixer to cream butter into sugar. The secret is in the use of whole milk (not skim or low fat), and in the combination of vanilla and lemon flavorings. So be sure not to leave those out, and may you . . . eat with blueberry joy!

Makes 6 standard muffins

1 cup blueberries (fresh or frozen)
2 teaspoons all-purpose flour
1 egg
1/2 cup whole milk (or half-and-half, aka light cream, or heavy cream)
1/4 cup vegetable or canola oil
1/4 cup white, granulated sugar
1 teaspoon pure vanilla extract
1/2 teaspoon fresh lemon zest (grated lemon peel, no white pith)
1/4 teaspoon kosher salt (or 1/8 teaspoon table salt)
1 teaspoon baking powder
1 cup all-purpose flour
1 to 2 tablespoons coarse finishing sugar such as turbinado or Demerara or a white

coarse sugar to sprinkle on before baking (optional)

Step 1 — Prep oven and muffin pan: Preheat oven *at least 30 minutes* to 375°F. Line 6 muffin cups with paper holders (yellow makes a nice presentation); lightly coat papers with nonstick spray.

Step 2 — Prep blueberries: If using fresh blueberries, de-stem, wash, drain, and pat dry. They can be a little moist, no worries. If using frozen blueberries, use them right out of the freezer, do not thaw. Gently toss the fresh or still-frozen blueberries in the 2 teaspoons of flour. Take care not to crush the berries as you toss them, keep them whole. The flour will absorb excess juice during baking and prevent your muffins from turning gray. Set aside.

Step 3 — Create batter with one-bowl mixing method: Crack egg into a mixing bowl and gently beat with a whisk. Add milk, oil, sugar, vanilla, lemon zest, and salt, and whisk until well blended. Now add baking powder and whisk very well, until dissolved. Switching to a spoon or spatula, mix in the flour until all the raw flour disappears and a lumpy batter forms. *Do not overmix* at this stage or you will develop the gluten in the flour and your muffins will be tough instead of tender. Finally, *gently* fold in the flour-tossed blueberries, again, taking care not to crush them. Keep them whole.

Step 4 — Prep for baking: This batter makes 6 standard muffins. Divide it up evenly among your paper-lined (and lightly sprayed) muffin cups. *Clare does not use finishing sugar.* But you may like this addition. If using a coarse finishing sugar, sprinkle over each unbaked muffin top . . .

Step 5 — Bake in your *well-preheated* 375°F oven for 25 to 30 minutes. Muffins are done when tops just begin to become light golden brown.

Note: The muffins are delicious with or without finishing sugar, but beware: although muffins with sugar on top will stay crunchy the first day, the sugared tops will go soggy on you if you wrap them in plastic for storage. So if you're baking these a few days in advance of serving, leave the extra sugar off.

Toothpick method for de-panning hot muffins: If muffins are left in hot pans, bottoms may steam and become tough. Gently insert a toothpick on each side of muffin. Use the toothpicks as handles and lift the muffin from pan. This is a quick way to remove muffins without squashing them.

To store: Once completely cool, store muffins in a resealable plastic bag or plastic container. If your weather or climate is warm, also place in refrigerator. They will keep well several days that way. Muffins *can be reheated* easily (10 to 15 seconds) in microwave.

THE VILLAGE BLEND'S CHARMING CHOCOLATE CHIP MUFFINS

"The crumb is delectable," Clare told Agent Cage about this muffin, "and if you sip your espresso as you eat the muffin, the rich roasted flavor of the coffee mingles on the palate with the bits of chocolate in a mind-blowingly sensuous dance . . ."

Sharon Cage, who'd had a rough morning leading an army of Secret Service personnel, stared in a kind of silent foodie shock at Clare's description, a tiny drop of saliva glistening at the corner of her mouth. Yes, the woman had skipped breakfast — and she was slowly charmed by Clare Cosi and these amazing muffins. The triple espresso helped, too.

Makes 6 coffeehouse-style muffins or 8 smaller muffins

1/2 cup whole milk or buttermilk
1/4 cup (1/2 stick) unsalted butter, melted and cooled
1/4 cup granulated white sugar
1/4 cup light brown sugar
1 large egg, lightly beaten with fork
1 1/2 teaspoons pure vanilla extract
1 1/2 teaspoons baking powder
1/2 teaspoon baking soda
1/4 teaspoon table salt (or coarse sea salt)
1 1/4 cups all-purpose flour
3/4 cup mini semisweet chocolate chips*

*Mini chips notes: For the best results, you should absolutely use mini chocolate chips in this recipe. In a pinch, you can chop standard-sized chocolate chips or discs, but do not use standard-sized chips for these muffins.

Step 1 — Prep oven and pan: First preheat your oven to 425°F. Line 6 muffin pan cups (or 8 cupcake pan cups) with paper liners and lightly coat the papers with nonstick spray to prevent baked muffins from sticking. Or use a nonstick muffin pan and lightly coat the pan with spray.

Step 2 — One-bowl mixing method: In a mixing bowl, whisk together the whole milk (or buttermilk), melted butter, white and brown sugars, egg, and vanilla. Whisk in the baking powder, baking soda, and salt. Switch to a rubber spatula or large spoon and stir in the flour, but do not overmix at this stage. Stir only enough to form a batter, making sure all the raw flour is incorporated. Finally, fold in the mini chips. Batter will be thick.

Step 3 — Bake: Divide the batter into the 6 muffin cups (or 8 cupcake cups) and bake at 425°F for 5 minutes. Now turn the oven down to 375°F and bake for another 12 to 15 minutes, depending on your oven. Let the muffins cool for 5 minutes in the pan and then remove to prevent the bottoms from steaming and becoming tough. To store, place completely cooled muffins in a plastic, airtight container.

CLARE'S CORN MUFFINS
Clare often makes these corn muffins for Mike Quinn. They enjoy them with coffee in the

morning. If reheating the muffins, simply warm them up for 10 seconds in the microwave and melt a bit of butter on them — amazing! For dinner, she'll reduce the sugar and pair the muffins with a bowl of chili or barbecued ribs or chicken. Note her variation suggestions in both cases. If you prefer savory corn bread, simply reduce the sugar to 2 tablespoons and (if you like) fold in some sweet corn kernels, a finely diced jalapeño, maybe even some shredded cheddar cheese. Make it your own and bake it with joy!

Makes 6 muffins

1 large egg
3/4 cup milk (whole, 2%, or skim)
1/2 cup sour cream (drain off any visible liquid)
1/2 cup granulated sugar (for savory cornbread reduce to 2 tablespoons)
1/2 teaspoon kosher salt or 1/4 teaspoon fine table salt
1/4 cup canola or vegetable oil
2 teaspoons baking powder
1/2 teaspoon baking soda
1 cup all-purpose flour
3/4 cup yellow cornmeal

Step 1 — One-bowl mixing method:

Preheat the oven to 350°F. In a mixing bowl, whisk together egg, milk, sour cream, sugar, salt, and oil. When the mixture is well blended and the sour cream smoothly incorporated, whisk in the baking powder and soda. Finally, measure in the all-purpose flour and cornmeal.

Switch to a spoon or spatula and stir until all the dry ingredients are incorporated into a loose, lumpy batter, but do not overmix or you will develop the gluten in the flour and your corn bread will be tough instead of tender.

Step 2 — Prepare the pan: Prep a muffin pan by lightly coating the muffin cups with nonstick cooking spray. Put a little on the top, too, in case your muffins spread. Pour your batter into the cups, distributing the batter evenly.

Step 3 — Bake: In a preheated 350°F oven, bake muffins for 20 to 25 minutes. When a toothpick inserted in the center comes out with no wet batter clinging to it, remove from oven. Remove muffins from pan quickly or the bottoms may steam and become tough.

CLARE'S BIG, CHEWY CAFÉ-STYLE OATMEAL COOKIES

Wonderfully crispy around the edges with a delightfully chewy center, these big, round oatmeal cookies are bakery quality — Clare Cosi's amazing version of the All-American oatmeal cookie. Two textures of oatmeal is her secret, along with a combination of nutmeg, cinnamon, extra vanilla, and dark brown sugar. They're extra popular with Clare's coffeehouse customers, including Stan "Sticks" McGuire, who enjoyed a plate of these with a hot cup of joe as he sat down with Clare for an eye-opening discussion about her difficult chef.

2 dozen big, bakery-style cookies, 3-inches in diameter

1/2 cup (1 stick) unsalted butter, softened
1/2 cup brown sugar, packed (light or dark brown? See Clare's note)*
1/2 cup white, granulated sugar 1 egg, whisked with fork
2 teaspoons vanilla
1 1/2 teaspoons ground cinnamon
1/4 teaspoon ground nutmeg
1/4 teaspoon salt
1 teaspoon baking soda
3/4 cup all-purpose flour

1 1/2 cups old fashioned rolled oats (divided)
3/4 cup raisins

*Brown sugar note: You can use either light or dark brown sugar for this recipe. Choose dark brown if you'd like a deeper, richer winter-spice flavor with a note of molasses. Choose light brown for a lighter colored cookie with a taste more like traditional oatmeal.

Step 1 — Prepare dough: Using an electric mixer, cream the butter and two sugars together until they resemble smooth and creamy peanut butter. Add the egg, vanilla, cinnamon, and nutmeg and mix well. Now add the salt and baking soda and blend until smooth. Stop the mixer. Measure in the flour and 1/2 cup of the rolled oats. Take the remaining 1 cup of oats, dump it into your food processor and pulse until it has the consistency of flour. Add this "oat flour" to the bowl, turn the mixer on low, and blend everything into a smooth dough. Make sure all of your flour is blended into the dough, but do not over-mix at this point. Finally, fold in the raisins.

Step 2 — Chill and form: Tuck plastic

wrap around the dough in your bowl and chill in the refrigerator for 30 minutes — this brief chilling allows the butter in the dough to harden up so you can properly form your cookies into balls. While waiting for the dough to chill, preheat your oven to 350°F and line a baking sheet with parchment paper. To bake, tear off pieces of the chilled dough and roll lightly in your hands to form walnut-sized balls. Space out the balls on your baking sheet to allow room for plenty of spreading. Using your palm, press down gently on the dough balls, flattening them into a circle roughly 2-inches in diameter.

Step 3 — Bake with care: Bake in your preheated 350°F oven for 10 to 12 minutes. The edges of the cookies should appear baked with the centers still soft and underbaked. That's okay. Take them out of the oven and allow them to finish cooking for 10 full minutes on the hot baking sheet. (*This method is the best for creating perfectly baked, wonderfully chewy cookies while preventing the bottoms from browning too much, which is the easiest way to ruin an otherwise delicious cookie.*) After 10 minutes on the hot pan, your big, beautiful oatmeal cookies are ready for you and your loved ones to eat with joy!

CLARE'S QUICK-RISE 30-MINUTE DINNER ROLLS

In just 30 minutes they're in the oven! Yes, this is the very recipe Clare baked up for Mike Quinn in the wee hours of the morning. Of course, she had an ulterior motive — snooping. But Quinn didn't care. The tender, warm fluffy interior of these rolls with the crispy golden crust made the invasion of his privacy worth it — and, after all, he did leave his smartphone in the kitchen with his message box unlocked.

Makes 12 rolls

1 cup plus 2 tablespoons warm water
1/3 cup vegetable oil
1/4 cup white granulated sugar
4 1/2 teaspoons RapidRise yeast (or any quick-rising yeast)
1 teaspoon kosher salt (or 1/2 teaspoon table salt)
1 large egg, lightly beaten
3 1/2 cups bread flour (or all-purpose flour)
Egg wash — 1 egg lightly beaten with 1 teaspoon of water (optional)

Step 1 — Prepare yeast: Preheat oven to

425°F. In a mixing bowl, stir together the warm water, oil, and sugar. Now whisk in the RapidRise yeast until dissolved and allow it to sit for 10 minutes. *Yeast note:* It's important that you use yeast that has not passed the expiration date of its packaging. At the end of this "proofing" step, you should see evidence that the yeast is alive. Watch for a slight foaming of the liquid — this is the yeast eating the sugar and producing carbon dioxide bubbles. If you don't see that, your yeast is dead. Start over with new yeast. In the meantime, prep a 9-by-13-inch metal pan by coating bottom and sides generously with nonstick cooking spray.

Step 2 — Make dough: Using an electric mixer with a dough hook attachment, mix in the egg and flour with salt mixed in. Using floured hands, knead the sticky dough in the bowl for 3 minutes, until it appears smooth.

Step 3 — Form rolls: Break off pieces of dough. Work each lightly in your hand like Play-Doh, then form the rolls this way: Flatten the piece of dough into a little pancake. Press your thumbs into the center and draw up the edges to form a little purse. Pinch the purse closed, turn it upside down, and place the smoothly formed roll into your well-greased baking pan. Form a total of 12 rolls. For even baking, they should be about the same size.

Step 4 — Rest the Rolls: Allow the rolls to rest in the pan (out of the oven) for 15 minutes.

(Optional egg wash: This recipe will give you beautiful rolls with a slightly browned top. For a shiny, bakery-style browning on top, brush the rolls with the egg wash immediately before baking.)

Step 5 — Bake: To bake, place pan in preheated 425°F oven. Bake for 13 to 18 minutes, depending on your oven. Pull out a test roll and split it. If the roll is overly doughy, continue baking the rolls for another 5 minutes or so, but be careful not to burn the bottoms. Remember, once the rolls come out of the oven, they will continue to bake as they cool, especially if you leave them in the hot pan.

CLARE COSI'S PRIME RIB ROAST

Mike Quinn would have come home even earlier if he knew what was waiting for him in Clare Cosi's kitchen — an herb-crusted prime rib roast. A rib roast is an amazing thing, delicious, tender, buttery. For beef lovers it's hard to beat. Clare made it a day in advance of Mike's homecoming to slice thin and serve with her American-style au jus. That savory recipe follows.

Serves 6

6 garlic cloves, finely chopped
3 sprigs fresh rosemary, chopped
5 sprigs fresh thyme, chopped
1/2 cup kosher or pink salt
3 tablespoons whole peppercorns (or fresh-ground black pepper)
3/4 cup extra virgin olive oil
1 small prime rib roast (3 to 4 ribs), about 6 pounds

Step 1 — Create a crust: Preheat oven to 325°F. In a bowl (or food processor) mash together the garlic, rosemary, thyme, salt, peppercorns, and 1/2 cup olive oil to make a paste. Smear the paste generously over the entire roast. Lay the roast, fat side up, on a rack in a walled baking pan. Drizzle with the rest of the oil.

Step 2 — Roast: In the preheated oven, roast for 1 1/2 to 2 hours — about 20 minutes per pound. When the internal temperature of the roast reaches 125°F, it is medium rare. (Prime rib should not be cooked beyond medium rare.) Remove the roast to a carving board, cover with foil, and allow it to rest for at least 20 minutes. During the resting process, the internal temperature of the meat will continue to rise, up to 10 degrees.

Step 3 — Serve: Strain the pan juices. Use the juice to serve with the meat, or to add extra flavor to your au jus (see the recipe below).

CLARE'S EFFORTLESS AU JUS

Slow cooking of a prime rib roast renders a lot of juice, but is it really enough? And what do you do a day later, when the beef tastes even better, but you've run out of the succulent, beefy gravy? While a traditional French dip uses beef juices, Americans have their own style of "au jus," and Clare is happy to share her version.

Yield: 2 cups

1 tablespoon olive oil
1 stalk celery, chopped
1/4 cup red onion, chopped

1 teaspoon garlic, minced
1 tablespoon water (or white wine)
1 tablespoon Worcestershire sauce
2 1/2 cups beef broth
1 teaspoon Wondra flour

Step 1 — Prep the veggies: Coat the bottom of a medium saucepan with olive oil and heat. Chop celery, onions, and mince the garlic. Caramelize the onions in the olive oil. Add celery and cook for 2 minutes. Add garlic and cook for 2 more minutes.

Step 2 — Simmer: Deglaze the pot with the water or white wine, then add Worcestershire sauce and cook for another minute, stirring constantly. Add the beef broth and bring to a boil. Reduce heat and simmer for 30 minutes.

Step 3 — Strain and finish: Pour hot broth through a strainer, then return it to the pot. Add the Wondra flour and simmer 5 minutes or until it thickens slightly.

Serving tip: When reheating the au jus for a beef roast, add some of the meat drippings from your main dish to the pan for added flavor and richness.

CLARE COSI'S CHERRY AND PORT–GLAZED PORK TENDERLOIN, WRAPPED IN BACON

The sweet-salty combination of the cherry-port glaze with the "barding" of the tenderloin (in strips of delicious bacon) is out of this world, which is where Clare Cosi sent Mike Quinn the night she served this dish to him, popping champagne at the dinner table to celebrate a victory over "Hopkins the Horrible." The cherries are dried, which makes it easy to enjoy this dish through the fall and winter. As for the port, as Tito would tell you, a "tawny" or "vintage" port has been aged for several years and is delicious sipped after dinner. This recipe will work just fine with a much less expensive, younger, "ruby" port. You can even substitute another sweet, fortified wine, such as a sweet Marsala.

Serves 3 to 4

For the pork loin

1 to 3 pounds boneless pork loin roast
6 to 8 pieces of thin-sliced bacon

For the dry rub

1/2 teaspoon chili powder
1/8 teaspoon cayenne pepper

1/2 teaspoon salt
1/4 teaspoon cumin
1/4 teaspoon cinnamon

For the cherry-and-port glaze

1 tablespoon cornstarch
1/4 cup chicken stock
2 tablespoons butter
1/3 cup chopped onion
Pinch of ground allspice
1/2 cup port or another sweet red wine
1/2 cup or so dried cherries
1/2 cup dark brown sugar, packed

Step 1 — Preheat oven to 375°F. Line a roasting pan with aluminum foil. Rinse the tenderloin in cool water and pat dry. Let the meat reach room temperature (about 15 minutes). Meanwhile create your spice rub. In a small bowl, combine your dry rub ingredients. When the tenderloin is ready, use your hands to massage the flavors into the meat.

Step 2 — Now it's time for "barding" the pork, the traditional term for wrapping something in fat before cooking. For this recipe, Clare is using bacon. Wrap the bacon around the rubbed tenderloin one piece at a time, starting at the ends and meeting in the middle. Cover all of the pork with bacon. Place the tenderloin in the center of the foiled pan. Roasting times vary. Roast 45 to 50 minutes if your tenderloin is 2 pounds or under. 50 to 60 minutes if it is 2 1/2 to 3 pounds.

Step 3 — Make glaze: While the pork is cooking, make the glaze. Whisk the cornstarch and stock in a small bowl until the mixture is smooth, and set the bowl aside. Melt the butter in a skillet, over medium heat. Add the onion and cook until tender but not browned. Add the allspice and cook for 1 more minute. Increase the heat to medium high and add the port (or other sweet, fortified wine), cherries, and brown sugar to the skillet. Bring this mixture to a boil. Reduce the heat to low. Cook the glaze until the mixture is slightly thickened, stirring occasionally to prevent burning. Add to the skillet the cornstarch mixture you made earlier. Cook and stir until the mixture boils and thickens.

Step 4 — Glaze pork: Drizzle this glaze over top of the pork roast (after you've roasted it for 45 to 60 minutes, depending on size) and continue to roast for about 30 minutes longer, or until internal temperature gets to 160°F.

Step 5 — Serve: Once out of the oven, you must let it rest for a short time to allow the meat to recollect its juices. If you cut it right away, you risk dry meat. After 10 to 15 minutes' rest, slice the tenderloin into servings about 1 inch thick.

LUTHER'S BUTTERMILK FRIED CHICKEN WINGS

In a bit of culinary magic, Luther Bell caramelized bacon bits, Vidalia onions, red pepper strips, and green beans in a sweet-tart glaze using hard cider. (That recipe follows this one!) The first tangy bite made Clare Cosi swoon with its bright and colorful flavors and al dente beans.

But the balanced pairing wasn't complete without a plate of buttermilk fried chicken wings — a deceptively simple dish that requires its own magic to prepare properly. Luther uses chicken wings exclusively. Unlike bigger pieces, which often end up burning on the outside before cooking all the way through, wings fry perfectly.

The buttermilk bath is the second key to success. The acid in the buttermilk is an excellent marinade, softening and sweetening the meat before it touches flour or oil.

Serves 4

3 pounds fresh chicken wings
1 quart regular or light buttermilk
3 cups all-purpose flour
1 tablespoon kosher salt
1 tablespoon pepper, ground very fine
2 tablespoons sweet paprika
2 tablespoons McCormick Poultry Season-
  ing or your favorite chicken spice blend
1 teaspoon cayenne pepper (optional)
Canola oil for frying

Note: This version calls for 3 pounds of whole chicken wings. That's about 12 wings, or 24 when divided, yielding 6 pieces each for a family of four.

Step 1 — Cut the wings into 3 pieces, discarding all wing tips (or you can boil the tips with carrots, celery, onion, and spices to make chicken broth). Place cut-up chicken in a plastic or glass container. Pour buttermilk over the chicken wing pieces and marinate in refrigerator for up to 3 hours (but no more).

Step 2 — Mix the flour, salt, pepper,

paprika, chicken spice, and cayenne pepper thoroughly in a paper or plastic bag.

Step 3 — Remove chicken pieces from buttermilk and discard excess liquid. Shake off loose buttermilk (do not rinse). Drop wing pieces into the bag 2 or 3 pieces at a time. Shake well until each piece is evenly coated.

Step 4 — Heat canola oil in a pan or pot deep enough to allow wing pieces to be submerged in oil (at least 2 inches deep). Shake off any excess flour on your chicken wing pieces and slowly place pieces, one at a time, into hot oil. (Note: you know the oil is hot enough for frying when a dough ball made from a bit of buttermilk and flour sizzles when dropped into the pot.) Make sure your pan is not too crowded; otherwise, oil's temperature will drop dramatically, and you will end up with greasy chicken.

Step 5 — Fry each batch for 8 to 10 minutes, turning occasionally until chicken is golden brown and cooked evenly. (Watch oil temperature. Keeping the oil hot enough is the key to good frying.) Place finished pieces on a metal rack over a cookie sheet pan to catch excess grease. Place rack in a 220°F oven to hold the chicken while the other pieces fry.

LUTHER'S HARD CIDER
GREEN BEANS

Luther's Hard Cider Green Beans showcase the bright tang of cider, which mingles perfectly with the bacon, onions, garlic, and red pepper to create a balanced dish that is smoky-sweet, slightly tart, with a bright, crunchy finish that dances on the tongue. As for the hard cider, that pre-dates America's founding. Apple seeds arrived on the Mayflower, and within a century the fruit was ubiquitous. Because nothing was ever wasted, fruit that was deemed too bitter or acidic to eat was made into hard cider for imbibing, or cider vinegar for pickling and preservation. The popularity of hard cider grew with the nation. Barrels of hard cider, freely given, helped George Washington win his campaign for the Virginia House of Burgesses in 1758. And after the Revolution, President John Adams drank cider to encourage more Americans to consume "local products," and hard cider quickly became the drink of "everyday Americans." After Prohibition, beer replaced cider as the working man's beverage, but today cider is making a comeback, both for drinking and cooking, and it works scrumptiously in this recipe!

Serves 6

1 teaspoon olive oil
6 slices bacon, chopped
1 cup Vidalia onions, sliced thin
4 cloves garlic, minced
1 red bell pepper, cut into slivers
1 1/2 pounds green beans, ends trimmed
1/2 cup hard cider
1/2 cup apple juice or apple cider
1 teaspoon sea salt
1 teaspoon freshly ground black pepper

Place a large skillet or Dutch oven over medium heat and add olive oil. When the oil is hot, add the bacon and cook until well browned (but not crispy), about 5 minutes. Add the onion, garlic, red bell peppers, and cook, stirring occasionally, until the onions are translucent, 3 to 4 minutes. Add the green beans and toss to combine with the bacon and onions. Increase the heat to medium high and add the hard cider and apple juice (or apple cider). As soon as the liquid begins to boil, place the lid on the pan and cook the beans for about 6 to 8 minutes. Remove the lid, season the beans with the salt and pepper, and toss well. Replace the lid and cook until the beans are tender, 1 or 2 minutes longer. Remove from the heat and transfer the beans to a serving dish or small platter.

LUTHER'S ALABAMA–STYLE WHITE BARBECUE SAUCE

In North Alabama, this vinegar-and-pepper-based mayonnaise sauce is king. Invented in Decatur, Alabama, at Big Bob Gibson Bar-B-Q in 1925, it is traditionally used to dress grilled and fried chicken. It's also a fine dip for chicken or other grilled meats and fish. It can also be used as a salad dressing or a pretzel or potato chip dip. "Everyone in Alabama has their own special version," says Chef Luther Bell. "Start with the basics, and you can always improvise."

Yield: about 1 1/3 cups

1 cup of mayonnaise
1/4 cup white or cider vinegar
1/2 teaspoon black pepper
Dash of cayenne pepper (to taste)

Mix all the ingredients in a tight container, seal, and shake madly. Good right away, or chill. It will thicken a little in the refrigerator. Store refrigerated for no more than seven days.

Chef's tip: You can spice up Alabama

White Sauce even more by adding, to taste, any or all of the following: garlic powder, horseradish, Worcestershire sauce, hot pepper or Tabasco sauce, white pepper, sea salt, dash of lemon juice.

LUTHER'S CAROLINA MUSTARD BARBECUE AND DIPPING SAUCE

Mustard sauce arrived on the American culinary scene in the 1740s, when the British paid thousands of German families to take up residence on free land in South Carolina. Carolina mustard sauce can be clearly traced to those settlers. Because it's made with dark brown sugar (no substitutes!) instead of the corn syrup often used to sweeten ketchup and tomato-based sauces, the mustard sauce won't roll off the hot meat when applied. It's also great for dipping fried foods, mini-hot dogs, pretzels, and raw vegetables. You can even use it as a salad dressing.

Yield: about 1 1/2 cups

1 cup yellow mustard
1/2 cup cider vinegar
8 tablespoons dark brown sugar (to taste)
1 teaspoon Worcestershire sauce
1/2 teaspoon of powdered cayenne pepper
1/2 teaspoon black pepper

Mix all the ingredients together in a glass or plastic container and shake until well blended. Chill for an hour or overnight for the flavors to properly blend.

LUTHER'S STICKY CHICKEN WINGS GLAZED WITH CAROLINA MUSTARD BARBECUE SAUCE

Here's a happy alternative to tomato-based barbeque sauces that pretty much everyone enjoys. It has the sweetness Americans have grown to love, with a special tang that comes from the mustard. Don't be fooled by this sauce's "raw" taste when you first mix it up. It mellows and sweetens with cooking, but never loses the special bite that only comes with mustard.

Serves 4

10 to 12 premium chicken wings, cut into thirds, tips discarded
1 cup Luther's Carolina Mustard Barbecue and Dipping Sauce (recipe above)

To cook in your oven:

Step 1 — Prepare chicken and pan: Prepare a shallow baking or roasting pan by lining with aluminum foil. (For easy cleanup). Coat the foil with a non-stick cooking spray. Place wings in the pan, at least an inch apart.

Step 2 — Bake and baste: Preheat oven to 350°F. Place your prepared pan of chicken wings in the middle rack. After 15 minutes, remove the pan and generously brush the prepared mustard sauce on top of each chicken wing. Cook for another 15 minutes. Then, at the 30 minute mark, flip each wing and brush the opposite side of the chicken wing. Bake for another 15 minutes. Flip the chicken pieces one last time and generously brush on a final coat of mustard sauce. Return the chicken to your oven for another 20 to 25 minutes. Total cooking time is a little over 60 minutes.

To cook on your grill:

Step 1 — Prep the wings: Roll chicken wings in vegetable oil and shake off excess. You want a nice, light coating. Sprinkle salt on all sides. If you are using a charcoal grill, you must create a cool area where there are fewer coals.

Step 2 — Grill: Lay the chicken wings on the hot side and grill for 5 to 10 minutes, depending on how hot the grill is (you do not want the chicken to burn). Once you have a good sear on one side, move the chicken pieces to the cool part of the grill (if you are using a gas grill, lower the heat to medium low). Cover and cook for 15 minutes.

Step 3 — Turn and sauce: Turn the chicken wings over and brush with mustard sauce. Cover again and allow to cook for another 15 to 20 minutes. Repeat, turning the chicken pieces over, basting them with sauce, covering, and cooking for another 15 to 20 minutes.

CLARE COSI'S COFFEE-GLAZED BARBECUED CHICKEN

Like a complex premium coffee, this glaze brings many flavors together. The earthiness of the brewed coffee blends beautifully with the smokiness of the charcoal and the sweetness of the molasses and brown sugar. The lemon brings brightness and the cornstarch is the magic trick to make the glaze thick. This recipe can also be baked in the oven. This glaze is the "secret" the President of the United States asked Clare Cosi to reveal at the Smithsonian's National Museum of American History. This one she was happy to give.

The other secret, which she hid close to her . . . ahem, heart — would remain Clare's.

Servings: About 10 pieces of chicken. Chicken thighs and drumsticks are good with this recipe because dark meat tends to remain juicier during grilling, but it works equally well with breasts and wings. Because the cornstarch makes the glaze stick, you can use chicken parts with or without skin.

1/2 cup brewed coffee or espresso
1/2 cup molasses (unsulfured, and not blackstrap)
1/2 cup light brown sugar, packed
5 teaspoons freshly squeezed lemon juice
3 tablespoons plus 1 teaspoon cornstarch (for thickening)

To make the glaze — Combine coffee, molasses, brown sugar, and lemon juice in a medium nonstick saucepan. Stir for a minute over medium heat until the sugar dissolves. Whisk in the cornstarch, 1 tablespoon at a time until it disappears.

While continuing to stir the glaze, increase the heat and bring the glaze to a simmer for 4 to 5 minutes. When glaze thickens enough to coat the back of a spoon (about the consistency of honey), it's done.

Troubleshooting: If the glaze seems too thin, increase the heat and bring it to a full boil while continuing to whisk. This should do the trick. If it doesn't, whisk in a little extra cornstarch (1 teaspoon at a time) and it should thicken up fast. If the glaze becomes too thick, simply whisk more coffee into the saucepan, a little at a time, and continue to heat and whisk until the glaze loosens to the right consistency for brushing.

To cook in your oven:

Step 1 — Prepare chicken and pan: Rinse your chicken parts, pat dry. Prepare a shallow baking or roasting pan by lining with aluminum foil. (You'll want to do this for easy cleanup.) Now coat the foil with a nonstick cooking spray. Place chicken in the pan, skin side up (if your pieces have skin).

Step 2 — Bake and baste: Preheat oven to 350°F. Place your prepared pan of chicken pieces in the middle rack of your oven. After 15 minutes, remove the pan and generously brush the prepared coffee glaze on top of each chicken piece. After another

15 minutes (at the 30-minute mark), flip each piece (so that the skin side is down) and glaze the unglazed side of the chicken. Bake for another 15 minutes. Flip the chicken pieces one last time so that skin side is up again and generously brush on a final coat of glaze. Return the chicken to your oven for another 20 to 25 minutes. Total cooking time is a little over 60 minutes.

Note on cooking time: If you are baking chicken breasts, which are bigger and thicker than thighs, you will need to add 10 to 15 minutes to the cooking time. For smaller pieces, such as wings, the cooking time should be shortened by 10 to 15 minutes.

To cook on your grill:

Step 1 — Roll chicken pieces in vegetable oil and shake off excess. You want a nice, light coating. Sprinkle salt on all sides. If you are using a charcoal grill, you must create a cool area where there are fewer coals.

Step 2 — Lay the chicken pieces skin side down on the hot side and grill for 5 to 10 minutes, depending on how hot the grill is (you do not want the chicken to burn).

Once you have a good sear on one side, move the chicken pieces to the cool part of the grill (if you are using a gas grill, lower the heat to medium low). Cover and cook for 20 to 30 minutes.

Step 3 — Turn the chicken pieces over and baste them with the coffee glaze. Cover again and allow to cook for another 20 to 30 minutes. Repeat, turning the chicken pieces over, basting them with sauce, covering, and cooking for another 20 to 30 minutes.

Finishing zap: Here's a quick and easy cheat to make sure your chicken is cooked through: Remove cooked and glazed chicken from grill and place in a microwave on high for 1 to 3 minutes. Then return the chicken to *the hot part* of the grill for another 3 minutes. This should take the meat to 165°F, and keep the seared skin nice and crispy.

LUTHER'S CHEDDAR-CORN SPOON BREAD

Spoon bread has its roots in a native American dish called subpawn, a type of cornmeal porridge. English colonists added eggs and milk to enrich the dish. Luther Bell built on the old, traditional recipe to create a more modern dinner side dish. Full of cheddar and corn flavor, this corn bread soufflé is easy to cook yet makes an impressive comfort-food side dish for fall dinners, especially roast chicken or turkey. Clare Cosi finds it hard to stop eating this one. May you, too, eat with Great American Joy!

Yield Note: This recipe is perfect for a 1 1/2-quart casserole dish. In a pinch, however, you can use an 8-inch-square pan. Whatever you use, be sure it is well greased with butter or cooking spray to prevent sticking. For a larger batch, double the amount of ingredients and use a 2 1/2-quart casserole dish or a 9-by-9-by-2-inch pan. Cooking time may be a bit longer for a larger casserole; check for doneness as indicated in the recipe.

2 cups sweet corn kernels (if using frozen, no need to thaw)
4 tablespoons melted butter
1 tablespoon white, granulated sugar
1 teaspoon table salt or finely ground sea salt
1/8 teaspoon ground white pepper (white looks better, but black will work)
1 pinch of cayenne pepper

1 1/2 cups milk, whole or low fat (1% or 2%, not skim)

1/2 cup water

3/4 cup cornmeal (yellow or white)

2 eggs

2 cups shredded mild cheddar cheese, yellow or white

2 teaspoons baking powder

Optional flavor additions: 1/4 cup crumbled bacon; 1/4 cup chopped roasted red and/or green peppers; 1/4 cup finely chopped, lightly grilled sweet onions*

First preheat your oven to 350°F. Into a medium-sized saucepan, place the corn kernels (still frozen is fine) and butter, warm over medium heat, stirring while butter melts. Add the sugar, salt, white pepper, and cayenne pepper and stir to blend the flavors. Add the milk, water, and cornmeal. Cook and stir this mixture over medium heat for 2 to 3 minutes, until mixture thickens and resembles porridge.

IMPORTANT: Remove from heat and allow the mixture to cool off for at least 10 minutes before whisking in the eggs, cheese, and baking powder. Transfer immediately to a well-greased 1 1/2-quart casserole dish. Bake in the preheated oven for 40 to 50 minutes (depending on oven). When the spoon bread is set on top (no longer liquid and jiggling) and slightly browned, it's finished cooking. As the name implies, spoon the bread pudding onto plates right from the baking dish and . . . eat with joy!

Reheating note: When Luther reheats this casserole, he often sprinkles extra cheddar cheese on top. It's amazing!

*If you'd like to add more vegetable flavors, such as chopped sweet onions and/or peppers, begin by sautéing them in the saucepan. Once they've cooked up, use the same pan to begin building the recipe, adding the corn, butter, milk, and so on.

LUTHER'S BOURBON HOT DOG BITES

After Abby's spectacular debut and the greenroom party, the after-hours crowd rolled back down to the Jazz Space. Gardner and his friends began an all-night jam session, and someone mentioned they were hungry. Unfortunately, the kitchen cupboards were bare. In their own foodie version of a perfect improvisation, Luther, Joy, and Clare played just the right notes — using simple ingredients to create an insanely delicious snack. First Clare found a few packages of wieners, then Luther threw them in a skillet with brown sugar, ketchup, and a generous splash of bourbon. Finally, Joy suggested using small, thin bar pretzel sticks to spear the Bourbon Hot Dog Bites, and the combo of salty crunch with tangy-sweet sauce made it the perfect foodie finale for the Village Blend's big night.

Serves 6

1 pound of your favorite hot dogs (beef or pork hot dogs)
1 cup Simply Heinz Ketchup (or other ketchup without corn syrup)
1 cup bourbon
1 teaspoon dry mustard
1 cup dark brown sugar

Step 1 — Divide the dogs: Cut both ends off each hot dog, then slice each wiener into 5 pieces, about 1/2 inch long. Set aside.

Step 2 — Prepare the mixture: In a large skillet or sauté pan, combine ketchup and bourbon and bring to a boil. As the mixture cooks, add dry mustard and dark brown sugar. Simmer for about 5 minutes.

Step 3 — Simmer: Add sliced hot dogs. When the mixture boils, lower the heat and simmer for 12 to 15 minutes. Serve warm.

Serving tip: Instead of the toothpicks or cocktail forks, serve with pretzel sticks. The salty-crunchy flavor combined with the sweet bourbon bite is outstanding.

LUTHER'S PIMENTO CHEESE

Luther confessed using a little cream cheese in his Pimento Cheese spread, his secret ingredient to making it nice and smooth. This "Caviar of the South" was offered in the Jazz Space, served with black pepper crackers and celery stalks.

Yields 2 1/2 cups

1 8-ounce block of extra-sharp cheddar cheese
1 4-ounce jar of pimentos, with liquid
1 cup mayonnaise
1/4 cup cream cheese
1 tablespoon yellow, brown, or Dijon mustard
1/4 teaspoon garlic powder

Step 1 — Cut the cheddar cheese into 1-inch squares and place the pieces in a blender. Add the entire jar of pimentos, including the liquid, the mayonnaise, cream cheese, mustard, and garlic powder. Blend until smooth.

Step 2 — The mixture will be somewhat loose. Transfer to a tight container and refrigerate for at least 1 hour, or overnight.

LUTHER'S BOURBON AND BROWN SUGAR STEAK

This was one of Clare's favorite dishes on the new Jazz Space menu. The sugar forms a crispy, sweet-savory char when grilled, the bourbon lends an amazing richness, and the pepper flakes a light spice. Inside, the meat is pink, juicy, and delicious. Slice against the grain and you have sweet-savory perfection.

Serves 4

1/3 cup bourbon
1/3 cup firmly packed dark brown sugar
1/2 teaspoon red pepper flakes
1 1/2 to 2 pounds flank steak, about 1 inch
  thick

Step 1 — **Marinate:** In a medium container or Ziploc bag, combine the bourbon, dark brown sugar, and red pepper flakes. Seal and shake vigorously until the sugar is dissolved. Add the steak to the bag, making sure to cover the steaks with marinade. Set aside for 20 minutes at room temperature or up to 3 hours in a refrigerator.

Step 2 — Grill: Heat up your grill pan on medium high, or fire up your outdoor grill. As you remove steaks from bag, shake off excess marinade. Do not rinse or pat steaks dry. Grill for 3 to 4 minutes, until the edges are a little crisp. Turn the meat sideways after 2 minutes if you want nice cross-hatched grill marks. Flip steak and cook for another 3 to 4 minutes, turning sideways once. A total cooking time of 8 or 9 minutes should result in an exterior that is nicely seared, the interior medium rare. Let the steaks rest for at least ten minutes so the juices have time to recollect. Cut the steak against the grain for juicy, tender slices.

CREAMY PENNSYLVANIA DUTCH NOODLE CASSEROLE WITH BAKED VIRGINIA HAM

Pennsylvania Dutch cooking is simple yet delicious, and versions of this casserole are common in the Northeastern region of the United States. There are versions that use canned soup, but Clare Cosi added a combination of fresh milk and evaporated (the latter for richness). For color, texture, and nutrition, Clare added peas and diced carrots. This dish has been made with many cheese combinations, but Swiss and sharp cheddar, with the salty ham, bring plenty of flavor, along with the tang of sour cream and a bit of mustard powder. Clare likes the flavor and brightness these bring. Though simple, the casserole is amazingly satisfying — one of America's great comfort foods, which is why Clare served it in little cups at the party in "America's Attic," the Smithsonian's National Museum of American History.

Serves 6

1 tablespoon vegetable or canola oil
1 tablespoon salted butter
2 cups cooked Virginia ham, diced into small pieces
1 1/2 cups frozen peas and diced carrots (do not thaw)
1 can (12 ounces) evaporated milk
1 cup fresh milk (splash in more for extra creaminess)
1/2 cup sour cream
1/2 teaspoon mustard powder
1 cup shredded Swiss cheese*
1 cup shredded sharp cheddar cheese*
1 12-ounce package of extra-wide egg noodles, cooked and drained

Salt and pepper to taste

*Or your favorite cheese. You could use mild cheddar, or Colby, Colby-Jack, and even Velveeta (though it's so mild you should combine it with either shredded Swiss or extra-sharp cheddar for better flavor).

Step 1 — Sauté Virginia ham and vegetables for flavor: In a large (at least 4-quart) skillet or saucepan warm the oil and butter over medium-high heat. When the butter is melted, add the ham and sauté for a minute or 2. Add the still-frozen peas and carrots and toss them to coat. (Do not try to cook them in this step, but do toss them enough to get their exteriors glistening with the butter and oil for good flavor in the final dish.)

Step 2 — Create the creamy sauce: Stir in the can of evaporated milk, the fresh milk, sour cream, and mustard powder. Heat to boiling. Reduce the heat to medium low. Now add the shredded cheese and stir until everything is melted and smooth. Remove from heat, cover, and set aside.

Step 3 — Cook the noodles: Use directions on package. Al dente is best; do not overcook. The minute they are well drained, add them to the pan of creamy ham and cheese and heat everything through until bubbling. If you find the sauce on the thick side, splash in a bit more fresh milk. Add salt and pepper to taste.

Noodle note: While you may be tempted to cook the noodles first, and set them aside while you make the sauce, Clare's advice is don't. When egg noodles cool, they stick together like the dickens. The result will be a heartbreaking noodle-blob that will ruin your casserole. So be sure to add the egg noodles right after they have been drained, while still hot, and you shouldn't have any problems.

LUTHER'S BEST-EVER PECAN PIE BARS

Is there anything better than a caramel pecan filling in a tender, buttery crust? Pecan Pie Bars are a classic American treat, and Luther Bell's version is amazing. It's sweet but not cloying, rich and incredibly satisfying. Clare believes Luther's recipe is the best she's ever tasted, and here are her reasons why.

Cream Cheese Crust: *Cream cheese dough is much easier to work with than* traditional pastry dough. Because the cream cheese forms layers, it's just as flaky, but the cream cheese does not melt as easily as butter, so it's a more forgiving dough to work with. Luther adjusted the ratio of flour to fat to create the perfect press-in crust, one that's tender yet strong enough to hold its shape for a bar. And the amount of crust is perfect, too, not overly thick or so thin that the bar will fall apart. But the primary reason Luther uses this crust is for flavor. Jewish bakers know the joy of that flavor. Rugelach, a classic Jewish cookie served at Hanukkah, uses such a crust. And in this recipe, the slightly tangy (yet incredibly tender) crust creates a delicious counterpoint to the very sweet pecan topping. It's a marriage made in culinary heaven!

Chopped Pecans: Luther's bars use coarsely chopped pecans instead of whole halves like many other recipes. The reason is simple: chopping the nuts allows more surface area to be exposed to the hot sugar, thus creating more caramelization per centimeter. Technically speaking, this produces more yums per inch of bar.

Combo of Dark Corn and Maple Syrups: Maple syrup gives a beautiful flavor to pecan pie and some bakers use it instead of corn syrup. Luther splits the difference for two reasons: Maple syrup can be pricey. But that's *not the only reason. The earthy flavor of dark corn syrup (or old-school cane sugar syrup) is such a classic flavor in pecan pie that leaving it out would be, well, just wrong. So Luther's recipe uses half maple and a small amount of dark corn syrup for economy but also for traditional flavor.*

Troubleshooting: *Yes, you can find recipes that are short and sweet, 100 words and you're done. But they won't give you tips to prevent disaster. Luther's little reminders in the recipe will help you achieve a nearly perfect end product.*

To see step-by-step photos of this recipe, stop by Cleo's online home: coffeehouse mystery.com.

For the press-in cream cheese crust

1/2 cup butter (1 stick), softened
3/4 cup cream cheese, softened
1/2 cup white, granulated sugar
1/4 teaspoon table salt (or 1/2 teaspoon kosher salt)
1 1/2 teaspoons pure vanilla extract
2 1/4 cups all-purpose flour
1 egg white (save the yolk for the filling)

For the whisk-together pecan pie filling

2 tablespoons unsalted butter

1/2 cup maple syrup

1/4 cup dark corn syrup

1 tablespoon cornstarch

1/2 cup light brown sugar, packed

1/2 cup white, granulated sugar

1 1/2 teaspoons pure vanilla extract

3/4 teaspoon table salt (or 1 1/2 teaspoons kosher salt)

2 large eggs plus 1 egg yolk (save white for crust)

1 3/4 cups coarsely chopped pecans (measure after chopping)

Step 1 — Prep pan: In your 9-by-13-inch baking pan, create a sling out of parchment paper so you can remove the slab of pecan pie and cut it into bars. (Tips: If you butter or spray the pan first, it will act like glue to keep the parchment neatly in place. Luther also suggests lightly buttering the paper or coating with nonstick spray.)

Step 2 — Make the easy press-in crust: Using an electric mixer, cream the butter, cream cheese, sugar, salt, and vanilla until light and fluffy. Stop the mixer. Add the flour. Blend until the dough makes coarse crumbs.

666

Pour these crumbs into the pan and press it evenly along the bottom and *up the sides of the pan* at least half an inch. This crust edge will prevent the loose filling from spilling beneath the crust and ruining the bars. Here are a few more helpful tips to create perfect bars.

Tips for perfect press-in crusts: Cover the crumbly dough with plastic and use the side of a glass to roll the dough into an even layer. Use the bottom of the glass to press the corners into a smooth crust.

Once again: Make absolutely sure you press the crust at least half an inch up the sides of the pan. This is important because it will keep the filling from spilling over the edge, which will ruin the bars. You can flute the edge or use a fork. This is not necessary. Whatever you prefer is fine. *Re-cover with plastic wrap and put the pan in the fridge and chill it for 30 minutes.* This is very important to getting good results. The chilled dough going into the hot oven will make a flakier, more tender and delicious crust. Now preheat oven to 375°F. You want a nice hot oven and a 30-minute preheating time will ensure the temperature is hot enough.

Step 3 — Make easy filling: While your crust is chilling, place a *large* saucepan on the stove. Over low heat, melt the butter and remove from heat. Stir in maple and dark corn syrups. Then add the cornstarch and whisk until fully dissolved (no clumps). Add the 2 sugars; vanilla; and salt. Fork-whisk the eggs separately and stir them in. Finally fold in your chopped pecans and coat well. Set aside.

Step 4 — Prep crust and bake: Take the chilled crust from the refrigerator. Remove the plastic wrap. Prick the crust all over with fork tines to prevent it from rising up during baking. Create an egg white wash by whisking the egg white with a few drops of water. Use a pastry brush to lightly coat the bottom and sides of the crust. You are creating a barrier between the crisp crust and wet filling. Bake about 12 to 15 minutes in your *well-preheated* 375°F oven. The crust will turn a light golden brown. When you first pull it out of the oven, you may see areas that are puffed. That's okay. Allow it to sit a few minutes and the crust will settle back down.

Step 5 — Final bake: While the crust is still warm, *slowly and carefully* pour on the filling; you can even ladle it on to make sure that none of it sloshes over the crust edges and beneath the crust, which will ruin the bars. If you're afraid the pan is getting too full, simply hold back a bit of the filling. It *should* all fit *if* you followed the directions and pressed the crust at least half an inch up the sides of the pan. No matter what, keep every bit of that loose filling inside the crust's edges! Return the pan to your 375°F oven. See bake time in next step . . .

Step 6 — Baking time notes: To prevent the ends from overbaking and the middle from underbaking, place foil loosely over the top of the pan after the first 10 minutes of baking. Carefully rotate the pan (don't spill the filling), and bake another 15 to 20 minutes — for a total of 25 to 30 minutes' baking time. You are watching for the top of the filling to set. There should be no liquid-looking areas. When you gently shake the pan, some areas may be *slightly* jiggly. If the tops of those areas are set (no longer liquid), then you can bring the pan out of the oven. Otherwise, bake 5 minutes more and check again. Remember that after the bars come out of the oven, they will continue to cook in the hot pan (so don't overcook the bars *in* the oven)!

After removing the pan from the oven, allow the pecan pie bars to sit in the hot pan, undisturbed for 1 hour. The bars *must cool off completely* before cutting. Luther advises slipping the pan into the fridge for an hour. Then carefully use the handles of the parchment paper to lift the slab of pecan pie out, cut into bars, take a bite, and you will be in buttery-sweet pecan heaven!

LUTHER'S NEW ORLEANS–STYLE BEIGNETS
Makes about 18 to 20 beignets

3/4 cup lukewarm water
1/4 cup granulated sugar
1 1/2 teaspoons RapidRise active dry yeast (a little more than half of a 1/4-ounce envelope)
1 extra-large egg, slightly beaten
1 small (5-ounce) can of evaporated milk (a little more than 1/2 cup)
2 tablespoons canola, vegetable, or another neutral-tasting oil
1/2 teaspoon kosher salt (or 1/4 teaspoon table salt)
3 1/2 cups bread flour
A little extra bread flour for dusting and rolling
Nonstick cooking spray

Vegetable oil for deep-frying
1 1/2 cups powdered sugar (approximately)
  for coating beignets

Step 1 — Make the yeast mixture: Combine the water, sugar, and yeast in a container. Allow to sit for 15 minutes. The mixture should appear active and produce foam. If not, the yeast is dead. Trash the mixture and begin again with fresher yeast.

Step 2 — Create a batter: In a large mixing bowl, fork-whisk the egg. Whisk in the evaporated milk, oil, and salt. Pour the yeast mixture into the egg mixture. Whisk in 1 cup of the flour until dissolved. Continue to add flour, stirring as you add. Flour your hands and knead the dough within the bowl until smooth. Remove the dough. Clean the bowl, lightly grease it with oil or coat with nonstick spray. Place the dough back into the bowl and place the bowl inside a plastic shopping bag (that's the very best method for rising dough — or you can cover the top with a small towel). Allow the dough to rise in a warm place for at least 2 hours.

Step 3 — Roll: On a lightly floured surface, roll out the dough a thickness of about 1/4 inch. Cut into squares — traditionally 1-by-

1-inch in size, but you can make them smaller or larger, your choice. If not using a fryer, pour oil (about an inch in depth) into a skillet or cast-iron pan. Preheat the oil to 350°F — the oil must be *very hot* and remain hot (don't crowd the pan) or you will end up with greasy, unappealing beignets.

Step 4 — Fry: Deep-fry. As you see the beignets rise and puff up, flip them over. Look for a golden brown color on both sides. Remove with a slotted spoon and allow to drain well on paper towels. While still warm, dust generously on both sides with powdered sugar and serve.

LUTHER'S BLACK MAGIC CAKE

While Hershey's created the original recipe, Chef Luther Bell worked his own culinary magic to boost this classic cake's texture and flavor. Now he'll share his secrets with you. First, Luther exchanged half the original recipe's oil for melted butter, which gives a richer texture and flavor to the cake. Why not use all butter? Because that bit of oil helps prolong the cake's shelf life, keeping it moist for a longer period of time. Next, notice how Luther improves the chocolate flavor of the cake by "blooming" the cocoa in the hot cof-

fee before mixing it with other ingredients. Luther also uses dark brown sugar for a more sultry result. Finally, Luther melts a bit of bittersweet chocolate with the butter (read more about bittersweet chocolate below). The result is a cake with a richer texture and deeper chocolate taste than the original. And now, here is the very cake Detective Mike Quinn — along with the customers of the Village Blend, DC — raved about: Luther's own version of the classic Black Magic Cake.

Makes 2 cake layers for 8- or 9-inch pans

1 cup espresso or strong brewed coffee
3/4 cup natural, unsweetened cocoa powder
4 tablespoons (1/2 stick) unsalted butter, softened
2 ounces bittersweet chocolate★
2 large eggs
1 cup buttermilk or sour milk (see note below★★)
1/4 cup vegetable or canola oil
1 1/2 cups granulated, white sugar
1/2 cup dark brown sugar
1 teaspoon pure vanilla extract
1 teaspoon table salt
2 teaspoons baking soda
1 teaspoon baking powder
1 3/4 cups all-purpose flour

*Bittersweet chocolate is a dark chocolate that is not as sweet as semi-sweet chocolate but has some sugar and other ingredients added, so it's not as harsh as unsweetened chocolate and it's often easier to melt. Look for a good quality bar of 60% to 70% cacao, make sure it's fresh by checking the expiration date, and bake with joy!

**Sour milk can be used as a substitute for buttermilk. To make it, simply combine 1 tablespoon of lemon juice or vinegar with enough milk to make 1 cup.

Step 1 — Prep pan and "bloom" the cocoa: First preheat your oven to 350°F. Next brew up some hot coffee or espresso. Measure out 1 cup and stir your 3/4 cup cocoa into it. You are blooming the cocoa for better flavor. Set it aside while you prepare two 8-inch or 9-inch, round baking pans by lightly coating with non-stick spray or buttering them and placing a round of parchment paper on the bottom of each. This parchment paper will give you foolproof results, so don't skip it. After the paper is in place, lightly spray or butter the paper.

Step 2 — Melt the chocolate: Using your

microwave (or a double boiler), melt your 2 ounces of chopped block chocolate with your 4 tablespoons of butter. Be sure not to overheat this mixture. Low and slow is the way to go. You do not want to boil or burn the chocolate or you will have to discard and start over. Once the chocolate and butter are melted together, set the mixture aside to cool.

Step 3 — Mix the batter: Using an electric mixer, beat the eggs. Stop the mixer and measure in the buttermilk, oil, sugars, and vanilla. Also add the coffee (with the cocoa already mixed in) and the melted and cooled butter and chocolate. Blend these ingredients until smooth. Stop the mixture and add the salt, baking soda, and baking powder. Blend well. Finally add the flour. Beat the mixture well for a good two minutes. Your batter will be thin.

Step 4 — Bake: Pour this batter evenly into the two prepared pans. Bake for about 30 minutes, or until a toothpick inserted in the middle comes out with no wet batter clinging to it (just moist crumbs). See Luther's "Chef Tip" below for proper cooling and de-panning. Then frost with his Special Chocolate Frosting for this cake (recipe follows this one).

LUTHER'S CHEF TIP: Would you like to avoid cake layers cracking, crumbling, sticking to the plate, or breaking on you? For foolproof cooling and de-panning of any cake, be sure to keep your cake layers in the pan for one full hour before removing. To de-pan, run a butter knife around the edges to release. Then cover a plate with plastic wrap, place the plate firmly over the top of the cake pan and flip both over. Remove the pan and gently peel off the layer of parchment paper on the bottom of the cake. Wrap the cake layer in the plastic and place it in the freezer for at least one hour. Repeat with the second layer. Now the cake layers are ready for you to frost.

LUTHER'S "SECRET INGREDIENT" CHOCOLATE FROSTING

This luxurious frosting pairs wonderfully with Luther's Black Magic Cake, enrobing the moist layers of deep chocolate in a silky, sophisticated finish. Luther's secret ingredient is a small amount of cream cheese, which brings smoothness to the texture with a hint of background tanginess, enough to prevent the finished frosted cake from becoming cloying. The espresso powder deepens the com-

plexity, as well. Like Clare and Mike's ending in this mystery, the result is a rich and satisfying treat — with just enough sweetness to make life good again.

Makes 2 to 3 cups, enough to frost a two-layer round cake (of 8- or 9-inches), or one 13-by-9-inch sheet cake, or 24 cupcakes

4 ounces good quality bittersweet chocolate*
1/4 teaspoon espresso powder
1 cup (2 sticks) unsalted butter, softened
2 ounces cream cheese from a block (not whipped), softened
1 1/2 teaspoons pure vanilla extract
3 cups confectioners' (powdered) sugar

First melt the chocolate, taking care not to burn it. If using a microwave, cook it in 10 second bursts, stirring between each. If using a saucepan on a stovetop, keep the flame very low or, even better, use a double boiler. After the chocolate is melted, stir in the espresso powder and set it aside to cool. Using an electric mixer, cream the softened butter and softened cream cheese together until they have the consistency of smooth peanut butter. Beat in the vanilla and your cooled chocolate (with the espresso powder already mixed in). Finally, beat in the powdered sugar one cup at a time.

*To read more about "bittersweet choco-late," see Luther's Black Magic Cake Rec-ipe.

CLARE'S FAVORITE LIGHT AND CREAMY NEW YORKER CHEESECAKE

Though the New Yorker *published a version of this recipe years ago, it originated from the City University of New York Graduate Center cafeteria. This light and creamy cheesecake became so popular with students that it continually sold out, becoming the talk of the town. Emilio Brasesco, the cafeteria chef who'd created the recipe, was a lot like Chef Luther Bell, passionate about pleasing his customers, using fresh ingredients, and keeping standards high. So when the Village Blend, DC, kitchen ended up with far more cream cheese than it needed, this recipe for "University Cheesecake" came to mind. Unlike the typical New York cheesecake recipe, this one needs no crust. It bakes up quickly and chills fast, too, Yet the result is creamy silkiness on a plate. Clare made some tweaks for ease and presentation. May you eat with joy!*

Makes enough to fill a 9-inch-round nonstick cake pan or an 8-by-8-inch-square nonstick baking pan

1 pound cream cheese (2 8-ounce packages), softened
3/4 cup white, granulated sugar
4 tablespoons (1/2 stick) unsalted butter, softened
3 1/2 tablespoons cornstarch (or 3 tablespoons plus 1 1/2 teaspoons)
1 tablespoon fresh lemon juice
1 1/2 teaspoons pure vanilla extract
3 large eggs, room temperature
1 cup heavy cream

Step 1 — Preheat the oven to 375°F, and note that you will be turning the oven down when the cheesecake goes into it. Take a 9-inch-round nonstick cake pan and grease it well (both bottom and sides — be sure to grease all the way up to the top of the sides) using butter or Crisco. (Clare does not advise using cooking spray.)

Step 2 — The batter-mixing process will take about 15 minutes. Be "Zen" about it. Take your time and you will be rewarded. Beat the (room-temperature!) cream cheese as Chef Emilio originally advised: "slowly and well and thoroughly." Then beat in the

679

sugar and, in turn, the butter, the cornstarch, the lemon juice, and the vanilla. Again, beat these well. Add eggs (room temperature!), one at a time, beating between each addition — this is important. You do this to add air to the batter and prevent the mixture from separating. Finally add the heavy cream and beat for a few minutes (depending on the power of your mixer, this will take from 1 to 5 minutes). You are watching for the batter to thicken. Other recipes for cheesecake may tell you that the batter should be thin and liquid. Not this one! Beat the batter until it is as thick as cake batter and easily coats the back of a spoon or spatula.

Step 3 — Pour the batter into your well-greased pan. Place the pan onto a rimmed baking sheet or jelly roll pan or in a larger baking pan. Place these 2 pans in your oven and add tap water (about 1 inch deep). The French call this "bain-marie" and it must cook this way to provide a humid environment and a silky cream — rather than a dry and cracking — cheesecake.

Step 4 — Turn the oven down to 350°F and bake from 25 to 35 minutes (depending on your oven). You are watching for the cheesecake to puff up and set into a spongy firmness around the edges yet still jiggle in the center. DO NOT OVERCOOK this cheesecake — you do not want to cook it until the center is firm. This would be wrong! Remove the cheesecake from the oven while the center is still jiggling and allow it to sit in the pan, cooling on a rack for 1 hour. The cheesecake will firm up as it cools — and you want it to cool off slowly and gently — it will also sink a bit and reduce in size, pulling away from the pan sides enough that you can literally slide it from side to side.

Step 5 — After 1 hour, the cheesecake will be set enough to de-pan by placing a large flat dish or tray over the top of the pan and flipping it carefully. Place the cheesecake in the refrigerator *uncovered* for 2 hours. Then place it in a plastic container or wrap gently with plastic (using toothpicks to tent it away from the top). Chill 1 more hour. You can slice and serve it now and it will be absolutely delicious. You'll want to store the leftovers in a sealed plastic container to prevent it from drying out.

Troubleshooting note for humid climates: This is a light and creamy cheesecake that can be made denser in one easy step. Depending on your climate and weather, you may feel the cheesecake is a bit too moist. In that case, place it in the fridge uncovered for a few hours or even overnight. The fridge will draw out the moisture and the cheesecake will automatically become denser. But do not allow it to remain in the fridge uncovered any longer than that, or the cake will dry out too much.

LUTHER'S BOURBON STREET BROWNIES

These fabulous fudge brownies were a favorite of Luther's customers when he worked in New Orleans, the birthplace of our great American jazz tradition. Bourbon Street is famous in the French Quarter of that town, but the name of the brownie also tips its hat to America's brand of good Kentucky bourbon. Luther suggests you go whole hog and use bourbon vanilla, too. To get this recipe, come visit Cleo Coyle at her online coffeehouse: coffeehousemystery.com.

MINI CARAMEL APPLE PIES
(JOY ALLEGRO'S LITTLE TARTE TATINS)

Tarte Tatins (upside-down caramel apple tarts) are as common in France as our apple pie. Legend has it that the dessert was created around 1900 by a pair of spinster sisters, who sold them to make their living. The last name of these women was Tatin. And that's why this buttery sweet pastry is called tarte Tatin.

This recipe is a mini version of the more traditional single, large Tatin, and they are close to foolproof. They're elegant little treats that always look amazing on the plate, as if Chef Bell or Joy Allegro had "sauced" the apples with caramel. Because they're individual servings, the recipe works for small dinner parties as well as large family gatherings. Best of all, the tarts can be prepared in advance. Simply cover your ramekins with plastic wrap and store them in the fridge for up to 2 days before baking and serving. (Just be sure you follow the recipe and toss the apple slices with lemon, which prevents them from turning brown.)

To see step-by-step photos of this recipe, stop by Cleo's online home: coffeehouse mystery.com.

Makes 6 tarts

Filling ingredients

3 Golden Delicious apples*
1 1/2 teaspoons lemon juice
1 1/2 teaspoons flour

Caramel ingredients

3 tablespoons butter
6 tablespoons white sugar
6 tablespoons dark brown sugar

You will also need

1 package frozen puff pastry shells
1 egg white (to brush puff pastry)
6 ramekins (7- to 8-ounce size, greased well
  with butter)
6 dessert plates

*Apple note: The Golden Delicious variety is best for this recipe because it holds its shape during baking and won't turn to applesauce when you plate the dessert. Granny Smith and Jonathan will work, as well.

Step 1 — Prepare the filling: Peel and core 3 Golden Delicious apples. Cut apples into relatively thin, even slices, about 1/2 inch thick. Toss the slices in a bowl with the lemon juice first, then the flour, coating them lightly. Note: The lemon prevents the apples from turning brown and the flour will absorb excess liquid released by the apples. If you skip the flour, your tarts may be watery.

Step 2 — Prepare the caramel: Grease the bottom and sides of your ramekins with butter. In a small saucepan, melt the 3 tablespoons of butter. Add the white and brown sugars and stir over low heat with a rubber spatula (to prevent sticking) until the sugars dissolve completely in the butter. The mixture will become thick. While still warm, divide the sugar mixture evenly among your 6 ramekins. Use that handy rubber spatula to even the mixture out at the bottom of each ramekin. (The mixture will harden as it cools, and that's fine. In the oven, it will melt again into a sweet, buttery caramel glaze for your apples.)

Step 3 — Prepare for baking: Divide your apple slices among the ramekins, layering them on their sides. You can bake the ramekins immediately at this point or store them by covering each ramekin with plastic wrap and placing in the fridge up to 2 days.

Step 4 — Begin baking: When ready to bake, preheat oven to 400°F. Remove plastic wrap, place ramekins on a baking sheet, and bake for 20 minutes. (You are halfway through the baking process.)

Step 5 — Add puff pastry: Remove your

baking sheet of ramekins from oven and (remembering the ramekins are hot!) carefully set a fully FROZEN puff pastry shell on top of the layered apple slices of each ramekin. Brush the top of the frozen pastry with egg white. This will protect the delicate pastry and also help it turn golden brown.

Step 6 — Finish baking: Return ramekins to oven for another 20 to 25 minutes. Pastry is done when dough puffs up and turns golden brown and the apples are cooked through. (You can test the softness of apples with the tip of a sharp knife.) Remove ramekins from oven and set on a cool surface. Let rest for 5 minutes. Note: the resting is important because your caramel will be boiling hot and you need to let it settle down.

Step 7 — Plate: Remembering that the ramekins are still HOT, use oven mitts to place a dessert plate over a ramekin and carefully flip it (like pineapple upside-down cake). After you flip the tart, the flaky puff pastry will be on the bottom of the plate and the buttery sweet caramel will drip down over the entire tart and pool around it on the dessert plate as if a pastry chef sauced it. If slices of apples stick to the ramekin simply use clean fingers to replace it prettily over the tart. Serve warm as is or with whipped or ice cream.

CLARE'S CHOCOLATE WHOOPIE PIES WITH WHIPPED KAHLÚA-CREAM

Whoopie pies are beloved in many areas of the United States. In fact, two regions (New England versus Pennsylvania Dutch Country) recently had a feud over who invented them — and whose were the best. Clare isn't touching that one! She also has her own swingin' spin on this classic American treat with a lighter yet delicious chocolaty version of the sandwich cake and a creamy-sweet coffee filling. This is the very dessert she served Mike Quinn on the night she celebrated her little management victory at the Village Blend. With a little coffee liqueur spiking the filling, she hoped making whoopie pies for Quinn would get the man in the mood for making another kind of whoopee. (It did.)

Makes about 24 large or 48 small, soft brownie-like cookies

5 tablespoons butter, melted
1/3 cup oil (I use canola)
1 1/2 cups all-purpose flour*

1/2 cup unsweetened cocoa powder

1/2 teaspoon baking powder

1/2 teaspoon baking soda

1/2 teaspoon kosher salt or coarse sea salt

3/4 cup light brown sugar

1/2 cup white, granulated sugar

1 cup plain yogurt (you can use low-fat but do not use nonfat; you can also use sour cream)

2 large eggs, lightly beaten with fork

1 teaspoon pure vanilla extract

*To add more fiber to the recipe, consider replacing half of the all-purpose flour with "white whole wheat" flour.

Step 1 — Butter and oil mix: Preheat oven to 350°F. Next melt the butter in a saucepan. Stir in the oil and set aside to cool.

Step 2 — One-bowl mixing method: Sift together flour, unsweetened cocoa, baking powder, baking soda, and salt. Now add in your 2 sugars, yogurt, eggs, and vanilla. Finally add the cooled melted butter and oil mixture. With a spoon or rubber spatula, mix by hand until flour is completely incorporated into a thick batter. Now stir about 50 strokes to blend well. Do not overmix or you'll develop the gluten in the flour and your whoopie pie cookies will be tough instead of tender.

Step 3 — Make cookies: Line a baking sheet with parchment paper. Batter will be thicker than cake batter but thinner than cookie dough. Drop in small mounds with a few inches of space between. Use a table-spoon for large cookies, a teaspoon for smaller ones. Using the back of the spoon, lightly swirl the mounds into even, level, flattish circles.

Step 4 — Bake: Bake smaller cookies for about 8 minutes, larger ones for about 10. Remove from oven. Clare likes to slide the entire strip of parchment paper onto the wire rack — this saves time and avoids disturbing the shape of the cookies by mov-ing one at a time with a spatula. Once cool, create sandwiches with the Whipped Kahlúa-Cream Filling, recipe below. Or . . .

Try sandwiching these together with Lu-ther's No-Churn Coffee Ice Cream. Get the recipe at coffeehousemystery.com.

Note: If making ice cream sandwiches, be sure to cover your plate with wax paper or plastic wrap before placing in the freezer or the bottom half of your sandwich may stick to the plate. After filling each sandwich, wrap them separately and store in the freezer.

WHIPPED KAHLÚA-CREAM FILLING (OR FROSTING)

3/4 cup heavy cream, well chilled
1/2 cup cream cheese, softened
1 1/4 cups powdered sugar
1 teaspoon pure vanilla extract
2 tablespoons Kahlúa (or Clare's home-made coffee liqueur)*

*Clare's homemade coffee liqueur may be used instead of Kahlúa. Find this deliciously easy make-your-own Kahlúa recipe in the back of her thirteenth Coffeehouse Mystery adventure, *Billionaire Blend.*

Using an electric mixer, whip the very cold heavy cream until it forms stiff peaks. Set aside in the refrigerator. Meanwhile, in another bowl, beat the *softened* cream cheese, powdered sugar, vanilla extract, and Kahlúa until combined. Take out your whipped cream and fold it gently into the bowl of cream cheese, sugar, and vanilla. An amazingly delicious filling for your whoopie pies or optional frosting for Clare's

Double-Chocolate Espresso Cupcakes (see
the next recipe).

DOUBLE-CHOCOLATE ESPRESSO CUPCAKES

*These dark, dense, and delightfully delicious
little cakes topped by a light, creamy cloud of
frosting were the most popular dessert at the
Smithsonian party catered by Clare Cosi and
her Village Blend crew. While Clare shared a
sweet and heartfelt moment with Agent
Sharon Cage, the party-goers took Clare's
cosmopolitan cupcakes off the tray and into
their hearts. Always a favorite at the Village
Blend in New York City, the sinfully sophisticated cakes have been added to the Jazz
Space dessert menu and Clare's DC pastry
case.*

For the cupcakes

1 cup plus 2 tablespoons all-purpose flour
1/2 cup unsweetened cocoa powder
1 teaspoon baking powder
1/2 teaspoon baking soda
1/4 teaspoon finely ground sea salt (or table
 salt)
1/2 cup (1 stick) unsalted butter (softened)
3/4 cup granulated sugar
1/4 cup light brown sugar

1 large egg, at room temperature
1/2 cup whole milk
1 teaspoon pure vanilla extract
1/2 cup espresso or strong brewed coffee (cooled)
1 teaspoon instant espresso powder
3/4 cup mini semisweet chocolate chips (must be mini!)

For the espresso buttercream

1/2 cup (1 stick) unsalted butter, at room temperature
1 1/2 cups powdered sugar
1 1/4 teaspoon instant espresso powder
1 teaspoon vanilla extract
2 tablespoons brewed coffee or espresso

Step 1 — Prep pan: First preheat the oven to 350°F. Line a cupcake pan with paper liners. To prevent sticking of the baked muffins, spray lightly with non-stick cooking spray.

Step 2 — Mix dry ingredients: Whisk together the flour, cocoa powder, baking powder, baking soda, and salt, and set aside.

Step 3 — Make batter: Cream the butter and sugars together until fluffy. Beat in the egg. Stop the mixer and add the milk, vanilla, and the cooled espresso or brewed coffee (with the instant espresso powder dissolved into it). Beat in the flour mixture from Step 2. Do not overmix at this stage, but be sure all the raw flour is incorporated into the batter. Finally, fold in the mini chocolate chips. (They really should be mini chips for the best results. In a pinch, you can chop standard-sized chocolate chips or discs, but do not use standard chips for this recipe.)

Step 4 — Bake: Divide the batter among the 12 lined cupcake cups of your pan. Bake about 18 to 22 minutes or until a toothpick inserted in the center of a cupcake comes out with no batter clinging to it. (Be careful not to mistake melted chocolate chips with unbaked batter!) Be sure to cool your cupcakes completely before frosting them.

Step 5 — Make frosting: Using an electric mixer, whip the softened butter until light and fluffy. Reduce the mixer speed and add your powdered sugar a little at a time. After the powdered sugar has been added, scrape down the sides of the bowl. Whisk your instant espresso powder into your vanilla extract and brewed coffee and then beat it into the frosting until it is beautifully fluffy and ready for the tops of your delicious double-chocolate espresso cupcakes. Top with chocolate shavings or a chocolate-covered espresso bean!

RULES FOR GOOD COFFEE*

BY MARTHA WASHINGTON

Drip coffee: For every cup of water, 1 heaping tablespoon of "specially selected coffee, pulverized as fine as cornmeal." For breakfast, serve coffee black with sugar and hot milk. After dinner, serve coffee black with sugar.

*From *The President's Cookbook*

ABOUT THE AUTHOR

Cleo Coyle is a pseudonym for Alice Alfonsi, writing in collaboration with her husband, Marc Cerasini. Both are *New York Times* bestselling authors of the Coffeehouse Mysteries, now celebrating over ten years in print. Alice has worked as a journalist in Washington, D.C., and New York, and has written young adult and children's books. A former magazine editor, Marc has authored espionage thrillers and nonfiction for adults and children. Alice and Marc are also bestselling media tie-in writers who have penned properties for Lucasfilm, NBC, Fox, Disney, Imagine, and MGM. They live and work in New York City, where they write independently and together.